SAN FRANCISCO

For Bill Crossen, San Francisco was a city to be conquered. He had spent years perfecting his plans, and he had left nothing to chance. He was going to break all the rules.

For Marjorie Levey, San Francisco was a genteel prison, a city that demanded she follow all the rules. She was determined to break the mold— once and for all.

SAN FRANCISCO brings these two people from vastly different worlds together in a novel that is as vibrant and compelling as the city itself. Here, set against the tapestry of a city whose old-world facade belies the behind-the-scenes quests for power and money, are the Nob Hill *grandes dames,* the financial and political power brokers, the decadent rich, and the outsiders who will stop at nothing in their desire to become part of the charmed circle.

Other works by John Haase

Novels
Big Red (A Pinnacle Book)
The Young
Road Show
The Fun Couple
Erasmus with Freckles
Petulia
The Noon Balloon to Rangoon
The Nuptials
Seasons and Moments

Plays
The Fun Couple
Wall to Wall War
Don't Call Me Dirty Names
Erasmus with Freckles

San Francisco

The novel
by JOHN HAASE

PINNACLE BOOKS NEW YORK

This is a work of fiction. All the characters and events portrayed in this book are fictional, and any resemblance to real people or incidents is purely coincidental.

SAN FRANCISCO

An original Pinnacle Books edition, published for the first time anywhere.

First printing, February 1983

ISBN: 0-523-41866-3

Cover illustration by John Solie

Printed in the United States of America

PINNACLE BOOKS, INC.
1430 Broadway
New York, New York 10018

GRATEFUL ACKNOWLEDGMENT TO BETTE ALEXANDER FOR HER ASTUTE AND IMAGINATIVE HELP AND TO LES McALLISTER FOR HIS CAREFUL RESEARCH AND EDITORIAL SKILLS.

FOR A WRITER TO FIND AN EDITOR AND
A PUBLISHER WHO HAS NOT ONLY WIS-
DOM BUT ALSO COMPASSION IS RARE
INDEED.
TO ADD HUMOR AND A DASH OF FREUD
IS FROSTING ON THE CAKE.
FOR ALL THESE BLESSINGS THIS BOOK
IS DEDICATED TO PATRICK O'CONNOR.

SAN FRANCISCO

Part One

Chapter I

September, 1945

Bill Crossen, a gray-faced young man, twenty-four years of age, nearly six feet tall, weighing a skeletal 125 pounds, stood near the bow of the Liberty Ship *Fox*. A gray young man on a gray ship sailing on a ponderously gray sea.

The *Fox* was known as one of Smith and Welton's "specials"—one that did not sink at launching; still, it's bent shaft and its faulty bilge pumps had caused the normal twelve-day crossing from Manila to San Francisco to stretch into forty days. Crossen, facing a leaden wind, felt justifiably that all of life conspired to delay him. His Japanese internment had cost him four years, World War II had cost him his Ph.D. at Cal Tech, and merciless childhood poverty had cruelly robbed him of his youth. Standing near the bow, he looked through the haze and made out the Farallon Islands and strained

3

to see the graceful Golden Gate Bridge, built against all odds by that little Jewish engineer Robert Strauss.

So far, he had survived. He drew in a salt-filled breath of sea air and felt no small sense of victory after all the preceding hell and fury. Four years in prison camp had taught him to compartmentalize his emotions. Emotions with which he had to deal daily—fear, pain, self-pity, anxiety—were shifted to a lower center. One lived with them like a brace, which is heavy and cumbersome until one achieves the rhythm of infirmity. He had to free his mind, his intellect—which was considerable—for survival, for cunning, for scheming, in order to confront that inevitable faceless man who sat behind a desk, and whose power would shape the course of his life.

Beginning with his father, his teachers, his army superiors, his captors—all these Bill Crossen had learned to confront, often with silence, more often with stealth, using every range of emotion from subservience to forced (for him) ribald conviviality. These functions were also controlled and monitored by the will of a very studiedly unemotional man. Now only one man (undoubtedly behind a desk) stood between him and freedom from his service to his country.

He still could not make out the towers of the bridge and returned to his cabin, which he had painfully shared with an ebullient colonel from Kansas who planned to spend the next two weeks in San Francisco before returning home.

"I've got eight thousand bucks in back pay," the colonel had told him over and over again, "and I'm going to spend half of it and screw everything that's loose in the town. The old lady'll never know how much I got from Uncle Sam."

Bill Crossen knew about back pay, having received $7000 and a majority upon his release from prison. The greatest savings bank in the world, they had called it. He had almost doubled that sum by winning a number of poker games on the ship, mostly small sums to ensure his anonymity. His fingers rarely left the outline of his back pocket, and he almost envied the colonel's gusto for hedonism; but he also knew that one phase of his life had ended and another was about to begin. There was little time to waste in the interim.

He listened to the orders over the intercom, orders to the enlisted men on board. "Section A, section B, bring your gear to the cargo deck." These orders did not pertain to him. His duffel bag was neatly packed and sat at the foot of his bed. It contained endless notes, drawings, projections, graphs, bids. No Japanese hand grenades, no samurai swords, no satin pillows with cotton fringes. This war had not left him with a desire for memorabilia.

Crossen, by choice, had managed to leave San Tomas with a battalion other than his own. He hardly knew the sixty officers assembled in the ward room, some drinking coffee, others eating breakfast: powdered eggs, soggy biscuits, tinned butter.

The captain of the ship, a lieutenant commander in the merchant marine, entered and advised the officers that they could leave the ship before the enlisted men on a forward gangplank, that cabs and buses would be available to them at the end of the warehouses, and that they were expected at Letterman General Hospital that morning.

"I guess you guys don't want speeches," the captain said. "I'm sorry it took so long to get here. I didn't build this fucking tub. Considering what you men have been through, you deserved better."

There was gentle applause and the captain left, as did Bill Crossen, to take up his position once again at the bow. And now he was rewarded with a good view of the elegant bridge spanning the Golden Gate, its dimensions as graceful as a well-made classical harp. Behind it sat Alcatraz, like a granite whale. To the right, still partly hidden by fog, rose the steep hills of San Francisco, all gray and white. Coit Tower rose gallantly on top of Russian Hill.

So this is San Francisco, he thought. Baghdad by the Bay, as Herb Caen called it. The Paris of the West, the City of the Seven Hills. His engineer's eyes quickly assessed the grid pattern of the streets as they ascended from the Bay, and he recalled having seen pictures and commenting that if the city had been properly terraced more people would have enjoyed the view. There was an absence of trees and foliage, as if every square foot of space facing this magnificent natural bay were built up to take advantage of its proximity.

The Bay was busy. Tugs, tankers, even an occasional pristine white sailboat, but there was one other quality to the city that no one mentioned: its silence, its purity. No factories bordered the water, no smokestacks belched poison as they did on the eastern seaboard; there were no frantic sounds of cars blowing their horns, unlike New Yorkers, who had never mastered the motorcar or a sense of propriety about its usage.

Crossen sensed the uneasiness of the men around him. They were eager yet frightened to join wives, mothers, children after so many years of celibate existence. Clearly, emotions were mixed: They needed the warmth, the embraces, the love that awaited them; but they were returning much older than their years—more private, more introspective, more suspicious. They had shed the jacket with POW stenciled on its back, but the initials had been seared into their souls.

Already the tugs were pushing the stern toward the dock. The heavy hawsers were shoreside; stevedores had fastened them. Bill Crossen listened to a Salvation Army band strike up "California, Here I Come." Relatives and friends stood behind manila lines strung up by military police. He could see handkerchiefs waving, children lifted to shoulders, the first signs of recognition of kin. He returned to the cabin.

Crossen folded his red medical corps blanket and placed it on his bed.

"Whyn't you take it home? It'll come in real handy when you're camping," the colonel advised him.

"Naw. I can't stand the smell of the thing."

"Sure you don't want to hole up with me at the Palace?"

"I'm sure."

"Well, I'll see you at Vanessi's on Thursday night."

"You bet."

"Best 'Eytie' food you'll ever eat."

"Thursday night," Crossen agreed.

"Ask anybody. Vanessi's. They been there a hundred years."

Crossen nodded and extended his hand.

"And whatever I'm with, don't forget I'm single, and available."

"Single and available. And rich," Crossen added.

"Well, I don't know how rich I'll be on Thursday."

They shook hands. Crossen picked up his duffle bag, left the cabin and walked down the gangplank. He felt the tension of the two thousand enlisted men held back until he and the other officers had debarked. Somehow he enjoyed the privilege of rank.

He bypassed the Red Cross table, the handshakes of the official greeters, pretending to look for a face in the crowd he knew did not exist. Only Selda knew of his homecoming, but he had not apprised her of the day or month. He found the cabs where the captain had predicted, got in and told the driver to take him to Letterman.

"They got army buses for you guys, sir," the cabbie said, seeing the gold leaf on Crossen's shoulder.

7

"I know. I've ridden in enough buses."

"I'm sure you have."

He swung out of the cab line and headed down the Embarcadero.

"Bet you're glad to be home."

Crossen nodded.

"I been working the troopships for weeks now. I was telling the missus the other night, some of the guys just storm out of the boat. Where's the broads? Where's the booze? Where's Market Street? Other guys just say nothing. Nothing."

Crossen had never been to San Francisco, though he had studied it on maps, in magazines, guidebooks, everything Selda had managed to ship him, so that he felt now, uneasy as he was, that he had almost mastered its geography.

"That must be Van Ness," he asked the cab driver.

"Sure is. You a local boy?"

"No."

"Well, pretty soon maybe they'll get some new cars on this street again. This De Soto's got two hundred thousand miles on her."

The driver headed up Van Ness to Lombard Street and followed it until he reached the gates of the Presidio. The guard in the white hat and white boot covers saluted.

"Where to," he asked the driver, who turned to face Crossen.

"Letterman General Hospital. General Admission."

Again the guard saluted and waved them on.

The entrance of the hospital resembled a Southern mansion. Eucalyptus trees draped the portico. He paid the driver and entered the foyer.

He saw a sergeant seated behind an oak desk and asked where returning officers were to report.

"Can I see your orders, sir?"

Crossen handed him the manila envelope. "Go to room four, Captain Welsh."

"Thank you."

Again the pervasive smell of disinfectant, of ether, permeated the air. It made Crossen slightly nauseated. It had followed him from enlistment to prison camp to here. His clothes smelled of it, his blankets, his skin. Would it ever leave him?

Captain Welsh, in his early twenties, was in the Medical Administrative Corps. His uniform looked new. The caduceus on his collar seemed somewhat ludicrous, since he could neither heal or assuage misery. He was solely a paper pusher.

"Welcome home, Major," he said, standing.

"Thank you."

"Have a seat."

Bill Crossen sat and looked at a desk whose neatness betrayed extreme inactivity.

"I am in charge of officer rehab and therefore at your service."

"How long," Crossen asked, "will all this take?"

"A week, maybe two." The young captain shrugged his shoulders.

"You are talking about a variable of seven days," Crossen said, a certain steel in his voice.

"You know Washington."

"What does Washington have to do with it?"

"Field-grade officers are processed through Washington."

"What is the longest period you project?"

"Two weeks," the captain said. "We're pretty new at this."

"You may be. I'm not."

"I understand."

Crossen had managed quickly to make the young officer uncomfortable.

"Of course, you're not required to remain on base during this period."

"I understand. Do you have a vacancy in the BOQ?"

"I suppose so."

"Then I would like a room."

The captain scratched his head. "Did you understand me, Major? You are not required to live on base at all."

"I understand you, Captain. If the army detains me, then the army feeds me."

"Yes, sir."

"Yes, sir, Major," Crossen added.

"If you'll leave your orders, I'll have you assigned to quarters."

"I will appreciate that."

Crossen stood and waited until an enlisted man arrived. He could see the sun breaking through the eucalyptus. He said nothing further to the captain and followed the private to the BOQ, an old barrack with single rooms, two-story, wooden, but with an unforgettable view from his window. The entire Bay spread out before him, the water turning blue as the sun finally hit it. A lazy freighter carrying timber moved slowly out of sight.

He put his duffle bag on his bed, hung up his summer uniform, his shirts, and sat on the bed. He lit a cigarette and noticed a tin can that could serve as an ashtray. The very luxury of being in a room by himself was almost unbearable. Four years of sleeping with sixty men had left its toll. Their endless farting and belching, their constant profanity, their mock conviviality, were almost harder to bear than the work load, the watery food, the absolute confinement.

He opened the window and heard a platoon of soldiers marching past the barracks, a drill sergeant counting cadence, admonishing a rearguard recruit.

"I'll never stand in a line again," Crossen thought to himself. "I'll never wait for anything," he vowed. He fingered the papers in his duffle bag. Their content represented three years of intensive work, of stolen hours, of working by the light of a fiery steam generator.

He lay down on his bunk, still dressed, and put his arms behind his head. The ceiling above him was old and weathered. Endless coats of sanitary green paint had not obliterated old stains and water marks. It was two in the afternoon when he fell asleep, and seven in the evening when he awoke. He rose, stretched and splashed water in his face to wake up, reveling in the quiet and the luxury of inactivity.

He ate scrambled eggs at the officers' mess, avoiding the bar, noisy and active with men, and finally took a cab, asking the driver for the Tenderloin district.

"That's a big order," the cabbie said. "What are you really looking for? A girlie show? A house? Pinocchio's?"

"Burlesque sounds OK," he said. "Is there a good one?"

"I'll take you to the Kearney. That's the best. They got some real lookers."

He rode silently, watching the city. It was Saturday, the downtown area deserted except for the ghosts of office buildings, their windows dark, their lobbies empty; an occasional restaurant; or a bar, displaying a cocktail glass rimmed in neon, the inevitable maraschino cherry glowing red inside.

The cab driver stopped in front of a small, rundown theater in Kearney Street. The street itself was busy with Chinese still shopping in tiny grocery stores, their strange wares spilling in the street, Italians dressed in their Sunday best, occasional groups of tourists heading for Chinatown.

He paid admission to the theater, and found himself stumbling in the dark until an usher found him a seat with his flashlight.

He sat and when his eyes became accustomed to the

darkness saw that he was surrounded by stoic, aging Chinese men, watching a poorly projected Abbot and Costello film. Bill Crossen laughed little at the slapstick and noticed as the picture came to its conclusion that the Chinese were slowly sneaking to seats closer to the stage. He followed suit and found himself in the third row when the movie ended. The lights came on and a vendor went from aisle to aisle trying to sell Cracker Jacks.

The house lights dimmed suddenly and a comedian dressed in a shabby tuxedo announced the first dancer, a full-blown brunette who crossed and recrossed the stage to the sound of a pianist somewhere below the stage. She was a tall girl, more legs than trunk, who somehow managed ungracefully to get out of a green satin negligee. Her figure was good, although her boredom was infectious. The Chinese men sat and stared, almost confused by the ritual necessary to complete striptease.

It had been two years since Bill Crossen had seen a naked woman, and the memory of his single night away from the prison camp seemed almost too sacred to be confused with this performance; still, he hungered for the sight. The stripper finally removed her bra. She had large breasts, still firm, her nipples large and dark in the field of moving white flesh. Crossen felt an intensity to his stare; and yet in this sea of Chinese he was hardly noticeable.

A blonde dancer followed the brunette, a redhead followed her. The sequence was as stereotyped and mechanical as the dancing. Somehow Crossen needed to see a woman, perhaps to reassure him that they still existed, still looked like women. He left when the movie resumed.

He walked from the movie house and Kearney Street was mercifully deserted. The fog had crept into the city, crossing the street lights in swift, gauzelike patches. He continued to walk toward the Bay, ascending the ridge of Russian Hill then moving down toward Fishermen's Wharf.

San Francisco was busy. The end of the war, the returning servicemen, the thousands of workers who had flocked to the city during the conflict to work in defense, the first sprinkling of tourists, strained all the facilities of a city that normally took all in its stride. He passed a succession of cheap bars, nightclubs, the sounds of jukeboxes, of street combos drifting to the sidewalk. People had money to spend and they were spending it.

On Fishermen's Wharf he entered Alioto's, took a small table in the dining room and ordered lobster and a bottle of white wine. When his wine arrived he raised his glass and toasted his presence. It had been a long road back to this corner of San Francisco. It would have been good to have someone to talk to, but perhaps the solitude was more symbolic. He had survived alone. The victory was his.

The first week at Letterman General Hospital was uneventful. There were physicals and there was paperwork. There were inducement lectures to reenlist, workshops on rehabilitation and a session with a psychiatrist. All of this activity took up his mornings; the afternoons were spent roaming San Francisco on foot. It was not until the tenth day after Crossen's arrival that he was asked to see Colonel Obers at G-2. Obers was a large, florid man, his face a map of every drink he had ever consumed, tiny blue veins holding a mass of red flesh like fish caught in a net. He had a paunch and was visibly uncomfortable wearing a necktie. Another man behind another desk, Bill thought as he entered the room.

"Do you have any idea why you're here, Major?" the colonel asked, his bourbon-irritated voice filling the room.

"No, Colonel."

"I have your service record here." He pointed to a manila folder. "It looks to be in order except for one thing. . . ."

"What is that?"

"A very serious matter."

"Yes?"

"Evidence of cooperation with the enemy during confinement."

Colonel Obers held a document in front of him and then let it drop among the other papers in the folder before him. Crossen's face grew red, he felt sweat in his palms.

"There is a fine line between cooperation and survival."

"I understand, Major. Still, your battalion commander spoke of 'unusual privileges' which you managed for yourself during confinement."

"I was the sanitation officer," Crossen explained. "My work by necessity took me all over the compound."

"There was fraternization, your camp superior stated."

"I knew the commander at the camp," Crossen said. "We had gone to MIT together. We were not captor and captive. We were both captives."

Colonel Obers fingered the document on the desk and pushed his wooden armchair back. He placed two well-polished shoes on his desk blotter and lit a cigarette.

"Smoke?"

"No, thanks."

"I don't think that much can come of this. Your record is clean . . . except for this."

"What *could* come of it?" Crossen asked.

"These documents go to Washington. A C file like this one is sent to the judge advocate's office for review. Usually it's routine."

"How many copies of this C file exist?" Crossen asked.

The colonel looked at Major Crossen, then at the document. "This is the original."

Crossen reached into his pants pocket and counted three $100 bills and withdrew them. He placed the money on the desk in front of them.

"Do you play poker, Colonel?"

"No," he said, "but I shoot craps."

"Good."

The colonel opened his desk drawer and fished for two dice.

"I'll bet the whole three hundred," Crossen said.

The colonel withdrew the C file from the folder. "Shoot," the colonel said.

Crossen rolled the dice. "Snake eyes."

"Guess you lose," the colonel said.

Crossen pushed the $300 in the colonel's direction. The heavy-set officer handed him the document.

Crossen folded it carefully and placed it in the pocket from which he had withdrawn the money. The colonel carefully inserted the $100 bills into his billfold.

"I think," he said, now standing, "that we can process your discharge tomorrow."

"I would appreciate that."

"Certainly nothing in your file now that would prevent that."

"I'll take your word for it, Colonel."

"Nothing at all. If you'll meet me in the officer's club at six, perhaps you'll buy me a drink. I'd like to hear about those days in prison camp."

"I'll be delighted," Crossen said.

The two men shook hands and Crossen left the office and walked into the bright sunlight of the parade grounds. One more day, he thought. Poker winnings.

It was against his nature but he did meet Colonel Obers at the officers' club at six o'clock. The regulars were already well-oiled. At twenty cents a drink the army, Bill felt, encouraged drinking.

Obers spotted Crossen as soon as he entered, and the camaraderie was easy after the first four bourbon and sevens.

"I spent the whole goddamned war in the States," Obers admitted, "running from one G-Two assignment to another."

"Don't complain," Crossen said.

"I know, I know. When I see guys like you, the hell you've been through, it doesn't make me feel too good."

"I expect to sit out the next war in the States myself," Crossen said.

"The next war," Obers repeated, lifting his glass. "I was a gunnery officer in World War One."

"Well, you've done your bit."

"Yeah. Purple Heart and all; but I tell you, Major, sometimes it's easier to shove a shell into a howitzer than filling those endless manila envelopes with records, files, bullshit."

One more day, Crossen kept reminding himself. Stay with it. Another round. Another round. The great leveler.

"How about some dinner, Colonel?"

"Much obliged. Just let me finish this drink, I'm not very hungry."

"Neither am I," Crossen lied.

There was an atmosphere of confusion in the officers' club. The regulars from the Presidio felt almost like refugees in their own quarters. The end of the war had spurred activity. Officers returning from overseas crowded out the regulars. Outfits in transit placed strains on the facilities, everything seemed unsettled.

Officers who had fought the war resented those who

had administered it. Those men leaving the service lost contact with men who were remaining. The officers' club, once a haven, became only a depot; but for Crossen's purposes it was just as well. He wanted to preserve his anonymity. The drunken colonel gave him a good excuse to avoid the questions of others. He feigned intoxication; the colonel's was genuine.

He had lost count of the drinks they had consumed. At eleven the colonel suggested he could use some help getting home, and Crossen agreed. They walked across the parade ground, past the brig and climbed the eucalyptus-covered hillside.

Obers' quarters were spacious. Probably one of the original Spanish houses built at the turn of the century, when the base was founded. He insisted on having a brandy, although Crossen objected.

"Come on," Obers insisted. "The old lady's been passed out for hours."

He opened the front door and Crossen found himself in a musty front hall. Obers stumbled over a German shepherd and found the living room light switch. The furniture was well-worn GI issue: clumsy overstuffed chairs, couches, ancient parchment lamps, scores of aging photographs of military commands, other posts, other quarters. Obers returned with a bottle of brandy, two glasses, and settled massively in the center of the couch. He poured two snifters of brandy and handed one to Crossen.

"What are your plans, Major?"

"Engineering. I'm a civil engineer."

"Yeah, that's right. You went to MIT."

Crossen unconsciously felt the piece of paper in his pocket.

"Don't reenlist. That's my advice."

"I hadn't planned on it."

"Pretty soon you got ten years, and you think of retirement in ten more, and then its twenty, and you think of thirty . . . there just weren't"—he belched—"there just weren't any jobs for gunnery officers when World War One ended."

"I understand."

"Well, if you stay in this town, I want you to come see me."

"Thank you."

"This brandy isn't bad, is it?"

"It's very good."

"I get it from Puerto Rico. It was really nice of you to help me home."

"The blind leading the blind," Crossen said.

"Yeah," Obers laughed. "That's pretty good. You married?"

"No."

"That's good, too." He laughed and pointed upstairs. "In the first war the old lady started boozing because I was overseas, and in this war she boozed because I was home." He slapped Crossen's knee hard. "Except damned women can't drink."

Crossen nodded.

"I mean, they put it away, but then they get nasty, and then they pass out. . . ." He put down his drink on the coffee table and leaned back on the couch. A minute later he was sound asleep. Two minutes later he was snoring loudly.

Crossen rose from his chair, crossed the room quietly and left the house. He almost ran down the hill to his quarters. It was two in the morning when he placed his watch on the dresser. This, he devoutly hoped, would be his last day in the service. He was almost too excited to sleep. He made certain that his room was locked, and then he unfolded the damaging C report he had extracted from his service record.

18

From Colonel Dunby
Camp San Tomas
Phillipines

To G-2

Subject: Lieutenant William Crossen

This officer, although one of the best young civil engineers in my command, conducted himself suspiciously during his period of internment from 1942 to 1945.

His work at San Tomas, consisting primarily of sanitation projects, allowed him access to the entire camp. Nevertheless the Lieutenant was rarely found among his own command. His rapport with his fellow internees was poor. He was at best a loner, and at worst a traitor. To qualify this last serious charge I shall enter in evidence the fact that Lieutenant Crossen at *no* time would participate in plans of escape, stating repeatedly that he felt it pointless and a waste of his energies, and though he managed at times to produce drugs needed for some of his men, repeated questioning did not produce satisfactory answers as to the source of his supplies. He was engaged constantly in affairs of his own during his off-duty times, writing, reading, and by virtue of a working knowledge of the Japanese language, managed to have a constant intercourse with the enemy. On Dec. 12, 1943, he was seen leaving the prison camp in a Japanese truck by several witnesses in my command. He stayed away for a total of eight hours, claiming only, after interrogation by the undersigned, that he had gone with the enemy to a supply depot to order drainage pipes, pressure gauges and other material. It was observed that during his period of internment he received more mail, letters, books, periodicals, than any other prisoner in my command, which, I know, is not a treasonable offense but adds to the suspicions about the conduct of this officer. It is only because of the general malaise caused by extreme malnutrition that more vigorous questioning was not conducted and I urge G-2 to pursue this matter now.

Signed

Colonel Dunby (Lt. Col.)
USA Corps of Civil Engineers
Manila

Bill Crossen stared at the document in its entirety for a minute. The walls of his room seemed to disappear and he could see the view from his compound at San Tomas. He saw the barbed wire and the expanse of swamp land, the leaden sky, the endless rows of huts. There was a guard tower on his left and a guard tower on his right, crude structures of telephone poles topped by a platform containing a Jap guard, a searchlight, a machine gun. He felt the never-ending heat, the humidity; and he heard the voices of his captors, always taunting, high-pitched, humorless; and he saw the vacuous stares of his fellow prisoners, their minds working on meals, sleep and evacuation. Pushing the scene from his mind, he lit a match to the indictment and held it until the paper turned into a sheet of brittle carbon. It held its shape for a long minute before it crumbled to the floor, black ashes to be swept away by an orderly in the morning.

Four hours later he heard reveille. He showered and dressed and at noon he stood his last review. The commanding general handed him his honorable discharge, his formal field promotion, his decorations and a handbook for newly discharged veterans, including a small golden eagle he could wear in mufti.

At one o'clock Bill Crossen was registered at the Marina Motel, a modest eight-unit establishment near the Bay. He picked up the phone to contact Selda Cohen.

Chapter II

During the thirties and forties, Judaism in San Francisco, like Gaul, was divided into three parts: At the bottom of the economic ladder were the mostly Orthodox McAllister Street Jews of Polish, Russian and Eastern European extraction. The men were tailors, butchers, owners of modest shops, dry-cleaning establishments and second-hand furniture stores. Many of them lived in quarters behind these shops, in airless, narrow rooms, their lives hectic and cacaphonous, with neighbors in merciless proximity, streetcars, autos, a never-ending parade of children playing in the streets, women leaning out of windows yelling at the children in the street.

In the middle were the Richmond district Jews: professionals, teachers, civil service workers, shop owners, soft-goods manufacturers. They rented apartments along the Golden Gate Park, the level streets paralleling Geary Street, shopped on Clement Street and occasionally went to the beach on rare warm, windless days.

Neither group infringed on the upper class, old-line Jews, the Zentners, the Fleishmans, the Rosenwalds, the Roths, the Hillers—who were San Franciscans first, Americans second and Jewish only in its most Reformed sense. Their daughters came out in gentile cotillions; their worship (such as it was) was conducted at a temple whose rabbi, handpicked by one of the matrons, was well paid, socially facile and religiously undemanding. This last, wealthy group, despite the holocaust, still felt that Zionism was a Communist plot, that most McAllister Street Jews were "Polacks," and that it was as important to straighten their own offsprings' noses as their teeth. Rich Jews dominated some of the finest mansions on Pacific Heights, Russian and Nob Hills. They commanded the best views of the Bay and felt secure on their Olympus. *Their* grandfathers had come West with the Forty-niners, they had owned the small trading posts, the general stores, often exchanging land for unpaid goods. They came from true pioneer stock; and the shrewdness and astuteness of their forebears, the prudent investments, the thrift and energy had earned them the right to now enjoy the fruits of all these past wisdoms.

They emulated the Brahmins of Boston. One lived only from dividends. The capital was never touched. And despite the limousines, the mansions, the yachts, the country estates, men still took the Number 3 streetcar downtown; they used Ivory soap instead of French soaps with "dirty scents"; they tipped correctly, but not generously; treated help with rectitude but let them know they were servants; and let Royce Brier of the *Chronicle* shape their views of the world—but rarely past ten o'clock in the morning when the shops opened for the women and the men were beginning to think of lunch.

Their daughters attended Sarah Dix Hamlin (segre-

23

gated religiously) and Stanford (somewhat segregated for the same reason), their sons, eastern prep schools or San Rafael Military Academy. And despite the heinous behavior of Hitler they still felt that intermarriage was a worthwhile institution and readied their children for a gentile world, which was, for most of them, the secret dream.

Selda Cohen belonged squarely in the center of the Richmond District. She was thirty-one years old, the only child of Abraham and Lisa Cohen. Abraham was a second cousin of Bill Crossen's father. Her parents had both been teachers. Abraham taught mathematics at Lowell High, Lisa biology at Galileo. They had lived in a pleasant apartment on Fourteenth Avenue near the Golden Gate Park, withstood the depression because of their tenured positions in the public school system, and devoted their lives to raising their only child. There were monotonous Sunday excursions to Mount Tamalpais, an annual two weeks on the Russian River and the smugness of looking forward to a secure retirement.

Abraham Cohen, unlike his cousin in the East, had always been bookish. He had studied at CCNY and at Columbia on a scholarship, and wasted little time fleeing the cauldrons of New York's ghetto life. He had been hired to teach migrant farm workers in California in the twenties and finally entrenched himself at Lowell High School, unquestionably the most academically oriented high school in all of California.

Abraham Cohen, from a family of eight, and his wife, from a family of eleven, purposely limited their progeny to one, and Selda's memories of her parents were warm and complicated. They spoiled her academically (a set of encyclopedia on her ninth birthday, piano lessons at seven, a tutor in French at the age of ten) and neglected her femininity. A dress would do for another summer, another winter; shoes were utilitarian objects, not for adornment. Underwear was something Selda's mother sewed by hand with such ineptitude that Selda remembered skipping physical education because she was embarrassed to undress with her classmates, fearing their taunts about her shapeless bloomers.

Selda had been a nice-looking child, slightly chubby, dark-haired with a good complexion. It was only her mother's lack of taste, her extreme frugality that gave Selda so little style, and, consequently, a lack of confidence. She was extremely shy, hiding in the library during recesses, in a corner of the cafeteria during school dances; and it was with relief that she graduated at eighteen from Washington High School with honors, commendations and a scholarship to Mills College in the foothills of Oakland.

She loved the beauty of the campus, the elegance and graciousness of the public rooms of her dormitory. She reveled in the lack of formality of learning, the presence of Darius Milhaud on campus, the youthfulness of the school president, who was fresh from Stanford.

It was, however, a short-lived dream. Far from being an escape from the inane and childish social pressures of high school, Mills, Selda soon discovered, was more a social institution than a university. Her roommate, a long-necked girl from Connecticut, occupied the same room as her mother before her; the school revolved more about the calendars of Fraternity Row at Berkeley or Palo Alto than the logic of Kant or Hegel, the wisdom of a Ghandi or an Einstein.

Selda soon discovered that Milhaud was merely the decoration on a very soggy educational sponge cake, and that the young ladies (as they were constantly addressed) were more interested in solid matrimony than solid geometry, that classes in home economics were more popular than philosophy, and there were more discussions about Emily Post than about Eleanor Roosevelt.

Abraham Cohen sensed his daughter's dissatisfaction earlier than her mother did. He could see the lethargy, and felt her mediocre grades were more a revolt than an inability to perform. He had discussed it with his wife the night before they were killed in an automobile accident on Geary Street on the way to Oakland to visit Selda for the weekend.

Her parents' death, sudden and dramatic, detailed in all the city's newspapers, gave Selda, that quiet, chubby girl in Swarthmore Hall, an aura of notoriety; and though for a while everyone treated her with a superficial kindness, she soon realized that without her parents' support, Mills was not the school for her.

A cousin who husbanded the trust and the insurance money left to her by her parents fortified her in her determination to leave Mills and its social pretensions and enter the University of California at Berkeley, where the emphasis was on education and where the student body included many Selda Cohens—insecure, lost, frightened. But nevertheless the campus was a fertile ground for dedicated teachers to build ideas, to lay some groundwork for a career, to stimulate and nourish educational appetites.

At the age of twenty-one, Selda claimed her inheritance—a sum somewhat over $50,000—and against her cousin's advice took a year off from school to attend the Sorbonne for a semester, to travel from Florence to Rome, from Rome to Siena—a year so totally beautiful that its memories would heal many scarred periods of later life. She slept with a sailor on the transatlantic crossing and with the son of the concierge of the pension she lived in in Paris. She had an affair with a middle-aged art historian in Florence and with an umbrella vendor in Siena. She had money for clothes, and for lingerie; she had funds for little dinners with good wines; she had her majority, and the pain of her parents' death to justify her hedonism.

She had also inherited her mother's practicality, all the while attending to school, performing her assignments even as she pursued her pleasures, and always considering her next step. In those quiet hours after intercourse with her middle-aged lover, they often discussed her future.

"I'm interested in art history," she had said, and he'd listened carefully with that consideration middle-aged men have for younger girls.

"What else?"

"I like libraries. I feel at home in them, secure. It is all logical, pure . . ."

"You have answered your own question."

"How?"

"I love you, Selda. I've watched you. You know I have watched you . . ."

"What do you mean?"

"You are a passionate girl, but also a pragmatist. I think you would be happier in a library. Art, all fields of art, are a fever. It is too hot or too cold. You'd never be happy."

She had returned from Europe and heeded that advice, returning to Berkeley and changing her major to library science, then an infant discipline. She was more content, less unsure of herself. She had discovered beauty in Europe and beauty in herself. She had experienced pleasure and had given it in return. She rented a small apartment near Telegraph Avenue in the foothills of Berkeley, decorated it with memorabilia of Italy and France and pursued her studies with devotion and personal equanimity. After graduation (again with honors) she remained in the research library as a junior librarian.

There was no question that her trip to Europe had fulfilled her hopes for sexual excitement and these desires had not disappeared upon her return. However, her social life as a "working young lady" was circumscribed. Still, she took some comfort in her relative youth and hoped that that situation would improve.

She accepted a position at higher pay with the San Francisco Public Library and moved to the city. She wanted to take advantage of San Francisco's richer resources, its music, art and, she hoped, its broader contacts.

She started and headed the business branch of the public library in the financial district of San Francisco. These three rooms, closely packed in the Russ Building, a thirty-structure office complex, were her domain. There she ministered to the needs and the hopes of the academically inclined executives of San Francisco, some bookish, some statistically oriented, some greedy, some very withdrawn. It was *her* library, and her club, and though she ran it with the utmost professionalism, it became home, work, play, almost to the exclusion of a private life.

Her income was adequate. The dividends from her inheritance allowed her small luxuries. She lived in a well-furnished flat on Vallejo Street, bought occasional original drawings, held season tickets for the symphony and opera, was generous to offspring of distant relatives and rarely went to bed without a one-pound box of Blum's candy on the night table. She was gaining weight, and she knew it. She managed somehow to avoid heself in the bathroom mirror after stepping out of the shower.

She had gone through the depression unscathed. She had seen her country embark on World War II and watched the turmoil of armament, mobilization; she had seen the young men leaving Montgomery Street, Sansome, Kearney. She had watched the heads of her charges change to gray, balding men, and yet she prevailed.

The absence of eligible men almost relieved the pressure. She was well. She was comfortable. She loved her work, her apartment. Somewhere under that extra poundage she knew lay a passionate woman; there was no hurry to produce her, to suffer diets and exercise. One more lemon cream, one more chocolate pistachio nut, and that's enough. She'd turn off the light in her bedroom at eleven. At times she could see a neighbor undressing in the apartment across the street. He was lean and exciting and slept naked. On nights like those she would sleep naked, too.

It had come as a surprise, that first letter from William Crossen. At first she failed to recognize the name, remembering finally that he had changed it from Cohen (against the protestations of his family) before applying to MIT.

She had met her father's family only once on her return from Europe. Her uncle, an indigent cutter, lived in circumstances so frightfully shabby that Selda could barely wait to terminate her visit. The family had bought pastries and she ate them self-consciously under the jealous eyes of her younger cousins, whose hands were constantly slapped as they reached for the plate of confections. She was impressed by her aunt, a stern, handsome woman not unlike her own mother, who proudly recited the scholastic achievements of all her offspring. The peeling kitchen walls were lined with diplomas, awards, ribbons and medals from various Hebrew schools, Sunday schools, city campgrounds, museums and foundations. There were four boys at home at the time (William was at NYU) and her memories were of dark eyes beneath black yarmulkes, short hair, cut by the

29

father, thin legs, sallow complexions, almost like transparent fish in a fishbowl. All eyes and movement.

Although she had not met William, she had later heard about his progress. His penchant for mathematics and his acceptance to MIT on scholarship were a source of no little pride in the family. He had made Phi Beta Kappa in his junior year (she had sent a book), the National Engineering Honor Society on graduation, summa cum laude (she had sent another book).

She had heard of his plans to do graduate work at Cal Tech in Pasadena, but the war interrupted these plans and he was commissioned and placed on active duty right before Pearl Harbor. She had also heard of his capture and internment in the Philippines and sent him an occasional box of chocolates through the Red Cross when she supplied her own needs at Blum's.

"Dear Cousin Selda," she had read, admiring the precision of the printing displayed in the letter, the engineer's hallmark.

I am surviving. I can honestly say that. Our treatment is harsh but just and one cannot transpose western values to eastern incarceration.

I write you today to ask for some help. My mother has often spoken to me of your important position in San Francisco's financial district and my unique predicament has forced me into a number of decisions which at this point I consider prudent.

I managed to graduate the youngest in my class at MIT because I wanted to spend two extra years at Cal Tech to gain my Ph.D. Unfortunately, the war upset my timetable, and my imprisonment has taken additional time from my career.

I don't know when I'll be released; however, I am convinced now that I can't waste the additional time at Cal Tech, but should begin to earn money rather than invest more time in school.

I've given much thought to my future—one has a great deal of time to think in prison camp—and have reached the conclusion that my future belongs in the west—particularly San Francisco. There were several reasons for this decision. I think the move west will be very strong once the war has ended and that career opportunities for an engineer will be better than in the east. In addition, the east, and particularly eastern engineering firms, are much more prejudicial toward Jews.

If you could think of such a firm, or research that subject, I would be very much obliged. I am very confident about my qualifications and know I can contribute the expertise needed for the job.

Your serious thoughts in this matter will be most helpful to me. You may write me direct and bypass the Red Cross, which is most inefficient. The mail will reach me. My thanks in advance.

Your grateful cousin,

William Crossen

The letter was curious in many respects. Selda Cohen had never in her life laid eyes on William Crossen though they were third cousins. To her, he was some nebulous younger relative who had succeeded admirably at MIT. Period.

She did not blame him for writing her, although the tone of the letter offended her. There was a definite demanding attitude that she felt but could not explain. She had people like this in her library. "The *Journal of Finance* is misfiled," someone would announce, as if she were responsible for the accuracy of the placement of the 9,000 volumes in her care, day in, day out.

But the letter also saddened her. A boy of twenty-two feeling his life was being wasted, his family so relentlessly geared to turn degrees into dollars and advanced degrees into advanced dollars reminded her of her father's stories of Hell's Kitchen, of families that sweated and strained for their children's education, and educated children who later sweated and strained to support their elderly parents. And she knew engineering students. And engineers. They went through college without gaining finesse or élan, their minds like graph paper, filled with formulas, equations, tables, graphs. To them life was an endless sequence of problems that could be solved by shoring them up with two-by-fours, by rewriting the equation, by drawing curves from profits and losses.

She did nothing when she first received the letter. It was an affront. William Crossen was only seven years younger than she. She was neither a crusty librarian nor a social arbiter in San Francisco. She was a well-functioning young woman who had finally found some peace amid turmoil.

However, the letter was more of a threat than she realized. To turn down a relative imprisoned by the Japanese was truly selfish. She must help; how much she helped would be *her* decision.

She was familiar with that top layer of Jews in her city, since many of them frequented her library. These men, she knew, were proper, conservative, polite and often selfless. Their dress was somber. Gray or navy blue suits, their white shirts from the White House meticulously washed and ironed, their small, textured neckties from Bullock and Jones in muted blues and maroons, their shoes buffed by the bootblack in the basement of the St. Francis. Their gold wrist watches from Shreves were usually wedding presents from their wives.

They were civil, these men, and intelligent and honest and hardworking. They performed often complicated jobs with a great deal of modesty and very little fanfare. Selda was respected for her intelligence and her professionalism. Her position as librarian in itself commanded respect; however, the warmth and the respect ended on Friday at five.

Occasionally she would be invited to a home for a library tea, a fund-raising drive, and again everyone was proper and pleasant.

"You are the librarian in the business branch," a matron would ask.

"Yes."

"That must be fascinating work."

"At times."

There were always questions about her work, about her library. No one asked whether she was single, married, had children, where she lived, whether she suffered or not. The teas would end at four. Children would enter the house but not be introduced. There was a public nature to these functions, the home per se was not to be invaded.

And still Selda would sometimes wander through those mansions on Broadway, Jackson, on Pacific. She would admire the lovely private libraries, the leather-bound volumes gracing the shelves, the roaring fires in marble-sheathed hearths, and she would walk to the windows and pull aside the toile to admire the view those precious hills afforded of the Bay below.

She knew what Bill Crossen wanted, and yet she was unsure whether she should help. Unsure how that help, if such it was, would reflect on her life. At thirty-one she herself wavered between benign spinsterhood and a desire for attachment, perhaps even marriage. She made no real efforts toward that end. Her weight, her desire for independence, her pleasant little life belied any great urges for commitment.

Selda Cohen was, nevertheless, a fair woman. She knew that her life was basically selfish. Alone, without dependents, her income and the returns from her parents' trust allowed her to live extremely well. She denied herself very little.

She was getting into a rut. A comfortable rut, she knew, yet it was well worn. Perhaps this boy, this maverick, might prove exciting. Perhaps he would prove stimulating. She carried the fantasies further, and laughed. He would return from overseas, hungry for life—and a woman. Who knew?

"Dear Bill," she wrote, after several weeks.

I am happy you are well, and that you have been receiving my parcels. If we are to get anywhere I want you to stop referring to me as Cousin Selda. I am your third cousin, slightly more than seven years your senior, and hate to be labeled as some sort of family relic.

I was amazed at your request. To feel at twenty-four that you are too old to continue your schooling seems foolish to me; however, since I've not been through what you are experiencing I can't judge your frame of mind. Since I do understand your anxiety about some sort of answer, I will tell you that whether I approve or not, I have done some checking, and can answer your question this way.

There is a firm in San Francisco by the name of O'Gara and Levey. I realize it sounds like a strange combination. O'Gara and Levey are partners because they are both civil engineers, San Francisco-reared and of different religious origin, in that order. They are both veterans of Boulder Dam and their firm is one of the largest of its kind in the West. Perhaps you have heard of them. They worked on Boulder, TVA, Hetch Hetchy, the bridges, aqueducts, airfield, big stuff.

O'Gara and Levey is a very large, very sound and very respected firm in San Francisco. Perhaps the presence of Henry Levey, a jew, might alleviate some of your fears of discrimination.

Since research is really my forte, I am giving you what you want, although it is not what I would counsel. A young man of your background and education should feel the world is his oyster; however, since I asked you to stop calling me cousin, I should stop talking like one.

If I can be of further help, please let me know.

Best wishes,

Selda Cohen

She mailed the letter in the evening and walked across the street to view the Bay. It was an unusually warm summer night in San Francisco. She walked slowly down Mason Street toward Columbus Square. There the street consisted of old, four-story frame houses, most of them with eight airless apartments. Windows were open and she caught the scent of garlic and oregano. Older men hung out the windows, men in undershirts, T-shirts, staring aimlessly at the street below. Young children played hopscotch around streetlights, older youngsters clustered around service entrances, cupping cigarettes in their hands. Corner grocery stores were still open, their vegetables slightly wilted, their owners labeling paper bags for tomorrow's specials. Chinese men hurried toward Grant Avenue, the alleys around Stockton. A few soldiers, their caps cocked rakishly, poked into liquor stores or corner bars. The city was alive, sweating. The last band of crimson in the night sky around the Gate belied a bloody war six thousand miles west. She heard Glenn Miller's band from one radio, the voice of Walter Winchell from another.

She walked past Columbus Square, still alive with people on the grass and benches. She saw the doors to Grace Cathedral open repeatedly. Women, their heads draped in black, praying for sons or husbands. She passed by bakeries and restaurant supply shops. She stared at huge copper kettles, zabaglione pans, elegantly fashioned wooden spoons, fish cookers, steamers, aprons and chefs' hats.

Cabs arrived at Bimbo's 365 club. Servicemen alighted, some with dates, others alone. She could hear the sound of music inside, see the neon lights behind the glass facade. She finally reached Fishermen's Wharf, almost deserted, a few merchants still steaming clams in open cans, cracking crabs for dinner guests of their establishments.

She ordered Olympia oysters and ate them from a paper cup as she walked along the docks of the fishing fleet. The seiners, the Monterey clippers were slowly getting ready for their night at sea. Men straining under wads of nets, puttering with one-lunger diesels gave off an odor indigenous to fishing boats.

She loved the wharf, and often wished she had the courage to ask one of those Italian fishermen to take her along as they pushed out to sea at two or three in the morning. She had watched them as they pulled out, like a covey of birds, defiant yet fragile with their kerosene running lights, their brightwork worn from years of salt, the men in sturdy woolen sweaters and caps, their fingers red and rope-scarred. Perhaps it was their nightly escape that she envied, or the seeming simplicity of their lives, or perhaps the complexities of the sea.

She walked to Jones Street and boarded the cable car for home. It was past eleven and she was the only passenger. The conductor, an older Irishman, joined her in the closed section of the car.

"My last trip for the night," he said, almost to himself.

Selda nodded sympathetically.

"Don't mind working a night like this."

"Beautiful evening."

"Yeah, where I live the heat stays all night."

"The fog will be rolling in soon."

"You're right. Always follows the heat."

Selda handed him a dime.

He placed it in his coin changer and rang it on the overhead chain.

"You want a transfer?"

"No. Just going a few blocks. Nice to take a walk."

"Sure, but you got to be careful. City ain't what it used to be. All those niggers and soldiers coming in."

Selda nodded. She neither had the distance nor the inclination to argue. She left the car at Vallejo and heard the jingle of the bell as it continued down Hyde Street.

Chapter III

It was nine-thirty in the morning when Crossen finally woke in the Marina Motel, and he was angered at having overslept, though he had to admit that this was his first night in a civilian room for almost four years. He stretched out on the bias, luxuriating in the space of a double bed, his eyes wandering from the flowered patterns of the drapes to the easy chair and circular table across from him. The sun was shining and he heard the noise of traffic outside his window.

He had wanted to be up early, phone Selda and make full use of the day. She would be at work now, and he considered the propriety of phoning her at the library. He rose, stretched and ran a shower; he caught himself soaping his lean body in the space of fifteen seconds, forgetting that now for once he could use more than a minute's supply of hot water. He stood under the hot stream of water, almost transfixed, feeling a warmth, a true warmth going through his body he had not known for years, although he had lived in the tropics. He reached for a towel and rubbed himself dry while looking at his reflection in the full length mirror attached to the door.

He was thin. Painfully thin. He could see the outline of his rib cage, the protruding bones of his clavicles, his hip bones; even his face seemed harsh and angular. His hair, which had always been sandy, almost reddish-tinged, seemed grayer, less lifelike, and yet he felt well. He had marched past the bodies of his buddies on Bataan, he had survived the hospital at San Tomas, he had not contracted malaria, beri-beri, pellagra or dysentery.

He had been neither physically abused, as had so many of his fellow prisoners, nor had he suffered badly from malnutrition. He cared little about food and ate what was given him, and somehow managed to receive enough from his captors to survive. The meat would return to the bones, he knew. The bones were unbroken. The foundation was still sound.

He dressed, finally, in his uniform. He owned no civilian clothes as yet. The army had issued the clothes in the Philippines along with his gold leaf of majority. The bookkeeping had been immaculate and his promotions were waiting for him after he was repatriated, but now all of it seemed wasteful, the olive green coat the pinks, the shirts, the insignia and shoulder patches, new and glistening as if the army were sparing the folks back home the sight of men in prison garb: shapeless, colorless, anonymous, POW stamped on their backs—too harsh a reminder that wars were fought on many levels, some of it actually in trenches, in foxholes, jungles, in field hospitals and even in prisons.

He ate breakfast at a small diner and finally found a phone booth. He dialed Selda's phone number at work. She answered readily, "Public library, business branch."

"Selda?"

"Yes."

"This is Bill Crossen."

"Bill Crossen. My God. What are you doing here?"
Bill sensed a genuine surprise, almost a panic.

"I've been discharged."

"The war is barely over," Selda said. "How did you
manage to get here so soon?"

"I managed."

"I know, I know," Selda caught herself. "I didn't
mean to sound rude, I'm . . . just simply surprised. Why
didn't you let me know sooner?"

"I've been in quarantine. I just left Letterman General
Hospital."

"Where are you now?"

"I'm staying at the Marina Motel on Lombard Street."

"I know where that is. You've caught me off guard,
Bill, I'm sorry. Let me pick you up tonight."

"I don't want to trouble you."

"No trouble, just give me time to get home from
work, do a little shopping. We'll have dinner."

"You're sure it's no trouble?"

"I'm sure. I'll pick you up at eight."

"Thank you."

"Oh, Bill . . ."

"Yes?"

"It is nice to hear your voice after all this."

"Thank you."

"Have you called your parents yet?"

"No. I'll see you tonight."

Selda placed the phone on the receiver and stamped
a couple of books for one of her older acquaintances.

"That was my cousin," she said, still flustered. "He
just got out of a Japanese prison camp."

"Poor devil. Is he all right?"

"He sounds all right."

"We'll be getting the real story soon enough with all
those boys coming home."

"I guess we will."

Selda had known that one day this would happen. After the cease-fire it was inevitable that Bill Crossen would simply appear out nowhere, although she had thought that the processing of prisoners of war would be lengthy. She had not expected him for months. She sat in the library that day lost in thought, mechanically going over a number of unimportant details. She would go to Goldsberg Bowens for meat and vegetables, catch a cab and stop at Blum's for an almond cake. She had wine and Scotch at home; she would use her "best" crystal, inherited from her mother, linen tablecloth and napkins she had purchased last year . . . the good silver . . . she had candles.

She ate no lunch that day but knew she wouldn't lose the twenty pounds she'd meant to lose for months. . . . She knew, she felt that there would be pain. Cousin Selda, the go-between.

What must it be like, she wondered, to be in prison for four years? To be afraid of your captors for four years? She was no stranger to pain herself. Of course, there had been well-meaning, loving relatives: aunts, uncles, nieces, nephews who had sincerely rallied around her after the sudden death of her parents, but having been an only child she had been used to a closeness that could never be replaced, and she, too, had become a prisoner within herself. She had been jack-knifed into maturity and she did not like it.

Bill Crossen had studied that map of San Francisco that Selda had sent him as carefully as everything else he had studied. He had also received *National Geographic* issues on the city as well as books, pamphlets and histories, and as he walked now from Lombard Street toward the Bay, his engineering mind followed the route he had committed to memory.

It would take eight blocks to reach the Marina, and from there it would be twenty blocks to Fishermen's Wharf. He would cross Van Ness Avenue, one of the city's northeast arteries, and reach Hyde Street. He followed this route and was rewarded. Indeed, his memory served him well and the city came out as he had studied it, but this was not his only emotion.

He was simply not prepared for the beauty of San Francisco. As an engineer he noticed the preponderance of wood, and the absence of brick as a choice of building material. Wood was warmer, and safer during earthquakes. Endless rows of Victorian homes climbed up the streets of Telegraph Hill, Russian Hill, Nob Hill. He marveled at the filigree work; the small, prudent gardens; the flower-filled window boxes. There was an intimacy to the city so unlike New York, as if all San Franciscans were kindred to the Bay, and all of them were bound by the physical beauty of the city, the vicissitudes of the weather, the fog, the winds, the crystal-clear skies.

There were small flower stands on the downtown street corners and cable cars, toylike and noisy, gripping a cable running endlessly like a steel serpent under the middle of the street.

Bill Crossen noticed the men, most of them hatless, wearing dark suits, dark overcoats or British raincoats. The women, trim and also hatless, their legs encased in natural-colored silk stockings, wore tailored little suits, and clutched small purses and white cotton or leather gloves. And yet in that melange around Telegraph Hill there were Chinese, Italians, Filipinos, Slavs. Children were returning home in clusters from parochial schools, their black uniforms offset by multicolored sweaters. Little Chinese girls in socks and saddle shoes, their parchment-colored skin stretched tightly over good bone structure passed by. They resembled the dolls sold in Chinatown as souvenirs.

Bill returned to his room about six in the evening. He had walked and walked in the city and felt a warmth in its provincialism, and knew that for all his planning, this intimacy, this small-town atmosphere, would both help and hinder him. He had never known any chauvinism. The Lower East Side had only one uniting factor: All those who lived there worked to get away from it. The only common denominator of its inhabitants was poverty and hatred for the landlord, the police, the Mafia, the neighborhood gang.

After changing the shirt of his uniform, Bill realized that he should have a present for Selda, a souvenir, perhaps some flowers. It had simply not occurred to him on his walk, and now he felt it was too late to find a store that was still open. He could scarcely deny that Selda had done much for him these past years. Hardly any request went unanswered. Not only was she meticulous in her research but she often proposed astute alternatives and made meaningful suggestions. He had been truly fortunate.

The shortsightedness in not bringing a gift bothered him briefly. Bill knew that if he wanted for one reason or another to get into the social whirl, he would have to eliminate this innate boorishness of his. It was something he knew he could not get from a slide rule or a book of tables . . . and yet, at this stage of the game it was of prime importance. He had doubts, but they passed as he picked up a phone book and looked up the name of Henry Levey. He was listed twice, once on California Street under O'Gara and Levey; the other listing gave his home address, 1800 Broadway. Bill took out his street map and discovered that the home was on top of the hill behind him.

He left the motel and walked to the corner of Lombard and Broderick streets. He looked straight up until he saw the mansions gracing the hilltops. The last rays of sunset were reflected in the large sheets of glass in the well-washed bay windows. He was looking up, up like a tourist, and he wondered when he would be looking down.

He returned to the room to slip into his jacket and wait for Selda to pick him up. Feeling listless, he plopped down on the bed and tucked a pillow behind his back. A pillow, he thought, now so aware of all the small luxuries even this motel room provided: a pillow, a stack of clean towels, soap. Light. Extra blankets, sheets. A telephone, a heater in the bathroom, a seat for the toilet, a mirror, clothes hangers for his uniform . . . and he remembered how painfully one gave up these amenities.

Although he had never met Selda, he knew she was part of his family, and their presence flashed suddenly before him. At home there were two younger brothers, frail and frightened as he himself had been of a driving father, an unsympathetic mother. It had not been a home nor had it been a family. It had been a clearing-house. All religion and education.

Meals were served sullenly and eaten silently. The smells and sounds of poverty hung over all. There had been no play that he could remember. No roughhousing, no sports. Clothes had to be preserved for the next boy in line. There was the Torah and bar mitzvah and he had received a fountain pen. There were books upon books and numberless trips to the public library. There were tests and examinations, and endless sarcastic questioning by his father. "You got a B in biology? A B, you got? Goyim get B's. You get A's. You get A pluses. *Pluses*, do you hear?" And there were his father's rough cutter's hands pulling at his ear, slapping him mercilessly across the face when he dared to speak up, when he *knew* he was right and also knew (oh, God, how early he knew) that he was never right in that house. Each book was followed by another, each test was followed by another, each day was followed by another and the *schul* provided no succor, no love, only a cruel teacher in Hebrew school, a stern rabbi administering the Torah.

A family. That, too, he had missed in prison camp. He could not share memories of home with the other captives. There were no hayrides, no Christmases, no smell of freshly baked pies, no family picnics. . . . He had nothing to share, except misery. His inventory of childhood was as barren as the cupboards in the kitchen. He recalled only the card catalogue at the library, that stained oak box that almost became an extension of himself. Childhood had been references and cross-references, dictionaries, thesauruses, charts, tables, graphs, lists, summaries, appendices, large print and fine. Footnotes, footnotes . . .

He heard a horn. That would be Selda.

Chapter IV

Selda was younger than Bill Crossen had expected. Her face was round, somewhat cherubic, her hair was dark and reflected much care; she was shorter than he had imagined and chubbier; her bustling manner did not betray in the least her rather austere profession nor her skill.

When he got into the car, there was an awkwardness about kissing or not kissing that ended with Selda pulling his face toward her own, giving him a squeeze. It was not until they had become somewhat less tangled, Bill moving to his side of the car, that they could study each other.

"You're all skin and bones," Selda said, now finally focusing on Bill. "Those clothes just hang on you."

"It's the uniform," he said almost apologetically. "I think they all come in one size."

"Let me see who you look like. Your mother? You think you look like your mother?"

Bill reddened. "I don't know. . . ."

"Have you called them? How are they? I haven't seen them in ten years. Are you cold? Roll up the window."

She was bustling. Nervous.

"I haven't called them yet," Bill said.

"Why not? They must be worried about you."

"I . . . I just can't talk to them yet. They'd want me to come home."

"You've got to call them."

"I know, I know. All in good time."

"Where are your things?"

"At the motel."

"Well, bring them," Selda commanded. "I have a guest room."

Bill hesitated, almost blushed. "The motel is quite comfortable."

"Nonsense. Check out. I'll wait. Can't have you living in a hotel room."

Prompted by frugality, Bill complied. He fetched his one valise, paid his bill and rejoined Selda.

Selda put the car in gear and headed toward Telegraph Hill.

"I think you just like to surprise people."

"No, Selda. It's, well . . ." he stammered. "There's much you don't understand."

She listened sympathetically.

"One of the medical officers explained it last week before I was discharged. He talked about releasing emotions. Imprisonment does many things to a man."

Selda shook her head. "It didn't do anything to your intellect. I can tell you that."

"It's nice of you to say that. I can't thank you enough for all your efforts."

"Don't mention it."

"I will mention it," he fumbled. "I'll also mention the fact that I didn't bring you a present. . . ."

"Please, Bill . . ."

"I'm still numb, I guess. You sit and wait for the end of war. Weeks, months, years. Every night the same bunk, the same food. You suspect it's going to end sometime, and then it does end. It *is* all over, but you're insecure. Every time somebody blows a whistle you want to fall in."

"Well, there are no whistles in my house. Get out and open the garage door for me, will you?"

Bill carried several large brown paper bags as he followed Selda up one flight of stairs. She fumbled with her keys, finally managed to open the front door, and stepped aside to let her guest enter.

"Welcome, Bill Crossen," she said looking at him, his arms laden with groceries. "Welcome to my humble home."

The flat was warm and lovely. There was no view of the Bay, but the living room, decorated in light beiges and pastels, overlooked a small, manicured garden in back of the house. There was a living room, dining room, a kitchen and two bedrooms, one of which was obviously Selda's study.

The flat was book-filled, flower-filled. Small etchings framed in passe-partout hung along the walls and framed photographs of Selda's parents graced her dresser, among silver combs and brushes and a tray filled with bottles of perfume.

"There is some Scotch and soda on the coffee table," Selda shouted from the kitchen. "Make us a couple of drinks."

"I rarely drink," Bill answered, "but I'll make you one," which he did, and brought it to the kitchen. Selda had removed her overcoat and tied an apron around her silk dress.

"What kind of soldier doesn't drink? Here, open the wine. Surely you'll have some wine."

"Tonight," Bill nodded. "Tonight I'll have some wine. What a wonderful home you have."

"It's comfortable."

"It's beautiful."

"No, it's not beautiful. I still have so much furniture from my parents. I should get rid of it. They've been dead thirteen years now."

Bill said nothing, still wandering through the living room, studying pictures, admiring a small inlaid rosewood box, a volume of views of San Francisco, a vase full of carnations; and Selda studied him while steaming string beans, broiling steaks, and stirring a Bernaise sauce.

She lit candles in the dining room, and finally said, "Well, dinner is served."

Bill entered the dining room and pulled a chair out for Selda.

"Oh, God!" she said, "I've still got my apron on."

They sat and Selda raised her wine glass in toast.

"Home is the hunter, or how does that go?"

Bill ate quickly, much too quickly for conviviality.

"More vegetables?"

"No, thank you."

"Potatoes?"

"No."

"Here"—she cut half of her own steak and put it on his plate—"finish it," she commanded.

It reminded him of his mother. She had invariably cleaned her utensils with her fingers and then licked them. He had detested the habit, but now ate the extra half of Selda's steak dutifully.

"That's the best dinner I've had in years."

Selda laughed. "I guess the Japs aren't much competition."

49

"That was a gauche statement, wasn't it? But it *is* the truth. . . ."

"I'm glad to see you can still smile. Here, let's have more wine."

Bill refilled the glasses.

"Have there been a lot of shortages during the war?"

"No, not really. Just gasoline . . . men . . ."

She made the remark honestly. Bill Crossen did not pursue it. Selda went to the kitchen and brought back a large chocolate cake.

"This has been my major vice for several years now. As you can tell, no doubt."

"No, no." Crossen's face reddened.

"This is the best thing in San Francisco. A chocolate fudge cake from Blum's."

"I can't eat any more."

"You've got to try it."

"A little later, perhaps."

They finally got up from the dining room table. Bill offered to help with the dishes but Selda stopped him. "Just leave them."

They entered the living room. Selda lit the kindling in the fireplace, placed a log over it and adjusted the fire screen. She dimmed some lamps, shut off others.

"How about some brandy?"

"No, thank you."

"That's the main reason I live here," Selda said, pointing to the fireplace. "Only the old flats have fireplaces. My folks had one, but they never lit it. My mother was afraid of the mess. My father wouldn't spend the money to buy wood. . . ."

"We didn't have one at home," Bill said. "I lived in a boarding house at MIT where the landlady had one in the parlor. She kept it going all winter."

"Well, well, well, Bill Crossen. Do you feel like talking or what would you like to do?"

Selda's warmth was genuinely affecting.

"I have lived by the clock for four years," Bill said. "Not by the hour, but by the minute. It seems I've looked forward to this evening forever."

Even during the brief time they had been together it became quite evident to Selda that Bill Crossen, although quite proper and courteous, had also been very deeply scarred. She could not tell how much damage had been done during the war and how much in his early childhood. He had shied away from all discussions of his family.

"You must be very tired," she said. "There is plenty of time to talk tomorrow."

"No, no," Bill protested, "I need to know so much. I'd love to talk, unless you're tired."

"I'm not," Selda said, pouring herself some brandy.

He rose and walked to his room and gathered maps, notebooks, graphs, drawings. All these he laid out in meticulous order on the dining room table.

"Before you start," Selda said, "I'd like to ask a question."

"Ask," Bill said.

"You've been a prisoner for four years. I can't imagine what you've been through. Wouldn't it be better if you relaxed for a while? Take a vacation, a trip, be in the sun, go to the mountains."

"I can't afford that luxury now," Bill said.

"Why? Do you need money? I'll give it to you."

"No, no, Selda. I don't need money. Thank you. You've given so much already."

"Nonsense," Selda said, "although I admit you were demanding."

"I'm sorry."

"Don't be. It all became fascinating after a while. How do all the pieces fit?"

"Let me show you," Bill said, his eyes becoming alive. He pointed to a map of California with a pencil.

Selda held up her head. "No, no, I don't want a lecture now. I want to know how all the pieces fit with you. How do you *feel*? How do you *really* feel?"

Bill pounded his chest. "Sound as a dollar."

"What does it feel like to be released after all these years?"

"I don't know," Bill said. "I don't really know yet. I remember the first night I spent at the Presidio BOQ. It was the first time I had a room to myself in years."

"What did you miss the most," Selda asked, "girls, food, drink, what?"

Bill blushed. "Girls, I suppose, but you forget to think about it."

"Can you really? At your age?"

"Not right away, but it happens. Men stop talking about their wives, their girl friends. No one wants to be reminded of their forced celibacy."

"What about food?"

Bill shrugged his shoulders. "One was always hungry, but again the body compensates."

"You learn how to cope," Selda said.

"Yes. You learn how to cope."

"And you scheme," Selda said, almost sorry about the harshness of the word.

"Scheme, yes."

"So let's see how the pieces fit together."

"You're sure you're not too tired?"

Selda nodded. "I'm sure."

Again Bill pointed to the map of California. "If you follow the path of the rivers, here," he said, "here, here, it is evident that two thirds of the water is in northern California but two thirds of the arable land is in southern California. Clearly, a lot of water is lost through the delta into the ocean.

"I've read all the studies you've sent me. They were done before the war. A canal will be built. The war only delayed its construction. My guess is that a pumping station at Tracy and a hundred-mile canal will amply supply the San Joaquin Valley. Only a few contractors could handle a project of that size and O'Gara and Levey is one of them. With the innovations I've perfected, I'm convinced that that firm could land the bid and come in at a profit."

Selda was both impressed by the young man's acuity and uncomfortable with his almost brutal directness. She listened further as he outlined more and more of the details of this proposed canal.

"You seem very sure of yourself, Bill, but you've done all of this on paper, in your head."

"Not true," Bill countered. "I've built this canal. In miniature, but to scale. It works."

"How could you do all that? You were a prisoner."

Bill managed a feeble smile. "I speak Japanese fluently, and the Japanese are avid students. Aside from my duties as sanitary officer for the camp—and I was good at them—I ran daily classes for them. They are very ambitious people."

"It's fascinating," Selda said. "I can't believe it."

"We reproduced the entire state, from Mount Shasta to the Salton Sea. Every river, every delta, every lake and desert."

"And how did your fellow prisoners take to this?"

"It was difficult, but I managed." Bill made it clear he did not want to elaborate.

They spoke for three hours. Construction, financing, population shifts, rainfall tables. At one o'clock, Selda stood up.

"All right. So you're convinced there'll be a canal. I would think every construction firm in California is poised for that project."

"No doubt," Bill said. "But I do have an ace in the hole." He rose and disappeared into his room and returned with two models, beautifully constructed and looking almost like abstract sculpture.

"What in God's name are these?"

"This"—he pointed to one of the models—"is a canal liner. This is a canal trimmer. Once built they'll save endless man-hours. My first step is to patent these inventions."

"They look intricate," Selda said. "How do they work?"

"They are simplicity itself," Bill said. "Their ingenuity—*my* ingenuity, and I don't mean this boastfully—is to use railroad tracks. Not the usual tracks, set three and a half feet apart, but set aside for the width of the canal. Both trimmer and liner work on top of these tracks and all the machinery to trim and to line are in bridges running along this track. Nothing could be more accurate and nothing could be faster. . . . Do you understand?"

"I suppose," Selda said. "But who will build them? They'll be expensive, won't they?"

"Yes. But I think Levey will back me."

Selda pushed back her chair and looked at all the data on the table, the computations, the graphs, the models, and then she looked at her cousin.

"There's no question you've done your homework."

"I suppose I have," Bill said.

"All you need now is a certain amount of polish. . . ."

"I don't quite know what you mean."

"I mean," she said rather sharply, "you may be one hell of an engineer, but you are still the kid from the Lower East Side of New York."

"I don't know if I understand you. . . ."

"Mr. Levey," Selda said, "comes from a very smug, very exclusive circle of Pacific Heights Jews."

"They'll object to my background?" Bill asked innocently.

"If you're not fourth-generation San Francisco—forget it."

"How about *you?*" Bill asked. "You're old-line San Francisco."

"Old-line in years, yes, but I'm from the Richmond district. Middle, middle class. My parents were teachers, not professors—not a chance."

"What would it take?"

"If you were a goy."

"*Any* goy?"

"Just about. They've all wanted to be goys themselves." She looked at him. "You've already changed your name. You look like a goy. Maybe you could pass."

Bill scratched his head. "No, I'm not going to do that. Despite its drawbacks, I like the intellectualism of Judaism."

"I'll drink to that," Selda said.

"There are other engineering firms, I suppose," Bill said.

"Yes, there are. There are fourth-generation gentiles in San Francisco, too. . . ."

Bill seemingly took no offense at Selda's lecture. "You are saying I still need polish. . . ."

"I am," Selda agreed. "You may be the brightest young engineer to come down the pike, but nobody is waiting for a pushy Jew."

"I suppose what you're saying makes sense," Bill said.

"That's mighty generous of you, Major," Selda said, standing and heading for her bedroom. "I've left some towels at the foot of your bed, and a key to the apartment. I have to work tomorrow. Good night."

She fell asleep mercifully soon, unaware that Bill had never gone to bed. He was still at the dining room table when she rose.

"Did you work all night?" she asked.

"Yes. I've learned to manage on two hours' sleep."

"You haven't even had that."

"I'm going to bed now," Bill said, rolling up his charts.

She heard the bedroom door close and fetched her purse and left for work.

Chapter V

When she returned home that evening, Selda noticed the military neatness with which Bill had made the bed. The dishes were washed and the apartment looked dusted.

They had finished dinner and Bill was about to continue his lecture from the night before, but Selda stopped him. She was somewhat annoyed that Bill, who had had a whole day to himself, still had not given her some token of appreciation, not for its material value, but for the thought.

"I don't mean to say I'm not interested in your plans. Your research seems meticulous. However—"

She pushed her chair back from the table.

"Yes?"

"You still don't really understand what I was trying to tell you last night. . . ."

"You said I wasn't a fourth-generation San Franciscan."

"I *did* say that. And there is nothing I or you can do

57

about that. However, I *can* tell you about the kind of man they respect."

"What kind of man is that?"

"He'll have to have social graces." She paused. "He *may* be ambitious but can't look eager. You'll have to buy the right kind of clothes, a car. You'll have to attend their parties, play their game."

"*What* game?"

"Dances, Sunday picnics, dinner parties. You said you have some money. How much?"

"Thirteen thousand dollars. I meant to ask you. I need to find a bank."

"Are you willing to spend any of it toward your career?"

"Yes. Whatever it takes. I had calculated some of that."

"That's the right word for you. How about your emotions?"

"They may be troublesome," Bill answered, quite openly.

"Well, I'm glad you realize it."

Selda did not wash the dishes or have brandy that night but went to bed early.

The following morning, noticing that Bill was asleep, she took off her pajamas, brushed her teeth and combed her hair. Moving quietly into his room she slipped into his bed naked. He awoke suddenly like a frightened animal and sat up quickly. But it took him only a split second to realize that Selda was lying shamelessly beside him.

"Selda."

"Yes?"

"We're cousins."

"Third cousins."

"I know, but . . ."

"Am I so repulsive?"

"No, no, but I . . ."

"But what?"

"You don't understand."

"Put your arms around me," she commanded, and Bill, used to orders, followed one more, gingerly feeling the nakedness of her buttocks.

"It's been a long time," Bill said. "A very long time. Where I came from men even gave up masturbating."

"I don't want much from you, Bill. I only need a masculine arm around me."

Bill complied and felt her ample breasts against his chest. He felt Selda opening her legs and felt the moistness. He caressed her with his fingers, but when she held him in return he remained limp.

She kissed him on his lips and said, "Don't worry so much. Don't worry at all. It's the worst thing you could do. You are a very good-looking man. Remember that!"

Then she rose and returned to her room, and Bill's eyes followed her out of the room. He went back to sleep.

It had not been right, Selda thought, doing this to a frightened boy, but there was no question that his presence in her house had excited her. Her life had been quite monastic since her return from Europe; and yet her memories were crystal clear: "You are a very warm, very vibrant girl," her lover had said in Florence. Ansell Eisman, the curator of a small Boston museum, had been on a sabbatical. (She had sensed he was on a marital sabbatical also.)

He had taken her to the studio of a friend of his. "Perhaps the best draftsman in Western Europe," he had said. "I want him to paint you." She had accompanied him to a small garret near the river. It was warm and smelled of chestnuts, and linseed oil, she remembered. She was introduced. The curator spoke Italian, but she didn't.

"It is agreed," her friend had said. "He wants to paint you."

"I'm flattered."

"You should be. I only hope I can attend the showing when it's finished."

"When will he start?"

"Now. The dressing room is over there."

"Dressing room?"

"I'm afraid, my love, you'll have to take off your clothes."

"He wants to do me in the nude?"

Ansell had come over to her and put his arm around her. He said something in Italian to the painter, and they both laughed. Selda was twenty-two. A protected San Francisco girl from a very middle-class family.

"An artist is like a surgeon," Ansell had said, and Selda went into the dressing room. She removed her dress, and she unfastened her silk stockings and slid them down her legs. Mercifully, there was no mirror in the small cubicle. She undid her bra, removed her panties. She stood naked and shivering, covering her pubic area with her hands, nervous, excited. There was an old robe on a nail, and she wrapped herself in it and reappeared in the atelier.

The artist, perhaps fifty, fifty-five, had arranged a series of canvas-covered boxes on a small platform, and was lighting it with a tin-covered floodlight. He took no notice of Selda at first, fussing with backdrops, lights and shadows. Finally he asked Selda to step up. She came forward. He motioned for her to take off the robe. She hesitated for a minute, then threw it off. The painter said nothing and placed her on the platform. He moved her legs, and her arms, and her face and touched her hair, all firmly, professionally. Selda sensed Ansell's burning eyes and the eyes of the painter on her body, still young, firm, ripe, her skin olive and smooth; she felt her nipples rise. . . .

They had gone to the painter daily for three weeks and it became a ritual. She undressed more easily each day, and slowly the air became clearer in the atelier. Ansell and the painter would converse in Italian. Ansell would translate. They commented on her coquettishness. They would talk about her breasts, her fanny as if she and her body were separate entities, and after the sitting they would rush back to Ansell's room and revel in warm, fierce lovemaking. Later they would go to the corner restaurant, a modest peasant establishment, and they would eat ravenously, and get heady with wine— all of it, the afternoon and evening, revolving around her, her body, her sexuality. . . . Those weeks had served her well, these many years. . . .

There had been sexual advances after this, mostly at work and all of them from married men. But Selda's sense of propriety would not allow these to flourish, and with the war and the scarcity of men, she had become quite celibate—but not by choice. This morning had only proved to her her needs; and her guilt was almost gone by the time she had packed her lunch, taken her raincoat out of the closet and skipped down the steps of her house on her way to work.

Bill awoke at noon with an erection. It was the first one since his captors had taken him to a Filipino whore two years earlier. They had allowed him less than an hour, and the girl, or girl-child—she was very young—had been so warm and compliant he was grateful that for one solitary hour he could forget the stumps of beheaded men on the march from Bataan, the mangled legs, the arms, the hundreds of men who had died of dysentery, malnutrition, heat stroke, malaria. Few of them died well, incontinence and vomiting being the usual farewell gestures. One had to shut all this off in a special room as well.

Selda had clearly caught him off guard, both physically and emotionally. And though he could not deny the enjoyment of a naked girl in his bed, the texture and the warmth of her body, yet he could not classify his emotions, something that was always troublesome for him.

When Selda returned from work bearing heavy grocery bags as usual, Bill surprised her.

"No cooking tonight," he said. "Allow me to take you out."

"My goodness," Selda said. "Look at the flowers. Where did they come from?"

Bill smiled and she kissed him lightly on the cheek.

"Well, let me get some of this ink and glue off my hands, dive into a shocking gown and we'll be off. I swear that Mr. Sullivan makes me get the 1941 Dow Jones compendium from the top shelf every day so he can look up my dress when I get on the ladder. . . ."

Selda had chosen a small inexpensive restaurant on Russian Hill called Julius' Castle, whose windows looked out on one of the most dramatic views of the San Francisco Bay. There were candles in old wine bottles, their drippings covering the neck like multicolored rosary beads. They ordered rex sole and green salad. The table groaned under stacks of sourdough bread, butter, Parmesan cheese. . . .

"This is a very pretty spot," Bill said, looking at the Bay below him, its outline circled by a ring of diamondlike lights.

"I should apologize," Selda finally said, putting her hand on Bill's.

"Why?"

"I don't usually just jump into bed with men."

"Please, don't apologize," Bill said. "You're a very pretty girl."

"No," Selda said. "I am not a very pretty girl." She shook her head and the candlelight caught the sheen of her dark hair. "But inside this plumpish body *is* a very pretty girl."

"I thought about you a great deal today," Bill said.

"That's nice to know," Selda said.

"Do you want me to move out?"

"Why would I want you to do that?"

"What if *I* jump in bed with *you*?"

"What if you do?"

There was so much fear in the boy's face, Selda noticed. Fear, anger, repression. . . . "What a god-damned conversation," she said lightly. "I'll get the prince consort ready for the ball, don't worry—and if there is a little hanky-panky in the servant's quarters who will be the wiser for it?"

"God damn," Bill said. "God damn this Cohen family."

"Why are you saying that?"

"Because they *are* bright. So bright. My father . . ." he hesitated.

"Go on," Selda said.

"My father was a cutter. He sweated all his life and yet I knew he was bright, as was my mother, as *you* are. . . ."

"Then why don't you call them?"

"They were bright," Bill said, "but stupid. Do you know what I mean?"

"Not totally."

"They were poor. Desperately poor, and so they used their children, me, my brothers, to build a bridge to a better future. My brothers did not excel. *I* did. I was the keystone to that bridge."

"But you can't blame them for that."

"Oh, yes I can." Bill was silent and finally said, almost

to himself, "You can only hammer that keystone so much. I got a scholarship to NYU. I got it just in time. I have learned in engineering that you can put just so much force on a bridgestone."

When they returned to Selda's flat, they drank a little brandy and Bill slept in Selda's bed. She recalled the next morning that his lovemaking was hasty, nervous, but there *were* times when he evoked memories of Florence, when she felt happy that the naked man was not in an anonymous window across the street, but in her own bed.

Time passed and Selda made headway with her new charge. She had supervised his purchases at Roos Brothers, at Bullock and Jones, at the White House and Emporium. She had helped pick out his suits, his shirts, had chosen his neckties (rep), his shoes (wing tips), and though he had chafed at the high prices at first, he bought good English wools and well-made shirts. He *did* see the wisdom in quality and correctness in his dress. Perhaps more important to Selda was the fact that he was now, willingly, sharing her bed, and her gentleness and womanly intuition slowly brought forth some of the sexuality long suppressed or perhaps never discovered. Selda's feelings were mixed, for she was growing attached to Bill, and not only physically.

She had learned these past weeks that this boy—yes, in many ways at twenty-four he was still a boy—was very stern. Not only with others, but certainly with himself. He had no indulgences, and all the new clothes, new luggage, the watch, the automobile, were there for a purpose, not for pleasure.

One evening after making love Selda sat up in bed.

"Let's say you succeed, Bill."

"I will."

"I'm sure you will. Then what?"

"I don't understand."

"Why? What will it bring you? Nothing really seems to give you much pleasure. Food, clothes—I don't even know whether you enjoy making love to me."

"I do enjoy it, Selda. I reach a climax now, don't I?"

"Yes," Selda said, almost pensively, "*you* reach a climax."

"What do you mean?"

"Nothing," Selda said.

"You've been very good to me," Bill said. "I am really grateful."

"But where will it all lead? You have a nice car, you rarely drive it. You have new clothes; you never wear them. Then you'll have bigger cars, even better clothes. . . ."

"I really only aim to be successful to have power."

"What kind of power?"

Bill thought for a minute.

"A power so great that I can tell everyone to go to hell."

Chapter VI

It had not been difficult for Selda through her contacts at the library to gain Bill some entrée to San Francisco's Jewish society. It had been customary during the war to invite isolated, well-behaved young men to dinner, and this custom prevailed now in the first afterglow of victory. As a major, as a prisoner of war, as a fine-looking young man whose ribs had filled in from Selda's cooking, Bill Crossen found himself quite popular with seemingly little effort.

He was quiet, intense, some said shy; others found him insecure, but he appeared, particularly to the older generation, as serious, bright and very decisive. He first met Marjorie at a small dinner party at the Lehmans', their lovely mansion on Jackson Street. He was unaware at first that she was the daughter of Henry Levey, whom he had planned to approach for a job. He had heard about this girl at other parties and from Selda, who had remembered that she was a brilliant pianist. He liked her looks. She was almost frail, but full-busted. Her face, framed by short hair, displayed a great deal of intensity and yet reflected an inner peace. Her nose was definitely aquiline but well shaped. Above all it was her hands and fingers that fascinated Bill immediately: their expressiveness, their strength and delicacy; the way the girl used them, guarding them like a Stradivarius.

"Major Crossen," she said, "I've heard so much about you."

"Please call me Bill," he said. "Your reputation precedes you also."

"Sounds ominous," Marjorie said.

"No, no. I am a great admirer of musical genius."

"Please, please. Someone is overstating my case."

But Bill contined undeterred. "I like mathematics, some say I'm gifted in that field. I think that music is the highest form of mathematics."

"Perhaps that's true, but a little feeling doesn't hurt it either. I seem to be having most of my problems along that line."

"Why?" Bill asked. "You seem like a very sensuous person to me."

"That is a very nice compliment, Major."

"Bill."

"Bill."

"But you still haven't answered my question."

"That's right." She brushed some hair away from her face. "Technique is one thing. One comes *close*, remember, I said *close* to mastering it, but one must reach the soul of the music. *That* is difficult. At least for me. Once you have accomplished that, then you begin to interpret. Rubinstein reads Brahms differently from Horowitz, but who is to say who is right?"

"It is hard to ask Brahms," Bill said, and Marjorie laughed.

"Yes, and Beethoven, Haydn, Bach. . . ."

"But what about, say, Rachmaninoff? If the composer plays his own material, isn't that the ultimate reading?"

Marjorie studied Bill intently. "They say that Horowitz plays Rachmaninoff better than Rachmaninoff. But now we go back to technique."

"And so you are at the mercy of the critics."

"Yes."

"And how objective are they?"

"It varies from critic to critic," Marjorie said, "but on the whole, respected critics have earned their reputations."

Mrs. Lehman, a gray-haired matron adorned in brocade and jade, came between them.

"I'm sorry to interrupt," she said, "but dinner is served."

They entered a lovely room in which an oval table was set for twelve. The chandelier was reflected in a small army of sparkling wineglasses; the linen napkins, crisp and starched, seemed almost too precious to soil. A butler and maid served a delicate shrimp salad and Bill (despite Selda's tutoring) picked up the wrong fork, and Marjorie, observing this, followed suit.

Mrs. Lehman noticed quickly and with a glance pointed out the gaffe to Marjorie, but said nothing.

Mr. Lehman, noticing the tense atmosphere, caught Bill's eye.

"You're an engineer, Major, I am told."

"Yes, sir. Civil."

"Planning to stay in San Francisco?"

"Those are my plans at present."

"Then you've not gained employment?"

"No, sir, only weight. I weighed a hundred and twenty-five pounds when I was released from San Tomas."

"Rotten Nip bastards. Truman should have blasted them all to kingdom come."

"Harold," his wife half shouted, indicating a Japanese maid.

"I'm sorry, Kimo," Lehman said. "You know what I mean. . . ."

The girl retreated from the dining room with tears in her eyes.

"Welcome to gentility," Marjorie said to Bill. "They all got rich in this war, and now they're all experts."

"There seem to be some people who have kept their heads," Bill said.

"Who?"

"You, for one."

"I hope so," Marjorie said.

"What was it like during the war," Bill asked.

"Here? In San Francisco? Not much changed. There was a shortage of butter, nylons and men. The dinner parties continued, the opera continued, everyone on Pacific Heights had illegal gas coupons. . . . The picnics still took place, the weekends in Tahoe, Carmel."

"What did you miss the most?"

"Men," Marjorie answered forthrightly.

"The deferment rate, as I understand it, was very high in San Francisco?"

"Quite right. Most of the sons of the rich were able to get 'classified' jobs. I think Darwin had somethnng to say about that."

"Then there *were* men," Bill said.

"If you want to call them that," Marjorie answered. "I minded my mother," she continued, "and attended all the obligatory parties, and I would come home and wish I had put in the time at the piano. . . ."

Dinner was over and, not unlike the British, the men retired to the library while the women hovered about the dining room.

Mrs. Lehman came up to Marjorie. "I am sorry I chided you, Marjorie," she said, "but I almost feel like you're my own daughter."

"Major Crossen," Marjorie said, "picked up the wrong

fork. He said for four years in prison he ate all his meals with a spoon."

"The Major," Mrs. Lehman said, "has a valid excuse. *You* do not."

"I was taught to watch my escort. If he commits a gaffe, you follow suit. I think it is called noblesse oblige."

"Oh, Marjorie, why must you always be so *direct?*"

Mrs. Lehman walked to the butler's pantry and Marjorie joined Bill and the men in the library.

They had been at the Lehman house on Monday and at the Green mansion on Thursday where the entire dinner conversation revolved about the pedigree of dogs and horses, trainers, stables, owners' colors, Virginia and Kentucky. Halfway through that meal Bill turned to Marjorie and said, "I seem to be totally at sea here. I never had a dog, much less a horse, in my life."

"You're missing the *whole* point of this theater," Marjorie said, and Bill, a lover of precise language, noticed the word *theater.*

"This is gentile talk. Not gentle. Gentile."

"I heard you," Bill said.

"These Jews," she pointed around the table, "don't give a damn about horses or dogs, either, but they have so much money now, they can finally indulge in the playing fields of the gentiles. Stables of horses, hunting, hunt breakfasts, steeple chasing, stable boys. . . .

It was after that second dinner that Bill returned home to Selda and reported his admiration for Marjorie Levey, a report that pleased Selda, but also hurt her. She was getting used to having a man in bed.

Bill phoned Marjorie after the Greene dinner and asked her to have dinner with him at the Mark Hopkins. She accepted and he sent flowers in the afternoon before picking her up.

When Bill arrived at the Leveys' home, a butler opened

the door and he was shown into the spacious drawing room.

"Would you care for a drink, Major?"

"No, thank you," Bill said.

"Miss Marjorie will be right down."

"Miss Marjorie *is* down," Marjorie said, stepping out of the adjoining library, "and I'll have a martini."

"Very good, miss," the butler said and retreated.

"Welcome," Marjorie said. "The flowers were lovely. Many thanks."

"My pleasure."

They heard footsteps on the stairway.

"Here comes Mother," Marjorie said.

"Major Crossen," Hortense Levey, a handsome woman in her midfifties, said with mock enthusiasm, "so happy to meet you. I've heard about you from Alice Lehman, Myra Green. . . ."

"Yes," Bill said. "I'm no good at musical forks."

"Oh, that," Hortense half laughed. "Etiquette seems to play a very large role in these circles."

The butler entered and handed Marjorie her martini.

"You're not drinking, Major?" Hortense asked.

"I seem to have lost the taste during the war."

"Really. Perhaps you could be a good influence on Marjorie. In *my* days girls never *drank* by themselves and *never* drank martinis."

"Well, here's to the village drunk," Marjorie said, raising her glass and downing its contents almost in one gulp.

"I am sorry," Hortense said, "that Mr. Levey can't meet you, Major. He is indisposed."

"Kindly give him my best wishes," Bill said as Marjorie went to get her coat.

Marjorie and Bill were seated in the lofty dining room of the Mark Hopkins surrounded by waiters in cutaways.

71

They could hear the bland music of Ernie Heckscher emanating from another room.

Bill was pondering Marjorie's statement about her father. He had asked her about Henry Levey's health on their drive to the hotel.

"My father," she said, "is not indisposed. He is sitting by the fireplace in his bedroom finishing his fourth martini and eating a large filet mignon."

"He eats alone?"

"Mostly."

"Why?"

"He hates my mother."

Bill finished his vichyssoise and looked at Marjorie.

"You are," he said, looking directly into her eyes, "a very forthright girl. I like that."

"Thank you. Forthright," Marjorie mused. "My mother has told me that despite an older brother and sister, every gray hair in her head was because of me."

"She must be proud of your talent."

"I'm not too sure. She's of the children-should-be-seen-but-not-heard school."

"And your father?"

"I am glad you asked."

"Why?"

"I'm sorry, but I made him sound like an aging alcoholic. He is anything but that. He's a brilliant engineer and I love him dearly."

"The firm of O'Gara and Levey," Bill said.

"Yes. Do you know of them?"

"Yes. I know almost every engineering firm in San Francisco. I do have to *gain* employment soon, as Mr. Lehman put it."

"Why don't you talk to Daddy?"

"I intend to."

Dinner was served, and also wine. Bill apologized for

not asking her to dance. "I've gotten pretty rusty the last four years."

"And where do you live now, Bill?" Marjorie asked.

"With a distant cousin. Selda Cohen. She's a librarian."

Bill looked at Marjorie and help up his hand. "Crossen, Cohen. I *will* explain. I changed my name to get a scholarship at MIT. A matter of expediency."

"The same nonsense as the horses and the dogs."

"Yes," Bill said. "My parents haven't spoken to me since."

Marjorie was impressed with the gravity of that statement and, sensing that she should probe no further, let the matter drop.

More parties ensued, at the Schlosses' and the Ellmans', at the Goldmans' and the Bodenheimers'. More dinners followed these (always preceded by flowers), at the Fairmont, the Huntington, the Blue Fox, at Jack's. It was after the last of these elegant meals that Bill parked the car in front of Marjorie's home and she turned to face him.

"We have covered everything from *War and Peace* to emerging computer technology. We have discussed dissonance and Disraeli, and I'd like to make a summation."

"To wit?" Bill asked.

"For an unemployed major I would like to ask you to stop spending money so freely, and secondly, if you won't kiss me good night, I'll kiss you."

Bill embraced her and kissed her quickly, clumsily, but Marjorie made light of that. She opened the car door and turned to face him.

"Next time—Foster's Cafeteria. They make the best English muffin in town—and stop the flowers, although I love them."

"You're quite a girl," Bill said.

Hortense was waiting in the living room when Marjorie entered.

"You've been seeing a good deal of this Major Crossen," she said.

"Yes," Marjorie said, "why?"

"All those flowers. What do you know about him? His family?"

"In what order, Mother?"

"Don't talk to me like that. Your lipstick is smeared."

"Thank God for that," Marjorie said. "I'm going to bed. Good night."

"I am not finished talking to you."

"I know. But I am. Good night, again."

She ran up the stairs to her room. After closing her door she wiped the lipstick from her mouth with a tissue, folded it and put it in a drawer.

Bill arrived home in high spirits and was surprised at Selda's testiness as he continued his enthusiastic revelations about Marjorie's spunk and wit and good humor.

Selda still seemed cold.

"What's wrong?" he asked.

"You can't understand anything, can you?"

"What?"

"Don't you think you mean anything to me? Do you think you can come home from night after night with that girl, make love to me, turn over and go to sleep?"

"I'm sorry, Selda."

Selda was crying. "Well, that's a step in the right direction. Pretty soon you can forget me, just like your parents."

"We'll always be close."

"Sure, sure," Selda said through her tears. "We'll see each other, but not in here. San Francisco is a very small town. I'm a very provincial girl. I don't sleep with married men."

She paused and thought to herself, Maybe my life would be easier if I did.

She watched Bill sleeping and was ashamed of her

outburst earlier. She had jumped into bed with Bill. *She* had been the aggressor. Bill had not lied. Not since the first letter she had received from him. It was *her* need that had initiated the lovemaking; she was certain that Bill would not have pursued it.

From the day of her parent's untimely death, she had learned quickly that to survive in this world she needed to be mature and she needed to be fair. The tragedy speeded the first quality; her innate goodness did not make it difficult to develop the second.

There was no reason now, even though she felt a deep involvement with this boy, to discard either maturity or fairness, she decided.

Chapter VII

BUDDING CONCERT PIANIST MARJORIE LEVEY
AND WAR HERO
MAJOR WILLIAM CROSSEN A NEW ITEM. SEEN
IN
ALL THE BEST PLACES.

Herb Caen
San Francisco Chronicle

"Jesus Christ," Bill said to Marjorie as they sat around
the pool of her father's Menlo Park estate. "You'd think
I'd won the Nobel Prize. Every one of your friends
keeps bringing up that item in that Caen column."

"They're not all my friends," Marjorie said, "but Herb
Caen looms very large in this city. I understand you can
hire press agents to get mentioned every three weeks."

"Curious," Bill said. "So goddamned curious."

"Why do you think I hide behind the piano?"

"That reminds me, young lady," he cupped her face

and kissed her, "when are you going to let me hear you play?"

"All in good time. I sound like my mother, don't I?"

It was a very warm summer for Bill and Marjorie. They had stopped the Mark Hopkins, Fairmont, Huntington circuit and now were picnicking in Muir Woods, spending weekends on the Russian River. They took long walks on the beach and grew more intimate, but Bill respected Marjorie's self-proclaimed virginity.

"I know," she had said, "that it may sound hypocritical coming from me, impulsive little Marjorie, but I *am* a virgin and perhaps some of those endless lectures of my mother had *some* impact."

Bill was not upset with these restrictions. He found himself drawn to Marjorie in a way he had never known. Perhaps she *was*, as Selda had cautioned, a fourth-generation San Franciscan; perhaps she *was* the daughter of Henry Levey. Yet she made him feel close, warm; her intellect was challenging, her repartee exciting.

It was only a few days after her proclamation of virginity that Bill drove to Marjorie's home on the spur of the moment. He heard the piano as he stepped from his car and was almost overwhelmed by the power of the sounds emanating from the keyboard. He mounted the steps and rang the bell. The maid answered the door and Bill put his finger to his lips and sat down outside the drawing room. He could barely see her between the fronds of a potted palm and watched as she made run after run, watched her make notations on the music, going over it again and again. Exercises for the left hand, exercises for the right hand, arpeggios and passage work. He was transfixed.

He must have sat there two hours when he heard her gently close the keyboard.

He rose and startled her.

77

"Sorry for the ambush," he said, watching her wipe perspiration from her face.

He sat on the piano bench and kissed her. He had never kissed her so fervently that she could remember.

"I can't believe it."

"What?"

"This talent. This sound. This intricacy."

"I should be very cross with you."

"You should."

"You said you were going on interviews."

"I did. But I didn't."

"Obviously."

"Something more pressing came up."

"What?"

"I've decided to ask you to marry me."

"Look at me," she said, "in an old sweat shirt. I'm drenched to the skin, no lipstick, no makeup."

"That's no answer," Bill said.

"What should I say?"

"Say yes," Bill offered.

"Yes."

"That is—" Bill hesitated, "if you're interested in an unemployed civil engineer."

"It's still yes."

"I'll speak to your father tomorrow."

"I'll speak to him tonight."

"Please," Bill said. "Please let me talk to him first. Say nothing for now."

It was almost a command.

Chapter VIII

The Levey home sat foursquare and four stories high on Broadway almost next to the pine forest of the Presidio. All of its well-washed northern windows commanded the best view of San Francisco Bay; and its Italianate structure, its furnishings—mostly from Gump's and Shreve's—reflected good solid, restrained taste. There was a fine library with leather-bound books, a large living room, an equally large master bedroom and ample quarters for all the children, all the help, all the Spode in the pantries and the luggage in the attic.

Henry Levey was taking his last brandy of the evening and watching the dying embers in his marbled hearth.

"I am worried about this Major Crossen, Henry," Hortense said.

"Why? I haven't seen Marjorie so happy in a long time."

"He was here this afternoon. He came unannounced."

"A criminal offense," Henry answered, yawning. "She's a grown woman. She's twenty-three."

"She's just a child."

Levey changed his mind and poured another brandy from a handsome cut-glass decanter.

"She is not a child. She is a very good student, a very fine pianist. I see no reason to deny her happiness."

"What do we know about this boy," Hortense snapped. "Is he a goy? Crossen—what kind of name is that?"

"His name is Cohen."

"How do you know that?"

"Marjorie told me."

"That's even worse."

"Why worse? He went to NYU, to MIT on scholarship. I can understand his motives."

"And where are his parents?"

"New York," Levey said.

"Polacks," Hortense said bitterly.

"Shut up, Hortense."

"Cohen from New York. You *know* what that means."

"It means only that he's not from San Francisco. So what?"

"Only the poor Jews stayed in New York. You know that as well as I do."

"Yes, like my grandfather."

"I don't want to discuss that anymore."

Levey laughed. "Still bothers you, doesn't it?"

"It's not the issue," Hortense said.

"What *is*? One Polack in the family is enough?"

"Stop shouting it, Henry."

"Afraid the children might learn the truth?"

"There's only Marjorie. Remember? I had Linda's nose fixed and she married a Seiff. Marjorie refused to have her nose fixed, and here we are."

"Well, where are we? Are you saying Marjorie is a *mieskeit*?"

"Don't use those words."

"What words would you like me to use?"

"She could have looked better."

"And married what? Another charming boy like your son?"

"Leave him out of it."

"Why? His only admirable quality is that he's from San Francisco."

"Why don't *you* shut up?" She ran toward the bathroom and slammed the door; and Marjorie, who had overheard the entire conversation, tiptoed to her room, locked the door and cried.

She lay on her bed and looked about her room. It looked like dozens of other rooms of her peers in San Francisco. It had twin beds so she could have friends overnight. Friends of her own sex. There were high school diplomas and honors, and camp certificates. There were felt flags from Stanford and Barnard and a collection of teddy bears and old dolls. There was her piano and its bench, a metronome. Her closet held all the clothes she needed for any social event on the calendar: cashmere sweaters, suits, tweed skirts, and bathing suits and clothing for skiing. There were signed photographs of piano virtuosi she had met and pictures of her niece and nephew, Linda's children. There were wedding pictures also, of her brother, of her sister, pictures of her catching the well-aimed bridal bouquet that Linda had thrown. And looking now at that picture, she knew her legs were a little too straight, too shapeless, her breasts a little too pendulous, her nose a little too long. She did not need the substantiation of a photograph to confirm her self-image. She had known the cruelty of her friends for too many years to have any doubts about her popularity in the group, and she was fully aware now of the talk, the gossip, the speculation that surrounded her alliance with Bill Crossen.

He was a silent man. This she had learned. He did not like being questioned. This, too, she had learned, and she had complied. He was troubled, she felt, almost afraid, and yet, he was there.

She had gotten much comfort from academia, and more from her music. She had survived a twelve-hour day with sixteen hours of activity. This had often worked. It would work for weeks, months, perhaps, but it did not work completely. She was a young woman. She wanted a man. She looked at the well-made twin bed next to her own, and she no longer wanted it occupied by another troubled or bubbly or equally frustrated girl friend over for the weekend. She wanted a double bed, shared by a man. It was time. It was high time. Whatever her family wanted, she cared less; and whatever her friends wanted, to hell with them. The slumber parties were over.

She picked up her phone and reached Bill at Selda's apartment.

"Bill?"

"Yes. Marjorie?"

"Yes. How quickly can you get packed?"

"Why?"

"I want to elope."

"You can't be serious."

"I'm very serious."

"Your parents . . ."

"To hell with my parents! How quickly?"

Bill said nothing.

"I'll be over in an hour. What's the address?"

Bill gave it to her and rose from the couch. Selda was in the dining room cataloging.

"What's up?" she asked.

"That was Marjorie."

"At this hour?"

"Yes. She wants to elope."

"That wasn't in your script, was it?"

"Not exactly."

"What now, Bubba?"

"I'll elope."

"Tell me why?"

"I don't want to lose that girl."

"What about Levey and O'Gara?"

"Let it fall into place," Bill said.

"Her father might think you married her to get a job."

"To hell with her father," Bill said. "There are other engineering firms."

Selda rose and kissed him.

"You know, Bubba, there's hope for you yet."

Chapter IX

Marjorie wore a light beige cashmere sweater, a tweed skirt. She carried a small valise and a dark blue blazer. Feeling slightly shaky, she pressed the buzzer to Selda's apartment, entered the small lobby and half ran down a dark hallway toward a shaft of light that promised an open door.

Bill caught her in his arms and led her in.

Selda rose and extended her hand.

"I'm Selda Cohen, Bill's cousin," she said. "Welcome."

"I'm terribly sorry," Marjorie said, "to burst in on you at one in the morning."

"Come here," Selda said. "Sit down. You're shaking."

Selda put her arms about the girl as Bill watched.

"I know this is incredibly rude, and I really *do* apologize. . . ."

"Bill," Selda said, "leave us alone for a few minutes, will you?"

Bill nodded and, looking confused, went to his bedroom and closed the door.

"Now," Selda said, "don't make me feel like a Jewish mother. I'm only eight years older than you."

Marjorie looked at her, at that kind, warm face.

"Bill told me why you're here, and I want to tell you that he is very fond of you. I make no apologies for him," Selda said. "He's quite a remarkable young man."

"I know."

"I want you to do me a favor, and that is quite simply to ask yourself how much you're going to hurt your parents by eloping."

"It's going to hurt them," Marjorie agreed.

"My parents were killed when I was eighteen," Selda said, "and I know how hard they struggled to give me everything."

"I'm sorry," Marjorie said.

"I don't mean to say that I haven't done impulsive things in my life or that all those impulses were wrong."

Marjorie put her beautiful hand on Selda's knee.

"You are very sweet but my mind is made up. If Bill agrees, that's all that matters."

"There is something about Bill that I should tell you, Marjorie, because I like you already."

"What's that?"

"He's been living with me for months now, and though I know a great deal about him there is much more I don't know. Four years in prison camp is a long time. He is fighting demons, I do sense that. It is hard for him to get through a night."

Marjorie now took Selda's hands in hers.

"I have my own demons to fight," Marjorie said. "I sit at the piano six hours a day. I have very strong shoulders."

"All right," Selda jumped up and walked to the ice box and withdrew a bottle of champagne. "On with the nuptials."

She walked to Bill's door and knocked.

"Mr. Major," she yelled, "come sip the wine."

Bill came in and sat next to Marjorie. He put his arms around her.

"What about your parents?"

"They'll survive."

"We've already covered this," Selda said, fumbling with the cork. "Here, Bill, you do this before I drop the bottle."

Bill popped the cork and Selda brought some lovely cut-glass wineglasses. When they were filled, Selda raised hers in a toast.

"To impetuosity," she said.

They clinked glasses and sipped champagne.

"I haven't got a ring," Bill said, and Selda rose and walked to her bedroom. She returned with a simple gold band.

"This was given to me in Florence. The situation was almost as hectic as this one."

"May I see it?" Marjorie asked, and Selda handed her the ring.

She read the inscription inside: "TO THE MADONNA OF THE ATELIER." She did not question the inscription, but thanked Selda with sincerity.

"I still don't have a job," Bill said.

"I am going on blind faith," Marjorie said, smiling, and Bill kissed her.

"Well, where are you going to run to? Las Vegas?"

"Las Vegas is fine," Marjorie said. "What do you think, Bill?"

"I am a very good poker player. You may never get me off the tables."

"Well, get packed, Bill."

"Wait," Marjorie said. "I'd like one more favor." She looked at Bill. "Could we take Selda with us?"

"Will you come?" Bill asked.

Selda clasped her knees and rocked back on the couch. *"You bet."*

"What about the library?" Bill asked.

"The business branch will stay closed. Everyone can buy their own *Wall Street Journal* today. The world won't crumple."

"Great," Marjorie said. "May I use your phone?"

"There's one in my room," Bill said and watched Marjorie leave and close the door behind her.

"It's all right, Bill."

"What is?"

"Everything. She's more than you deserve. She's like a breath of fresh air. . . ."

"I know," Bill said, "but as you said . . ."

"What?"

"It wasn't in the script. I feel kind of helpless. That's not like me."

Marjorie returned full of smiles. "Now I know everything is all right," she said.

"You called your mother?" Bill asked.

"No. I called Brogan. She raised me." She paused and looked at Selda. "You might say I called my mother. Brogan is saying a prayer for me at Mass this morning."

Selda packed a picnic basket and the three of them headed out of a foggy San Francisco to emerge hours later into the brutal desert of Nevada. They dozed in shifts and it was almost six o'clock when they pulled up in front of the Rancho Vegas Hotel, a drawn-out, neo-Western structure, its hundreds of rooms spread about a swimming pool, its casino already humming with guests. The clink of the slot machines could be heard, the monotonous chants of the crap dealers, the whirr of the wheels of fortune. They rented two rooms and headed for one of the dozens of wedding chapels strung along the highway.

The wedding was as plastic as the bouquet Bill purchased for Marjorie from the "Reverends'" wife. They refused the recording of the ceremony, which was brief, uninspired and cost $25. They duly signed marriage certificate, which was all the credence the ceremony had, and all of them headed for the nearest bar to consecrate the marriage in spirits that had been lacking in the chapel.

They returned to their rooms to change for dinner. Marjorie had packed a lovely long linen dress and emerged from the bathroom to ask Bill to do up its buttons at the back, which he did clumsily.

She spun around and asked, "Do I look virginal enough, Major Crossen?"

"I would like to know who buttoned these buttons before?"

"That is a good question. I'll let you wonder."

They ate dinner with Selda and when they returned to their room found another bottle of champagne waiting for them. Its note said simply, *Begin. Love, Selda.*

And they did begin and it was quick and clumsy and Bill was asleep before Marjorie, who, though she felt confused sexually, was convinced about the wisdom of her decision.

Chapter X

The firm of O'Gara and Levey occupied three floors of the Hibernia Building on California Street near Sansome, and though its offices and drafting rooms looked like most other engineering offices Bill Crossen had ever seen—wooden desks, linoleum floors, oak desk chairs and drafting stools—he was amazed not only by the size and activity of the firm, but also by the elegance of Henry Levey's private office. The walls were panelled and held a wonderful collection of ship models: schooners, square-riggers, ketches and yawls, some under full sail, all of them glass encased and well lit by small brass lamps. There was no desk in the room at all—only comfortable armchairs and a large coffee table. The only utilitarian objects in the room were a phone, a large white note pad, a silver pen and pencil.

Bill was dressed in a gray flannel suit, a blue and white shirt, a solid blue necktie. He wore blue, knee-length socks and well-polished black shoes. The gold eagle of honorable discharge was evident in his left lapel. He had the training to stand tall and straight and shifted easily into the role of the unassuming young man.

"Major Crossen," Levey said. "I think we have things to discuss. . . ."

Marjorie had agreed that Bill should see her father first on their return, but standing now in this elegant office, he felt uneasy.

"Well, now, Major Crossen," Levey said, "have a seat, have a seat."

"Thank you, sir. You have a lovely office."

"I do," Levey admitted. "I finally swore after all these years not to have a desk or cubbyholes full of plans, but we have other things to attend to don't we?"

"We do." Bill shifted uneasily. "I'll tell you the sequence of events and Marjorie has made me swear that I tell you the truth."

"Go ahead."

"On Monday afternoon I had asked Marjorie to marry me and she accepted. I told her that I would speak to you the next day and she finally agreed to that. However, at midnight on Monday she phoned and said we should elope.

"She seemed upset on the phone and arrived at my cousin's apartment at one o'clock. I assure you that both my cousin Selda and I tried to reason with Marjorie, but her mind was made up. I had the choice of losing her or following her plans. I did the latter. We drove to Las Vegas and got married. I am a very lucky man."

Levey said nothing for a long time, studying his well-manicured fingers.

"Marriage is not a crime," he finally said. "Not always the best state of affairs, but not a crime. I know how headstrong Marjorie is, and this decision of hers to elope comes as less of a surprise to me than you think. It's been a long time since I've seen Marjorie as happy as she's been since she met you, and I respect her very acute intelligence. I don't think she acted foolishly."

"Thank you, sir."

Levey looked at Bill rather sternly now. "You are aware of her great talent?"

"I am, sir."

"Do you intend to encourage that?"

"By all means, sir."

"She is a different person at the piano. It becomes an obsession. She becomes transfixed. . . ."

"It is the way I approach engineering, Mr. Levey."

Levey glanced over the remark. "I doubt whether she has ever washed a dish before, mended a dress, hemmed a skirt or could fry an egg."

"I'm not afraid of starving," Bill said.

"Nor should you be," Levey said, standing and pacing his large office. "You're well aware that Marjorie is a rich young woman."

It was a tough statement and Bill understood the innuendo.

"Marjorie, like all my children, owns ten percent of this company."

"I was *not* aware of that, sir."

"Well, money," Levey continued, "has its blessings and its curse."

"I intend to stand on my own two feet. I have a master's degree in civil engineering from MIT, I'm Phi Beta Kappa, and graduated summa cum laude. I have published several papers."

"Very admirable," Levey said. "But an outsider marrying my daughter will not sit well in San Francisco. How tough are you, boy?"

Bill said quietly, but emphatically, "Goddamned tough."

"That's good. You'd better be. There's not only San

91

Francisco and Pacific Heights, but also Marjorie's mother, Hortense. She will eat you alive."

"I survived the March on Bataan, sir," Bill said.

"Child's play," Levey said, now embracing the boy. "Welcome to the family and stop calling me sir."

"Well now," Levey continued, "with those credentials we should find a slot for you here."

"That is very kind of you, sir, but I've already taken your daughter. I don't expect your money, too."

Levey laughed. "That's well put."

"I *have* been spending a good deal of time since my arrival in San Francisco at the Mechanics' Library, studying postwar projects. Everything seems to point to a canal which will be built in the Central Valley."

"The Delta-Mendota Canal," Levey said.

"I didn't know it had been named."

"It has," Levey said, "and we're bidding on it."

"I have some ideas about this project which I think would help land that bid and secure me a job at the same time."

"Really," Levey said, quite surprised. "Since you are now a member of the family, would you care to share them with me?"

"I would have to get my projections and my drawings. It would take some time."

"Let's have lunch tomorrow," Levey said. "Come back to the office."

"Yes, sir," and Bill remembered the admonition, "I'm sorry—Mr. Levey."

"Now, if you will excuse me for a few minutes, I have some letters to sign, some calls to make and then we'll go home and have a wedding feast."

Chapter XI

Hortense was in "rare form," as Henry would put it, pacing her bedroom like an agitated lion tamer.

"There is only *one* solution," she said to Marjorie, who was sitting on her father's bed. "I've already spoken to Milton Ganz this morning. Annulment."

"What did you say?"

"Annulment. Imagine running off to Las Vegas like a common shopgirl, staying in that horrid city with a man who has *no* job, *no* family. How could you do such a thing to me?"

"Annulment," Marjorie said calmly, "can only occur when there has been no sexual union. You are no longer looking at a virgin."

"Stop that language," Hortense shouted.

"I was not aware of improper language."

"I did not raise my children to be this explicit."

"I thought you raised your daughters to get rid of this explicitness."

"If you must persist in this vein, yes, that is right. But lose it to the right man."

"And how do you define the *right* man?"

"Family, background, breeding."

"Money," Marjorie added.

"Yes, money is important."

"What if I told you I had enough money already?"

"You have a share in the business, that is *yours,* no one else's."

"Was Daddy rich when you married him?"

"That has nothing to do with it."

"Why not? Where's the difference?"

"Times were different. Times were harder."

"Not like the fun years of World War Two," Marjorie mocked.

"I don't intend to continue sparring with you. We will not tolerate this behavior."

"Who is *we?* How does Daddy feel?"

"You have hurt him very badly."

"Is that what he said?"

Hortense reddened. "I don't have to tell you what your father said."

"That's right," Marjorie said. "You don't have to tell me. I'm sorry you're taking this so hard. I did not reach this decision lightly."

"Lightly," Hortense yelled. "You haven't even been engaged. A two-year engagement in our group is normal. You must see whether that boy fits into your group. You must see whether he makes friends, whether he is accepted..."

"I still say, I am sorry you feel the way you do. I don't give a damn whether my group accepts him or not. I would suspect they won't anyway."

"And why do you feel that?"

"Because he's not from an old-line San Francisco family; he comes from poor Jews in New York; he is not rich, he doesn't know which fork to pick up . . . Trivia," Marjorie said.

"It may be trivia to you, my dear, but you are committing yourself for a lifetime. You have always been a headstrong girl." There were tears in her eyes.

Marjorie came over to her and kissed her lightly on the cheek.

"I am not going to apologize any longer."

"Where are you going?"

"I am going to start my life." She rose and left the room.

Marjorie was just leaving the house when her father's limousine pulled up and she watched him and Bill alight. Henry Levey stretched out his arms and his youngest child fell into them. There were tears in her eyes now, but he kissed her and congratulated her.

Bill stood aside, not quite comfortable with all the emotion.

"Where are you going?" Levey asked.

"I'm leaving."

"But, why? We're going to have dinner. Open some wine, champagne. Let's celebrate."

"You celebrate with Mother. Discuss annulment with her. Come on, Bill, we're going."

Crossen looked perplexed. He looked at Marjorie and then her father.

"Lunch, tomorrow," Levey said. "At twelve o'clock."

Henry Levey found his wife near hysteria when he walked into the room with a martini and a shaker.

"Annulment, eh," Henry said. "That's how you welcome home your daughter? Annulment?"

"I don't want to discuss it any further." Hortense said.

"I do, goddamnit. What kind of a mother are you, anyway?"

"I really wonder," Hortense admitted. "My daughter running off with an unemployed Polack from New York."

"He won't be unemployed tomorrow. I'll give him a job. He's an engineer."

"You do *that*," Hortense rose, "and *everybody* will think he married Marjorie for her money. . . ."

"You run the house. I'll run my business."

"You don't even know whether he's any good."

"He couldn't be any worse than your son. I've got stockboys who are more able, and the legal advice I get from your son-in-law ends up in the wastebasket, and I use Levy and Coulter for advice. For that futile exercise I pay ten thousand dollars a year."

"Milton Ganz said we could find grounds for annulment."

"Milton Ganz is full of shit. Can't you remember that Marjorie is a full-grown woman? She is twenty-three years old. If you hadn't insisted on her virginity so much, perhaps she'd know more what she's getting into. . . ."

"I will not hear that word bandied about any more. Do you hear?" Again Hortense cried. "What are we going to tell our friends?"

"The truth. And keep the innuendos out of it."

It was a difficult night for Bill and Marjorie. He was aware of the scene that must have ensued at Marjorie's house.

They had rented a room at the Mark Hopkins and Marjorie, wearing a chaste white slip, was sitting on the bed.

"Do you want to talk about it or not," Bill asked.

She looked at him. He was so straight, she thought, so earnest, so beautiful. "I just want you to put your arms around me."

Bill sat next to her and complied.

"What did Daddy say?"

"I like him. He warned me about San Francisco, your mother. . . ."

"And you?"

"I said I could handle it."

"Can you?"

"If you help."

"You don't have any doubts about that, do you?"

"Not if you say so."

"Good. I did not want a scene with my mother, but it was inevitable."

"Your father asked me about your money. *That* seemed to concern him."

"My interest in the business?"

"Yes. I didn't know."

"When I was very young my father decided to give ten percent of his interest in the business to each of his children and his wife. It is a very respectable sum—I don't even know the amount. I receive about four thousand dollars a month in interest. I rarely touch it." She looked at Bill. "I know that may sound cold, but I can't apologize for the money or the fact that it means so little to me."

Bill looked perplexed.

"I *am* aware," she said, "that people are poor. I *am* aware that people struggle. I *do* help young artists, I *do* contribute where I feel it proper. . . ."

"I didn't marry you for your money," Bill said.

"I believe that."

"I feel confident enough to know I can support us. I have the credentials. . . ."

"I still want you to talk to Daddy."

"I'm supposed to have lunch with your father tomorrow. He wants to give me a job."

"Then take it," Marjorie said.

"No, I don't think I will. I can get a job anywhere. There's so much talk about money already."

Marjorie turned to face him. "You will not hear about money from me. You never have. You never will. Nor will I tell *you* what to do. Ever. You have my word. But *do* have lunch with my father. I see no reason to hurt him."

They went to bed, and attempts at making love were difficult. Finally Marjorie sat up in bed.

"I feel so sorry for you," she said, half crying. "I made you the eye of a hurricane. . . ."

"I said I could handle it."

"I know, I know. My mother is so unreasonable. It had to come to this, but I shouldn't have involved you."

"Mrs. Crossen," Bill said, "enough."

"Is that an order?"

"Yes."

"Good."

Chapter XII

After a hearty luncheon at Sam's, whose white table clothes, mahogany chairs and beveled mirrors on the white wood panelling symbolized understated elegance in San Francisco, Bill Crossen returned with Henry Levey to his office. He not only spread out his maps, graphs and notebooks of calculations, but also produced the two beautifully constructed models of a canal trimmer and a canal lining slip form.

Levey, both an experienced and very scholarly engineer, listened carefully to the young man's exposition. It was a recitation that lasted almost two hours, and its content left very little to chance for the success of the project: the building of the Delta-Mendota Canal.

"From studying California practice," Crossen said, "I expect that the canal project will be bid in segments. If the original successful bidder can finish ahead of schedule, he should be awarded the next assignment. My research shows this to be the precedent.

"I've studied the topography of the canal and have paid particular attention to the content of the sub soil. Many of the bids will rely on compacting. With my trimmer and lining slip I expect to line the entire project with concrete and can complete the first segment in less than half the time allowed."

When Bill Crossen had finished, Henry Levey asked a number of pointed questions. But after receiving Bill's invariably logical and ingenious answers—he simply drew back his chair from the conference table.

He fondled the two models on the table, admiring their precision. "These devices will not be cheap."

"No, sir. I have an amortization table. They should pay for themselves in three months."

"What about the displacement of labor? What about the unions?"

"The unions," Bill Crossen said, "will become increasingly more adamant. They have been held down by years of wage controls. Anyone who can turn to mechanization will realize a great profit. In addition, there is a lot of wetback labor in that valley. I can pick up all I need after the harvests."

After Bill Crossen had finished his proposal and Henry Levey had finished his questioning, Levey could say only one word: "Masterful." He paused. "I do have some further questions, however, Bill."

"Shoot."

"This data—" he said, indicating all the graphed figures on his coffee table, "no man could compile all this data in six weeks at the Mechanics' Library."

"Very true. It was compiled by me and two associates using the computer at MIT."

"That is a new science, I understand, but how can you trust it?"

"Because a computer is built on very logical mathematics."

"It's only a machine."

"That's true. You have to trust the man who programs it."

"And who is that?"

"Me."

"I've read about computers; I've heard they are the coming thing. Developed at Cambridge, weren't they?"

"Yes, and perfected at Pennsylvania and Harvard."

"And how do you pay for this service?"

"With money."

"Whose money did you use?"

"My own. These printouts before you cost me five thousand dollars."

"Do you have that kind of money?"

"I received seven thousand dollars in back pay when I was released from prison camp. I played some poker on the ship and arrived with thirteen thousand dollars in my pocket."

"That represents a lot of faith in that machine."

"It does. And in myself."

Levey rose and paced the room. "I have become rich because I've always gambled and I've rarely lost. I will gamble on you, boy. Consider yourself hired."

"There is only one condition," Crossen said.

"What's that?"

"I don't care what you pay me. However, I must be supervising engineer of the project."

Levey looked at him.

"How old are you?"

"Twenty-five."

"Do you think I could put you ahead of men who have worked for me for thirty years?"

"That's the choice you must make," Bill said, gathering up his data.

"You're right," Levey said after a moment.

"About what?"

"You *are* one tough son of a bitch."

"Should I take this data away or leave it?"

Levey looked at him steadily.

"Leave it and please leave me alone."

Bill stood, shook hands and departed.

Levey watched the boy leave. He cared little about Hortense's objections of the night before. He cared little, really, whether the Delta-Mendota Canal came in early or at a huge profit. He worried only about himself. Not because he feared Bill Crossen, or worried about his ambition. He worried about the fact that he had lost a closeness with Marjorie, whom he loved, or thought he loved, a girl, *his* daughter, who was, unfortunately, at this minute as much a stranger to him as was Bill Crossen.

He did not admire his grandfather, that Polish presser, for his skills or his poverty, but he remembered being there each Seder evening as a child, and he remembered what a family really was. What had they wrought in San Francisco, in all those mansions, with all those governesses, with all the civility and propriety? Did Emily Post cover emotional distance or estrangement in her book? Or did she teach that only through correctness, surrounded by the right silverware and glassware, all used in proper sequence, you create a regal atmosphere, the trappings of a phony kingdom?

What had he done, really, besides make money? Had he sold out everything in his own life? Had he lost that warmth and love he had known in his own family and behaved like the automaton Hortense demanded? Henry Levey, the public figure, the solid citizen, the properly dressed, housed and socially correct figure among other figures in a relatively small group of Jews in San Francisco. All that he had mastered, to be sure. What had he lost in the interim?

Part Two

Chapter XIII

On his first day at O'Gara and Levey Bill Crossen was introduced to Mr. O'Gara, to various department heads and other key personnel, and assigned a small office facing an air shaft. The office contained an oak desk and swivel chair, a drafting table and a stool and several gooseneck lamps. None of this spartan environment bothered Bill as he spread out his drawings, maps, drafting tools, pencils and pens. He was deeply absorbed in his work when Henry Levey, Jr., came to his door at noon.

"Let's have lunch, Bill," he said.

"I'm sorry, I can't."

"Why not? You have to eat."

"I never eat lunch. Besides, I've got a lot of catching up to do."

"You've only started this morning."

"I know. I appreciate the invitation."

"Don't get off to a bad start," Henry Jr. said. "I'm going to have lunch and then play a round of golf."

Crossen watched the boy leave and laughed to himself. "I started this job four years ago," he thought.

It took Bill only two weeks to fully understand the workings of the firm.

There were five large construction companies in San Francisco with the manpower and equipment to bid on major projects. And although most of these jobs were awarded to the lowest bidder, a certain savvy could circumvent this legality. O'Gara, a beefy, bourbon-voiced man, had that political savvy. He knew his way around city hall, whose office holders were mostly Italian or Irish and whose needs—women, booze, money—he understood even better.

It was graft, pure and simple, that brought the firm ample work; however, it was Levey's superior engineering skill that managed to complete most jobs to everyone's satisfaction.

The end of the war had brought a cornucopia full of projects long delayed because of manpower and material shortages during the conflict; and O'Gara and Levey quickly found themselves with millions of dollars' worth of projects on their hands.

Levey had prevailed over O'Gara's objections and had decided to name Crossen supervisor of the Delta-Mendota project if it came their way, and after three weeks Crossen met with Levey to show him his finished proposal.

Although they had discussed the project in general terms before, Levey now studied the final plans carefully. After a question-studded hour he finally rolled up the plans and looked at the young man.

"This is one of the best proposals I've ever seen."

"Thank you, sir."

"There is only one thing wrong with your bid."

"What's that?"

"It's too low."

"Using my trimmer and lining slip, I assure you we'll come out at a profit."

"It's *your* neck," Levey said, "and mine. You can imagine how popular my decision to appoint you supervisor was."

"I appreciate it."

Levey handed the data to Crossen, but Bill was not finished.

"I've made some other studies."

"Yes? What other studies?"

"The Nimbus Dam, the Peach Bowl Bridge, the Fish Hatchery project. We're spread too thin. We don't have the talent or the manpower to bring these projects in at a profit. They'll only detract from work on the canal."

Levey resented the "we" Crossen had used. "Leave those decisions to me," he said.

"But . . ."

"No buts," Levey commanded. "It has never been the policy of this firm to put all its eggs in one basket. We haven't even won the Mendota Canal bid yet. Not even the first stretch."

"It's as good as ours," Bill said. "No one can come close to our figure."

"If that's the figure we use," Levey said.

Bill left and Henry Levey paced his office. The plans, he had to admit, were the finest and most innovative drawings he had laid eyes on in years. They were extraordinary. But Crossen's meddling in the other affairs of the company was presumptuous; and Levey considered discussing it with his wife, but decided not to add fuel to an already smoldering fire.

Henry Jr. picked him up for lunch and they drove to the Concordia Club. After saying hello to half the city's leading Jews, who were already seated in the large dining room, they landed at a small table by the window and ordered some gin.

"What do you make of this Bill Crossen?" Henry asked his son.

"He's an enigma."

"Why do you say that?"

"He's polite, but curt. He won't even have lunch."

"All right, he's either asocial or shy."

"Or ambitious," Henry Jr. said.

"Yes," Henry Levey said, "or ambitious."

"I've tried very hard, Dad, to make him feel at home in the firm, show him around; but he's so intense, he always makes me feel I'm intruding. His mind is on one thing—work. He's demanding and impatient. He hardly says hello or good-bye to anyone. . . ."

"He's an engineer," Henry said. "A good one, from what I've seen. Maybe he could teach you more than you could teach him."

"You're not going to start that stupid argument again."

"There's nothing stupid about it, Henry. I got you through the war by declaring you essential. I would do that again. The war is over, son. You'd better find some skills you can be proud of."

"I thought the purchasing department ran very well."

"That took no brains during the war. We purchased whatever we could get our hands on. Things will change now. There'll be plenty of raw materials and the shrewd buyer can make or break a project."

"They don't teach you buying in college."

"Maybe they do, maybe they don't. They sure as hell don't teach it on the golf course."

Chapter XIV

The war between Marjorie and her mother had not come to an end. However, through diplomacy and instinct Henry Levey had been able to negotiate between them. He finally persuaded Marjorie that a wedding reception was in order, because it would put the family's imprimatur on the marriage and allow Hortense to maintain her status in San Francisco society.

Hortense had ordered a sit-down luncheon at the Crystal Room of the Fairmont Hotel. Two hundred guests were invited and San Francisco knew how to cater such an affair with grace and elegance. There was a small dance floor and a small band and Bill danced the first dance with Marjorie, then danced with other members of the family and finally with Selda.

Bill was keenly aware of the scrutiny of all the guests, particularly the women. They were a good-looking lot, taller, it seemed, than the girls in New York. Their faces were fresher. Their hair more lustrous, and a good many of them, he surmised, had had their noses fixed, their teeth straightened.

Unquestionably the prettiest girl of the crop was Elyse Wolf, who was married to Lewis Wolf, one of San Francisco's richest young men. But there was more to her than her pedigreed looks; her reputation was equally fascinating. Each young man Bill had met at party after party would either volunteer that he had "possessed" this beauty at one time or another, or if he had not been so fortunate himself, had a catalog of friends who had been.

Tonight Elyse wore a black satin dress slit to the waist, but her faultless carriage revealed no cleavage. She was about five feet, four inches; her black hair, drawn severely back, was as luminescent as an Oriental's. Her eyes were the shape and color of almonds, her cheekbones high, her lips full, her cheeks lightly rouged.

"Hello, Major," she said very calmly and openly. He danced with the girl and her lightness and grace easily made up for his clumsiness.

"Let's stop a minute," he said, and they walked to a corner of the room and picked up two glasses of champagne. "To you," he said.

He raised his glass in toast. "You are structurally the most beautiful girl I have ever seen."

"That is the most clinical compliment I've ever received."

Bill blushed slightly. "I knew no other way to phrase it."

"Don't try," Elyse said, "you've been married scarcely a week."

The music ended and they walked to Elyse's table. Bill was introduced to her husband, a jolly, flushed little man, friendly and warm.

"Sit down," Elyse said, and Bill joined them.

Elyse looked at him quite innocently. "I like you," she said.

"Thank you," Bill answered, perspiring lightly.

"I heard about the wrong fork," she said.

"Already?"

"It's a small town."

"Not small." Bill said. "Petty."

"Quite right. But they're formidable. I should know," Elyse said.

"You? How?"

"I come from 'wrong-fork' territory myself. McAllister Street. Have you heard of it?"

"No," he said. "Not really."

"It's the San Francisco version of the Lower East Side. Herring barrels, yarmulkes, street vendors. . . ."

Bill looked at her. "You are not creating a feeling of nostalgia in me," he said.

"Nor me," Elyse agreed. "I think you'd better get back to your wife. As I said, it's a small town."

Bill rose, still admiring the girl's beauty, but not *only* her beauty—also her confidence in it.

"Will I see you again?"

"I think there is a very strong possibility of that."

Lewis Wolf leaned forward. "What do you do?" he asked Bill.

"I'm an engineer."

"For a living?"

"I hope so. And you?"

"I just drink and make love to my wife. Pretty, isn't she?"

"Very," Bill said. "I mean, what do you do for a living?"

"I just told you," Lewis said. "I haven't got time for work."

It was a hurried, almost compulsive honeymoon. Marjorie felt protected, even loved during the three days. But she also sensed Bill's hurry to go back to work. She

111

felt rushed even in bed and she wondered about all those sensual tales her sister Linda had spun so feverishly after returning home from dates.

They took walks. Long walks along the lovely beach of Carmel and they sat on rocks overlooking the Pacific.

"It's strange," Bill said. "New York City is surrounded by water and there are beaches there, too, but I think I've only been to Coney Island once. I hated it. All sweat and bodies and dirty water. . . . But here, in California, it seems that all of it is pointed at the beach."

"In California," Marjorie said, "people are drawn together on the beach. The beaches, the mountains, the lakes, the rivers, they all unify the nomadic Californians."

"I wouldn't call your crowd nomadic," Bill said. "They seem as rooted as the trees on Pacific Heights."

"It's not *my* crowd, Bill. I want you to realize that."

"I didn't mean to insult you."

"I know," Marjorie said. "A lot of that 'heritage' is sham, and I've hated it since I've been able to think for myself."

"You're a pretty good rebel," Bill said.

"You bet." Marjorie faced him and put her arm around his shoulders. "I want to be part of a crowd," she said. "Us."

Bill put his arm about her waist and continued to look at the incoming waves.

"I'll try," he said. "I am a pretty sullen son of a bitch. I'll admit that. But I'll try," he said.

"I can't ask for more than that. There *are* things I want in our marriage," she continued.

"What's that?"

"Peace," Marjorie said. "I want peace. I'm tired of rebelling. I am tired of fighting my mother, my relatives . . . I want it all with us. . . ."

"I'll be working hard," Bill said. "Very hard. Long hours. . . ."

"That doesn't frighten me. My father's an engineer. And I don't exactly intend to sit on my butt myself."

Bill kissed her and she tousled his hair.

"Come on," Marjorie said as she stood. "We've got one night left. I know you hardly drink, but let's make an exception tonight."

They walked slowly up the beach, and then along the souvenir-filled shops of Carmel. They ate dinner by candlelight at Galliene's and drank heavily: first gin, then wine, then brandy. When they finally fell into bed Bill made love to her. But neither the wine nor the candles had the effect Marjorie had hoped for. It was still hurried and austere in the dark.

He had turned over afterward and fallen asleep, and Marjorie felt alone but also convinced that all of it was better than having a girl friend stay overnight.

Chapter XV

San Francisco was burgeoning after the war. Thousands of servicemen returning from the Pacific theater had fallen in love with the vibrant city gracing the steep hills above the Bay. During the war thousands more had been drawn by work in the shipyards and on the docks and now found little reason to return to the drabness and provinciality of the Middlewest, the oppression of the South, the cold and filth of the East.

There had been as well a great influx of blacks, Okies and people from New York and New Jersey, none of whom were welcomed by old-line San Franciscans. New neighborhoods sprang up. Endless, ugly stucco duplexes were built on the sand dunes of the Sunset district and on the flatlands of the peninsula.

Previously, no one had waited at counters of I. Magnin, the White House, the Emporium, and now one had to be content to be served by salesgirls who had neither the tact nor the subservience of the former employees.

Restaurants like Julius' Castle, the Blue Fox and the Cornelian Room now required reservations and longtime patronage no longer guaranteed special treatment.

The city was crowded with tourists and newcomers. It was losing its intimacy. There were suddenly too many blacks, too many midwesterners, too many New Yorkers. There were foreign tongues and foreign manners (or mostly lack of them). One could no longer park where one pleased, get the window table one was accustomed to; and the mention of one's Pacific Heights address did not provoke awe.

Families just starting out moved into the new, ugly tract houses while the young and unattached clung to the lower reaches of Russian Hill, and North Beach and streets like upper Grant Avenue and Union Street. The area around Columbus Square was filled with coffeehouses, secondhand book stores and art galleries. Craft shops appeared selling merchandise totally foreign to the conservative tastes of the "city," as old-line residents referred to San Francisco, to distinguish it from Los Angeles, its equally burgeoning but terribly gauche and unconcerned rival to the south.

Henry Levey had spread Bill Crossen's drawings on his coffee table and tried to explain their intricacies to O'Gara, but the effort was futile.

"You know goddamned well, Henry, this stuff doesn't mean anything to me. If you say they're good, they're good. I don't know one end of a slide rule from the other anymore. What's the bid?"

"Twenty-one million dollars."

"That's pretty goddamned low."

"It is," Levey admitted, "but I've checked and rechecked it, and Crossen's figures make sense."

"Quiet kid," O'Gara said.

"Yes. Quiet."

"Understand he scarcely drinks," O'Gara said, almost accusingly.

"It's a new breed."

"Yes," O'Gara said, scratching his balding head. "Everything is new."

It had been a good partnership, spanning over thirty years now. O'Gara the outside man and Levey the engineer had prospered.

They were not small-minded. There was no need to be. The business earned them enough money for the good life and neither the difference in their religions or backgrounds nor the disparity of their life styles concerned them at all. They could hardly recall a squabble between them.

"I've got things pretty well greased at city hall. I think we could go another four million safely."

"Agreed," Henry Levey said, "but Crossen feels that this hundred-mile canal will be bid in eight sections. If he comes in according to his projections, he figures on getting the whole canal."

"That's one hell of a big canal," O'Gara said.

"We're only trying to save the taxpayer money."

"Yeah, the taxpayer." O'Gara laughed. "Shit, some coon tried to buy a drink at Murphy's Saloon yesterday. They almost threw him out head first."

"The world is changing," Levey said.

"The *world* may be," O'Gara said, "but I'm not. I'm getting too old for that."

Chapter XVI

Elyse Wolf had not only been blessed with great physical beauty but also with a very keen mind. She had been born and raised behind a tailor shop on McAllister Street, her bed in the hallway never more than ten feet from a herring barrel whose pungency lingered in her clothes, her hair, even her skin, she felt. There were two younger sisters, an older brother studying for the rabbinate, a life centered around the Torah, Hebrew school and poverty.

She attended Lowell High School because of her superior grades and suffered the strain of poverty even more in this school populated by the rich sons and daughters of the San Francisco gentry. She wore no cashmere sweaters, no freshly polished saddle shoes; she could not talk of months in Europe after summer recess; and her religious background and parental domination very severely limited her social life.

A full scholarship at Stanford changed all this. She

was on her own financially. Her beauty had only deepened. She dated all the eligible young men she had only known casually in high school and partly out of revenge, partly out of frustration, she let her new friends exploit her to the fullest and soon got the reputation not only of being pretty, but also "easy." She knew all that and cared little, enjoying for the first time the freedom she had so lacked when she was younger. She spent weekends at Tahoe and in Palm Springs; she made trips to Rosarita Beach and to Hollywood, but soon sensed that though she never lacked for male attention she was rarely asked to the young men's homes, she never met their parents, and she found that any "serious" discussions about the future, about commitments, were usually laughed off or shoved aside.

She returned home only once after her freshman year to show her parents her report card which displayed a straight-A average.

"You're a hure," her father had screamed and raised his hand ready to strike her. And seeing quickly that her mother, her own mother, did nothing to defend her, Elyse fled before he touched her.

"I am a hure," she had said that night at the Fairmont Hotel to Charlie Feldman, an eligible, rich young man; and they toasted that statement with French champagne. Then Elyse celebrated her final break with her parents by giving full credence to her father's charge.

Lewis Wolf III had attended Stanford for only six weeks. He came from one of the oldest and richest families in San Francisco and his father took great pride in telling his son that no one in the Wolf family could ever recall having worked a day in his life. Lewis's announcement that he would go to Stanford had been greeted with a certain amount of disbelief and much merriment. It gave rise to yet another roaring party, which the great house in Pacific Heights seemed to host endlessly.

Lewis Wolf III had not had the academic credentials to enter Stanford. He had occasionally attended some private schools at Menlo, Ojai and Exeter, always being expelled for bad conduct and/or drunkenness, none of which bothered his father too much. He had lost his wife when Lewis was four and had raised him only with love and indulgence. Discipline had not been a household word.

Lewis Sr.'s endowment of a botanical library at Stanford assured his son's acceptance, and it was true that, outside of drinking and whoring, Lewis III did have a passion for pressing flowers; and his collection was quite impressive, filling numerous Webster's dictionaries and elegant botanical presses with flora he had collected on endless trips.

Lewis Wolf III was twenty-four years old when he entered Stanford. He was five feet eight and comfortably chubby. His brown, slightly curly hair always seemed somewhat unkempt as did his clothes, which, though faultlessly tailored and of expensive English cloth, always looked as if he had slept in them, which was more often true than not.

His face was pleasant with a short, broad nose, blue, somewhat bloodshot eyes and a mouth with a humorous, roguish cast to it. Lewis's face and overall demeanor reflected, in fact, a very sunny outlook on life, as well they might. He had been reared (even in the depression) in luxury and freedom, and with much fatherly love.

His serious academic career stopped two weeks after he had entered the university. It was at eleven o'clock on a Monday morning when he spotted Elyse, wearing a clinging white tennis dress, carrying her racquet and a can of balls, her lovely hair held behind her head by a silver clip.

119

Lewis simply stepped in front of Elyse, almost tripping her.

"Excuse me," Elyse said.

"Jesus H. Christ!" Lewis answered loudly.

"What did you say?"

"Jesus H. Christ. You are the most beautiful girl I have *ever* seen."

Elyse looked at Lewis in bewilderment, but she could hardly get angry. His face was open and smiling, and it was not the first time her looks had spawned a similar reaction.

"Well, I thank you for the compliment, but I've got to change and make my chemistry class."

"Nothing of the sort," Lewis said. "One class just leads to another. I've got a much better idea."

"Really? What's that?"

"How would you like to go to Acapulco?"

"Acapulco?"

"Have you ever been there?"

"No, I'm afraid not."

"Splendid. My name is Lewis Wolf the Third."

"I'm Elyse Hearsh," she said, "the First."

"Good. Brains, too. Now, then, Elyse the First, when can you be ready?"

"First you practically run me over, and now you're being slightly ridiculous."

"Slightly ridiculous? My dear girl—as my father would say—how about dinner this evening?"

Elyse looked at the boy, whose smile had never left his face.

"Dinner it shall be. I live at Ardmore. How about seven?"

"I don't know how I can wait that long, but seven it is."

Elyse had that fortunate beauty that needed only a shower and a comb to bring it out in all its fullness, and she possessed such a small wardrobe that it was only a matter of taking her one good dress out of the closet. It was white and had a pleated skirt and scalloped collar. She picked up a navy blue cardigan sweater that she held on her arm as she descended the broad steps of Ardmore Hall. Lewis Wolf, sitting in a large Chrysler convertible with its top down, jumped out and gallantly opened and closed the door for her.

It was a warm October night, and they drove to La Bastogne, reputedly the best and most elegant restaurant in Palo Alto.

He ordered Moet et Chandon, a new adventure for Elyse, and raised his glass in a toast.

"To Mexico," he said, smiling.

"You're still talking about that?"

"I've thought of nothing else." He reached into the inside pocket of a blue blazer slightly less rumpled than the tweed jacket he had worn that afternoon.

"Here are the tickets." He spread out an array of folders. "Plane tickets. The biggest suite at Casablanca, the whole bay below your feet. First cabin all the way."

Elyse was overwhelmed and somewhat frightened. "Hold on, hold on, Lewis the Third. You hardly know me."

"I know all I need to know. You're beautiful. I love you. What else do I need?"

"You don't know anything about me."

"Should I?"

"Perhaps. Do you know Peter Trowbridge, Buddy Feiger?"

"Their names sound familiar."

"You live in Pacific Heights?"

"As a matter of fact, I do. Why?"

"Then you must have gone to school with them."

"I never went to school long enough to make any close friends. You're not drinking."

121

"*You* are."

"Yes," Lewis said, that boyish grin on his face, "quite a lot."

"Well, I think it's very generous, the offer of this trip, but I *do* go to school. The semester isn't a third over."

"I go to school myself. That is, I did until I saw you."

"You mean you'll quit?"

"Of course. I have found everything that Leland Stanford, Jr., University has to offer."

Lewis signaled for more champagne. He ordered dinner with great finesse; and though this was not the first rich, spoiled young man she had dated, there was a wonderful freshness and openness about Lewis.

Later they sat in Lewis's car in front of the dormitory. It was still warm, the air fragrant.

"I can't go with you, Lewis," Elyse said, holding both his hands. "I'm here on scholarship. I need a better reason than a trip to Acapulco if I want to be reinstated. My father is a very poor tailor living on McAllister Street. You can fill in the rest. . . ."

"*My* father," Lewis said without any guile, "is *very* rich. Even *I* am very rich. If I brought you home he'd be the happiest man in the world. There are only three of us rambling around that big mansion. My father, my brother and myself. You'd be the freshest flower to enter those musty halls. My father would say this was the first sensible thing I've ever done."

"What, to take me to Acapulco?"

"That's only part of it. I intend to propose."

"You've never even kissed me."

"I intend to settle that right now." He did lean over and held her face between his hands and kissed her. It was a gentle, warm kiss. He did not try to fondle her breasts or slide his arm around her backside.

"Well, my love, what do you say?"

"I think you're crazy."

"Everyone knows that, but that's an observation, not an answer."

Elyse looked at this curious young man. "Let me meet your father, then I'll give you an answer."

The following morning they drove up the driveway of one of the largest mansions in San Francisco. A maid dressed in black opened the front door. Elyse could see a butler standing at the foot of a lovely curved stairway and watched a man in his early sixties hustle into the foyer and fondly kiss Lewis on the cheek, tousling his hair.

"How is my academician," he said. "Who is this lovely child?"

"Father, this is Elyse Hearsh."

"What a beauty." He stood back as Elyse blushed. "An *incredible* beauty."

"I thought you'd appreciate my taste. I've asked Elyse to marry me."

"I can't believe," Lewis Sr. said, "how much they've taught you at Stanford in only two weeks."

"He has asked me, sir," Elyse said sweetly, "but I haven't accepted."

"Insists she wants to talk to you, Father."

"Alone," Elyse said.

"Come, come," the elder Wolf motioned. "Let's go in the library. I'm beginning to like this girl better by the minute."

It was a lovely room. They sat in well-proportioned chairs facing each other, a verdant, well-tended garden visible behind an open French door.

"I've only known your son for two days. He is charming, but not very practical, I'm afraid."

"You seem to know him better than you think. Lewis *is* charming and he is *not* practical. Neither is his father."

"I have dated other rich young men," Elyse said

123

forthrightly. "None of them has asked to marry me. My father is a poor tailor on McAllister Street, my mother speaks better Yiddish than English . . . they no longer speak to me at all since I've given up Orthodoxy."

Lewis Sr. studied the girl carefully.

"You are very forthright for such a young woman. I admire that. . . ."

He stood and paced the room, speaking but not looking at her. "Since my wife died sixteen years ago, I've raised both Lewis and his brother Jake. I haven't done an admirable job. I can't force them into a profession or commerce, since I pursued neither myself. I am not ashamed of our fortunate financial circumstances, but I'm certain it has weakened the fiber, both in myself, and in the boys."

He looked at Elyse now. "But I *love* them, and I think the feeling is returned. A poor tailor from McAllister Street has, I'm sure, accomplished a great deal more than I have in my lifetime, and I presume if we went back far enough into the Wolf genealogy we'd find a poor tailor or builder or some sort of merchant who started all this." His hand swept the room. "I think the question really is, Elyse, not whether we want *you*. It is whether you want *us*."

Elyse was taken aback. She did not expect that generous response.

"I make no demands on young Lewis—I have no right. If you decide to say yes, I'd like you to move in. It is a big house. There's room for more love. Frankly, I've hated the weeks that Lewis has spent at Stanford."

"What will people think of me," Elyse asked. "They'll think I'm a gold digger."

"Fortunately we are secure enough that we don't give a damn what anyone says. At times we drink too much, wench too much. As long as we don't hurt anyone, we do as we please."

It was a statement Elyse would never forget. She rose and kissed Lewis's father, who held her about the waist as he called in his son.

"It's all settled, Teddy Bear," he said. "Elyse has consented to marry me."

"Unhand my bride," Lewis III said and now embraced Elyse. "We're going to Acapulco," he said.

"No, no," his father said, "not Acapulco first. Mexico City first. We have friends there. *Then* Acapulco."

"All right," Lewis said to his father, handing him the tickets. "*You* work out the itinerary. If you have the time. I want to leave on Saturday."

"*If* I have the time. That's a family joke, Elyse."

"I can't believe any of it."

"Now, Teddy Bear, call up Mrs. Solomon and have her take Elyse to Ransohoff's. Tell her to dress and coif that girl like a queen. Top to bottom."

"What about the wedding?"

"Do you want a big wedding, Elyse?"

"No. Please, no."

"All right. I'll call Judge Wertheim. You name the day."

"Tomorrow."

"A girl with spunk." Lewis Sr. clapped his hands and rubbed them together.

Chapter XVII

To the outside observer, Bill Crossen seemed to slip quite gracefully into San Francisco's social scene: his marriage to a proper girl; their new, well-furnished apartment in the Marina district (a good neighborhood); his job with his father-in-law at O'Gara and Levey, a fine firm to belong to. All this was deceiving, however, since Bill Crossen, though he had been in San Francisco for over two years now, was still very much in San Tomas and very much in the back alleys of the Lower East Side of New York; and certainly, as Marjorie could attest, he was very much with himself.

And there was little that San Francisco society did to help him, to make him feel at home. There were, at parties particularly, endless weighted questions. Where did you go to prep school? What clubs does your family belong to? Do you buy off the rack or do you have a tailor? The men would ask what sports he participated in and Bill would answer, *none*. The women would ask who monograms your shirts, and Bill would say, My shirts are not monogrammed.

And after each party, after each gathering, each function, Marjorie would take Bill home and nurture him.

"Most of them are bastards, Bill. 'Where do you have your shirts monogrammed?' What bilge. . . .Why don't you show them the scars on your back, why don't you tell them about your malaria attacks?"

"It's all right, honey," he would say, "they're not getting to me."

"Then get to *them*. Tell them you fought this goddamned war so they could have their shirts monogrammed, their pubic hair waxed, their feet pedicured. . . ."

"I have better things to do. There were men from San Francisco that died in the war."

"I know, but they're not giving you trouble. Almost every son of a bitch in our crowd had a 'safe' job or was deferred."

"It was the same at MIT, Marjorie. I had a scholarship to Cal Tech to get my Ph.D., but I was drafted. The old-line boys all stayed in school."

"Would you like to go back to school? I have enough money. . . ."

"No, no. Not now. I haven't got the time."

"You're only twenty-six."

"I know. I *do* appreciate the offer."

Marjorie rarely spoke about "her" money. And Bill never knew or intended to ask how much she had. It mattered so little to her. She practiced piano six hours a day: four hours at the academy, two hours at home. This strict regimen was observed six days a week and Bill admired her strength. It was amazing to watch her, and as her father had said, she did become transformed; but Bill himself would work equally hard at home poring over blueprints, calculating, writing.

Hortense had remarked that their living room with its piano and drafting table looked more like a factory than a home.

Bill's new acquaintances, the young men and women of old-line families, were now beginning to enjoy the hedonistic life denied them by the war, despite some consternation on the part of their elders. They knew there was money, there had been the war and now was the time to enjoy life. They bought big cars, the wives shopped endlessly for clothes, they travelled to Hawaii, to Europe, to Acapulco. They skied, they sailed, they played golf, tennis, built modern Japanese-style homes. They partied and they nightclubbed. They made the social and entertainment columns constantly. They were Herb Caen's raw material; and many a matron, usually while still in bed, would pick up the *Chronicle* from her breakfast tray and read avidly the doings of her children and those of her friends and realize that the old way of life, of chaste elegance, of reserve, of understated wealth and low-key behavior was quickly going by the boards.

"I keep seeing Henry's name all the time, I see Linda's name mentioned. But I never see Marjorie or Bill's name in the paper," Hortense said one morning as Levey tied his tie.

"His name where?"

"In Herb Caen's column."

"He works for a living," Henry said. "He hasn't time for that nonsense."

"It might hurt him socially," Hortense said, "being an outsider."

"He is an outsider, pure and simple. Sitting around those nightclubs doesn't land us contracts. Just leave him alone."

*   *   *

Marjorie complained little about their spartan social life. She was an intelligent young woman with a serious career of her own. She *did* force Bill to attend some affairs, since she could not insult all of her old friends; however she hoped that by joining in his reclusiveness it might bring them closer. But even there her great sensitivity (which she certainly did not inherit from her mother) taught her not to nag her husband (and she *had* learned that from observing her mother), not to pressure him, in the hope that in time he might slowly shed the layer of armor with which he surrounded himself, though she wondered just how many layers of armor there were.

She had heard no objections when her grand piano was moved into the living room, no complaints as she practiced relentlessly, no remonstrations as teachers and fellow performers crowded her life. Perhaps the only admiration, true admiration, Bill ever expressed was after she finished a long and difficult passage, the perspiration light on her forehead, her fingers finally lifting from the keyboard with that practiced finality of a virtuoso. Then, and only then, she could see Bill watching and listening in awe, and occasionally he would comment.

"It is incredible, Marjorie. You were wonderful. There is much that I can master, but that instrument is a total mystery to me."

"No more than your graphs or your slide rule are to me."

"Yes, more. There are only a handful of virtuosi. There are thousands of engineers."

"First of all, my love," she said, sitting at the end of the piano bench, "I'm far from being a virtuoso. Secondly, Daddy has spoken very highly of your engineering."

"That's nice," Bill said. "I hope I can put it to the test soon."

"Let's make love," Marjorie said. "Chopin always makes me romantic."

And they *did* make love, but as always it was fast and almost mechanical, and left her sexually up in the air. Marjorie did not complain, but pressed her body to Bill's naked back and finally fell asleep.

The bid for the first section of the Delta-Mendota Canal was awarded to O'Gara and Levey; and despite the protestations of O'Gara and a number of senior officers in the firm, Levey named Bill Crossen supervising engineer. It was Levey's wife who put forth perhaps the strongest arguments.

"They will accuse you of nepotism," she said. "They will say you are getting senile, it is an affront to your own son."

They had returned from the symphony and were undressing in their spacious bedroom. A fire was playing in the hearth, the Bay below them was full of tugs and ships. The bordering coastline of Sausalito, Tiburon, Berkeley was shimmering beautifully.

"They can say what they want if we fail. But we won't."

"All right, it's only *one* project, I'll grant you that, but you still haven't said anything about Henry Jr."

"Henry Jr. is not an engineer."

"He's been in the firm for five years. Certainly he must have learned *something*."

"He hasn't learned engineering. You learn that in engineering school. You may remember how long he lasted at Case even after I gave them a handsome endowment."

"Then what *does* he do in your office?"

"That's a good question. He's in purchasing. Most of the time he's on the golf course."

"He has a lovely wife."

"Agreed," Henry said, untying the laces of his highly polished black shoes. "A lovely girl from a lovely rich family. Henry will *always* be all right."

"I detect some resentment in your voice. Do I hear echoes of your Polish grandfather?"

"Shut up, goddamnit. There was nothing wrong with my Polish grandfather. He made an honest living as a presser."

"Except he forgot to press his own suit for our wedding."

"Shit."

"What did you say?"

"I said shit. That's what I said. It was thirty years ago, our wedding. I wasn't born with a silver spoon in my mouth. It may have been silver plated, but not silver."

"You are being vulgar, Henry."

"Vulgar, hell. Everything in this house I built with my own two hands. What did *your* elegant ancestors contribute?"

"Entrée, Henry. Entrée."

"Sure, entrée. Entrée to *what?*"

"To the people who finance your bridges, your dams, your ships."

"My entrée is O'Gara, who can't even remember his father. O'Gara and the open palm and the grease in city hall. That's what gives us entrée."

Hortense was now settled in bed, her hair in curlers, her face lubricated. She poured a glass of water from silver pitcher sitting on a silver tray on her night table.

"Are you identifying with that boy?"

"What boy?"

"Bill Crossen."

"I *know* his last name."

"You didn't answer."

131

"I will answer you. The answer is *no*. I am identifying with the success of that canal." He pointed his finger at her. "The success of that canal and *every* other success will keep up this house, and my membership at the Concordia, and the debts I'm paying off for your crooked brother's liquor business, and the house in Menlo Park to which I am now going."

"It's midnight," Hortense said.

"That's right. It's midnight. Call them and tell them to expect me, and call the office in the morning and tell them *not* to expect me."

Henry Levey drove toward Menlo Park and Meadow-brook, his fourteen-acre estate whose name—very gentile—and whose appearance—very British: formal gardens, espaliered trees, boxwoods—gave him extreme pleasure. He was aware of the gossip (true) that he would reside there for fourteen days on end while his family was in Europe, using a different bedroom and a freshly made bed every night that he was in residence. It was the same with the Bentley he was driving, and the two-dollar Havana he was smoking: he had listened to his own father's advice, which was, "There are days, *only days*, when a man should spend all the money he has made on himself. Then you know what you're working for."

As he waited for someone to open the gates to his estate, Henry Levey reflected that he had always liked that lecture.

The following morning, Bill Crossen was upset that Levey was not in his office that day. He had just encountered O'Gara in the hall, who had apprised him of the fact that they had landed the Delta-Mendota Canal project.

"We got it, kid," O'Gara had said. "And we *did* get four million more than you proposed."

"A mistake," Bill said.

"Cocky little Jew, aren't you," O'Gara said.

Crossen stared reflectively at a point in space over O'Gara's head. Finally he looked at the florid Irishman.

"I was in the march at Bataan."

"So I heard."

"The Irish shit in their pants, just like the Jews, before they whipped their heads off."

"I see," O'Gara said. "I'd like to take you to lunch and talk about it, but I understand you don't eat lunch."

"That's right. And I don't eat breakfast, either."

"No breakfast? No lunch? What the hell do you do for fun?"

"I *think*," Crossen said, and O'Gara left.

"I think," Crossen thought to himself and he remembered Selda's lecture about his self-denial.

"You have a car, you don't drive it. You have new clothes, you don't wear them. . . ."

And Selda had been right. He had very few material urges and assumed that this feeling was shared by most people. He could not recall when Marjorie had ever expressed a wish for anything. Selda was too generous herself to covet things, and yet this afternoon, knowing that his numerous patents were making a rich man of him already, he decided for once to splurge.

He walked into Gump's, that venerable Oriental bazaar and was almost overwhelmed by the splendor of Steuben glass, the intricacy of Spode chinaware, the lovely inlaid lacquer boxes, the richly embroidered silk kimonos, the paintings, the etchings, the jade.

He was equally awed by the prices of these objects but nevertheless bought Selda a lovely jade brooch and Marjorie an even more delicate jade necklace.

His first stop was at Selda's, who was not only surprised by his unannounced visit but delighted by his gift.

"What's all this? It's not Chanukah."

"I don't know," Bill said. "I just never spent four thousand dollars in one afternoon." He showed her the necklace for Marjorie.

"It's beautiful," Selda said. "How is that sweet girl?"

"Fine. Just fine. Married to her piano."

"By choice?"

"I hope so. Why do you ask?"

"Are you happy, you two?"

"Of course," Bill said. "Again, why do you ask?"

"I ask because I love you both. Sometimes I worry the way you both bury yourselves in work."

"I'm right on schedule," Bill said. "I start in Tracy next week."

"And Marjorie?"

"I'll be home weekends. She knows what the life of an engineer is like. They don't give the jade away at Gump's."

"No, they don't," Selda said. "And here you've bought me this lovely gift and I play Jewish mother."

"How have you been, Selda?"

"Busy." She shook her head. "The library, the meetings, the Blum's candy. A little lonely at times. . . ."

"Are you dating?" Bill asked.

"Occasionally. It seems all the best men are married. I'm not much at casual conversation. I still prefer a good book to a dull man. I guess—" she hesitated, "I guess you really do what you want to do. So I don't get married. It won't kill me."

Bill had no answer. "You're young," he lied. "You've got lots of time."

"*You* lecture me about time? You'll own San Francisco by the time you're my age. . . ."

"Not if I keep shopping at Gump's. They showed me a watch, for myself. It was a thousand dollars."

"So? Did you buy it?"

"No," he said. "I couldn't. A watch is a watch. A thousand dollars. Boy, you have to deliver a lot of newspapers for that."

He kissed her and left, and Selda, fondling her jade pendant, thought of Bill still measuring his time by the newspapers he had delivered.

Bill caught Marjorie at the piano as usual and carefully slipped the jade necklace over her head.

"What's this," Marjorie said, looking at her gift and turning to face him.

"Crossen's folly," Bill said. "I finally decided to turn those ever-growing ciphers in my bank book into something tangible. . . . I invaded that evil bazaar called downtown San Francisco."

"I love it," Marjorie said and kissed him. "I don't know what to say."

"Enjoy, as Selda would counsel. I bought her a brooch also."

"How sweet. And you? Did you buy something for yourself? Look at those clothes you're wearing. You're coming out of your elbows."

"I really hate to shop," Bill said.

"Then go to Daddy's tailor. You know how well dressed Daddy is."

"I hate tailors, too. I can't stand people handling me."

Marjorie understood that statement. She felt the pain she knew was there . . . but she kept her counsel.

"If you're so flush, Major, how about taking this lovely necklace to dinner? I'd love to show it off."

"I'll make a reservation," Bill said and Marjorie returned to the piano and played the last four bars of Brahm's second concerto.

"Beautiful," Bill said.

"Not really, I just can't leave Brahms hanging in mid-air." She did not like that feeling herself.

Chapter XVIII

Tracy, California, population 7,000, was, despite the postwar boom, a sleepy, pleasant agricultural town raising beets, lettuce, sugar cane and barley. There was still a town square with a bandstand, a rodeo ring, a good and bad part of town. The advent of O'Gara and Levey went almost unnoticed at the beginning. Bill Crossen had leased twelve rooms on the second floor of a brick office building on the outskirts of town, torn down the partitions between offices, (save his own), and built a stark but efficient drafting room for his engineers. He furnished his own office with a simple oak desk, a drafting board and a stool. Only his master's degree (summa cum laude) from MIT graced one wall. A fluorescent light was soon turned on and never turned off during the tenure of the project. He had found himself an equally spartan room in a railroad hotel, a room that he occupied five nights a week, eating his meals in the hotel dining room, returning to San

Francisco Friday nights to keep his still-young marriage alive.

He had drawn on the best talents of Levey's firm for his staff, but had also hired three young classmates from MIT whose expertise was more current, and whose language Crossen spoke with greater ease.

It was true that engineering had not changed basically over the past fifty years. The laws of nature, of stresses, loads, of parabolas and suspension had remained constant. What *had* changed—and many of these changes had been pioneered at Pennsylvania, Cambridge, Harvard—were methods of calculation. Gone were the endless sheets of graph paper, yellow foolscap, handwritten notebooks, most of them replaced now by accordion-pleated computer readouts. Man had finally harnessed mathematics, to the point where often months, even years, could be saved by calculations done in seconds, minutes. Not only did this miracle machine, the computer, save time, but if it was properly programmed, it was almost infallible and certainly dispassionate.

The computer, aside from its speed, not only allowed engineers like Bill Crossen to gather the data they needed, but also permitted the extravagance of making conjectural projections that previous projects could rarely afford because of time and expense.

Crossen had mastered the computer as he had Japanese. He knew that strange invention as an extension of his brain and he had hired the best men from MIT to utilize this tool.

Although O'Gara and Levey at first balked at the immense cost of computer time, Levey quickly realized that this tool, properly used, allowed Crossen to base his choice of materials on its results, allowing him to order lightweight steels instead of heavy beams and to project the necessity of equipment and materials at proper times during construction, thereby eliminating the often-plundered, usually wasteful stockpiles of equipment and raw material necessary with most major construction projects.

Bill Crossen was innovative, even daring, on this huge project, there was no denying that. But even more remarkable was the foresight and dogged determination of the older man, Levey, who was willing to step into a new era in his profession, using the canal building as a pilot project. Night after night, in the early days of the project, he had to face O'Gara and other old-timers of the firm, explaining the high construction costs. Worse yet, he had Hortense at home, fired up by her son's stories that Crossen was literally ruining the firm.

Levey was a complicated man. His engineering skills were flawless. His business acumen, by his own admission, was average. He had become a millionaire through a combination of his own professional know-how and the craftiness of O'Gara. He generously gave credit to that man for his contribution and carried his lack of financial sophistication into his private life. At Hortense's insistence, his stock in the company had been equally divided into five parts: one share for him, one for Hortense, and one for each of the three children. He cared little about this disposition, but he did care, more than ever now, that *their* ownership, which had been made possible through his and O'Gara's labors, allowed them a voice in the affairs of the company.

But Hortense was an astute woman and she urged Henry to invest that hard-earned money in all the amenities she felt were due them. They built a large home in Pacific Heights, a second estate in Menlo Park. She increased the domestic staff, and their travels (particularly to Europe) became more frequent. They entertained elegantly and expensively, dressed well, ate well; and against his better judgment Henry joined the Concordia Club, bought a limousine and hired a chauffeur.

139

John Haase

He had enjoyed his children when they were young,
no doubt of that. He loved the outings on Mount
Tamalpais, the summers at Lake Tahoe, the first trips to
Europe; but as the children grew, Hortense calculatedly
took over. She dictated their schooling, their pleasures,
the state of their teeth, their clothes and, in the case of
Linda and Henry Jr., even their noses. Only Marjorie
had rebelled. Poor little Marjorie, who had been the
biggest genetic loser of their union, had guts. She *did*
rebel as much as she could against this strong woman.
She did not consent to having her nose fixed, she vetoed
braces on her teeth, and it was only her musical talent
that gave Hortense some excuse for relaxing her rules
and standards, labeling the child "odd," or "possessed
by a rare talent," a child she could not quite press into
the Pacific Heights mold.

And it was Henry Levey who had encouraged Marjorie to develop her gifts. He provided the best in teachers, in tutors, in master sessions, which allowed Marjorie
to flourish easily and early. But even here he was thwarted
to a degree by Hortense's endless diatribes about the
girl's looks, her habits, her lack of conformity, until he
slowly withdrew from even that endeavor and retreated
deeper and deeper into the elegant recesses of his private office. Later, when he was in his fifties, he chose to
come home and retire early, having his drinks and dinner sent to his bedroom, feigning endless colds, mi-
graines, backaches, but truly yearning for the anesthesia
of sleep and the luxury of total silence, for the pleasure
of a good book and the lack of confrontations with
Hortense. He knew that many a visitor to the house
speculated about his vague "illnesses" as the butler
brought a large tray containing a very thick steak and a
bottle of wine to his bedroom. However, that position,
that pedigree, which Hortense had so carefully cultivat-

140

ed, could serve him now, as he enjoyed these small amenities and rose above any criticism.

Such was not the case this evening as Hortense at her shrill and cutting best tore into him.

"I told you," she said, "that Henry Jr. said you are bankrupting the firm. Your stubbornness in listening to that upstart Crossen has already cost you the services of five men who have been with the firm over twenty years, and resentment is mounting daily."

Henry listened.

"Your son says that his job has practically been eliminated by some young upstart from MIT who spends his time going over figures spewed out by some new office machine."

"Are you trying to tell me how to run my business?"

"It is not your business."

"My half of the business," Henry said. "I know O'Gara owns half."

"You don't own the other half."

"Who does?"

"You own ten percent. The children and I own forty."

"I find that very amusing."

"Do you, now?"

"Yes. Perhaps you and the children who by the grace of my largesse have become major stockholders would like to run the business. I have worked hard all my life. I would be happy to retire to Menlo Park and we can pay ceremonial visits to each other. Weddings, funerals, bar mitzvahs, the high holidays. . . ."

"Don't be foolish."

"Foolish. I am not being foolish. I pay your son two thousand dollars a month for nothing. I have stock boys who make forty dollars a week who show more promise. I pay Linda's husband ten thousand dollars a year as legal counsellor, and I throw his work in the wastepaper basket and use the firm of Coulter and Jones to give me usable advice.

"If I step aside, I shall make you a present of these two socially prominent young men whose combined IQs hover around room temperature.

"With my ten percent I'll take Bill Crossen and start my own little firm. You are even welcome to O'Gara. I'm beginning to see the end of *his* era, too, poor devil. City hall is beginning to clean up. There are fewer and fewer open palms. The bids will soon be won by the performers, not by the grafters."

Hortense countered with her only reserve weapon: tears.

"Dry your tears, Hortense," Henry shouted now. "There is no salt in them. I will tolerate anything, almost anything, but no one tells me how to run my business, even if I only own ten percent of it."

"Then it *is* Bill Crossen," Hortense said coldly, changing tacks.

"Bill Crossen is nothing to me, except that he represents the state of the art of engineering after World War Two. I can teach Bill Crossen a good many things, but unfortunately Bill Crossen at the tender age of twenty-six can teach me more."

"That is a sad admission, isn't it, Henry?" Hortense was gaining strength again. "Are you trying to tell me you haven't kept up with your profession?"

Henry laughed derisively.

"We have just come through a war. A rotten, miserable, costly war which has killed a great number of innocent boys, some of whom we knew intimately. That war, however, has made us rich. Not only us, but every other major engineering firm. All that was needed was a modicum of brains and a maximum of equipment. We had that. So did the others. Welton and Smith built Liberty Ships"—he pointed—"right across the bay in Sausalito.

More than half of them sank when they launched them. Do you know why? Because neither Welton nor Smith knew anything about shipbuilding. They didn't even care. The poor government was so happy to get the fifty percent of the ships that floated at *all* that they paid and paid and paid.

"Sure, there'll be lawsuits and Smith will settle it out of petty cash and three expensive hookers."

"Henry!"

"Oh, Christ, stop acting prissy. The key word during the war was *expediency*, and O'Gara and Levey were very expedient. And got very rich while millions of Jews died overseas because of another type of expediency."

"Don't be maudlin."

"Maudlin? Shit, Hortense. What did the Concordia Club raise for the victims of Dachau? Eight hundred seventy dollars. Henry Goldman loses that much at bridge before lunch. . . ."

"It was a sad period," Hortense said.

"A sad period. Is that how you justify our financial cannibalism while millions of our brothers died? Do Jews come in different colors?"

"Yes. They do. Orthodox, Reform and Liberal."

"And do they monitor their guilt quotients?"

"I don't want to discuss it."

"*Of course* you don't. You're just like O'Gara, the Catholic, who can wash away all his whoring sins through a young, awed priest in a booth on Sunday morning. Your goddamned Temple Beth El serves the same purpose."

"Meaning what?"

Henry was shouting again. "Meaning exactly what you know. Dear, handsome Rabbi Gold, who's fucking elegant, young Kip Fein while her son goes through the sixth year of bar mitzvah lessons. He runs a bloodless, token temple. No fire and brimstone, no exhortations to

143

morality. Just bring in the dollars and your meager religious needs are fulfilled. Available for weddings, births . . . bar mitzvahs, the lot. Afternoon discussions of interreligious cooperation, lectures on Freud, Jung, for the ladies. Available for all social events—covered by Herb Caen—and all travel assignments—covered by Stan Delaplane."

He pointed a finger again at his wife. "There have been times I've wanted to rip the vestments off that phony and strip the few symbols of a basically decent religion from that building that is nothing more than a Pacific Heights travesty."

"You will go to hell, Henry Levey, for saying this."

"Take care of your own posterity. Perhaps you should read the Old Testament once or take a run to a McAllister Street temple. If you could get a passport."

"You're horrid and vulgar," Hortense said.

"My offer is still good," Henry said. "I'll make you a present of O'Gara and Levey."

"What do you know about Bill Crossen, this wonderful Bill Crossen?"

"Personally, nothing. He's been scarred. Deeply scarred. I've worked around construction stiffs long enough to know that."

"What about his family?"

"They're from New York," Henry said.

"They didn't attend the reception."

"That's right. His father is probably a presser. A Polish presser. Bill was ashamed to bring them here to the Levey's of Pacific Heights. The Great Untouchables."

"Poor Marjorie," Hortense feigned sympathy.

"Poor Marjorie, hell. She's not complaining. She married the only workingman in the family, besides myself."

"The workingman, God bless the workingman," Hortense said. "Your eternal idol."

"Well, let me tell you, those thin mints from Blum's

that you will devour before you go to sleep were bought by someone who worked."

"Just shut up, Henry, I've got a migraine."

"I thought that was my excuse," Henry said as he turned the lights off.

"It's like an armed camp," Hortense said in the dark.

"What?"

"Our marriage."

"You might call it that," Henry agreed. "First the scouts, then the patrols and finally the heavy artillery. . . ."

"I don't get vulgar, like you," Hortense said.

Henry turned in his bed to face hers. "There is a dictionary in the library. I'd suggest you get a proper definition of that word."

"I know what the word means."

"I doubt it, Hortense. Vulgarity covers more than the use of the language."

Chapter XIX

Elyse Wolf had no real complaints. The carnival of her trip to Mexico with Lewis, the extravagance of her marriage, the love and kindness of her new husband and of her father-in-law and brother-in-law were truly overwhelming. Nothing that Lewis's father had predicted had failed to come true.

Her husband had been born entirely without guile. Nothing he had ever wanted had been denied him: a car, a sailboat, a house at Tahoe, trips, clothes, fine watches, jewelry, cameras. His apartment in his father's mansion, which resembled a rich college student's fraternity room, housed a collection of photographs, memorabilia, pennants, ashtrays, empty imported beer bottles, steamer trunks and pornography.

The entire house, Elyse soon discovered, was a college dormitory, loosely presided over by Lewis's father, who, while lacking his son's energy, was equally hedonistic.

Jake, Lewis's older brother (rumored to be the result

of an illegitimate union), was homosexual, but inoffensively so. He and his string of male lovers occupied the top floor. Lewis Sr.'s playground was the fourth floor, and in deference to holy matrimony, the first three floors were alloted to Lewis Jr. and Elyse. The basement held rooms for a Chinese couple, a cook, a second-story maid, a butler and a chauffeur.

Lewis Wolf III was a lovable man. Or was he a man? Elyse often wondered. His entire function, outside of pressing flowers, was holding, caressing, teasing, fondling and screwing his wife.

It was perhaps fortunate that Elyse since breaking with her family had scarcely led a celibate existence. She felt little guilt, really, about how many young men in San Francisco she had bedded, and she was sure that she was ready for *anything* that Lewis might ask of her.

But she was wrong. She decided one night that her husband, not bothered with prospects of earning a living, nor burdened with normal feelings of insecurity, had devoted all his energy to learning about sex. Lewis was a good lover—a marvelous, warm, generous lover—and he brought Elyse sexual gratification she had never known. He had ways, techniques of bringing her to climax after climax. He had taught her to orient her mind and her body totally for pleasure. His language was tinged with sex, his hands, even when he was drunk, found her erogenous zones (many of which she never knew existed). His reading material, his art, his culture were all channeled into one arena: sex, love, intercourse, eroticism, voyeurism, exhibitionism, whatever made up the parts of the whole.

Then there was Lewis's drinking. It started at ten in the morning. Gin. Neat, no ice, in a small, round tumbler. It seemed like an endless half-filled glass. There were tumblers all over the house for refills. For lunch there was white wine, vintage, from the cellar. There was more gin in the afternoon. More wines with dinner. Then brandies, liqueurs.

"I cannot remember," she told Bill Crossen later, "ever seeing Lewis without a drink in his hand."

And yet Lewis was an accomplished drinker. He never got raucous or particularly unsteady. His speech was not slurred. He dozed a lot, but a slight nudge would waken him, and he was as aware of the world about him as ever—an awareness that was not particularly acute except when it came to Elyse. She was an obsession with him and at the beginning it was flattering and welcome.

There was a room on the fourth floor, it had no particular name. It was filled with well-worn leather couches, overstuffed chairs, pinball machines, a radio, a fireplace, an almost atticlike collection of furniture, and it was to this room that everyone repaired after dinner, which as a matter of habit was usually formal.

The postdinner sessions in this room were usually begun with Lewis the elder's announcement: "Well, let's get down to some serious drinking."

There were tales of the day, and though each of the three men carried a very small itinerary, the most was made of all of it. A new suit. Yet another car. Reservations for a trip. Old acquaintances met, births, deaths. Elyse did not drink. There was no puritanical reason for it except her concern for her figure. She coveted her looks as much as her husband and his father did, and felt, amidst all this wealth and splendor, it was the only thing that was hers. Her appearance and health were sacred to her.

She had slowly been refurbishing the house: recovering chairs, replacing drapes, rearranging armoires and antique chests. She revitalized the garden and filled the house with flowers and sunshine. There was no end of appreciation for her efforts and never a limit on her budget.

She began entertaining. Entertaining the same group of acquaintances from Stanford, most of the men married now, and she took perverse delight not only in asserting her very firm position in the society previously denied her, but also in outdoing them in quantity or quality of food served or wine drunk.

"I'll spit in their teeth," she'd say to Lewis in bed after they left.

"Spit all you want, darling. We'll never run out of saliva."

"You don't know how much I want to hurt those bastards," Elyse said.

"The world is your oyster. You've heard Papa say that often enough."

"You're really sweet, Lewis. You're really sweet."

She could well remember the first evening that things went slightly awry. It was usually Elyse who descended to their bedroom first, undressed and slipped into one of the sheer nightgowns or peignoirs that Lewis was forever bringing home. She would wait for Lewis to come to bed, but soon discovered that he was reluctant to leave the pub above her. Habit and family ties made these nightly drinking bouts extremely important. She returned upstairs, most evenings, usually entering to the whistles of the men. On this particular evening her husband put her on his lap. His hand cupped her fanny.

"Papa has a present for you."

"Really. How nice."

Lewis Sr. patted the right-hand pocket of his vest.

"But there is a price."

"Really. What is it?"

"You have to take off your robe."

"I do? Why?"

"Papa said he can't stand it anymore."

"What?"

149

"Seeing the outline, but not the essence."

Elyse blushed.

"It's all in the family," the old man said.

"Go on," Lewis said, pushing her off his lap.

Elyse stood. She was transfixed. She thought of that long, dark hallway in McAllister Street. The smell of herring, of laundry being baled in the kitchen, the sound of trash being thrown down a metal chute. She took off her peignoir. She stood straight in her nightgown. It was sheer, so sheer that one could plainly see the nipples of her breasts, her not-too-ample pubic hair.

Lewis Sr. sat up. "A vision," he said. "You are a vision."

"You are lovely," Jake said quietly.

"Come here," Lewis Sr. commanded, and Elyse walked over. She stood in front of the man, unashamed, almost defiant.

He reached in his pocket and brought forth a small, elegant box and handed it to Elyse. She opened it. Inside lay a diamond necklace.

"Put it around my neck, Papa," she said, leaning over, knowing that the old man would see her nude, totally nude now.

He took his time unfastening the clasp, slipping the necklace around her neck and refastening the clasp.

She kissed his forehead.

"Enough," Lewis Jr. said, grabbing her by the hand and rushing off with her to bed. He had a huge erection, but that was not unusual.

"You were magnificent, Elyse. Magnificent."

She could say nothing, for Lewis made love so ferociously she was almost breathless. When they finally had stopped and lay in bed, Elyse, facing the ceiling, asked, "Didn't it bother you?"

"What?"

"Your father seeing me like that?"

"Of course not. I loved it. He loved it."

"But I'm your wife."

"You are a Wolf. We have our own code."

"Which is?"

"Never deny that which gives pleasure."

"But *you,* how did *you* feel?"

"I loved it. I love you naked. I love for others to see you naked. Let them eat their hearts out. You're mine. Mine." He turned and buried his head between her breasts.

"How far would you go?"

"What do you mean?"

"What if your father wanted to fondle me? To make love to me. . . ."

"That all depends."

"On what?"

"On my mood. If I thought it would excite me, if I could watch. . . ."

"Do I have a say, Lewis?"

"What do you mean?"

"What if I say no?"

"You can say no."

"No recriminations?"

"Of course not. . . ."

He sat up and cradled her. "You are so young, Elyse. So young, so lovely, so innocent. . . . You have so much to learn."

"I do. Don't I make you happy?"

"Happier than any girl I've ever known."

"What else then, Lewis?"

"There is no end to indulgence. No end to experimentation. You've hardly begun to taste the fruit."

"Much of it is foreign to me, Lewis. It's strange."

Lewis sat up and filled his glass with gin.

"There is a different code in the aristocracy."

"Do you consider yourself aristocracy?"

151

"Only financially, Elyse. My father once said we could buy the kingdom of Sweden. We even considered it. It seemed too much work."

He put down his glass and turned to her.

"I'm ready if you are."

"So soon?"

"I told you once you were not married to an ordinary man."

"I'm beginning to believe it. Go to it, tiger. It's better than lying here thinking."

But after Lewis was finally asleep, she *did* lie awake thinking, and the weight of the diamonds around her neck became heavier. She touched the necklace and cried, but she was not sure why. She heard the words of her father:

"You are a hure. You are a hure. . . ."

Chapter XX

Bill Crossen had been in residence in Tracy for one month, anxiously waiting for the state of California to finish the hydraulic tower that would ultimately lift the water one hundred feet to the canal he was poised to build. He had filled his complement of engineers and office staff, set up work camps, haggled with an endless procession of suppliers and subcontractors and finished most of the legal work that kept the local bureaucracy alive.

At ten o'clock one Tuesday morning a tall, bald, heavy-set man strode into his office unannounced and slammed the door shut behind him.

"Do you remember me?"

"I'm not sure."

"Well, I'll refresh your memory. I'm Colonel Dunby. We were in San Tomas together."

Bill *did* remember him. Seeing that man who had been his superior in prison camp shocked him. It threatened him. His presence opened wounds that had had no time to heal or form scar tissue.

"Now I remember," Bill said.

"And the letter I wrote about your suspicious behavior?"

"I remember that, too."

"What happened to it?"

"Nothing."

"The letter to G-2. We both know you were a goddamned traitor. You know you can buy anything when you have enough money. You seem to be doing all right, from all I know."

"And what do you know, Colonel Dunby? What do you *really* know?"

"I know what we both know, and whether you have an honorable discharge or not doesn't make a goddamned bit of difference. There were a lot of other prisoners at San Tomas, or had you forgotten?"

Bill was silent. He had not forgotten. Not for a minute had he forgotten. The work details he had formed . . . the heat, the deaths.

He looked at Dunby with less hostility and asked, "What is it you want? What do you want from me?"

"I want to see your ass in a stockade."

"Why?"

"I've already told you. I don't like traitors."

"That's your word, not mine."

"Let a court martial decide the definition of your behavior."

Bill looked out the window. "You're either a warped patriot or you're trying to blackmail me."

"You'd better be careful. I haven't asked for a thing. . . ."

"That's right," Crossen said. "And I could get the best attorneys money could buy and beat any rap you'd trying to hang on me."

"Perhaps you could," Dunby said.

"Are you still in the service?" Bill asked.

"What business is that of yours?"

"None. Are you?"

"No."

"What are you doing now?"

"Recuperating," Dunby said. "Trying to find work. There are a lot of bastards who never fought in the war who have *no* respect for a full colonel."

"I'll give you a job," Bill said.

"What kind of a job?"

"I'll be running a small army of Mexicans on this job. You were always a prick at handling men. I could use your talents."

Dunby was quiet for a long time, then asked, "What does it pay?"

"Five thousand a year. Good quarters, rations and benefits."

Dunby faced him. "If you think you can buy me off for five thousand a year, forget it."

"I'm offering you a job," Bill said. "Take it or leave it."

Again there was silence from Dunby. Finally he said, "The last time I applied for a job, this little shit said to me, 'There are twenty thousand chicken colonels looking for work. . . .' " He sighed heavily. "I'll take it, but what I said still goes."

Bill nodded his head. "I know. What you said still goes. Report to Feiffer at eight in the morning. I'll draw up the papers."

Bill saw no more visitors and took no more calls that morning and tried to analyze the wisdom of his decision to hire Dunby. He was bribing Dunby now, he knew, and he also knew that blackmail rarely worked in either direction. So what had he gained? Time, perhaps. Yes, time. He could keep his eye on Dunby and he would know that as long as he was on the job, Dunby would not spend time trying to crucify him.

Time, he thought. Yes. That goddamned time. He had to finish that canal. The canal would give him power. It would give him money. Power and money, he thought. But would it give him peace?

The following morning he met with the district supervisor of the Farm Labor Bureau. His name was Miller and he was dressed in neat dungarees, his shoes old but well polished; a chain on a leather belt held a large set of keys.

"Understand you wanted to see me," Miller said.

"Yes, I do. Sit down, please," Crossen said. "We're going to build the first section of the Delta-Mendota Canal, as you know."

"So I've learned."

"I'm planning to use a lot of Mexican labor."

"I've heard that, too."

"I'm going to have to house them."

"I guess that'll be your problem."

"I know, except . . ."

Crossen stepped to a map. "There are a lot of migrant camps along the route." He pointed. "Here, here, here."

"Oh, Christ, mister, they were condemned by the state years ago. Governor Knowland, I don't know, some do-gooder."

"I've inspected them," Crossen said. "They look all right to me."

"Do they, now? They look like the *Grapes of Wrath* to me."

Crossen faced the man across his desk. "I've spent four years at San Tomas prison camp in the Philippines. Those migrant camps look like palaces to me."

"Yeah, well, the spics—sorry—the Mexicans aren't prisoners. . . ."

"That's right, but the 'spics' are out of work between harvests. Where do they go?"

"Further south, some of them; back home, a lot of them."

"We'll pay them decent wages, but I need that housing. I won't need it very long. We'll move on in six months."

"It ain't for me to decide," Miller said.

"Who's it up to?"

"The county supervisor."

Bill Crossen put a large black checkbook on his desk. He opened it and displayed a row of three checks on a page. The book was over an inch thick.

"I know about county supervisors," Crossen said. "I know about county government. I'm willing to pay *somebody* to use those camps. Somebody will make use of this check."

Miller eyed the checkbook hungrily and thought of his wife, his three children.

"Somebody will, that's for sure."

"So let's say that I'll make it out to you. You name the amount. Make it big enough to take care of your boss."

"You're a pretty smart fellow. Once the news hits the papers about these camps, it'll get to Sacramento."

"That'll be a local newsman," Crossen said coldly. "I've got checks for him, too."

"How long you gonna use these facilities?"

"Six months at the most."

"Ain't too long. It'll never reach the governor by then."

"Give me a figure."

Miller, filled with hunger and fear, apprehensively said, "Eight hundred dollars? Figuring one-half for the supervisor."

"That's high," Crossen lied, "but perhaps you can throw in a little maintenance."

"We'll have it running like the Palace Hotel."

Crossen made out the check and handed it to the pale man with the pomade in his hair.

"Pleasure to do business," Miller said.

"Likewise," Crossen said, picking up the phone to dismiss the county man.

His next visitors were more sophisticated. They had traveled from San Francisco, they wore gray flannel suits and raincoats, and one carried a bulging briefcase.

"Sit down," Crossen said. "Is everything settled?"

"Everything," George Halverson, the attorney, said. "This is Al Smith, my partner."

Crossen reached over and shook hands.

"We have all the patents for your lining slip form and your canal trimmer. You are fully protected."

"How about foreign rights?" Crossen asked.

"Everything is covered."

"Let me see the documents."

Crossen studied them, and though he had been trained in engineering, he had some familiarity with legalese. He had asked Selda for several copies of copyright laws during his internment.

"I would say, if you plan to lease this equipment, you can pay for the legal fees out of your first job."

"I know I could, but my father-in-law is paying for the prototypes, so I think I owe him the first twenty miles on the house."

"As you wish. Our fee is two thousand."

Crossen opened his desk drawer, pulled out a personal check and made it out in that amount.

"Here are your patents," Halverson said, "and good luck."

"There is your check, and thank you. I hope to do much additional business with you."

"What the hell do these machines do, anyway?"

"These machines," Crossen said, "pave eighty feet of canal a day using ten men. That saves me seventy workers a day."

"Jesus Christ," Halverson said. "Are you selling stock in this invention?"

"Not until it goes sour," Crossen said and stood. It was a signal of dismissal.

Following this meeting, he phoned O'Gara.

"Mr. O'Gara?"

"Yes."

"Bill Crossen."

"What is it, Crossen?"

"I am planning to use three condemned migrant camps along the first stretch of the canal."

"They've been condemned," O'Gara said.

"I know that. I've just reopened them with eight hundred dollars."

"That's illegal."

"I agree," Crossen said. "The local man shouldn't have taken the bribe."

"You're very crafty," O'Gara said. "Why are you telling me all this?"

"I'll need these camps for six months. I don't want the governor to know."

"I know my way around San Francisco," O'Gara said. "Sacramento is another story."

"I think you can manage, Mr. O'Gara."

"Your confidence overwhelms me. Anything else?"

"No, that is all. Thank you." Crossen hung up the phone.

He walked out of his office and down the stairs. As he left the building he spotted Elyse sitting in an open convertible across the street.

He had seen her at dinner parties, weekend outings since his wedding, and he had noticed that she was drawn to him. She asked questions, probing questions about his life, his ambitions, his new environment, and Bill did little to discourage her curiosity. She was lovely, no question about that. He enjoyed simply looking at her. Her face, her figure, her very attractive movements.

"Well, well," Bill said, "what a pleasant surprise. What brings you here to this godforsaken town?"

She looked radiant, wearing a pair of yellow shorts, a white silk blouse, a red bandana pulling back her black hair.

"I'm on my way to Yosemite. I thought I'd see what a real workingman does all day."

Bill seemed flustered. "How about lunch?"

Elyse looked at her watch, which was diamond-studded and small. "Breakfast sounds better."

"Either one," Bill said, walking around to the other side of the car and seating himself beside her. "We'll go to Olsen's. It is the best in Tracy and not all that good."

They sat almost alone in a whitewashed room, the tables covered in a gingham, and they ordered bacon and eggs and coffee.

"And why, may I ask, are you heading for Yosemite, alone?"

"I need air," she said. "Air to breathe. Air to think."

Bill looked at her. "Elyse," he said. "There's something troubling you. Tell me. No one just happens into Tracy."

"You are always so direct, Bill."

"I know. Brutally direct. I'm sorry."

"I have nothing to complain about. Nothing," she said. "I have everything a girl could want. A beautiful house, adoring family . . ."

"Then what?"

"I'm bored. Four of us live in that big house and we wrack our brains trying to pile pleasure upon pleasure. . . ."

"*Do* something," Crossen said. "Do something constructive."

"Like what?"

"Go to school. Have a child. I don't know. I've never had the problem."

"I believe that. I wasn't raised to have that problem, either."

"You are the most coveted girl in town."

"Because of my looks . . ."

"That's nothing to be ashamed of. I don't think you lack brains, either," Bill said.

"Thank you, but if I have any brains left, what do I use them for?"

Crossen shrugged his shoulders.

"They're your brains, not mine."

"That's right. Oh, Jesus, Bill, I'm trying to have a child. I've thought of going back to school. What for? What good will more education do me?"

"It'll make you more educated."

"Yes. Stupid questions get stupid answers."

They both laughed.

"And tell me about yourself," Elyse said. "What are you doing here?"

"Come to the office and I'll show you."

They rose and drove to Crossen's stark office. He unrolled blueprint after blueprint for her, he showed her maps on the wall, he gave curt answers to curt questions from an endless stream of men entering his office and finally he escorted her to her car and asked her to drive to the hydraulic plant and down a stretch of road where the canal would be built.

He rarely stopped talking or gesturing, and it was almost sunset when they returned to his office.

"How long," she asked, "would it take to become an engineer?"

"Six years," Crossen said.

"Would you give me a job?"

He laughed. "If you wore *that* outfit," pointing at her sparse clothing, "you'd cost me one day of construction out of three. Did you see the rubbernecking going on?"

"I noticed your eyes didn't turn when I bent down."

Bill blushed.

"Could I get a room around here?"

"Why?"

"Why do you think, stupid?"

"It's a very small town."

"You're the head honcho here, aren't you?"

"That's the trouble."

"You mean you couldn't find your way to my room if I rented it."

"I didn't say that. I happen to have a great deal of respect for my wife. . . ."

"I didn't ask you to marry me. I just offered you a free fuck."

"Now who is direct?"

"I am. I used to steal kosher pickles from Levy's delicatessen but the bastard used to feel up my tits."

Bill felt an erection. "Try the Laurel Court. Ask for cabin twelve. It's way in back."

"You're not going to take me out to dinner?"

"No, the place has a hot plate. Improvise. I'll be there at eight."

"You seem to know it pretty well."

"*You* made the offer. . . ." Bill said.

"Yes, I did."

Bill returned to his own quarters and sat on the bed. "Not in the script," Selda would have told him and he would agree. And it also was true, he had not been able to take his eyes off the girl all day, not unlike every rich son of a bitch in Pacific Heights. He had indeed watched as she bent over and he could see the tops of those

162

lovely breasts, and he had watched that ripe young ass beginning below the bottom of her brief shorts.

He sat on his bed and put his head between his hands.

Why, why had that goddamned girl come up here? And he remembered Alfred Weinstein's remark at a cocktail party one evening as they both watched Elyse: "Do you have beautiful girls like *that* in New York?"

And Bill had remembered looking at this acne-scarred little bastard and wanting to say, "No, perhaps not, but I'll have her in bed before you will."

He took a shower and changed into clean underwear, denims, a blue workshirt and still felt an erection.

Promptly at eight he knocked on the door of Number 12, Laurel Court, and Elyse opened the door. She was wearing a bath towel knotted about her back. It was slit on the side and he could see her, half-naked.

"I just took a shower. God, this is a dusty town. I've made you a martini and dinner will be right up."

"I hope it's not a sit-down dinner," Bill said.

"Why?"

"I've had a hard-on for four hours."

Bill took a stiff drink. "You're not drinking?"

"Never do."

"Why?"

She ran her hand over her toweled body. "Have to protect the inventory. This is all I've got."

"It's enough," Bill said, standing and half throwing Elyse on the bed.

He undid her towel and kissed her. Hard, almost brutally, and Elyse wrested her mouth from his and opened his fly. She bent down and closed her lips on his stiff penis and Bill watched the beautifully coiffed head moving up and down. He watched one lovely breast, her sparse pubic hair.

"Hold on," he said, "hold on," and Elyse turned to face him.

"Come, goddamnit, come," she said, and he slid his hand between her moist legs and *did* come. In her mouth. He apologized.

She looked at him, amused. "You tall, good-looking bastards are all the same."

"What do you mean?"

"You're trigger-happy."

"I said I was sorry. What about you?"

"We'll get to me in good time. We've got all night."

"Until four," Bill said. "I've got to drive out of here in darkness."

"It seems so strange," Elyse said.

"What?"

"Lewis never has anywhere to go. Anything to do . . ."

"Is that why you're here?"

"Partly."

"What's the other part?"

"Jesus Christ, Bill, don't you realize you are one of the most attractive men in San Francisco?"

"I hadn't given it much thought."

"Don't you know that I realize that they are trying to hurt you?"

"Everyone except Marjorie," Bill said.

"That's true, perhaps. I have the Wolf family, but other than them I *know* what they're saying."

"About me?"

"No, about me."

She had managed a stew on the hot plate, bought a chocolate cake, and found a cold bottle of wine; and they sat now, both wearing cheap towels, in a linoleum-covered dinette area, eating in comfortable silence. After dinner Elyse spread herself naked on the bed, and Bill, after kissing her lips, her cheeks, her breasts, felt her hand guide his head toward her vagina, and he found his tongue exploring her with great gusto.

He watched her face, her beautiful face, her closed eyes; and then she said, "Now, *now*, get inside," and he did, and once more he reached a climax quickly and withdrew too quickly.

Elyse turned to face him.

"Well, Major Crossen, you are now one of a select company of young men who can say they have fucked Elyse Wolf."

"Don't say things like that."

"It's true. Do you know what my father's last words were to me?"

"No."

"He called me a hure."

"I won't tell you my father's last words."

"Baruch atah al hamayim" Elyse said.

"Besiach al gal," Bill finished.

"I will tell you one thing, Bill."

"What's that?"

"You are the first man I've slept with since I married Lewis."

"Why are you telling me this?"

"I'm not as bad as I made myself out."

He reached for her and cupped her fanny.

"I'll tell you one other thing," she said.

"What?"

"There's a lot Lewis Wolf could teach you about making love."

"And how would he feel if he knew about us?"

"It wouldn't bother him, probably. It would bother him less if he could have watched."

Bill looked at her. "I'm going to sleep, but I've reached one conclusion."

"What's that?"

"There's a hell of a lot they don't teach you at MIT."

Bill did leave at 4:00 A.M. and lightly kissed Elyse before going.

"The Christian work ethic," she said.

"It's not that. I just don't have the 'inventory' you have."

"I wouldn't be too sure," Elyse said. "It just needs practice."

He drove quickly out of the motel parking lot and, using various side streets, reached his own quarters. He felt—and he laughed at himself, because he classified them in his head—guilt toward Marjorie, lust for Elyse and annoyance about his apparent failures to please any one in bed.

Once more he showered and brewed himself a cup of coffee. At 5:00 A.M., he was at his desk, but this surprised no one. There were nights he never left it.

Chapter XXI

Bill Crossen dutifully arrived at his Marina apartment at six-thirty after a fast and grueling drive from Tracy. He had almost gotten used to seeing a navy blue or a charcoal gray suit laid out on the bed, along with a clean shirt, tie, shoes, socks. Like the rising and setting of the sun, young San Franciscans entertained each other lavishly over the weekends. There were small dinner parties at home for eight or ten, or large dinner parties for a hundred, mostly held in the dining rooms of the St. Francis, the Mark Hopkins, the Fairmont Hotel. There were almost always the same people, and usually the same conversations. Almost all these sons and daughters of the rich Jews in San Francisco believed firmly in this ritual. The small parties attested to some of the culinary imagination of the young women; the large parties essentially had the same menu: chicken, roast beef, turkey. There was always some drinking, but never to excess; there was always dancing at the larger affairs to the sounds of Ernie Heckscher or Tony Martin, smooth, slow, undemanding sounds.

They were a good-looking group. The men mostly tall, the young women handsome, well dressed, well coiffed. And for the most part they tolerated Bill Crossen, by virtue of his marriage to Marjorie, but they also let him know in not too subtle ways that he was not a member of the club.

"Where in the hell did you get that suit?" they kidded him, but Crossen was not amused.

"What do you mean you've never heard of Sally Stanford?" and Crossen was at a loss.

"You mean you've never heard of the Goldman scandal!" and again he was at a loss.

The women, more liberated after the war, were often equally aggressive.

"Do you think it's right to leave Marjorie alone five days a week after you've been married such a short time?" they asked.

"We're planning a week in Hawaii. Why *can't* you join us?" and he was filled with apologies.

He detested the weekends, and his frustrations almost rose beyond toleration on that lonesome drive from Tracy. He hated the small humiliations, the barely concealed taunts, the innuendos, the leading questions. And yet he knew that now, like his tenure at MIT and at San Tomas, he must put in his time with this useless, bitchy, fucking crowd.

It occurred to him that Marjorie, exhausted herself after a long week of practice, might be happy to forego these childish weekend games, but he was apprehensive about discussing it with her, since she might well agree, and that was a situation to be avoided. It would bring them closer and somehow he feared that. "Why, damnit?" he thought. She was a warm, lovely person. She was gifted. He respected her talent, her grit. What was it, then?

There was a certain mystery to the girl. Like himself, she was a very private, determined person. She said little that was not essential. She seemed to rise so easily above pettiness. He sensed the limits with which he brought pleasure to her in bed, but even here she was undemanding.

How well did he really know her? He wondered as he finished dressing for the latest round of weekend socializing.

"Hold on, Marjorie I'm almost ready."

"You look wonderful, Bill," she said as he emerged from the bedroom.

"You look pretty good yourself," he answered, and she kissed him lightly as they left for the next party.

Marjorie, like most of her peers, had been a virgin when she married Bill. She enjoyed his lovemaking but sensed an abruptness, a selfishness to the act, and yet she could not really judge. Of course, she had heard stories from her sister, from girl friends, she had read novels, but wondered how much that was told her was nothing more than romantic drivel. Bill was her man. The family could go to hell. She scarcely listened to the complaints of her brother and sister about Bill's domination of the firm; she dismissed her mother's constant probing, her endeavors to bring Bill "closer" to the family, to make him "open up." She also wished for a greater intellectual intimacy with her husband, but as reluctant as he was to get closer, whatever his reasons, she chose not to rock a boat that had been launched and was at present sailing in smooth, albeit shallow, waters.

*   *   *

169

There were times, particularly during Bill's absences, that Selda and Marjorie had dinner together.

"We'll have to find you a man," Marjorie said totally without guile one evening.

Selda laughed. "I don't know, Marjorie," she said. "I'm getting to be a slob and I don't mind it. I'm getting very set in my ways and I'm not sure I want to change the scenery too much."

"Don't you ever get lonely?"

"Of course. Don't you?" Selda asked.

"Not often." Marjorie was quiet for a minute. "I suppose I do. I turn to the piano. It's quite simple."

"I admire you for that. I turn to a box of Blum's candies."

"Are you happy with Bill?" Selda asked simply.

"Yes," Marjorie answered just as simply. "I realize he's . . ." she hesitated.

"What?"

"Different."

"How is he different?"

"He's terribly involved, he's driven, he's very quiet . . ."

"I noticed that, too," Selda said, "when he was living with me. He's very mature for his age."

"He's been through a lot," Marjorie said.

"Does he ever talk about it?"

"Never."

"Not to me, either," Selda said. "Sometimes, sometimes I wish he would. Maybe to you."

"Perhaps in good time . . . They say in music, never rush a forte passage."

"He's very lucky, Marjorie," Selda said. "You're quite mature yourself."

"That's a nice thing to say. I'm not so sure I am. I bury myself in the piano. That may not be such a good idea."

170

"I think it's wonderful," Selda said. "Do you realize I still open a package of books like a Christmas present? I get them every day. . . ."

"I know," Marjorie said. "I feel that way about a new score."

Chapter XXII

At ten o'clock Bill Crossen had assembled his senior staff in his office. There were few chairs, so most of the men stood while some sat on their haunches. They were older than Crossen, most of them veterans with O'Gara and Levey, but Crossen was not intimidated by their years or seniority.

He read to them from a Bureau of Reclamation bulletin: " 'The Delta-Mendota Canal is the largest single item in the postwar construction work on the Central Valley Project. The canal,' " Bill continued, " 'will be one hundred thirteen miles long, forty-eight feet wide, have a depth of sixteen feet and a lining thickness of four inches. The projected cost of the entire canal is in excess of seventy one million dollars.' " He looked at the men around him and saw sparks of interest.

"We have been awarded the first section of the canal and I am told there will be eight other bids until completion." His voice rose. "I mean to land *every other bid.*"

"Excuse me, Bill," Donovan, a senior engineer said. "I know we're a good construction company, but so are Hasler, Elliot and Parson, Everist. We've got a lot of competition. . . ."

"They all lack one thing we have," Bill countered.

"What's that?"

"A slip form and a trimmer." He spread out the plans for these giant, birdlike pieces of machinery so the men could study them.

"Jesus," one of the engineers said finally, "will these things work?"

"They'll work," Crossen said confidently, "I know they'll work. I've built models of them. They'll do just fine."

"And what's to prevent other companies from using them, too?"

"I hold the patents to them. *I* control their distribution. Of course, I'll license them out to other firms, but not on this job. . . ."

The men looked at him with a mixture of awe and misgiving.

"We never quite used to handle construction like this. If one outfit needed a steam shovel and we had them sitting around, we'd let them use it."

"Well, things have changed," Crossen said, picking up a sheaf of computer logs. "Competition is going to get rough. We're going to stay on top. These figures" —which were meaningless to most of the older men in the room—"prove we should come in forty percent ahead of time and thirty percent under labor costs."

The room was quiet. "Are there any questions?" Bill asked. There were none.

Donovan said, without much enthusiasm, "I think you've got the bases pretty well covered. I hope the hell you know what you are doing. What if these machines break down?"

"I have backups," Bill said.

"Where are you going to get men to run these things?" another engineer asked.

"They'll have to be taught," Crossen said.

"By whom?"

"By me. They work as easily as a tractor."

"That's some tractor," someone remarked.

"The trick is that the cement keeps flowing. That's your job, Blandy."

"I know." He scratched his head. "That's a lot of mud this thing spews out."

"A lot, yes," Bill said. "Can you handle it?"

The man nodded. "I can handle it."

"These liners and trimmers have several diesels on them," Bill continued. "Who is the chief diesel engineer?"

"I am," a small, heavy-set man volunteered.

"They take M-two fuel, and watch the bleeder valves."

"I know how to treat a diesel engine."

"Good. There will be engineers hanging around from other companies," Bill said. "We can't stop them. But my lawyers can. Are there any questions?"

"What about rain?" Donovan asked.

"What about it?"

"You going to work in the rain?"

"Hell, yes. You have a slicker?"

Bill looked around the room. He was not making friends, he knew, but he didn't care.

"Sure there aren't any more questions now?"

There were none.

Grady and Smith and Donovan were seated in a mock Mexican cantina, the walls covered with dusty wrought-iron fixtures purchased in Tijuana years ago, a few bullfight posters, a torn piñata. The men ordered beers and a heavy-set waitress placed taco chips in front of them.

"I don't know where the old man came up with that son of a bitch," Smith said. "This used to be a good outfit to work for."

"He told me, 'Hang in there Grady. I'm giving the boy *one* chance. He's got new ideas. Construction is changing. I want to see whether he'll work out.' "

"It's still a pile of crap," Smith said. "You, Donovan, have got the seniority. *You* should be supervising engineer."

"We work for a Jew firm, at least half of it is Jew. We've always known that. What about that lard-ass kid of Levey's? He doesn't know the difference between a broom handle and a two-by-four."

"Oh, shit," Smith said. "Old man Levey's all right. He's a good engineer. Maybe he knows what the hell he's talking about."

"Maybe he does, maybe he doesn't," Grady said. "Still doesn't give him the right to push some snot-nosed Ivy League engineer ahead of us."

"We'll get all eight sections of the dam," Donovan imitated Crossen. "What does he think? Elliot, Parson, Meehan are going to sit on their asses while we grab section after section?"

"Who knows? Maybe that fancy machine he's got will do the job."

"Bullshit," Smith said. "We've all seen fancy machines before. There's only one machine I trust on a job like this."

"What's that?"

"It's got two hands, a strong back and speaks Mexican."

The all laughed and ordered another beer.

That same day O'Gara and Levey lunched at Jack's. They were directed to a table in the middle of the room and after acknowledging the presence of half the diners already seated, they sat down to chilled martinis and a fresh loaf of French bread.

"Where did you find that Bill Crossen?" O'Gara asked bluntly.

"I didn't," Levey said. "He found me."

"Tough little bastard," O'Gara said.

"He's been through a lot," Levey half apologized for the boy.

"Called up one morning. Told me he was taking over three condemned migrant camps. Paid off some county politician."

Levey smiled. "You're just pissed off because you didn't think of that."

"Maybe," O'Gara said, "but when I pay off somebody, I *know* who I'm paying off. That kid could get our ass in a wringer. . . ."

"I'll talk to him," Levey said. "It's a point well taken."

"I didn't think they taught stuff like that at MIT," O'Gara said.

"They don't, I'm sure."

"Then where the hell did he learn that?"

"On the Lower East Side."

O'Gara nodded and watched the waiter bone his sole.

"He's not an easy kid to get to know," Levey said. "Smart, though. I understand he taught himself Japanese in three months. Marjorie said he's given himself six weeks to learn Spanish. . . ."

O'Gara looked into Levey's eyes. "Maybe he's smart, maybe he's a hell of an engineer, but . . ." He scraped some crumbs into a heap on the table cloth.

"But what?"

"Are you *comfortable* with him in the firm?"

Levey pushed back his chair and lit a cigar.

"Times are changing, O'Gara. He's a new breed of engineer. I've got a couple of old boys on the job that are reporting to me. When I feel I have to rein him in, I will."

"Well, don't give him too much head. I saw the bills for that slip lining form, that canal trimmer. That's not peanuts."

"Agreed," Levey said. "I argued with him about that. He said, 'Stop buying slum housing on Mission Street. Put your money where it counts.'"

"And how does he know you buy property on Mission Street?"

And now Levey looked O'Gara in the eyes. "That is a question I ask myself. How does he know so much? So soon?"

They paid the waiter, exchanged pleasantries with friends on the way out of the restaurant.

"There's *one* thing I *do* know," Henry Levey said as they walked down Montgomery Street. "I know where Henry Jr. will be when I get back to the office."

"Where?"

"On the golf course."

O'Gara shook his head. "Unless he's at the races with my kid. Maybe we weren't so smart after all."

"What do you mean?"

"Trying to keep them out of the war. Maybe they'd be men now."

"They're alive," Levey said.

"Are they?" O'Gara asked as they separated to go to their respective offices.

"Are they?" Levey pondered as he sat behind his desk. A set of complicated proposals soon ended his introspection.

Chapter XXIII

Most of the postwar changes in San Francisco were not only unpleasant for women like Hortense, but threatening as well. There were days when Henry needed the limousine and she was forced to take the Number 3 streetcar downtown. If the car was full, neither men nor children got up to offer her a seat, and those rattan seats were often so grimy one would soil one's clothes sitting on them. She had learned now to take two pairs of gloves: one pair made of leather, to use until she reached her destination; another pair, white, which she would don downtown; and she found her friends doing the same thing. Minorities had never before been a problem in San Francisco. When one thought of black people, one thought of Joe Shreve—so called affectionately and in true San Francisco-plantation style after his employer—a tall, elderly doorman at Shreve's jewelry store who opened the door of your limousine and the door of the store, but now black people were *everywhere*. They sat next to you in public conveyances, black ladies shopped next to you at Ransohoff's and black people taught your children.

The Chinese, of which San Francisco had a large population, were either confined to those tubercular quarters of Chinatown along Grant Avenue or lived in subbasements in the mansions facing the Bay. Many of them had been with families for generations and assumed the last names of their employers. There were the Charlie Zantners and the Tommy Fleishmans, sallow-skinned men who acted as butlers and chauffeurs, their wives acting as cooks, maids, laundresses. Of course, they had children, and one paid little attention to them, but those children had grown a foot taller than their ancestors after one hundred years of assimilation. They wore the same Block sweaters as the white families' children, they participated in athletics and often excelled. They won scholarships to universities.

Commercial streets like Fillmore, Polk and Clement, which had always been pleasant, solid middle class avenues, were becoming increasingly ethnic, and one "took one's life in one's hands," or so Hortense imagined, entering one of the little shops whose employees no longer showed deference to the patrons from Pacific Heights.

If she drove toward their country home in Menlo Park, she was appalled by the uniformity and lack of charm of the endless rows of stucco houses that lined the hills of Hunter's point, the area of Castro Valley. And Market Street, which had always been a point of division in San Francisco, was now almost an armed camp south of the Slot. The Mission District, always poor but somehow quaint, was assuming the character of Harlem; the Haight-Ashbury area filled with hundreds of lovely Victorian structures increasingly housed the poor.

She did not care to listen to what Henry or Bill Crossen said, that they, the Leveys, and many of their friends were profiting by these expansions, that the row houses, the tracts, the shopping centers were making them even richer. To her all this influx, this congestion, this racial mix spelled doom for this city she loved, where one parked one's car where one pleased (and the police were paid off), where one entered great restaurants like the Blue Fox, or Doros, or L'Orangerie, and the headwaiter seemingly had *their* table ready without reservations, and one could count on the other diners to be well-dressed, well-modulated and genteel.

Very little of this touched Bill Crossen. He had never known the "old" city nor had he ever enjoyed its peculiar life style. He was used to blacks in his neighborhood; he had lived with minorities in his childhood. He saw little merit in the endless complaints of Hortense, or even in those of Selda or Marjorie. He felt that he really did not belong here any more than anywhere else he had been in his life. His apartment was comfortable. The view of the Bay, when he occasionally walked along the yacht harbor, was inspiring, and he knew that his arguments that the tourists and newcomers filled the coffers were grudingly acknowledged, but officially condemned.

Not all his contemporaries merely sat in the board rooms of their fathers, or sailed their yachts or inhabited their mansions. Some, like Bill Crossen, felt that change in the city and profited from it. Peter Fels expanded his clothing business. Apartment homes were built, grocery chains developed, car dealerships multiplied, and most people actually enjoyed the freer life in San Francisco. The secretaries along Montgomery Street, "the prettiest girls in the world," as young Herb Caen so often referred to them, were not only that, pretty, but less rigid morally. Sotto voce tales of office parties, of romps in

Marina motels reached Crossen's ear with increasing frequency. The ladies of the venerable whorehouses of Sally Stanford and Blackie Duveen were being replaced by hundreds of young women from Tennessee and New York, from Dubuque and Oklahoma City, who not only invited the young scions to their apartments but ended the meal with a guiltless romp in the hay.

It all faintly amused Bill Crossen, but he was isolated by the nature of his profession and the sheltered life he led with his wife, her family and friends. Construction on the canal had begun. His liner and trimmer worked flawlessly. With each day of construction he gained almost half a day on the schedule and Henry Levey could scarcely believe the progress being made in Tracy, receiving daily grudging compliments not only from O'Gara but from fellow construction tycoons.

The first segment of the canal was completed eight months ahead of schedule, and the almost uncontested awarding of the second section was no small victory for Crossen. He had pulled off a very masterful engineering feat using intricate machines that he had invented plus the complicated computer technology that he had so quickly embraced. He received congratulations from friends and grudging admiration from business acquaintances.

On Friday, Bill, as had been his custom, drove home to San Francisco where Marjorie met him, coiffed and well dressed, with a bottle of champagne sitting in a silver bucket.

"My, my," Bill said, "don't we look festive. What's the occasion?"

"Don't be so modest."

"Why?"

"Daddy phoned me. He told me you've won the second bid on the canal. He said you were the talk of the engineers."

"I'm right on schedule," Bill said.

"*Your* schedule."

"Yes, *my* schedule."

"Well, here's a toast," Marjorie said, lifting her glass. "To Bill Crossen, boy wonder."

"I'll drink a toast to you," he said.

"Strange, isn't it?"

"What?"

"To see me dressed for a change. You must get tired of seeing me in my sweat shirt," Marjorie said.

"I like you in your sweat shirt. Look at me, dirty boots, unpressed pants."

"And your truck in front of the door. Wouldn't you be more comfortable in a car?"

"To tell you the truth, Marjorie, I wouldn't know the difference."

"I *do* believe that. How does it feel to have so many men working for you? Do they resent you being so young?"

"There *is* resentment, but I don't let it bother me. The trick is to be ahead of everyone, to make the right decisions and never show an ounce of mercy."

"That's tough talk," Marjorie said.

"You bet. But everyone is testing me. They're all waiting for me to fall on my ass. I'd better not."

"I worry about you," Marjorie said. "I had dinner with Selda on Thursday night, and I told her about my fears."

"Don't worry, Marjorie. I can take care of myself. I learned that much at San Tomas."

"I love you, Bill, that's all. You know I'll never stand in your way, I have the same stupid drive, but Selda said correctly, 'Why, why that push? Where is it all going?' "

"I do know what it's like to be poor. I don't like it. I've been poor all my life."

It was one of the first times Bill had spoken of his past.

"You're no longer poor, Bill. Just marrying me ended that."

"I am not talking about *that* money."

"Well, it's there, and it's yours as much as mine."

Bill put his arms around her. "I know the way you meant it. Money is just a milestone, believe me. I don't really *want* anything materially. It's a measure, it's like getting those passages down on the piano."

"I understand that. I just don't want you to think you have to prove anything to me."

"It's not that," Bill said almost pensively. "Whatever I do is because I have to prove something to *myself*. This next section of the canal is going to be even tougher."

"Why?"

"I've gotten to know this crew now. I've learned to separate the wheat from the chaff. . . . There'll be a lot of heads rolling when I get back."

The statement gave Marjorie more cause for concern, but she said nothing. "I turned down an invitation to the Hellers tonight. I wanted to celebrate alone."

"That's good," Bill said. "Let me take a shower and we will play married couple."

"Great idea."

They ate quietly by candlelight, Marjorie full of local gossip, including the news that Elyse Wolf was pregnant.

"She told me," Marjorie said, "that she wondered why it took so long. She said she spends half her life with her legs apart."

Bill said nothing, remembering that headstrong girl in bed and feeling guilty as he made love to Marjorie that evening.

Goddamnit, he thought. Marjorie deserves better, and yet he could still feel Elyse's breasts in his hand, see her face on that bed.

She had called him after her return from Yosemite.

"Just wanted to let you know I got home safely," she had said. "Or were you worried?"

"It's nice of you to call," Bill had said.

"You didn't answer my question."

"I know. You're quite a girl, Elyse. Quite a girl."

"I shall take that as a compliment and hang up. Lewis just came in the house. Take care," she had said and hung up.

Could he put her into another room in his head? Bill wondered, and fell asleep.

Elyse also made love that night. It was nothing new. Lewis had taken her to bed after lunch and there was nothing new about that, either.

But unlike Lewis, who had consumed a full quart of gin, she did not go to sleep but lay thinking about Bill Crossen.

What was it about him that fascinated her?

He was good-looking. True. So were a good many other young men in San Francisco. They shared a poor Jewish background, but even *that* bond was tenuous. She did not like to dwell on her life on McAllister Street and could not remember Bill celebrating *his* ghetto upbringing. She did not find camaraderie along these lines with Crossen and, to be honest, she found very little else.

He was seducable. She had learned that, but most men, she had found, were seduceable. She was blessed with the face, the body. She knew all that.

She *envied* Crossen. He had not, as everyone expected, settled comfortably into the firm of O'Gara and Levey. He did not embrace the social privileges of Pacific Heights now available to him (as she had fully embraced them).

No. He was his own man. Brilliant, tough, headstrong, merciless and fighting, still fighting.

184

Perhaps that's what it all was. Envy. Where was she going? *She* was bright. She knew that. She was ambitious. She knew that also. And yet, outside of the materialism, what did she have to show for it?

A child. She put her hands on her stomach. Yes, a child. If it's a boy it would be Lewis Wolf IV. And could she make a man out of him? The environment was hardly conducive. Papa, Lewis, Jake, hardly a great tutorial group. Be honest, she thought. What about me? What great example do I set? It will be a handsome child, she knew that. But what will be his heritage? A drunken father, a mother who does *nothing*, nothing, really, all day . . . just dresses and looks pretty and opens her legs. . . .

Goddamn, she thought. Goddamnit anyway. She heard one of Jake's lovers descend the stairs, let himself out the front door and then she heard a car being started and pulling away.

We could buy Sweden, Lewis had said offhandedly once. We could afford it, but we thought it would be too much trouble.

To the manor born, Elyse thought, and she saw the dark, dark hallway of her home on McAllister Street; and then she watched the dying flames in the hearth in her bedroom. You have to be born to the manor. It was sad, but she still felt like a guest.

Chapter XXIV

Bill Crossen sat in Henry Levey's office. Even though he had been with O'Gara and Levey for almost three years now, he was still awed by his father-in-law's elegant office.

"Congratulations," Levey said. "Your new machines, the use of your goddamned computer have proven you right."

"Thank you, sir."

"I can almost believe you'll build that whole canal. I think you deserve a raise."

"I don't need a raise," Crossen said.

"Come, come, now. A young man should look out for himself, his family. Do you and Marjorie plan to have children?"

"We haven't discussed it."

"I see."

Levey reached into his desk drawer and pulled out a check. He started to hand it to Crossen.

"Well, here's a bonus," he said, but again Crossen

refused it. Instead he reached into his briefcase and brought out some folders.

"Since you financed the prototypes of my canal trimmer and liner I have allowed you to use them on this segment of the canal."

Levey looked at Crossen. "Go on."

"Both pieces of equipment were patented by me and I shall charge you a fee for the continued use of that equipment."

"I'll be a son of a bitch."

Crossen was unaffected by the retort. "As you can see from this list I have licensed forty-four rigs around the world."

"Where in the hell did you get forty-four rigs?"

"U.S. Steel is building them for me. They share in my royalties."

Levey stared at the three-page document almost in disbelief. "These figures project an income for you of over one million dollars in the next year."

"It will be higher," Crossen said unemotionally. "I have just signed with Kaiser Steel. They are building additional rigs."

"This sheet," Crossen continued, handing it to a stunned Levey, "will give you a cost breakdown on the Delta-Mendota project. You'll detect a profit margin despite the royalty. You can see it's still a handsome amount."

Levey dropped the sheet on the desk. "Has it occurred to you that you are part of the family? That it was *my* money, *my* faith which built those prototypes?"

"It has all occurred to me. The profit on the first segment of the canal has more than repaid you for your faith and generosity. I see no further need for nepotism. There is too much in this firm already."

The blood drained from Levey's face. "And what the hell do you mean by that?"

"Your son, and your son-in-law are luxuries which a firm this size can't afford very much longer. However, that's your business."

"Thank you."

"I have made four projections; The Nimbus Dam, the Friant-Kern Canal, the Peach Bowl Bridge and the Fish Hatchery project. I have spent many hours of my own time calculating and recalculating these ventures, and I have sent you endless reports proving that they will come in at a loss. You have chosen to ignore these studies altogether."

Levey rose and faced Crossen. "I've already had one heart attack."

"I am sorry, sir. I did not know that."

"Sorry, shit. Didn't your computer tell you that? I'd like to punch you right in the mouth. I'd like to kick your ass right out of this office, this town, my house."

"You can do so without physical exertion," Crossen said. "I shall be happy to resign."

"I bet. Have you already contacted the competition?"

"I have said nothing to anyone. You have my word."

"*Your* word. Shit. The word I want to hear is *family,* that's the word I want to hear. Does that mean *anything* to you?"

"I have tried to be a good husband to Marjorie," Crossen said. "Your 'family,' of which you're so proud, has hardly accepted me. I have heard every slur and felt every innuendo since I joined your 'family' and their friends. I have been called a kike behind my back, a Pole, a Polack, a foreigner, an outsider, by everyone except Marjorie."

"And me," Levey said, sitting down.

"That's true." Now Crossen paced the floor. "That's very true. I'm truly sorry that I didn't acknowledge that."

There was silence in the room as Levey sat thinking. He thought of Hortense's diatribes against this boy, the complaints of his son, his daughter, his son-in-law. He remembered the warnings of O'Gara and his old-time employees. And he remembered also his young days in San Francisco when the same epithets that were being thrown at Bill had been aimed at him.

"Are you a gambler, Crossen?" Levey asked

"No sir, I'm not."

"Well, I'm going to ask you to gamble."

"How?"

"You will make over a million dollars this year. Perhaps two. The forty-thousand-dollar royalties you want from me are pocket money. Waive those royalties."

"Why?"

"For *my* sake."

It was Crossen who was quiet now. Finally he looked up. "Consider them waived."

Levey nodded but said nothing.

"And what is *your* definition of family, Mr. Levey?"

"I don't need to give you that definition," Levey said.

"That's true."

The room was quiet and Crossen left. Levey put his feet on his expensive coffee table. He looked at the projections for Nimbus Dam, the Fish Hatchery project, the others scattered on its top; and he leaned back on the couch and closed his eyes, pressing the lids with his fingers, and did not know whether to envy or pity Bill Crossen—or whether to envy or pity himself.

Crossen returned home to find Marjorie highly excited. "Look at this," she said, waving a letter at her husband.

"Who is it from?"

"Solari. Pietro Solari. The *great* Pietro Solari. He has accepted me into his master classes. Imagine!"

"That's wonderful. When is he coming?"

"He isn't coming. I'm going, silly."

"Going? Going where?"

"To New York. For six weeks."

"When?"

"This winter. It's the first time he can fit me in."

"Alone?"

"Of course, unless you can join me."

"I wish I could. What will people say if you go alone?"

"*What* people?"

"Our friends, your family. Your friends," he corrected himself.

"To hell with what our friends will say. This chance comes once in a lifetime. . . . Solari just fit me in."

"I think it's wonderful," Bill said. "Congratulations. Perhaps I could visit you?"

"You can. You know you can."

Marjorie leaned back on the couch.

"You don't know how many recitals I've given. How many prizes I've won. How many competitions I've entered. . . . You don't know how many hours I've spent at that piano, that damned monster."

"I've watched you, Marjorie," Bill said.

"I know. I know, Bill. That instrument is a monster, believe me. . . . One can spend a lifetime trying to tame it."

"Is it worthwhile?" Bill asked. "Is it really worthwhile?"

"It is," she said slowly, "when you get an invitation from Solari. *That* is a milestone. It makes all the recitals, the hours of practice seem incidental. A letter from Solari is the first real step."

"To what?"

"A career," Marjorie said with great finality.

"Where will this lead, Marjorie? Where are you going?"

"With Solari's blessing, I could debut with any symphony in the world. I plan to play with the San Francisco Orchestra next spring at the Opera House."

"Is that the best?"

"Not the best," Marjorie said. "It's San Francisco. I've been a refugee myself here."

"What do you mean?"

"I have *eyes*, too, Bill, and ears. I have feelings. Perhaps *some* people will understand why a good-looking, bright young man like Bill Crossen would want a Marjorie Levey." She wanted to say a *mieskeit*, but prudently she didn't.

"It's been a day filled with emotion," Bill said, removing his tie. "Too much emotion. Could we stay home tonight?"

"And miss the Goldman party?"

"Yes."

"With pleasure," Marjorie said.

Chapter XXV

One month later, Bill Crossen arrived at his desk at seven in the morning after a two-hour drive from San Francisco, the day after Marjorie had left for New York. He had barely picked up the night-shift report from the wall when the phone rang.

"Bill."

"Yes."

"Henry Levey."

"So early. What can I do for you?"

"I want you to come to the office. Right away."

"I just arrived up here in Tracy."

"Can't one of your foremen handle it?"

"Of course."

"I'll see you about ten?"

"Yes, Mr. Levey."

There had been no hint, no clue as to the reason for this request and Crossen was truly puzzled as he sat across the coffee table from Levey.

"Coffee?"

"No thanks."

"I'll tell you why I sent for you. I feel somewhat like the Chinese engineers who, having tried the computer, agreed that it was a fine invention, but said, after we check the data on the abacus, it really doesn't save too much time."

Levey looked at Bill.

"This has been my dilemma. I *have* been studying your printouts and it is difficult to equate these cold figures with years of experience, with feelings, with intuition; but I must admit that your facts are right—mine are not. I've spent a week traveling from project to project: It only fortified your predictions."

"I wish it were otherwise," Crossen said.

"It isn't and that's it. Now I am talking to you as a member of the family, and I want it kept that way."

"Go ahead."

"As you predicted, we're going to lose our ass on all of these projects unless we do something. Now, this firm can stand that loss and still survive, but it won't help our reputation and as sure as hell won't help us on another round of bidding. Since by marriage you own ten percent of this company, I am asking for any and all suggestions. There is no pride involved."

"Do you have the projections here?"

"Yes." Levey spread them out and Crossen studied them intently. He took out a gold pencil and made some computations on a large note pad, figured silently for ten minutes and then looked at Levey.

"All right," he said, "first off, the Delta-Mendota Canal will build itself now. It doesn't need my presence. We might lose a few days, that's all. I can take over Nimbus Dam. That's got the biggest problems. I've got two men from MIT in Tracy. One can handle the Friant-Kern Canal, the other the Peach Bowl Bridge."

"What about the Fish Hatchery project?"

"You take over," Crossen said. "Do you good to get back in the field."

"What about the men handling the projects now?"

"Demote them or fire them. Your choice."

"That'll raise hell with the morale in the company."

"You want good morale or a profitable firm?" He looked at Levey. "The morale in Tracy stinks. Everybody gets paid every week. Everybody gets drunk. Everybody hates my guts—but everybody is back to work on Monday morning."

Levey nodded.

"Set up a phone hookup. We can keep in touch with each other every day. We've all got strengths, we've all got weaknesses."

"I never thought I'd hear that from you."

Crossen let the remark pass.

"All right," Levey said, "I'll cut the orders and talk to O'Gara."

"How will all this sit with him?"

"He likes money like the rest of us. What do you hear from Marjorie?"

"She sounds tired but ecstatic. She said to reserve seats in the Opera House in March."

Crossen returned to Tracy and broke the news to his classmates from MIT.

"I want you to handle the Friant-Kern Canal," he said to Bush. "And you, Everest, finish the Peach Bowl Bridge."

"How will this go down with the supers there?"

"Like a dose of clap," Crossen said. "Here are your orders: If you get any shit, tell 'em there's lots of starving black people in San Francisco looking for work."

"When do we start?"

"Tomorrow. We'll have the phones in by noon. Check with me at Nimbus."

"How in the hell can you rescue Nimbus? You've got less than a year," Bush asked.

"You build your canal, mister; I'll build my dam."

"You sound like the army," Everest commented.

"The army was easier. If someone didn't follow orders you could shoot the son of a bitch."

"What about *this* canal? Who'll finish that?"

"There are some O'Gara and Levey guys who've learned something in the first stretch. If they don't deviate from my orders, they'll be all right."

Bill Crossen was installed in the supervisor's quarters at Nimbus Dam by six the following morning. There was a short, unpleasant scene between himself and the on-site supervisor, but the power lay in Crossen's hands and he made short shrift of the affair.

"You can stay as my assistant or you can leave," Bill said. "Take your choice."

"How long have you been an engineer?" the older man asked.

"Long enough. Now move your gear. You're in *my* quarters."

Crossen assembled the supervisory personnel in his quarters one hour after he arrived. As had been the case on the Delta-Mendota Canal, everyone was older than Crossen, most of them veterans at O'Gara and Levey. He felt the resentment in the room, but he was used to it. He knew that the only way to deal with the situation was to ignore it and present irrefutable facts, and to assume an aura of command, which certainly would not elicit affection but might eventually provoke respect.

"Gentlemen," he said, "the progress of the Delta-Mendota Canal, of which you are aware, was achieved not because of my presence but because of the use of several of my pieces of equipment and for the most part by computer technology, for which I have to thank the University of Pennsylvania, Cambridge and Harvard."

He spread out sheaves of printouts on his drafting table.

"Many of you, I assume, are aware of this new technology; some of you are not. Quite simply, all these figures represent machinemade computations that took only days to produce, computations that the best engineering minds could not complete in a year.

"As you can see, I have made a series of studies: Engineering, stresses, materiel, weather, workforce. After collating this data, it has become clear to me and my associates from MIT—and also to Mr. Levey—that if we continue to build this dam in the present fashion, we will definitely come out at a loss.

"The most obvious reason that this dam is almost one year behind schedule is the time lost in moving equipment and supplies from one gorge to the other. We will remedy this by building a bridge across the chasm. Since the dam will top off at seventy-four feet, this bridge will be built at elevation seventy-six feet and not only give us access to the other gorges but will also assist us in pouring the concrete."

"How long do you figure for this bridge?" an older engineer asked.

"Two weeks," Crossen said. "We'll work around the clock."

"We'll need more men."

"True," Crossen answered. "Get them. I've got the figures right here."

"We'll need more housing, sanitary facilities, kitchens."

"They're all available in Vallejo. Army and navy surplus. We'll buy it ten cents on the dollar."

Another older man spoke up. "You're asking us to

change all our plans because of some goddamned machine."

"You're right, in a sense," Crossen said calmly. "The figures were reached by the goddamned machine. It is only that. The machine, however, will work only as well as the wisdom of the human input."

"And whose wisdom was that?"

"Mine," Crossen said, quietly and firmly. "And if you have any doubts, ask the men on Mendota. We rarely lost one hour, we never were overstaffed or understaffed and the material flow was so accurate we seldom had one two-by-four too many or too few." He scratched his head. "I'd suggest that if any of you have any doubts, you should visit the canal site. However, until the bridge is completed, all leaves will be canceled and we'll go on a seven-day week.

"Are there any further questions?"

There were none.

"All right," Crossen said, "let's go to work." He left the room, walked briskly to his office and shut his door. He neither wanted to see nor hear the skepticism he knew he had created, and picked up the phone to speak to the new supervisors of the other projects.

Henry Levey was almost as excited as a kid going to camp. His butler managed to find denims and work shirts in the attic and Levey was pleased they still fit him. He found boots and parkas, gloves, hats, even a theodolite he hadn't used in years.

"You're out of your mind," Hortense screamed. "A man your age heading for the wilderness."

"Best idea Bill Crossen ever had."

"I knew it was him. Does he know you've had a heart attack?"

"He knows. An honest day's work will be better for me than those goddamned lunches at Jack's every day."

"And where do you intend to sleep?"

"We've got quarters for engineers."

"Sure, wooden barracks with no heat."

"Sorry to disappoint you, Hortense, but things have changed since the unions. I expect my quarters to be quite comfortable."

"In that case, I'll come along."

"No," Levey said, "you won't. It's no place for a woman."

"I am your wife."

"I haven't forgotten. The answer is no. We don't allow engineers to bring their wives."

"You *own* the company."

"Not quite," Henry said. "*You* do, most of it."

"What will I tell our friends? We have a dinner party Saturday night."

"I think you'll manage."

"Why don't you send Henry Jr.? He needs the experience."

"You're right about that, but I can't. We haven't finished the golf course yet."

"I hate you, Henry Levey."

"I do believe that, Hortense. I do believe that."

Although Crossen and Levey worked within two miles of each other, they did not see each other for two weeks after arriving on their respective projects. When Crossen had finished the crude but sturdy bridge across the dam site, Levey visited his son-in-law in his quarters. Bill had ordered steaks from the mess hall, bought a good bottle of Scotch, and even managed to buy a comfortable armchair from a local hotel for his guest.

Levey had inspected and approved the bridge. He had finished his steak and now his third Scotch and soda. He looked at the meticulous but barren quarters of his son-in-law: the drafting table, the phone hookups, the neatly made army cot, the various garments needed for construction hung evenly on a lead pipe.

"Tell me something," Levey said, slightly drunk. "What was your father like?"

"Tough," Bill Crossen said. "Tough and mean."

"That figures," Levey said. "What did he do?"

"He was a cutter."

"Really," Levey said. "My grandfather was a presser."

"*Your* grandfather?"

"Yup."

"Jesus, I thought . . ."

"That I came from a long line of San Francisco royalty."

"Frankly, yes."

"Well, I don't. But you don't have to tell Hortense I told you."

"Don't worry."

"More Scotch."

Crossen refilled his glass.

"Did you ever have any love when you were a kid?" Levey asked.

"I don't remember," Crossen said. "I don't remember being a kid."

Levey nodded.

"How's the hatchery coming?"

"I won't know until I get water from your dam."

"You using those lightweight pneumatic drills?"

"Yeah, work like a charm. Why, you got a patent on them, too?"

"As a matter of fact, I do. . . ."

"You want royalties?"

"No."

"That's good. I'll buy the Scotch next time."

"I never drink Scotch."

"I do," Levey said, raising his glass. Then, looking at Bill he asked, "What are you going to do with all that money you're making?"

"Build a house," Crossen said, "like yours."

"That's a nice house," Levey said, "but it's not everything."

"What do you mean?"

"My quarters at present aren't much bigger than yours," Levey gestured with a small sweep of his arm. "I haven't been happier in years."

Crossen walked to the washbasin and picked up a water glass. He poured some Scotch into it and raised it in toast.

"I'm pleased about that, I really am."

Henry Levey finished his drink and took his leave. He walked back to his quarters, wishing he could teach his son-in-law what he had long ago learned and wishing that he could learn what Bill already knew. The night air sobered him and he wondered whether there was a whorehouse nearby. There wasn't much he could do anymore but a hundred-dollar bill would make some filly lie pretty good about his poor performance.

Chapter XXVI

It was after the second week of Marjorie's abscence that Bill visited Selda. He had asked to come to dinner and she, as usual, was gracious about having him. He had even acquired a touch of polish, bringing both a box of Blum's candies and a dozen long-stemmed roses.

"I can't believe it," she said, kissing him. "You've actually brought a gift."

"Yes," he said, shedding his raincoat. "The etiquette of the rich is beginning to rub off."

"Rub off, hell, Bubba. I read about your licensing agreement. The way you're going, you'll be richer than any of them."

Bill was surprised by her statement.

"How do you know about that?"

"You forget, my young cousin, I work in the business library. *Fortune* magazine carried quite a story about you and your machines."

"It did? I didn't know that." He sat down and stared into space.

"No one interviewed me. I thought no one knew except Henry Levey."

"When you're talking about two million dollars a year, *everybody* knows the story."

"Good God. I haven't even told Marjorie."

"She's in New York, I hear."

"Yes, with Solari. I spoke with her earlier today. She's in seventh heaven."

"I'm glad," Selda said. "I love that girl. And you," she asked, giving him a drink, "are you in seventh heaven, Bubba?"

He flinched at the word.

"Not really."

"I'm sure you've always wanted to be a millionaire."

"Every East Side kid wants to be a millionaire. So far it doesn't feel any different."

"Are you doing anything different?"

"Not really. Just working hard."

"For what?" Selda asked.

"You've asked me that before."

"For what, Bill?" she repeated.

"What's for dinner?"

"You're evading my question."

"I'm not evading it. I haven't an answer."

"You could work less. You could stop working altogether."

"Then what?"

Selda fussed with the table. She poured the wine, and Bill remembered his first dinner in this warm apartment.

"You don't want to talk, we don't have to talk," Selda said.

"Can I do something for you?" Bill asked.

"Like what?"

"What do you need? Anything. Tell me."

202

"I've got food on the table, wine in my glass. What do I need? You want to donate some books to the library, I'll give you a list."

"Done," Bill Crossen said.

"Have you spoken to your folks?"

"Don't ask me that."

"Sorry," Selda said. "You going to buy some new clothes? You're coming through your elbows."

Bill looked at his sport coat.

"I hadn't noticed."

"I bet. I bet you make another million before you'll buy some clothes. . . ."

"You could be right."

There was a pause. They sipped their wine.

"Well, there *are* some new things around here," Selda finally said.

"Tell me."

"I have a gentleman friend."

"Wonderful."

She cocked her head. "It's not everything. It's Wednesday night, and I can't wear perfume and he keeps some clean white shirts in my lingerie drawer. Feels kind of good to have a piece of a man here."

"You're telling me I'm not welcome here anymore."

"You're welcome anytime, Bubba, you know that. But not in bed."

"Why?"

"Not because of Mr. Wednesday."

"Why, then?"

"Because I love your wife. She's my friend. I want to be able to look her in the eyes."

"I see," Bill said, disappointed.

"Quit sulking. If you wanted a girl you could have dozens of them prettier than me. I'm just someone convenient. Safe."

"I don't want dozens of girls. . . ."

"I'm glad."

"Just one."

"Marjorie?"

"Not Marjorie."

"Then who?"

"I've cheated on Marjorie," Bill said, "once." It was unlike Bill to betray himself, and he wondered why he felt the need to tell Selda. "Her name is Elyse Wolf. Her husband is Lewis Wolf the Third."

"He's an alcoholic," Selda said.

"How do you know that?"

"Everybody knows it. And that tootsie?"

"Elyse Wolf is the most beautiful girl in San Francisco. Everybody in Marjorie's group is after her."

"Including you."

"I didn't initiate it. She drove to Tracy. She said, 'Rent a motel room.' " He avoided Selda's eyes. "I did and that was that."

"You did it to get even with all those other guys that are after her?"

"Partly, yes."

"What else?"

"I told you. She's a knockout."

"Good in bed?"

Bill nodded, then said, "But Marjorie doesn't deserve this. She is one of the finest people I've ever known. . . ."

"No, she doesn't. Is this thing serious?"

"No. I haven't seen her since. I hear she's pregnant."

"And if you had the chance, would you see her again?"

Bill ran his hand through his hair. "I don't know," he said, looking very troubled. "I'd better go. I've got to get up at five." He stood.

"Sit down for a minute, Bill."

He obeyed.

"You know you can't alter the universe."

"What do you mean?"

"I suspect you've been grown up since you were eight and an old man since you were fifteen. . . . You were an old man when you first walked in here. A boy of twenty-four sacrificing everything for what? Power, you said. Power, power to tell everyone to go to hell. And so you connived and you maneuvered, and you're succeeding . . . succeeding at being able to tell everyone to go to hell. But there is one demon you can't quite conquer yet."

"I know—Elyse," Bill said.

"Elyse is just a symbol. You can't conquer the fact that you're *human*. You thought you could plow through it all with a bulldozer, a computer, only now you're finding that little pieces seem to stick along the way. You have a heart. You do love Marjorie. You *have* balls. You lust for Elyse. Jesus *Christ*, Bill, get off it. You're not different from anyone else."

"What about Marjorie?"

"Maybe she has what she wants. She has her own battles to fight."

"Like what?"

"I don't know, Bill. She says very little. She's insecure, too. Her music is a compulsion."

"I suppose," Bill said, standing again. "Tell Mr. Wednesday I'm jealous."

"Mr. Wednesday," Selda half smiled as she stood at the front door. "There's a word in Yiddish for what I am doing."

"There's a word in Yiddish for everything," Bill said and walked to the elevator.

Chapter XXVII

Marjorie was comfortably ensconced in a suite at the Plaza Hotel, three blocks from Solari's studio. She unpacked, showered and dressed, nervous and anxious to meet the maestro. She left the hotel and walked along Fifth Avenue, unmindful of its elegance. She found the building, where a doorman ushered her into the lobby and an elevator operator took her to the top floor.

Solari had concertized for ten years; and though he was a fine, sensual performer, he finally realized that he would never approach the level of a Horowitz, a Rubinstein, a Schnabel. He had always loved teaching, and so he established his studio and was happy refining the skills of a number of formidably talented pianists on their way to the concert hall.

To Marjorie the very thought of meeting Solari, of spending six weeks under his tutelage was almost more than she could comprehend. The years at San Francisco Academy, at Juilliard, at Meadow Glen, the endless hours with Madame Polansky, with I. Glick, the competitions in Europe, in New York were all behind her; and as she sat in the elegant foyer, she wondered whether her fingers would move, her feet respond, her ears hear.

She wore a navy blue suit, a white satin Peter Pan blouse, white gloves, expensive middle-height pumps and carried a chaste leather bag, which held an envelope sealed and addressed to the master. It contained $5000.

The door finally opened and, back-lighted by an immense skylight, Solari stood straight, dressed in corduroy trousers, a cashmere sweater, a silk sport shirt open at the neck. He looked young and vibrant, his face warm, smiling and intense.

"Marjorie Crossen," he said, extending his arms and walking toward the girl, embracing her. "A kiss for the Maestro," and Marjorie complied. He released her, save one hand, and took a half step back.

"Let me look at you . . . lovely hair, full bust, good straight legs . . ." Marjorie blushed, and he said simply, "Come in, my dear, come in."

She entered the large, sunlit studio and he directed her to two white armchairs in the corner, strategically placed to face the Steinway, whose cover was open.

A sloping skylight enclosed a cream-colored room adorned with delicate etchings, a Matisse, a Picasso, scores of framed, signed autographs of great pianists.

Solari himself was a tall man, perhaps in his early forties, his hair black and speckled with gray and very full. His eyes were dark, his nose prominent, his face smooth, his hands firm and slender, his fingers long and muscular.

"This is charming," Marjorie said.

"Thank you," Solari said. "Art may flourish in a garret, but it need not be shabby. Matisse's studio looks like an operating room. Now," he said, patting her knee, "tell me, are you comfortable?"

"Very."

"Where are you staying?"

"At the Plaza."

"Good! We're neighbors."

He poured a green liquid into a couple of dainty crystal snifters.

"What's this?" Marjorie asked, smelling the liquorice odor.

"Pernod. The ambrosia of the left bank of Paris."

Marjorie sipped it. It had a foreign, bitter taste.

"You're married, Marjorie?" Solari asked.

"Yes, my husband . . ."

Solari placed his fingers on her lips.

"I don't want to hear a word about him."

Again she blushed.

"For the next six weeks you'll be married to me. Body, soul, fingers, feet, all of you. Can you take that?"

"I'm not certain I understand."

"Go to the piano, sit down. There are three measures of Mozart. Play them for me."

Marjorie stood.

"Take off your jacket," Solari commanded. She obeyed and he studied her large breasts more closely. He watched her walk to the piano and sensed a degree of aristocracy in her. She had been well schooled, well finished.

She sat, looked at the music and played. He stopped looking at her and closed his eyes. He listened to the sound, the phrasing, the rhythm and the precision of the rests. After she had finished, he said nothing, and finally Marjorie turned on the piano bench to face him and saw his eyes still closed.

"Was I terrible?" she asked innocently.

"I'm sorry," he said, "what did you say?"

"Was I terrible?"

He stood and walked over to the piano. He stood in

back of her. "Put your head back," he commanded and she did as told. He kissed her lightly on the forehead.

"When did you want to make your debut?"

"Next March."

"With San Francisco?"

"Yes."

"You'll be drowned in roses." He sat next to her on the bench and watched tears form in her eyes.

"I'm sorry," she said.

"For what? Tears?" He cupped her chin. "The life of performing artists is all tears and all joy. There is no middle ground. Can you learn that? That's the first lesson."

He kissed her moistened cheeks and Marjorie accepted the affection with a strange equanimity. Solari reached for a score and placed it in front of her. It was a simple five-finger etude.

"Today's lesson will be very simple. Very short. Today, however, is just beginning."

"I must be in the hotel at six," Marjorie said. "Bill will call."

"You'll be in the hotel at six. Play."

Marjorie played. It was a simple exercise. She had played it hundreds of times. Finally Solari whisked away the score and said, "Play without the score," and Marjorie followed instructions. She had done this countless times.

Suddenly Solari rose and stood behind her. "Keep playing," he said as he placed his hands under her armpits. "Straighten up," he said. "Be ramrod straight." His hands did not move away. She could feel the tips of his fingers holding the sides of her breasts, but she said nothing, and Solari sat down again.

"Straight," he said, "sit straight. Head forward, toward the woodwind sections." Marjorie played and replayed and noticed Solari shamelessly arranging her legs, touching her thighs; she was aware of her skirt slowly creeping up her legs, and made no move to correct that, nor did Solari try to remedy the minor impropriety.

The sun was almost setting and the light in the studio was very soft and subdued in such a harsh city.

"I must go back to the hotel," Marjorie said finally.

"Yes. Accept your phone call. Then put on your most shocking gown, your most illicit perfume and I will call for you at seven-thirty. Let me call a cab for you." He picked up the phone.

Marjorie could not remember the cab ride. She could not remember how she found her suite on the twenty-first floor, nor how she managed to sprawl on the large double bed.

She felt Solari's fingers on her breasts as if he had not taken them away, and she thought of the numerous nights her sister Linda had come to her room to mercilessly detail every sexual thrill she had experienced during the evening.

"He held my nipple," she would say, "his hands were right here," she would demonstrate and Marjorie would beg her to stop, to stop talking about it, and yet Linda persisted, coldly, almost boasting, leaving her sister in a pool of tears after she departed.

Where was all the eroticism that Linda had boasted about? Where was all the passion she had read about in books and been told about by girl friends in her darkened bedroom? And why did her husband fail to arouse her as Solari had?

The phone rang. It was Bill. "How is it going?" he asked.

"Just fine," Marjorie said, still feeling Solari's fingers on her breasts. "It looks like the San Francisco Opera House."

"That's wonderful, darling, wonderful."

"What's new with you, Bill? How is the canal?"

"I'm no longer on the canal."

"Why?"

"I've taken over the Nimbus Dam. It's too complicated to explain . . . even your father is back in the field."

"Daddy?"

"Yes. He's supervising a job two miles down stream."

"Does he like that?"

"He loves that."

"Then, you'll call tomorrow."

Bill hesitated. "I don't know. I'll try. We're just getting our phones in order. . . ."

"Don't worry," Marjorie said. "My hours are hectic, too. If I'm not here, you can leave a message and I'll call you. I think I'm in for a rough six weeks."

"Don't overdo it. How is that fellow Solari?"

"I can't tell yet," Marjorie said. "There'll be a lot of work."

"I know," Bill Crossen said, "I've got my own hands filled. Talk to you soon."

"Yes, Bill," Marjorie said. "I love you. Take care of yourself."

She hung up the receiver and looked at the dressing room, the elegant bath behind it. She looked at the black silk dress whose cleavage could be adjusted by black, silk-covered buttons. She picked up the phone and ordered a champagne cocktail from room service.

Chapter XXVIII

Marjorie glowed as she emerged from the elevator of the Plaza and quickly found Solari, dressed in a tuxedo, a light opera cloak slung over his arm.

"You look wonderful," he said, "except . . ."

"Except?"

"That dress is buttoned too high."

"The night is young," Marjorie said, and he swept her through the lobby holding her arm, guided her to a cab and ordered the driver to take them to the Waldorf Astoria Hotel.

The headwaiter was expansive. The linens on the table spotless, the glassware shimmered and reflected the candle, the single carnation on the table. The height of the ceiling, the vastness of the room, the inconspicuous service made them feel very much alone.

They started with martinis, then had a succession of wines with the paté, the sole, the chocolate mousse, and finally ended sipping brandy in the dark recesses of the

Oak Room of the Plaza. Marjorie, who had undone not one, but two of the buttons of her dress on her trip to the powder room felt quite drunk, quite wicked and strangely unafraid. Solari was a great raconteur of musical anecdotes, all of them revolving around great artists and many of them involving himself.

He, too, was getting slightly drunk and pushed his chair closer to the girl.

"Before you ask, Marjorie, whether I act like this with all my pupils . . . the answer is no. By no means do I wish to plead celibacy, however. . . ."

"I haven't asked the question," Marjorie said. "Besides, you haven't done anything except buy me a lovely dinner. . . ."

Her frankness startled him.

"I do intend to *do* something, Marjorie."

"I'm still not flinching," she said, "but why? Why me?"

He laughed. "I knew it wouldn't be long before you would ask a trite question—Why me?"

"Go on."

"Because you are a virgin, and I love virgins."

"You forget I'm a married woman."

"You're still a virgin."

Marjorie felt flushed.

"Sayings of a sage old man. . . ."

She put her hand on his arm. "Old, my God. How old are you? Forty? That's not old. I've never stayed out this late. Bill begins to yawn at eight o'clock. We're sound asleep at ten."

"I told you. You're a virgin."

They drank more. They danced. Night people stopped by the table to pay their respects to Solari. They finally entered his salon at four in the morning. He took off his tuxedo jacket and proceeded to the kitchen.

"A raw egg and a cognac. Rubinstein taught me that."

He reappeared in the living room and Marjorie downed the egg with as much enthusiasm as the earlier Pernod, and gulped the cognac like an antidote.

"Easy," he said. "That's two hundred years old."

"So was the egg," Marjorie said.

Solari had been right. She might as well have been a virgin. She only remembered laying back on the divan. She barely recalled her clothes coming off because it was done with such delicacy and finesse. Each part of her body was discovered, fondled, and smothered by kisses. She reached climax after climax by feeling Solari's tongue slowly reaching her pubic area on a journey started at her toes. She felt her breasts cupped and her nipples circled with his tongue. She felt his nakedness, his penis deep within her. And she heard herself moaning, crying, pleading, saying words she had heard but never uttered. She did not notice dawn arriving, or the harsh sun of full daylight.

It was ten-thirty in the morning when they finally lay on the bed, spent, exhausted, satiated. Solari rose and got two bathrobes. He donned one himself and handed her the other. She noticed it was a woman's robe and said nothing.

"Now we practice," he said.

"I'm exhausted."

He rose. "Only part of you is exhausted, Marjorie. You'll see, the artist is very much awake."

She followed him meekly to the grand piano, her feet suddenly cold on the well-polished parquet floor.

He opened the score for Rachmaninoff's *Rhapsody on a Theme by Paganini*.

"This," he said, "will be your debut concerto. My mind is made up."

"How did you find time for decisions?"

He laughed and took her hands in his and rubbed them.

"Proceed, little one. You're no longer a virgin."

Solari, unbeknownst to Marjorie, started a blank tape on a recorder; then he placed a recording of the orchestral part on the phonograph. He arranged the music, turned on a light and gave the downbeat.

"Proceed," he said, and Marjorie began the piece. Solari allowed her to play without interruption, simply turning the pages of the score when necessary.

She has been well taught, he thought. Classically, to be sure, thoroughly also. Her range was considerable, her fingering flawless, her reading intelligent. Solari knew full well that he was working with good clay. They were ready to begin.

When Marjorie had finished Solari said nothing more than "Come over here and sit down." Again they sat in the two facing armchairs. Solari put one leg over the arm and tilted his head toward the ceiling.

"What do you know about Paganini?" he asked.

"He was a great violinist, a great composer. Italian. Born 1782, died 1840."

"Music History One," Solari said, half-jokingly.

"Yes."

"You know nothing, then, of Paganini?"

"What do you mean?"

Solari half shouted: "Demonic, that was the word attached to Paganini; satanic. They said of his playing that the 'devil was at his elbow.' Did you know that?"

"No."

"He had a frightening nose, a lofty brow, white cheeks, an almost crippled physique due to a chronic spinal ailment, but he used it all in his creativity. He brought it all to bear on the use of his instrument: his amazing virtuosity on a single string, his uncanny left-hand pizzicati. He affected everyone around him, Rossini, Meyerbeer, Brahms. Liszt, rightfully called the Paganini of the piano, heard the great violinist at age twenty and was so inspired by his virtuosity, his presence, the frenzy he created, that he retired for several years, exploring ways of emulating the artist. When he emerged with the Twelve Etudes of Transcendent Execution, he unleashed a ferocity and intensity never heard before on the keyboard. But he did not inherit the devilish mantle of Paganini. He was too healthy-looking, too handsome, and was accorded adjectives like *Promethean, luciferous.*"

"Where was the deviltry in Paganini?"

"It was a label. He played the fiddle, the instrument of death, the devil, skeletons and cats, symbols of the Middle Ages. His virtuosity defied ordinary description. The allusions to the devil were most numerous and Paganini revelled in it. It was box office. He was a man who liked money.

"Now let's take Rachmaninoff. Born thirty years after Paganini's death . . . an equally brilliant performer, a fine composer . . . a different kettle of fish. *His* career was almost finished by his First Symphony. It had one dismal performance in Saint Petersburg and its reviews were so horrendous it took Count Tolstoy three days to give the boy some ego strength, and his young wife to restore vitality and creativity to the boy and later to the man. He never failed again. The Second Symphony, the Third, the *Isle of the Dead,* the unfinished *Mona Vanna* . . . He composed the *Variations on a Theme* at the age of sixty-one."

"Incredible," Marjorie said.

"Yes. Incredible since many critics had already pronounced a musical death sentence upon him, saying that separation from his homeland stultified his creativity. He threw the *Variations* right in their teeth. . . ."

Marjorie noticed Solari's clenched fist.

"All right ... What was Rachmaninoff really like musically?"

"A romantic, I'd say."

"True. Rachmaninoff always said that in the world of music there was one supreme ruler. Melody. Melody and harmonic fiber, that was Rachmaninoff. He detested experimental music, and yet with his wonderful, wicked playfulness he could outshock and outcompose all the flashy dissidents."

"You love Rachmaninoff?" Marjorie asked.

"Yes. Unquestionably.

"All right. It is 1934. Rachmaninoff is secure. His last two pieces, the *Three Romanian Songs*, the *Variations on a Theme by Corelli*, were well received. Perhaps it was his genius, or his own sense of security which prompted him to tackle Paganini, a piece which had already been used by Brahms, Liszt, not forgetting Paganini himself.

"The first thing a composer *must have*, and Rachmaninoff did have, is a slavish dedication to the theme he is addressing himself to. That dedication must be religious, reverential, and unquestionably it was."

Solari paused to emphasize his point.

"But once that devotion is affirmed the artist *must* question the original virtuosity. How did Paganini compose that theme? What manner of man was he? What were his motives, his feelings, his goals?"

Leaving this question still dangling, Solari rose quickly and walked to the piano, motioning Marjorie to follow him.

"Sit," he said, "next to me."

Again he started the accompaniment on the phonograph.

"Listen," he commanded. "Here is the theme. What would you say it was?"

217

"Modest," Marjorie said.

"Good, Modest is good. I'll give you a better word. *Skeletal.* Angular, emaciated. Rachmaninoff is seeing Paganini. Here comes the piano," and Solari began to play beautifully.

"You see," he said continuing to play, "the piano barely surrounds the theme—*there*"—he paused—"all the violins in unison are answering the theme. A tribute to the master's instrument, perhaps? Even the first six variations are quite like Paganini's own, another tribute . . . and *here,* listen, here in the seventh variation comes Mr. Rachmaninoff with his *Dies Irae.*"

His hands left the keyboard and he shut off the accompaniment.

"The *Dies Irae,* why the *Dies Irae,* that frightening part of the Catholic mass which graphically describes the happenings awaiting us on judgment day? Why the *Dies Irae*? It's been used by Liszt, Berlioz, Saint Saëns, Tchaikovsky.

"Why the *Dies Irae*? Was Rachmaninoff flirting with death? His own? Paganini's? His own, I presume."

"Both, maybe," Marjorie said.

"Both, perhaps. I've never considered that . . . but Rachmaninoff has used it in other works. . . ."

He resumed playing. "You see the tempo changing to moderato, the piano chants simple solemn harmonies, the orchestra hops and skips merrily. Here the *Dies Irae* reappears, here again. . . ."

But once more Solari stopped and faced Marjorie.

"Now, one thing must remain clear. The *Rhapsody* does not become a set of *two* variations. Never. Rachmaninoff's reverie is intact. Paganini is the theme. Here, I'll show you—" and he resumed playing, in the eighth variation.

"Paganini reigns supreme again. All right," he said getting up. "Begin."

Marjorie began to play.

"Leaner," he shouted. "Leaner" and Marjorie diminished her force.

"Think of the keys as eggs. You're breaking eggs. Quiet, quiet, better—that's better . . . no, no."

He sat down again.

"Forget the eggs. Think of the keys as cougars. You are afraid of the jaws. Think of sharks. Yes. Sharks. Leave those keys before they bite. . . ."

She watched his strong, lean hands and remembered them only minutes ago caressing her, and then she started again and now it was fine, fine.

"Yes," he said. "Yes. Yes.

"Now listen," he ordered Marjorie, "listen to variation nine. You see Rachmaninoff abandoning the theme. Listen to the orchestra. What do you hear?"

"Almost percussion," Marjorie said.

"Almost. There is a rattle of strings. The players are using the wood of their bows, there's the dry tapping of the side drum. Listen to the piano, it's offbeat, an agitated clatter of descending triplets. It's demonic, do you see?"

The sun had set. They had been at the piano almost seven hours, yet it seemed like minutes to Marjorie. No one had taught like this. No one had intellectualized music like this. It had always been technique—forte, mezzo forte. Brahms, Liszt, Tchaikovsky—they had only been names on top of the music . . . dim, dead men now, who had somehow managed to compose music. . . . Master classes with Solari . . . She was beginning to understand. She was beginning.

It was eight o'clock in the evening when they finished at the piano and Solari suggested that Marjorie return to her hotel and get a good night's rest. It had been twenty-four hours since she had left her suite, twenty-four hours of intense emotional, sexual, artistic activity.

She returned to the hotel and once more she sprawled on the bed, but she could not sleep. She felt every touch, every kiss, every caress. She knew that she had played as she had never played before. She realized that Solari was right, that the energies spent in bed were on a different level from the energies at the piano, and she saw now that the two worked together.

But there was guilt. She had betrayed Bill Crossen, her marriage vows, her own code of ethics; and no amount of rationalization would ease this feeling. At one in the morning she phoned Solari.

"I can't sleep," she said. "I feel terrible."

"I'll be right over," he said and hung up.

Solari sat in an armchair facing Marjorie on the bed. He could see she had been crying, but made no move to touch her.

"Let me say something, Marjorie, and then I'll shut up."

She looked at him.

"You feel guilty because you've betrayed your husband. And you wonder now whether my actions were Machiavellian or sincere."

Marjorie with tears in her eyes nodded. "Right," she said, "on both counts."

"Which emotion is stronger, Marjorie?"

"I don't understand?"

"The guilt of cheating or your doubts about me?"

"I don't know. And that frightens me, too."

"All right," Solari said. "Whatever I say you'll still think I'm manipulating you."

"Say it. I'll tell you honestly how I feel."

Solari rose and paced the dimly lit room.

"I take on six students a year and I have the pick of

the best. I don't choose students casually. I have spoken to everyone you've worked with and I have spoken to people who know you in San Francisco. The assessment was always the same."

"What was it?"

"You are a flawless technician. You have the ear, the timing, the proficiency. There is only one thing you lack."

"What's that?"

"Sensuality. True sensuality. Wait, wait"—he held up his hand.

"You have that, too. You saw that today. . . ."

Marjorie sat up erect and stared into the darkened room.

"I've never played like that before," she said, almost to herself.

"I expect that's true," Solari said, "but I know your next question."

"Was it all a game . . . ?"

"That's what I expected." He faced her. "I told you earlier that no matter what I say you still have the right to feel manipulated . . ."

"I know."

He sat in the armchair. "Music, Marjorie, is sensual. Sexual. That's something your teachers have never really taught you. A concerto is nothing more than sexual intercourse: foreplay, a theme, variations on a theme, a leitmotif, a drive, a teasing, fighting, slowly, slowly building to a climax. Is that right or not?"

"That's right."

"Have you ever felt that?"

"Yes."

"Has it ever been verbalized?"

"No."

"I thought not. Most great musicians, most great artists use love as a tool. Did you know that?"

"Not really."

"The greatest—and I know most of them—live in a cocoon. They live in a very sheltered atmosphere, in a hothouse. Great pianists have only the keyboard and the bed. They live only from sensuality to sensuality.

"If you are a great artist, Marjorie, then the world expects so much of you. You are constantly asked to 'give,' to perform, to provide miracles. Of course, you are rewarded materially, but to most of the great artists that's secondary. But in order to *give*, to perform, to sustain that output, there must be something to balance the equation. For some it's applause, accolades, fame; for others it's love or drink or food. Whatever it is, it's part of the bargain. Greatness has its own code, its own morality, its own demands, and a great artist doesn't agonize over it, he doesn't feel guilty about it; it is his to expect, and it is his to deserve."

Marjorie rose and walked to the window. She put her forehead against the cool glass.

"It's so much all at once," she said.

"And," Solari replied, "I didn't answer your question."

"No. You didn't."

"You are not the first girl I've made love to and you won't be the last. I will tell you honestly, however, that I've never slept with anyone I didn't like—love, if you prefer.

"There was—is something so fresh about you. Frightened, immature, the well-mannered, prim, proper upper-middle-class Jewess. And then you sat down. You played those small etudes, and I knew there was a different girl inside that shell.

"That is exciting for a man. The Pygmalion syndrome. Exciting for *this* man. You must believe me."

"And so," Marjorie said, turning to face him, "I'll ask a middle-class Jewish question. Where will it go?"

"We've had one night, Marjorie. For me a wonderful,

warm, exciting night. No one can take that away from us. We can have more nights. That's up to you. You are at the beginning of a very exciting career. I will always be a part of that if you want me to be. That's all I can say."

"And what about my husband?"

"Bill Crossen is your affair, not mine. If you are going to be the great artist I expect, then inevitably your lives will be conflicting."

"Why?"

"You are the artist. He is not."

"You may be wrong," Marjorie said steadily. "Bill Crossen, I've heard my father say, is a genius."

"Perhaps I've underestimated the man," Solari said. "I did not mean to belittle him."

"That's good," Marjorie said. "I'm tired. Confused."

"Do you think you can sleep now?"

"Standing up," Marjorie said and Solari laughed.

"Good," he said, getting up. "Tomorrow we'll work on the fourth variation again."

"The fourth variation," Marjorie said, collapsing on the bed, grateful that Solari did not touch her, kiss her, but simply left.

"I wish I could tell Linda about last night," she thought, but she was soon asleep.

Part Three

Chapter XXIX

Elyse's pregnancy had mercifully stopped the ever-increasing lasciviousness in the Wolf household. Elyse had come to accept the sexual promiscuity, the fondling, the pats on the fanny, everyone's unabashed nudity about the home.

Papa Wolf's generosity never ended, whether it was a ten-carat ruby ring, a new convertible, a weekend in Rome, a week in New York, she could have whatever her heart desired.

She had become used to the endless merriment in the house that revolved about her beauty, her youth, her openness. Lewis continued to drink. No event, she was certain, would ever relieve him of that crutch. However, he was always warm, always courteous; he rarely left her side, in bed or out.

She had accepted the presence of Jake's changing male friends; she joked about Papa's visits to the library, which they all knew were visits to any number of willing ladies; she even drank a little herself and laughed at the sexual escapades of the men in her house.

There was also true joy and anticipation about the impending birth. Papa Wolf himself had supervised the creation of the nursery, buying a lovely antique brass bassinet, hiring a fine Swedish woman to become the nurse, hosting a never-ending series of parties to hail the coming blessed event.

Elyse even listened with surprising equanimity to Lewis's plans for those weeks she'd be sexually incapacitated and wondered sometimes late at night how much she really *did* love that man or how much he loved her.

Up to now, she had cast the die. She had opted for luxury and security instead of challenge. She enjoyed telling Lewis about the propositions she received, because Lewis enjoyed hearing about them. There were times when she felt that he might even condone a liaison, if she were to relate it graphically or convince him it would help them sexually.

She had read about eroticism. The Wolf household had one of the finest libraries in town on the subject and she even began to understand the reasons behind Lewis's desire to share his wife to some degree with other men, even his own father. She learned that it was a form of latent homosexuality, a trait some men fought desperately, brutaly, but Lewis accepted unconsciously and with ease. She had never told Lewis about Bill Crossen, and now before going to sleep she wondered why, and she worried about it.

A healthy boy was born on Christmas morning. Buddy Feiger, *Dr.* Buddy Feiger, the glamour boy of Jewish society, had delivered the baby and instead of performing a routine postpartum examination on Elyse, he was fondling her breasts.

"What the hell are you doing?" Elyse asked, rising slowly from her hospital bed.

"What do you think I'm doing?"

"You're supposed to be a doctor. . . ."

"You've got a healthy son. Who do you think delivered him?"

"I did, you son of a bitch. Did that excite you, too?"

"Jesus Christ, Elyse, be reasonable."

"*Reasonable* about what?"

"We used to date at Stanford. . . ."

"So we did. I even liked you."

"So what has changed?"

"What has changed is that you couldn't bear to bring me home to your family. Remember?"

"It wasn't all that simple."

"It was simple enough for you to play with Rhoda Fels. Why don't you fondle her breasts, what little there is of them?"

"Elyse, please."

"Elyse, please, shit! I'm going to report you to the Medical Society."

"Would you really testify against me?"

"What have I got to lose? All you bastards treat me like a whore anyway. Why should I be a lady now?"

Feiger backed away from the bed.

"You're tired," he said. "I'll see you tomorrow."

"You will like hell. If you ever set foot in this room again I'll scream, *rape*, so loud they'll have to close off this wing."

"I'm sorry, Elyse," he said.

"Get out, you prick."

He left the room and Elyse cried. She cried bitterly and she was happy to hear Lewis tell her later that he had not had a drink for twelve hours and that Papa had physically kicked out Jake's latest lover.

"There'll be a child in this house," he had said. "Take your goddamned trade elsewhere."

Two months after Elyse had returned home with her child the aura of the event had worn off. Papa was returning to the whores, Lewis to the bottle, his brother to his lovers. Nothing had really changed. The baby was a beautiful boy, but since he was cared for primarily by the nurse, his presence did not alter Elyse's life as much as she had hoped. The birth was an act accomplished and everyone expected her to return to the role of house courtesan, the "flower," as Papa referred to her, the wife-whore that Lewis expected.

Chapter XXX

Elyse was restless and she was selfish. Of course, no one could match the material advantages that came to her from the Wolf family, but she needed more, and she reached out to Bill Crossen.

She had reached out once before in her marriage, although it had been more innocent. Arthur Donen had been in their circle of friends. Arthur Donen was San Francisco's leading impresario. Dapper, tall, white-haired, in his early fifties, he owned the two most successful legitimate theaters in town, and had an interest in a chain of movie houses, a theatrical agency, and a small publishing firm. His wealth and taste were reflected in his penthouse. It was large and spacious, its high-ceilinged, ivory-colored rooms filled with well-chosen Oriental rugs. French doors from each room faced an artificial garden, and all of San Francisco was spread out beneath it.

There were posters of plays produced by Donen; and countless photographs of stage and screen stars in silver frames, in *pas patou,* adorned the walls or stood like soldiers on the grand piano.

All this Bill took in as he waited for Elyse to appear.

She had phoned him in Tracy. "My stomach is flat as a board," she had said. "I'd love to talk to you."

"Where?"

"The Donen penthouse. Do you know it?"

"I know *of* it. Where's Donen?"

"In Europe."

"I'll be in the city on Thursday," Bill said.

"How about five?"

"Five it will be."

"I'll leave the front door open."

Arthur Donen, like many men, had fallen in love with Elyse Wolf. But Arthur Donen, by virtue of his looks and with the help of his wealth and the nature of his business, had known many beautiful young women. He had sensed that restlessness in Elyse developing early in her marriage and offered his shoulder, and Elyse had accepted.

"I'll put you on a long lead," he had said. "Don't be frightened. I'll always be here."

And so a loose alliance had begun. Donen spent most of his time in New York or Paris (he had quarters in both cities) and once gave Elyse a gold key inscribed THE PENTHOUSE. "It's yours when I'm not here. It's yours when I am. . . ." he'd said.

Elyse appeared wearing a scanty pair of panties and a very small bra. She came over to Bill and kissed him.

"You know," he said, holding her away, "you are going to make conversation very difficult, wearing this."

She put her hand over his fly. "I *will* say that you're easily aroused."

"Not by everyone," Bill said.

"I'll take that as a compliment."

"Do you always run around like this?" Bill asked.

"Most of the time I wear *nothing* at home. Lewis prefers it that way." She poured some wine. "Hard day at the office?" Elyse asked.

"They're all hard."

"Make another million today?"

"I hope so."

"I so admire you, Bill."

"Why?"

"I read that piece in *Fortune*. You're really sticking it down their craw, aren't you?"

"If I am, that's incidental. What I am doing is for myself."

She picked up his hand and studied it. "Look at this. A manicure."

Bill laughed and pushed his hand inside her bra. Once more he cupped those marvelous breasts. Firm, warm . . . (goddamnit! he thought).

He withdrew his hand. "Talk," he said. "You wanted to talk."

"We can talk later," Elyse said.

"No. Not later, now." He walked around the living room and stopped at a window to watch the sun cast its last orange rays over the busy waters of the Bay.

"That's some view," Bill said.

"Some view," Elyse agreed. "That goddamned view. Where I came from, on McAllister Street, all I ever saw was garbage chutes, back stairs, worn-out underwear drying on aging clotheslines.

"The first time I ever saw this view was when Loren Hilf took me to this hotel for a weekend while I was at Stanford. I was eighteen. He screwed me and fell asleep and I was up all night looking at this view. Chicago has the Lake, New York has the Park and San Francisco has the View."

"My view wasn't so red-hot either when I was a kid."

"I can believe that," Elyse said sympathetically. "I

vowed that night that I *was* going to have this view in this city."

"Well, you have it," Bill said.

"Yes, I do," Elyse said. "But the price is high."

"Why?"

"I feel so goddamned useless," Elyse said. "I thought having a child might make the difference, but it hasn't changed a thing. It's just another toy in the house. I envy you, Bill. You're not only accomplishing things on your own, but you respect Marjorie.

"I said to you that Lewis was good in bed. He is. He still is, but, Jesus Christ, there has to be more to life than that. If I divorce him, then what?"

"They'll eat you up alive. You know that," Bill said.

"What grounds? What grounds do I really have? My husband is warm, sweet, generous, none of the family knows what else to do for me. . . . Do you think I could go back to school?"

"Why not?"

"I never got my degree."

"I think it's a fine idea. What interests you?"

"Biology. Maybe medical school."

"What's stopping you?"

"I want you to help."

"How?"

"Give me the strength. Challenge me. Why don't you challenge me? Kick my ass. Tell me I am the lousy hure my father called me. He was right, you know. Oh, how right he was. . . ." She began to cry now, and Bill sat next to her and held her. They made love on Donen's bed, and he wondered how many ladies had been seduced in those luxurious surroundings. After eating dinner in the suite they made love once more.

Bill rose at four. One more time he fondled Elyse. "Kick my ass, you said. Some ass."

"Come here, Bill." Elyse sat up in bed. "Do you like me?"

"Yes," he said slowly. "Now ask me if I like my-self. . . ."

Elyse did decide to continue the education that had been so abruptly terminated by her marriage to Lewis, and even that event brought only further merriment to the household. Papa bought her a lunch box, Lewis a gold fountain pen and Jake a pair of saddle shoes. She rejected Stanford and attended the University of California at Berkeley, planning to get her degree in biology.

It was challenging and she was seriously tiring of the constant teasing she received at home. "My daughter, the schoolgirl," Papa would call her; "my wife, the coed," as Lewis referred to her. . . . No one in that household could see the sense of spending hours in the laboratory, the classroom, when, in their view, the world held so many other pleasurable diversions.

Only Bill Crossen seemed to understand.

"I admire you," he had told her one evening at the Lehmans.

"Why?" she had asked him.

"It would be so easy *not* to do this. . . ."

"I'm reverting," Elyse said.

"I'm not sure I know what you mean."

"We were brought up to respect learning, agreed?"

"Yes, but not for the sake of learning."

"That's right," Elyse said. "Education was a tool. A way out of the ghetto. It's all a Jew had as an escape. Both our parents drilled that into us. Why do I have to explain that to you? You've done it all on your own."

"Perhaps you're right, but I try not to dwell on the past," Bill said.

"You know you can't deny it. *They* fed you, they housed you, they made you go to school, to temple. . . ."

"Yes," Bill admitted. "They did all that. And still I wonder. . . ."

"What?"

"Did they do it out of love? Did they feel a sense of duty? Or did they do it selfishly?"

"What do you think?"

"They did it selfishly. That's what I think, and I don't like myself for thinking that, and yet I know it's true. . . ."

"And you've cut yourself off, like I have," Elyse said.

"Yes, I have. I've tried sending money—but they send it back."

"So that's that."

"Not really," Bill said. "I'd rather spend the money and get some sleep at night. I need all the energy I can get."

Elyse looked at him for a long time. She brushed his forehead with her delicate hand.

"You're not leading a life, Bill. You're making a series of investments."

"Perhaps I am," he said. "But they're not all paying off."

All the firm's projects were now in the clear—the Nimbus Dam, Peach Bowl Bridge, the Fish Hatchery, the Friant-Kern Canal—and he spent more time in the office in San Francisco studying future bids, making projections, doing analyses.

Marjorie had returned from New York. She had changed, Bill noticed. She was livelier, more assertive.

"I have two records to play for you," she said on her first night back, going to the phonograph. "This first record was an ambush. I didn't know it was being made. It was my first performance of the variations."

She played the record and Bill said quite honestly, "Very good. That's very good."

"Wait," Marjorie said, as she put on the second record.

"This was the best performance I gave at Solari's. Listen to the difference."

And Bill Crossen did listen. He was not musically inclined, but he did feel the passion, the sensuality of the playing, the absolute dominance over the instrument.

Marjorie closed her eyes and the last six weeks passed before her. She remembered all the exhortations at the piano. "D minor," he would shout; or, "Allegretto," he would say. She recalled phrases like *Marche au supplice* and words like *bravura*, and she remembered the love-making that had not ended that first night, as she had known all along it wouldn't.

"Incredible," Bill said after hearing the final bars. "Incredible. He must be quite a teacher."

"He is, Bill, he is that."

"I'm very proud of you, Marjorie," Bill said.

"Thank you," Marjorie said, truly feeling pain facing her husband.

Marjorie, so filled with guilt, thought of her mother, whose only rationalization for leading a rich matron's life was her endless protestation that she had spent most of it raising three children.

And it was true, Marjorie thought, that well-to-do San Franciscans did make a ritual of childraising. They had been schooled at Grant School, at Lowell High, some at Presidio Open Air, others at Sarah Dix Hamlin. Whatever academic choices were made, children were expected to perform. Laggards like her brother would get tutors, and she herself received all the musical tutelage she could absorb.

There were summers at Lake Tahoe and other summers in Europe. There were box seats in the Opera House for the Children's Symphony and basketball games at Julius Kahn's playground. There was dancing school, and etiquette lessons from a lady who wore a pince-nez. Innocent birthday parties with lamb chops with paper skirts gave way to dances, balls, the first taste of champagne.

Everyone wore the proper clothes (cashmere sweaters; plaid skirts; clean saddle shoes, polished nightly by the butler), the medical attention was careful, the children's rooms in the large mansions were comfortably furnished. Everyone had a record player, Glenn Miller records, Benny Goodman, Artie Shaw. . . .

But despite the affluence, the materialism, a code of ethics did prevail. Hortense, and Emma, a stern German governess, taught honesty, cleanliness, punctuality and courtesy.

All this had gone through Marjorie's mind on her three-day journey home aboard the Super Chief. Watching the endless wheat fields of the prairie, the drama of the Rockies, the lushness of Colorado flash by her window, she fought the urge to tell Bill of the affair with Solari. She had sinned, and she deserved punishment. That was her upbringing, that was the code. But she said nothing to Bill the first night, and nothing the second after they had made love. It was only Selda, her lovely friend Selda, who heard her confession after Bill had returned to his dam.

She had cried when she told Selda and Selda gave her a handkerchief.

"So, you're human," Selda said. "You've fallen off the pedestal."

"It's wrong," Marjorie said. "How could I do this to Bill?"

"It's wrong," Selda said, shrugging her shoulders. "I can't say it's right."

"What should I do? I haven't told Bill."

"Do you *have* to tell Bill?"

"I can't live with this lie. It's not like me."

"Wrong," Selda said.

"What do you mean?"

"You screwed the piano teacher. You did. You just said you did."

"Yes."

"So you did it. All right. You're no angel. Who is? You think I am?"

"I've never thought . . ."

"You've never thought I have urges, too?"

"I didn't mean that, Selda."

"Wednesday nights, a gentleman comes over here. Punctually at seven. No dinner, no drinks, sometimes one. We fall into bed and make love. He is married. He has two children. I'm not an angel either."

"I didn't know."

"Well, now you know," Selda said, "and I don't go around saying this isn't like me. That's crap. It *is* like me. I get horny. I need a man. *That's* like me. Do you understand?"

Again Marjorie was crying.

"What will you accomplish by telling Bill?"

"I deserve to be punished, Selda. Don't you understand?"

"Nonsense. You're a grown woman. You made a decision. Maybe not the right decision, but you made it, so live with it. *Grow up.* Maybe Bill will stray one day. Who knows, maybe you'll understand that better then."

"I wish he would."

"Why?"

"I don't know."

"It would take away some of the guilt."

"Perhaps."

Selda rose and walked around the table. She sat next to Marjorie and put her arm around the girl.

"I love you, Marjorie. You know that?"

She nodded.

"I really do. Don't think you're better than anyone else. I don't like that quality in people."

239

"I'm sorry."

"That's better." Marjorie dried her tears and managed a smile.

"Was he good?"

"Who?"

"The piano player."

"He was good, Selda. I reached a climax for the first time in my life."

"Well, as my father used to say," Selda said, "it shouldn't be a total loss."

Marjorie left and Selda knew that she had counseled Marjorie and she had counseled Bill; and she had advised them both to take life as it comes, to enjoy pleasures guiltlessly, and she wondered now about herself, about her Mr. Wednesday. She was, she knew, the "other woman." He had made no bones about it. But she enjoyed him. Perhaps she loved him, but, she thought, was it all so easy? Was it really so simple to compress love and sex into two hours a week? Who was there to counsel *her*?

Chapter XXXI

Henry Levey, Jr., had already built a home on Pacific Heights. It was not as stately as his father's; nevertheless it commanded an equally impressive view of the Bay. He had married a pretty girl from his own social circle and the parents on both sides agreed that ownership of a good home was prudent.

Henry Jr. was a tall, likable young man who had accepted all the largesse of his family with equanimity and good humor. By virtue of his father's war-related business, he had, like a number of his friends, been able to miss the entire war and thoroughly enjoyed those years when there was one eligible man for every ten eligible young women.

Joanne Freed, whose father's family owned hundreds of acres of prime vineyards in the Sonoma Valley, had moralized little about Henry's lack of patriotism. She had married him happily knowing that her family approved of the union, that Henry was fun, although perhaps a little dull, and that by keeping their social noses clean, their life with its impending trust fund and inheritances should follow a relatively untroubled course.

They had two children, a boy three, a girl one, whose welcome presence gave even more legitimacy to their ownership of an elegant quasi-Japanese town house with its carefully manicured small garden.

Joanne was pretty. Blonde, petite and lively, she was a good hostess, a pleasant mother, and with the aid of a household staff and a governess, she was able to share Henry's endless drive for the social life San Francisco had to offer.

There were dances, and dinners and brunches at Menlo Park Golf Club. There were hunt breakfasts and weeks in Hawaii, in Acapulco, and months in Europe. She spent as many obligatory hours as her mother and mother-in-law did in downtown San Francisco, shopping for or exchanging baubles. She was acquiring little antiques and paintings by promising North Beach artists, attending a number of lectures by far-out rabbis, farther-out poets, radical psychologists, and finally placed (like so many of her friends) an abacus over the telephone, hung paper lanterns in the entry hall and, unlike her forebears, furnished the house in Scandinavian furniture, which was too low for the comfort of the middle-aged and too deep for maintaining a decorous hemline. And she would, weather permitting, sunbathe in the nude on the roof terrace of her house, keeping a good tan, which was always considered a gauche trademark of Los Angeles.

It was Sunday morning. Breakfast had been served in bed; they could hear the sounds of the children three floors below them as they were lounging on their bed, knowing that ultimately it would lead to yet another round of lovemaking.

"You saw the article in *Fortune*," Henry said to his wife.

"I didn't read it, Henry," Joanne said, "but everyone *is* talking about it."

"They say that Bill will earn over two million dollars this year alone."

"Well, at least it's not your father's money he's taking. . . ."

"That's true, but I still don't trust the son of a bitch."

"Why?"

"You don't know what he's doing to the company."

"What?"

"Men that have been with us for years are getting fired, demoted. He's brought in a whole slew of young guys from MIT. He's even got Daddy supervising a job in the field."

"Daddy?"

"Yes. Near Tracy."

"Well, he and O'Gara must know what's going on."

"I guess they do. They never tell me."

"Do you feel threatened by Bill, Henry?" Joanne asked.

"Somewhat."

"You own ten percent of the company."

"I know. So does Bill Crossen."

"By marriage."

"Sure, but he's got Marjorie eating out of his hand."

"What the hell are you worried about? You can always go in business with my father."

"What the hell do I know about the wine business?"

"What the hell do I know about the construction business?" Joanne asked, and Henry looked at her.

"That wasn't a nice thing to say."

"I didn't mean to hurt you. I'm sorry."

Henry scratched his head and his wife lay back on the bed, one breast coming out of her flimsy night gown.

"You're a blonde bitch," Henry said falling on top of his wife.

They made love and finally Henry sat up in bed smoking a cigarette.

"How do you feel about guys like Crossen, about Buddy Feiger returning a full Commander and setting up practice, about Peter Fels, Bill Zellendorf?"

"I don't feel anything, Henry. We have a lovely home, we have beautiful children, we have a good life and you make me very happy in bed."

"A pragmatist," Henry said.

"I didn't know you knew that word."

"My mother made me read a book once."

"Did you enjoy it?"

"Not really. I enjoyed Iko better."

"Who was Iko?"

"A little Japanese girl who used to work for us."

"The great sex maniac."

"The great sex maniac and the blonde bitch. Not a bad title. Maybe I'll *write* a book. I've got nothing else to do in that office."

"Well, you've already got one word to start with."

"What's that?"

"Pragmatist."

He slapped her fanny. "We've got to get dressed. I am teeing off at noon."

"You shower first and play with the children for a minute."

"I always forget the children when I make love to you."

"I know," Joanne said. "We may have more."

"There's always relief."

"Or Grandpa Kahn."

"I wonder how much the son of a bitch is leaving us?"

"You are a bastard, Henry," Joanne said, sitting up.

"Why do you say that?"

"My father always said, 'All these fourth-generation bastards in San Francisco, living from inheritance to inheritance.'"

"I didn't force you to marry me."

"I know," Joanne said, standing. "I know you didn't. I think I'll play with the children." She left the room quickly and Henry followed her.

He was perplexed, but a good hot shower would take care of that.

Chapter XXXII

It was Christmas Eve in San Francisco and the city, freed from wartime restrictions and enjoying general prosperity, put on a good show. The windows of Podesta Baldocchi were a cornucopia of reds and greens, the little flower stands sold sprigs of pine with red bows, mistletoe and holly. The windows of Gump's were as beautiful and elegant as ever, displaying emerald jade under black light, delicate crystals and ornately embroidered Chinese housecoats. A lovely fog blanketed the city, diminishing the artificiality of a sunny California yuletide. Sallow Salvation Army lasses rang their strident bells into the ears of fur-coated women entering and leaving I. Magnin's in search of last-minute gifts. A few enterprising vendors sold hot chestnuts and pretzels.

Henry Levey sat at a solitary table at Jack's. He had ordered rex sole, was drinking a Guinness stout. His coat pocket was filled with envelopes containing checks for maids, the butler, the chauffeur, the gardener, children and grandchildren. "The annual bloodletting," he called this holiday, knowing that his pocket bulged with a sizable amount of money to reward those who served and to satisfy those who were related. Of course, he would receive his annual subscription to the *Reader's Digest* from Hortense, a gesture he reciprocated by giving her a book of Yellow Cab scrip totaling thirty dollars. He ate slowly and observed in the mirror next to his table that he was getting balder, paunchier, and that the veins in his nose were getting more prominent.

He ate slowly, reveling in the quiet of the room, the solidity of the meal. Once more he spread a thick slab of butter on a piece of sourdough bread, and he agreed when Otto (his waiter, who would also get a check) suggested brandy.

"All set for the holidays, Mr. Levey?" Otto asked.

"Set as I'll ever be. Going to be with your family?"

"I'm going to be with my daughter and her kids," the waiter said. "She had all her Christmas gifts stolen yesterday. The niggers are really taking over Daly City."

"I know," Levey said, "it's not like it used to be."

He finished his brandy, his coffee, wiped his lips with the starched napkin, gave Otto his check and one to the headwaiter, and left. His chauffeur opened the car door and Levey sat down in the gray elegance of his limousine. "Keep going," he felt like ordering the chauffeur, but he said nothing and closed his eyes briefly before the onslaught of the children, the grandchildren, the chore of carving a turkey, the greater chore of playing pater familias.

There was a lovely tree in the living room decorated with ornaments handed down from generation to generation in Hortense's family. Reform Jews always had trees, defending their presence as being American rather than Christian. There were the handknit stockings for the children and grandchildren on the hearth, an immorally large mountain of presents from the finest stores in the city and, mercifully, the butler with a double martini and a sly wink to soften the festivities.

Everything had gone exactly to schedule. Drinks for the adults, Shirley Temples for the children. Marjorie's beautiful rendition of "Silent Night" on the grand piano. The table, exquisitely set, groaned with food, the conversation was civil and lightweight and the opening of the presents brought forth the mandatory "oohs" and "aahs" and long lines at the department stores a few days hence when most of them were exchanged.

It was Bill Crossen who finally cornered Levey in the study and asked for a few minutes of his time.

"What's on your mind, Bill? Care for a cigar?"

"I don't smoke, thank you."

"And you don't drink Scotch," Levey said, lifting a Scotch old-fashioned in toast.

"I know that O'Gara wants to bid on the Broadway Tunnel."

"That's right," Levey said. "It's a big job."

"Forget it," Crossen said.

"What do you mean, forget it? O'Gara has the inside track on this one. The job is as good as in our pocket."

"I say again, forget it. You'll lose your ass."

He reached into his coat pocket and brought out his projections. . . .

"More of that?"

"Not that alone."

"What else?"

"Have you been reading the paper?"

"Of course. I get the *Chronicle* every morning. Have to keep up with Henry Jr.'s social life."

"Did you read about a mysterious explosion on Telegraph Hill?"

"As a matter of fact, I did. What was that all about? Nobody seems to know."

"I do," Crossen said. "I did a probe. I had to blast."

"What kind of probe?"

"Geological. I went down eighty feet."

"How?"

"At night. It's easy. I learned it in the Corps of Engineers."

"What did you find?"

"Everything I'd expect. I've got the samples at the office. Breccia, water, sand, clay, a tunneler's nightmare."

"I'll be a son of a bitch."

"You'll be a poor son of a bitch if you persist on that bid."

"This is O'Gara's baby. He's got plans for his hunting lodge on the profits of that job."

"Then let O'Gara build it."

"What do you mean?"

"Split up."

"We've been partners for thirty years."

"That's long enough," Crossen said.

Levey said nothing for a minute and studied Bill. He was handsome, no doubt. He had put some meat on those bones from the earlier days. His eyes were blue and steady, his hair was short, his clothes conservative, his shoes polished, his fingernails clipped short.

"Do you know it's Christmas Eve?" Levey asked.

"Yes, sir. Sorry. Yes. Thank you for the check. It was very generous."

"It's Christmas Eve and you are telling me to split with O'Gara after thirty years."

"That tunnel will break you."

"I asked you once about family. Do you remember?"

"Yes."

"Well, O'Gara is family."

"I also told you about nepotism," Crossen said. "I'll leave this data on your desk."

Crossen left the room and Levey stirred the logs in the study's fireplace.

Hortense entered the library. "What are you doing here? Little Michael wants you to assemble his dump truck."

"Tell little Michael to fuck his dump truck."

"Henry! It's Christmas."

"I know," Henry Levey said. "Merry Christmas. I'm going to bed. My chest is aching."

"There's Alka-Seltzer in the medicine chest. It's just your goddamned drinking."

Henry Levey walked slowly up the stairs. If Alka-Seltzer or aspirin did not cure you, you were not sick in San Francisco. He was asleep before Henry Jr. assembled the dump truck, which he did poorly.

Henry Jr. apologized weakly, saying, "I never said I was an engineer."

Bill Crossen had watched him coldly during the performance.

"What *are* you?" he wondered.

Chapter XXXIII

New Year's Eve was just another pearl in an endless string of parties. The red, white and blue bunting of the Fourth of July was replaced by the orange and browns for Thanksgiving, the red and green for Christmas, and was now exchanged for white ribbons, balloons and confetti at year's end.

The residents of Pacific Heights traditionally celebrated this night at the Menlo Park Country Club on the Peninsula, its golf course and lush grounds surrounded by many of the second homes of wealthy San Franciscans.

The tables were set, balloons suspended, and HAPPY NEW YEAR graced a wall in six-foot letters, its silver spangles mirroring the festive crowd.

There was French champagne and Russian caviar and the traditional duck dinner. Everyone was formally dressed, the men in black, the women in long gowns reflecting the best of Paris' designer's latest efforts.

Ernie Heckscher and his band from the Fairmont

Hotel lured diners from their tables as an atmosphere of great good cheer spread over the room. There was security in the select company and a general feeling that the new year would bring another cornucopia of good fortune.

The older generation remained until shortly after midnight, and until that hour the dancing was traditional—sons and mothers, fathers and daughters, in-laws and in-laws, the room generally subdued and well-mannered. But once the band had played "Auld Lang Syne" and after each proper toast had been made and the last bit of confetti had been brushed from their clothes, the limousines arrived at the portico, the mink coats were retrieved from the check room and the club belonged to the young.

The lights grew dimmer, the waltzes gave way to the rhumba, the rhumba to the cha-cha. The drinking became heavier, the voices louder, more animated and the inevitable game of musical partners began. Some of it had been planned months in advance, some of it was spontaneous, New Year's Eve was simply the best excuse about.

Levey had explained it all to Bill on the Fish Hatchery project, months ago.

"It is all a matter of mathematics. There are just so many 'right' young men and women, and eventually they marry each other because it is simply easier."

"Why easier?" Bill had asked.

"Financially, primarily. The merger of two powerful families is always good insurance. And easier because announcement of intention to marry the proper boy or the proper girl is usually met with parental approval. Much is overlooked: dullness, premature baldness, obesity, all minor flaws as long as the pedigree is there. I once heard Linda say that when she got engaged to Bob their respective mothers got married.

252

"But once the honeymoon is over, and the wedding presents have been tactfully documented, when the drapes are hung and the paintings placed, a lot of the carefully overlooked flaws loom larger, the lack of looks, the bad habits, the strange mannerisms get closer scrutiny; and many a little girl quickly learns that although Charlie Solomon may come from the third-richest family in California, his cock is just too short to satisfy her, 'until death do us part.'

"Of course, there are good marriages. Attractive unions, despite the money. It is not *all* that evil. But the others, the others . . . and there are lots of those . . . play—" he hesitated, "games."

Levey had stopped and then looked at Bill.

"Games. Yes, we played them in our times. You'll play them in yours. Perhaps this generation will change. Divorce was never the pattern of Pacific Heights in my day. There were some, to be sure, but they were scoffed at. I've known men who married their mistresses after their wives died, and I know the same was true of the women. I even know of men who got new mistresses after their first ones got older.

"That was the way it was done. It wasn't good, but it was acceptable."

"And then there was me," Crossen had said, and Levey had laughed.

"Yes, and then there was you," and again he paused, "and before you there was me."

"You?"

"Me," Levey said almost bitterly. "You think my life was straight as an arrow? *Bullshit.* Hortense, although you may not realize it, was quite a pretty girl—a *very* pretty girl—but she'd never let me forget my questionable background. Never. I was dynamic. I was bright. I worked. I prospered, but it still wasn't enough."

He filled his glass with Scotch.

"Did you ever hear of Winthrop East Boulton?"

"No. Should I have?"

"Winthrop East Boulton, M.D.," Levey said sarcastically. "He was not only socially prominent, he was *gentile*. That's as close to royalty as you can get on Pacific Heights. Winthrop East Boulton, M.D. The children's pediatrician. He treated them until they were eighteen. Jesus. Every cold, every sniffle, every minor cut found Winthrop East Boulton, M.D., in our house.

"He was always hanging around. I've watched that mediocre physician become dean of the medical school of the University of California, *not* by his abilities, but by his looks and his charm and women like Hortense whose money and power as auxiliaries in the hospital were eventually paid off politically."

"Why did you stand for all this?" Bill asked.

"It was a long time ago," Levey said, staring in his glass, and Bill realized that the man did not want to reveal any more.

All this Bill Crossen remembered this evening, watching the liaisons, the soulful looks on the dance floor, the hands on the knees, the bodies pressed together, all this he remembered as he sat on the portico with Elyse Wolf, staring at her white bodice, chastely scalloped at the neckline but revealing those full breasts, her nipples punching the light material mercilessly.

"Did you rent the tux or is it your own?" she asked him.

"Only *you* would ask such a question."

"Only me, that's right, and you haven't answered me."

"I own it," he said. "And I hated to buy it, but in this town you amortize one of these suits in a month."

"You figured that out on your computer?"

Crossen laughed. "No, I could figure this one out on a slide rule."

"Still fighting, eh, Bill?"

"Still fighting," he nodded. "Yes, still fighting."

"Why?"

"Because you *have* to fight to stay above water in this town."

"From all I've heard you're not only above water, Bill, you could *walk* on it. . . ."

"Don't believe everything you hear."

"Modesty does not become you," Elyse said.

"Nor you," Crossen said, looking hard at her breasts. "Do you know what I'd like to do?"

"What?"

He closed his eyes and there was silence. Finally he looked at her. "Nothing," he said.

Elyse rose and bent down. She kissed him lightly on the cheek. "Happy New Year. I'd better find my teddy bear before I have to fish him out of the swimming pool."

Crossen watched her leave, his eyes on her undulating buttocks, and he wondered whether she wore *anything* under that dress at all.

Alcohol was the great liberator at this hour of the evening. Crossen walked through the semidarkness of the public rooms of the Menlo Park Country Club. He recognized faces and he heard whispers. He caught the movement as strange hands felt breasts of other men's wives, as hands slipped under long dresses or into the recesses of tuxedo pants. There were the genuine drunks, like Lewis Wolf, Charles Leventhal, like little Charlie Munsel or Rosy Weill, but there were mock drunks who continued or initiated sexual encounters under the guise of alcoholic anesthesia, which would tomorrow serve as an excuse for being on the porch, on the stairs, in the library, in the arms of, under, over, half-naked, whatever.

Bill and Marjorie left at three and returned to the Levey mansion at three-thirty. They were both filled with mixed emotions. Bill felt a certain victory over his old-line peers knowing that he had bedded Elyse Wolf, their perennial cheerleader, and Marjorie felt guilt about her affair with Solari, and still they could not help but discuss the party.

"They all seem restless," Bill said. "It's like a giant game of Spin the Bottle."

"Perhaps," Marjorie said. "I see it differently. . . ."

"How?"

"You probably won't agree with me, but I have no use for the 'good' people of Pacific Heights, you know that. They have totally abrogated their Judaism. They are pursuing rich white Christianity with a vengeance."

"But you're not particularly Jewish," Bill said.

"No," Marjorie answered, undressing for bed. "Not in a religious sense. But musically I am very close to Jewish performers: Horowitz, Rubinstein. . . . I have a great respect for a culture that can produce that much talent."

"That's an interesting point. . . ."

"Whoever heard of a Jewish country club a generation ago?" Marjorie asked. "They're playing a game. Beat the gentiles at their own game. Don't you see that?"

"Do you think infidelity is just a gentile trait?" Bill asked.

The question caught Marjorie by surprise.

"Perhaps not," she said. "Maybe it's not fair to lay all the blame on the Christian altar. Rank has its privileges. How's that?"

It was a strange, cold remark for Marjorie, Bill thought, but his own guilt about Elyse ended the discussion on his part.

SAN FRANCISCO

The fog was rolling in to Menlo Park and Bill closed the window. Rich San Franciscans believed in cold bedrooms and sterile bathrooms. He knew that, but he had known enough cold as a boy.

Chapter XXXIV

It was only a few days after New Year's that Crossen faced Levey in his office. Perhaps his barren youth, his imprisonment, his studied unemotionalism allowed him to face this man without a trace of guilt or pity. He understood the camaraderie of a good partnership, the mutual trust, the shared experiences, but in his mind, none of that could interfere with logic.

"If," Levey said after admitting Bill, "you are going to throw me those sheets of figures to convince me about the Broadway Tunnel job, forget it."

"I'm not," Crossen said. "I gave you the core samples."

"I have them," Levey said. "I saw them all. The breccia, the mud, the sand. . . ."

"It's more than that," Crossen added. "It is the *sequence.* I can shore against sand, I can shore against mud, but I can't shore when I have nothing to shore against. The sequence, particularly in the center of the tunnel, is disastrous."

"We can pressure against it," Levey said.

"You can't," Crossen answered. "You can't get enough pressure against all of Russian Hill."

"They built caissons in the Bay to build the bridge. They had to put pressure against the whole Pacific."

"It was a known pressure," Crossen said. "They knew *exactly* what they were up against. It was measurable. A hundred probes into that hill wouldn't give you that answer."

"What the hell am I going to do? I can't tell O'Gara all this."

"*You* have to make that decision, Mr. Levey. *You* have to decide whether this is a business or a social club."

Levey turned toward him, red-faced. "You *are* a brutal son of a bitch, aren't you?"

"Not really. Just a realist."

"How is Marjorie?" Levey asked, surprising Bill with the abrupt change of subject.

"She is fine. Working, working, working. Her concert is in three months."

"Is she happy?"

"Engrossed," Crossen said.

"That's not the same thing."

"I know," Bill said. "I don't ask her whether she's happy."

"I can believe that," Levey said. "Is that all?"

"That's all," Crossen said and Levey stood.

"Thank you," he said formally and turned toward the window, waiting for his son-in-law to leave.

He has presence and elegance, Crossen thought. He has the height and the leanness and the right amount of gray hair. He knows how to wear expensive clothes and he has a sense of command. Henry Levey has much to teach me, he thought.

* * *

Levey called O'Gara and they met at Jack's in one of the private booths. Levey asked the waiter to draw the green velour drapes after he had served their martinis. They were alone.

"I've made a decision," Levey said.

"What's that?"

"I'm not going to bid on the Broadway Tunnel."

"Why?" O'Gara asked, already excited. "It's in the bag."

"The bid, yes," Levey said. "The tunnel, no."

"You've been talking to Crossen again, haven't you? His fucking computer came up with zero, I suppose."

"Not his computer."

"What, then?"

"His core samples. They're in my office. You've got everything in that hill. Mud, breccia, sand, faults. I'll be glad to show them to you."

"Fuck the core samples. I've been through scores of tunnels. All you need is men's backs and guts."

"You're not going through this one with Chinamen, you're going through with union labor. With safety inspectors, with city engineers."

"They can all be bought," O'Gara said. "Has pussy gone out of style? Is the hundred-dollar bill out of circulation?"

"I won't bid on it," Levey said.

O'Gara looked at him for a long time. He picked up his chilled martini.

"I will."

"I thought so."

"You know what this means?" O'Gara asked.

"Yes," Levey said, "and I don't like it."

"Nor do I," O'Gara said. "It's been a good partnership."

"The best," Levey said. "Let someone else bid on that tunnel."

"No," O'Gara said. "It's not just the tunnel. . . ."

"What?"

"It's that goddamned kid. *He's* your partner, not me. Nothing ever came between us before that Crossen showed up."

"I can't argue with you," Levey said, "but you have to admit he knows what he's doing."

"Luck," O'Gara said. "Beginner's luck."

"No, I disagree with you. The Mendota Canal, maybe. It was hard to miss on that one, but on a lot of other projects, we might have had serious problems."

"What's the use of arguing about it," O'Gara said. "It's all academic now."

"True," Levey agreed.

"We'll just split up. I'll build the Broadway Tunnel, we'll divide the rest of the work."

"If you want to share offices," Levey said, "it's all right with me."

"No," O'Gara said. "If we split, we split." He offered his hand. "No hard feelings."

"None whatsoever," Levey said. "The best of luck. You know I mean it."

"The same to you, Henry. Don't let that kid bully you. The next thing, he'll get rid of you."

"That has occurred to me," Levey said. "I might beat him to the draw."

"How's that?"

"Retire."

"That's not a bad idea," O'Gara said. "It's just . . ." he paused, "you put in so many years . . . and there's no one in the family who can take over."

They finished lunch in silence, each man with his own thoughts, and Henry Levey went home from the restau-

rant, though it was only one o'clock in the afternoon. He did not want to see Crossen and he did
not want to face Hortense. Seeing her car in the
driveway, he ordered his chauffeur to take him to
Menlo Park.

Perhaps it was Levey's coldness that morning or the
fact that he had not returned from lunch that prompted
Bill to discuss the matter with his wife. It was a rare
phenomenon.

"I don't see," Marjorie said, "why you should take it
all on your shoulders, Bill. You pointed out the problems with that tunnel, you didn't urge O'Gara's leaving
the firm."

"That's true, but if O'Gara insists on building the
tunnel, that is what will happen."

"Then I would say it's *their* decision, not yours."

"You *know* what will be said, Marjorie."

"By whom?"

"Your mother, your brother, everyone in the family."

"I've told you before, Bill"—she looked at him
steadily—"I don't give a damn. Our life is our life. Their
life is theirs."

"You really believe that, don't you?"

"Of course."

"You're a strong girl, Marjorie."

"I'm not so strong. I'm tough, maybe. I've learned to
be tough."

"But who has hurt you? You've had everything you
needed."

"Materially, yes. Everything. That was the easiest thing
my family could provide."

"Everyone is proud of you."

"Now, perhaps," Marjorie said. "Now, that all those
grueling hours at the piano may be paying off. It wasn't

always that way. Until I left home I always found the greatest warmth in the kitchen."

"The kitchen?"

"We had a maid. Brogan. Remember, I called her the night we eloped? An Irish immigrant girl. I never knew how old she was. Brogan was mother, father, *everything* to me. When no one asked me to a dance, Brogan would take me to a movie. When Henry or Linda had friends for the weekend and I was alone, I slept in Brogan's room. When my mother put me on a merciless diet, Brogan sneaked cookies to me."

"And where is she now?"

"Here, in San Francisco. My parents fired her."

"Why?"

"She erred once. She was ill. That's all."

"So what happened to her?"

"I support her."

"How?"

"I have money of my own."

"I know."

It was a curious statement. This gifted young woman, this emotionally scarred girl, who on one hand clung to an Irish immigrant, could on the other quite naturally exercise her financial independence. "I have money . . ." she had said, and he saw Hortense. . . .

"If O'Gara leaves," Marjorie said, "you should become a partner in the firm."

"It doesn't matter to me."

"It should."

"Why?"

"You deserve it."

"I don't have that ambition."

"What is your ambition, Bill?"

"To succeed. Maybe on my own."

Marjorie thought for a while.

"You'd leave Daddy?"

"Perhaps. I think I could stand on my own two feet."

"I don't question that at all, except . . ."

"What?"

"Anywhere but here. Here, San Francisco."

"What do you mean?"

"This is a vicious town. You should know that by now. They'll blame you if O'Gara leaves. Leaving Daddy would be the final blow. . . . You couldn't win a bid no matter *how* low it is."

Bill took Marjorie's hand in his. "I never realized . . ." he said.

"What?"

"I never realized how much you knew, I never thought that you ever took an interest in the business."

"You never asked me," she said, smiling somewhat coyly.

Bill Crossen nodded silently. "That's right," he said, "I never asked you."

She withdrew her hand and placed both of them around his neck. "You fight your demons, and I'll fight mine. I've never believed that a marriage works because the partners pool their insecurities."

"Do you feel our marriage is working?" Bill asked, and Marjorie averted his eyes.

"I don't feel answering a question like that is beneficial."

Marjorie sensed the coldness of her own remark. "I have a great deal of respect for you, Bill. I respect you more than any other man except for my father."

"That is a very high compliment."

"It was meant to be. I sense you feel the same for me."

"You know that."

264

"Well, let's dispense with this Freudian bullshit and go to bed." That night Bill made love to her with greater fervor than ever before, not fully understanding whether he admired this toughness in his wife, whether it was a challenge, or whether it was a mirror of himself. For once he thought less of Elyse Wolf and Marjorie less of Solari.

Chapter XXXV

"I see by the papers," Selda said to Bill Crossen, who was sitting in her living room, "that the firm of O'Gara and Levey has become Levey, Levey and Crossen."

"Yes," Bill said. "Blood runs thicker than talent in San Francisco."

"Come on, now, Bubba, what did you want? First billing?"

"No, no, not that. But that asshole, excuse me, that flaccid kid—a partner—Jesus!"

"He *is* the son."

"Hortense's son."

"What does that mean?"

"It means Hortense has the most shares."

"Oh, Jesus, Bill. I didn't ask you over for that. . . ."

"I'm sure. How are you?"

"There, that's a step in the right direction. You actually *asked* me. Something is rubbing off. What is it? Marjorie? How is she?"

"Incredible," Bill said. "Absolutely incredible. She's at that piano sixteen hours a day."

"Forget the piano. How is she otherwise?"

"She's quite a lady."

"How about that—what's her name—that tootsie?"

Bill Crossen winced. "Elyse?"

"Yes, Elyse."

"She's around. She's still around."

"Still the goddess?"

"As pretty as a goddess, I'll say that."

Selda frowned and offered Bill some wine. He declined and she poured a glass for herself.

"All right," Crossen said, "what's on your mind?"

"What kind of a question is that? How much time have you allotted me? Are you worth so much an hour now?"

"I'm sorry."

"Well, maybe I should keep my mouth shut," Selda said. "Maybe I should hope you're worth a lot an hour."

"What's going on?"

"Mr. Wednesday . . ."

"Yes."

"You remember Mr. Wednesday?"

"I do."

"He's an engineer, too."

"I didn't know that."

"Yes, a petroleum engineer. He works for Standard of California."

"What about him?"

"He's been transferred to Saudi Arabia. For six months. His wife isn't going because she doesn't want to take the kids out of school. . . ."

"But you *are* going, I take it," Crossen said.

"I'd like to."

"What's stopping you?"

"My job. I love my job and they won't hold it for me for six months."

"*Who* won't?"

"The city. The Department of Libraries."

"Bullshit," Crossen said.

"Bullshit to you, Billy boy, not bullshit to me. You once told me that the only one who knew his way around city hall was O'Gara. . . ."

Crossen laughed. He stood and cupped Selda's face. He kissed her fully.

"Still bullshit. You think I didn't learn anything from O'Gara when he was in the firm?"

"You can fix it?" Now Selda smiled like a young child.

"I can fix it. What happens in six months?"

Selda sat back and let her head rest on the top of her sofa.

"Six months . . . it seems like an eternity now. Mr. Wednesday will turn into Mr. Monday, Tuesday, Thursday and Friday. I'll tell you in six months."

"I'm happy for you," Bill said.

"That's good," Selda said. "I'm happy you're happy for me."

"He's getting a very fine girl."

"All compliments accepted. All cautions to the wind, all sensibilities stored with my mother's unused linens— Away we go. . . ." She smiled.

"Away we go," Bill echoed. "Do you need some money?"

"No."

"Luggage, clothes, *anything?*"

Selda looked at him and tears formed in her eyes.

"I need your arms around me and I need you to say, 'Go, you wicked woman, and enjoy!' "

Bill complied and added, "Go and tell him he's a lucky man." Then he stood and said good-bye. The following day he sent over a handsome set of luggage.

Chapter XXXVI

Hortense and Henry Levey's master bedroom was twenty-five feet by thirty-two feet. Its colors were cream and beige. The room contained two twin beds with monogrammed bed spreads, night tables and marble-topped armoires. There was a lovely fireplace with two small couches flanking it, a Duncan Phyfe oval coffee table between them. There were Oriental prints and photographs of parents, grand-parents, children, grandchildren, all framed in *pas patou*.

The most frequently used piece of furniture, however, was a yellow chintz chaise longue, which faced the window overlooking the Bay. It was Hortense's throne, and similar couches served as similar thrones throughout Pacific Heights.

It was considered slothful and middle-class to spend the day in bed (unless there was illness), but perfectly proper for a woman like Hortense, showered and coiffed, to lie on the chaise until midmorning wearing a dressing gown and a pair of Oriental slippers.

It was at this command post that servants received their orders for the day, that breakfast was eaten and the paper read. It was from here that supplies were ordered by phone, appointments made, children delegated, and later (also by phone) that Hortense conversed with other ladies similarly situated about the last twenty-four hours. There were recordings of deaths and births, illnesses and good fortunes. There were the usual gossipy speculations, a good deal of truths and a share of lies.

Whatever the day's activities (shopping, clubs, bridge or lectures), the chaise longue once more received Hortense at four, after she had changed again into something fresh, looser and comfortable, having been buffeted by traffic, rudeness or reality during the day.

Her son was now sitting at the foot of that chaise this early evening explaining in detail O'Gara's departure and the ensuing uproar in the firm.

"You have no idea what's going on, Mother. The firm is getting larger and larger, but all the hiring is done by Bill. We seem to be the new home for graduating engineers from MIT, Cal Tech, and Case. The older men in the firm are getting very annoyed."

"Your father said that the firm is making more money than ever."

"Right now it is, but as Linda pointed out, what if the boom recedes, then what? We're stuck with all those high-priced engineers. . . ."

"Why do you listen to Linda? You're right *there.*"

"So is Bob. He knows the legal end better than I do."

"What end do *you* know?"

"Oh, Jesus, Mother, you sound like Dad."

"Well, do you think you could run that firm?"

"I've never thought of that."

"Well, who is going to run it after your father? Linda?"

"What are you saying?"

"I am being realistic, Henry." She put her arms about his shoulders. "Maybe you should think about all that."

"I just told you what's going on. . . ."

"I appreciate that," Hortense said and wanted to add, "now go back and play," but she resisted.

It was Henry Levey, Sr., who would get the barrage when he returned home from work.

"I don't see," Hortense half sneered at her husband, "how you, knowing you're a minor stockholder, could make the decision to split with O'Gara. None of us would have ever let that occur."

"I am going to tell you calmly, Hortense, just once. O'Gara wanted to bid on the Broadway Tunnel, but none of his data holds water."

"According to Bill Crossen."

"And myself. I used to be an engineer, remember?"

"Why split up over *one* job?"

"That's what I told O'Gara. I suggested that we not bid on the job at all, but he refused."

"You know what will happen now?"

"No. What?"

"You will be known as Levey and Company."

"Levey and Crossen," Henry said.

"A *Jewish* firm. A Jewish construction firm."

"What is that supposed to mean? Goldman is Jewish. Fels is Jewish."

"Goldman is in the banking business. Fels is in the clothing business, traditional Jewish businesses. Construction is not."

"We've been in business for thirty years."

"And you've had O'Gara as a shield."

"Shield, my ass. O'Gara knew his way around city hall. That's all. He knew as much about engineering as Whitney East Boulton, M.D., knows about medicine.

The only thing these guys have in common is the fact that they're gentile."

"You're horrid," Hortense screamed. "You *know* you forced me into that affair."

"*I* did?"

"Yes. You seem to forget Milton Ganz's stag party, the whore he had. The stories about some naked red-head on your lap. . . ."

This had been the rationalization all these years, Henry thought. A naked redheaded whore who had sat on his lap some thirty-five years ago, and he had been stupid enough to admit the incident.

"It was a stag party. That was all. I never knew the girl's name. I never screwed her. She didn't hang around this house like Boulton. She didn't take my money like Boulton did, and there is more, and you know it."

"Whitney East Boulton has had a stroke. I wish you'd remember that."

"I hope it paralyzed his cock. There wasn't ever any brain to affect in the first place."

"You're as crude as ever." Hortense's tears were flowing now. "You always revert to the gutter when you're trapped. . . ."

"I don't want to discuss it any further. Where's my martini?"

"I've spoken to Henry Jr. He agrees with me. So do Linda and Bob. We won't allow the dissolution of O'Gara and Levey."

"I'm sorry, Hortense, that has already been done."

"You can't do it. Not legally. I've spoken to Bob."

"You make me laugh." He imitated her: " 'I've spoken to Bob.' That idiot couldn't defend the Pope against a rape charge. I may not have the majority of the stock, but I *am* the managing partner. That's all the authority I need. Did Bob tell you that?"

"No."

"Of course not. He's never read the articles of incorporation, has he?"

"I don't know."

"Sometimes," Levey said, "I fear for your own intelligence, when you start asking Bob for legal advice."

"Then it will be Levey, Levey and Crossen," Hortense said.

"That makes it sound even *more* Jewish, doesn't it?"

The butler arrived with the tray of martinis and left the charged atmosphere of the bedroom quickly.

"Levey, Levey and Crossen," Henry raised his glass. "That has a nice ring to it. Like lymphogranuloma inguinale."

"What's that?"

"It's a venereal disease you catch in Borneo. If left untreated, your balls fall off, unless you consulted Whitney East Boulton, M.D. Then your balls would fall off, anyway."

"I am begging you to be civil," Hortense said.

"Civil," Henry said sarcastically. "What a strange word to come across this battlefield. . . ."

For once Hortense said nothing. Even *she* knew the definition of finesse.

Four blocks east of the Levey mansion, Henry Jr. sat at the dinner table watching his pretty wife, his pretty children eating a well-cooked, well-served meal.

"I have some news," he said, and Joanne looked up as did the children.

"Today the name of our firm changed. It is now Levey, Levey and Crossen. I became a partner."

The children looked uncomprehending and Joanne looked puzzled.

"What happened to O'Gara?"

"He's out."

"Why?"

273

"Daddy and he split. Some bid they fought over. I don't know."

"And Bill Crossen is a partner, too?"

"Yes."

"I don't like it," Joanne said.

"Why? He's been good for the firm."

"He's been good for Bill Crossen."

"Jesus Christ, Jo, what do you know about it all?"

"More than you think."

"Bill Crossen can't hurt me. I've got as much stock as he has."

"Bill Crossen has been hurting you all along. You don't know what people are saying."

"What people?"

"Our friends."

"What are they saying?" He looked at the children's upturned faces. "To hell with them," he said conspiratorially. "I don't want to hear about it. Let's have some wine. Some champagne. This calls for a celebration."

Joanne followed him into the kitchen. "You *know* everyone hates Bill Crossen."

"They don't hate him, honey. He's just different."

"They don't like his coldness. His indifference. I wonder how Marjorie stands him."

"I couldn't tell you. She's so busy with her music she hardly talks to anyone herself."

"Do you think they have any fun in bed?"

"How would I know? Why don't you ask her?"

"She's *your* sister."

"What would you like me to say? Do you enjoy screwing your husband?"

"Oh, forget it. You don't care *what* happens."

"What *can* happen? You've always said I could go into the wine business."

Joanne looked at him pensively. "You really don't care much, do you?"

"I've got you. I've got the kids. A nice home. Why should I get upset?"

"You know you didn't earn any of it."

"That's true, I suppose. And what contribution have you made to society?"

"I am a woman. I'm a mother. . . ."

"For about an hour a day."

"Would you feel better if I washed the diapers?"

"I'm not complaining. You are."

She looked at him and then she put her arms around her husband. "I really need you, Henry, you lovable boob. I just don't want Crossen to hurt you."

"I can take care of myself. There's still my father."

"He won't live forever."

"That's true. When he dies we'll inherit even more money."

It had been a cruel statement for Henry Jr. to make and its cruelty hit Joanne harder than he realized. The only daughter of successful vintners in Napa County, she had been reared with much love and wisdom. She was vivacious, cheerful, she had friends, lots of friends. She lived in a large home surrounded by vineyards. It was benign country.

At the age of fourteen she had been thrown by her horse and what originally seemed nothing but a bruise eventually turned into a spinal paralysis. She had spent months at Johns Hopkins and further months in traction in bed at home. Nothing was spared in medical aid and nothing was spared in parental love to see her though this ominous year.

She had watched her eternally tanned skin turn to a sickly white. She had watched the edges of her cast fester her young and tender skin. She suffered through the beginnings of menstruation helplessly encased in a body cast, and only through the ministrations of a warm family: father, mother, two older brothers did she regain her health and her beauty, and her only penalty was the admonition that she could no longer ride, she could not ski; and though she could otherwise live a normal life, it would of necessity be one of restricted physical activity.

That year of confinement and the following years of physical restrictions had made her more introverted. She was still beautiful, or once again beautiful. The color returned to her skin, the luster was restored to her hair, and as she entered the mainstream of social life as a young woman in San Francisco, she was unquestionably a prize catch.

Henry Levey, Jr., was himself attractive. He was kind and he was warm and he had always been understanding of her physical limitations. She was able to make love, and seemingly that was all that he cared about. They had raised a lovely young family and Henry did make her happy in bed.

Of course, she was aware of his lassitude. She was aware of his blatant acceptance of his birthright; and still, she remembered that year, when she knew, despite the family's protection, that she might not survive it, or even if she did, she might be paralyzed from the waist down. She had made a covenant with herself that year, that if she survived it, that if her life resumed its former sunny existence, then she would try to propagate that loving, protective existence in her own marriage. She had been fortunate. Henry was basically sweet, they had lovely children, a lovely home. She felt blessed.

The cold mention of death, the death of Henry Jr.'s father, a man she loved, did not sit easily with her; and though she made no point of his statement, it frightened her and made her wonder how much he was his father's son, and how much he was his mother's.

She could bring him home, to be sure, and she could get him a job in the vineyards; but if Henry's statement about his inheritance was really true, then he would not fit in that sunny climate of her family, nor even into *her* life. Nevertheless, she took comfort in knowing that few of Henry's statements were rigid or particularly thoughtful. She had to focus on his love, which *was* real, and ignore the rest.

Chapter XXXVII

Not all went well on Nimbus Dam before its completion. Bill had a general strike on his hands. The issue was not money, since Crossen paid his men top wages. The issue was a Mexican man in his early forties named Rodriguez.

Even though Crossen might have a thousand men on his project, he made it a point to know all of them by name, and to know their weaknesses and strengths. Rodriguez's quick thinking and raw courage had averted what could have been a major catastrophe: A giant bucket of cement descended from the gorge as had hundreds of others before. But this bucket went wild and threatened to fall on the men below. Rodriguez lassoed that bucket and guided it safely to the ground. Bill had watched the whole performance and had called Rodriguez to his office.

The tough, slightly paunchy Mexican man stood before Bill, and Bill rose and shook his hand.

"That was a very brave thing you did with that wild bucket. I am very grateful to you. From now on you will be lead man of section four."

"Me," the Mexican said with true astonishment. "Me, lead man? You don't understand, boss. I'm Mexican."

"I understand," Crossen said. "Go to the office and get a new badge. And a new hat."

"*Santa Maria.*" The Mexican scratched his head. "Thank you." He was still scratching his head an hour later.

In that hour every lead man assembled in Crossen's office. A stocky white man with red hair, a man in his fifties, faced Crossen. His name was Murphy.

"You name Rodriguez lead man?"

"So I did."

"You gonna have a spic lead man, and you're not going to have a dam."

"Why is that?"

"Because we're going to strike."

"Who is we?"

"All of us. All the lead men."

"I see," Crossen said calmly. "Where were you white wonderboys when that bucket went wild? I can count twenty-four of you in this room right now who were closer to it than Rodriguez."

"He lucked out."

"Luck, my ass. He could have been whipped in half."

"Well, what do you say, Crossen?"

"I'm going to have four trucks in front of my office and I will give you four hours to decide. After that I'll take you off the site, off the job and hire men away from the Benson Company."

"Is that it?"

"That's it," Crossen said. "Get out of my office."

The news reached Henry Levey before the four hours were up and reached the newspapers that evening.

Henry, deeply concerned, called Bill. "I'd better get down there."

"Stay just where you are," Bill said. "These chicken bastards will never walk out. We pay them too well."

"I'll wait four hours," Henry said. "Call me. Then I'll decide what to do."

"Very good."

Carter, one of Crossen's MIT men, entered the office.

"I happen to agree with you, Bill. I don't think they'll walk out, but what about Rodriguez?"

"What about him?"

"I don't want to see him as a corpse."

"I hadn't thought of that. I'll handle it. Call in Dunby."

Ten minutes later Dunby appeared.

"You wanted to see me?"

"Yes. I've named Rodriguez lead man."

"I heard. A dumb mistake."

"I didn't ask for your opinion."

"Then what do you want?"

"I don't want anything to happen to Rodriguez."

"Hell, I can't protect him from a thousand men."

"If *you* can't, I'll get someone who can. *You've* got three hours left to decide."

"I told you," Dunby shouted, "I still know things about your past."

"Three hours," Crossen said.

At four o'clock Murphy appeared in Crossen's office. "We ain't leaving, we decided, but Rodriguez's life ain't worth a plugged nickel."

"I'm way ahead of you, Murphy. I've got guards around him. If anything happens to him, you won't have to strike. I'll can every one of you."

The phone rang. It was Henry Levey. "It's all over," Bill said. "We're going to work a little late tonight. I'm going to get my four hours back."

"It's all over the *Examiner,* too."

"I bet," Bill said. "There's a reporter outside from the *Chronicle.*"

"Well, I would speak to him. Tell *our* side."

"I will. Don't worry."

"Some tough son of a bitch," Henry said.

"Who?" Bill asked.

"You," Henry said and hung up.

And Crossen did talk to the reporter and the following morning the headline of the *San Francisco Chronicle* read, LABOR BREAKTHROUGH AT NIMBUS DAM, and the story that followed was as Bill had told it. The writer had been good. There was mention of Sacco-Vanzetti, there were accolades for Bill. It was a reporter's dream story.

Marjorie read the paper and began to tremble. She could barely manage to dial his number and was relieved when he answered the phone himself.

"Darling," she said.

"Yes."

"How *are* you?"

"Fine, just fine. Why?"

"I read the story in the *Chronicle* this morning. You made the headlines. . . ."

"No kidding?"

"I'm afraid for you."

"Why?"

"I really respect you for what you did, but I am worried about *you*. *You*, Bill, *you* don't have to take those risks."

"Look, sweetheart," Bill said. "I've spent my whole life taking risks. I'm an old pro."

"Well, I don't care if you're an old pro, I want a *live* pro."

"Marjorie," Bill said, genuinely moved, "I love you. Go back to your piano and I'll run my dam."

"I have to admit something," Marjorie said.

"What's that?"

"It felt good seeing your name in the paper."

"Well, go to the del Prado for lunch and stick out your chest. . . ."

"Bullshit. I've got work to do."

"That's my girl. Take care."

Elyse Wolf also read the paper, and she felt Bill Crossen's hands on her breasts. "That son of a bitch," she said.

"What, darling?" Lewis asked.

"Bill Crossen, there's a story about him in the *Chronicle*."

"Bill Crossen—" Lewis said, "just looking at him tires me out. Where is my gin?"

"You probably drank it. I'll ring for the butler."

"Thank you."

Elyse turned the page and reread the story.

Hortense was truly at bay. "What does this mean?" she asked Henry, who was dressing for work.

"You can read, can't you? What do you think it means?"

"The way I read it, it means that the Leveys have embraced the Mexicans."

"No, Bill Crossen embraced *one* Mexican and made a hero out of him."

"He probably didn't hurt his own cause, either," Hortense countered.

"And what's that cause?" Henry asked.

"I wish I knew."

And there was a small group of men in San Francisco, men who met at the Bohemian Club, at the Pacific Union Club, who also read the story, and they had heard (even in those gentile corridors) of Bill Crossen before.

"We ought to look into this guy," Benson said at the Pacific Union Club.

"What for?"

"He is getting a lot of exposure. Good exposure. Prisoner of war, self-made millionaire, he's young, good-looking. . . . What more do you want in politics?"

"He's Jewish," Kellog said.

"I know. There are a lot of Jewish votes in San Francisco. And *more* in L.A."

"That's right," Kellog nodded, "and now you can add the Mexican vote."

"Sure, if they know where to put the X."

"We should get him on some commissions. Police, parks, something, see how he performs."

"That's not a bad idea, Alfred. Not a bad idea at all."

Chapter XXXVIII

Bill Crossen, undeterred by the loss of O'Gara, rented the vacated space of the former partner to establish a separate firm called Crossen Development. He was convinced now of the inestimable value of computer science and hired four young engineers from Harvard to staff his enterprise. He realized that he would soon lose the exclusivity of this valuable tool and reasoned that he could sell his expertise to other engineering firms.

"I'd be happy to sell you some shares in this company," he said to Henry Levey, but Levey declined.

"At my age," he said, "I have no urge to expand. We've got all the business here we can handle."

The white urban flight was very pronounced now in San Francisco. Many young professionals, financial managers, or sons of the rich were fleeing to San Mateo, San Raphael, Palo Alto, Sausalito, Tiburon, where schools were still white and neighborhoods safe. Many of them built lovely country homes, others occupied tract houses now mushrooming all over the Bay Area. There was not only a building boom, but an explosion. New tracts demanded new amenities. Shopping centers came into being, schools were needed, hospitals, parks, highways, and all of these demanded engineering, and much of it was dropped into Levey, Levey and Crossen's lap.

"I've been thinking," Bill said, "that these shopping centers we are developing make sense."

"How?" Levey asked.

"The formula seems quite simple. You need a few seed stores, a Sears Roebuck, an Emporium, a Joseph Magnin, a good-size parking lot, and the other stores fall into line."

"That's true. I'd expect there'll be a good number of them."

"So do I. But why do we only provide the engineering?"

"What do you suggest?"

"We can develop them ourselves. *We* could hold the master lease. Truman has called the housing shortage our biggest problem."

"To hell with Truman. I have never been deficit-oriented. I'm not about to kiss Goldman's ass to borrow money at this stage of my life."

"I'm not above that, but why do you need Goldman's money? I can get eastern financing."

"You get eastern financing in this town and *try* and get the Emporium or I. Magnin. . . ."

"It's *that* clannish, is it?"

"You bet."

"Well, then, *I'll* ask Goldman."

"You're twenty-nine, Bill. Jesus Christ. You're *already* starting another company. How much do you want? How much do you need?"

"Personally, I need very little, but these opportunities are just too good. I have patented and licensed eleven new processes in the last six months. I've got to put my money to work. Otherwise I just give it to the government."

"Would you like to buy an aging engineering firm?"

"Which one?"

"Levey, Levey and Crossen."

"Don't be funny."

"I'm not being funny. I could just go around the world—Paris, London . . . Venice—I love Venice."

"You couldn't stay out of harness for more than a week."

"That's what everybody keeps telling me. Old Henry, he just loves to work."

"Don't you?"

Levey put his feet on his lovely coffee table and stretched back on the couch.

"I used to. When I was your age. I no longer have that drive. I can only eat one steak at Jack's at one time and ride around in one limousine. . . ."

"Why don't you take a long vacation? You and Hortense could go to Europe. I'll hold things together here."

Levey smiled. "I bet you would," and he sensed the sarcasm in his voice. "I didn't mean that the way it sounded. No," he said, "I'd prefer working to two months in Europe with Hortense. God save me."

Bill left Levey's office, but he did not leave Levey's mind. Listening to Crossen was like looking in a mirror twenty-five years ago. He, too, had had that drive and he, too, had succeeded.

But had he really? he wondered. Financially, certainly, and Crossen had succeeded financially. Emotionally? No, he, Levey, had not succeeded emotionally. His marriage was a failure. It had been a failure for many years. And he had compensated, sure. But how? With homes and servants and lovely old books and fine antique furniture. He had compensated with big houses and a liveried driver and a limousine, tailor-made clothes, and percale sheets on his beds.

Of course there had been affairs. Most of them short, most of them revolving about his money and his power, perhaps a few that could have given him some lasting pleasure.

And now Crossen, this young, headstrong, brash, tough son of a bitch . . . Was he happy? He seemingly didn't care for material things. What *did* he want? Did he find love with Marjorie? Was it love, or was it respect or was it easier to stay married as it had been for him?

He would see the envy on the shoeshine boy polishing his oxfords every morning at ten o'clock, or the waiter at Jack's holding his overcoat. He was aware of being watched as he strode into his office every morning, and was used to the obsequiousness that had became part and parcel of his life.

He could not deny that this brought pleasure. He could do what he wanted, when he wanted to. No one told him what to do. There was little he could not possess; he was obeyed; he was catered to; his time was coveted; and yet how often did he feel an arm about his shoulders, a kiss on his forehead, a woman in his arms? How often did he hear a word of praise or encouragement?

How often, he thought, did he laugh? And how often had he seen Bill Crossen laugh?

Chapter XXXIX

Despite supervising the construction of Nimbus Dam, it was Bill's custom to spend Fridays at his home office in San Francisco. And although the dam was within five days of completion and he had begged off attending the ceremonies celebrating that event, there was still much administrative work that necessitated his being near the accountant, the attorneys, the men from the state offices.

It was exactly ten o'clock in the morning (he knew without looking at his watch because the sun would begin to illuminate the edge of his oak desk). The phone rang. He picked it up. It was Dunby.

"They've hanged Rodriguez," he said coldly.

"They *what!*" Bill shouted.

"Hanged him. Strung him up on a tree. He's dead."

"*Who* did it?"

"I don't know."

"What do you mean you *don't* know? You don't hang a man like you shoot him. There had to be more than one. A mob, I suspect. He's only been a foreman for four months."

"I told you. I don't know," Dunby repeated.

"You *were* being *paid* to protect that man. You're *supposed* to know."

"I wasn't there. That's all. What do you want me to do? There's a bunch of sheriffs and state cops here."

"Do *nothing*," Bill commanded, "until I get there. Can you get that straight?"

Dunby hung up and Bill covered his eyes with his hands. He sat immobile for what seemed like hours.

He recalled Rodriguez's face when he had promoted him to foreman. He remembered it had reflected both fear and pride. He recalled warnings about the danger he was placing the man in . . . and he recalled all those nightmare visions of death at Bataan, at San Tomas. He had seen men decapitated and men shot in the back, he had seen men drop almost gracefully from exhaustion and malnutrition . . . he had seen men hanged.

There was a gentle knock on the door. Bill looked up and dried his tears.

"Come in," he said reluctantly and Henry Levey entered, carrying two glasses of brandy.

"Here, drink this," he ordered, and Bill complied, coughing.

"I killed him," Bill said, finally looking at Henry. "I killed him just as surely as if I had strung him up myself."

"Bullshit," Levey said.

"I didn't know, I didn't know," Bill almost pleaded.

"You didn't know what?"

"How strong that prejudice was. I didn't know how much they hated Mexican labor. . . ."

"What you did," Henry said, "was something that needed to be done. You were the first who had the guts."

"The guts," Bill said. "The guts, shit. All I've got on my shoulders is Rodriguez's guts. I have a tough time sleeping as it is. . . ."

The remark puzzled Levey, but he did not pursue it.

"You're an engineer," Henry said. "A good one. A damned good one. Didn't they teach you death ratios at MIT? They did me, at Cal."

"They taught me," Bill said quietly. "I know *all* about death ratios. Those actuarial figures are arrived at by studying the relationship of terrain, weather, heavy machinery to the frail human worker. I know all that. I have, as you know, a very good safety record."

"Extraordinary," Henry said.

"Rodriguez was not killed by terrain, weather or heavy machinery. He was killed by *me*."

"Stop it," Levey said. "I thought you told me you were one tough son of a bitch."

"Well, you're watching him fall apart right in front of your eyes. . . ."

The room was silent for a long time. Finally Levey said, "I am not happy about Rodriguez's death, but I *am* pleased to see your reaction."

"Why?"

"Because for a long time now I've wondered whether you *feel* at all. That's why."

"You'll have my resignation this afternoon," Bill said.

"I won't accept it."

"No, damnit," Bill said. "I cause death, don't you understand? I cause men to die." He rose quickly and headed for the door, but Levey blocked him.

"Where are you going?"

"To Nimbus."

"Why?"

"I'll find the bastards who did this."

"Don't," Levy said. "There are better men to do that."

"Sure. White sheriffs, white state troopers, what the hell do they care about one more dead spic?"

"You are not the Creator," Levey said. "You're a supervising engineer. You'll only get yourself killed."

"Perhaps," Bill said, "that is the proper atonement. Please," he said gently, "step aside," and he left the office. A minute later Levey could hear the sound of his truck being started and the squeal of the tires as he left.

He crossed over to Bill's phone. He called Riley at Nimbus. Riley, the old Golden Gloves champ whose father had worked for O'Gara and Levey and whose muscles now served the firm.

"Riley . . . ? Yes, Mr. Levey . . . Yes, I heard. I have a job for you."

"What is it, Mr. Levey?"

"You'll see Bill Crossen arrive at Nimbus in a couple of hours. I want you to watch for his truck and I want you by his side."

"Why?"

"He's off his head. I don't want him in trouble."

"I understand, Mr. Levey. I'll do my best."

"I know that, Riley. Thank you."

Levey picked up the phone again to call Marjorie. He told her what had happened.

"My God, Daddy. Why did you let him go," she said, after hearing the story.

"There was no way I could stop him. I have a guard waiting for him. He'll be all right."

"How can you be sure? I'll go up myself," she said.

"No," Levey ordered. "For once, Marjorie, no, please . . ."

"I'll suffer more here than at his side."

"Then suffer, Marjorie, like I will suffer. But you don't belong there."

"I'll wait," Marjorie said.

291

"Good." He paused before ending the conversation. "Tell me," he asked, "does Bill have trouble sleeping?"

"Yes. Why?"

"He told me about it."

"I've tried to help," Marjorie pleaded.

"I'm sure," Henry said, "I'm sure of that. I'll call you back soon."

"Thank you."

Crossen scarcely remembered the drive. He was met at his office by a sergeant of the state troopers.

"We followed your orders, Mr. Crossen, but we've got to cut down that spic."

"That spic," Bill yelled, "had a name. It was Rodriguez. He has a wife and two sons named *Rodriguez.*"

The sergeant looked at the screaming man and said, "I didn't mean nothing by it. . . ."

"I know," Bill said, "it doesn't mean anything to you at all."

He rode in the sheriff's car to a remote area of the dam. The law officers had roped it off, and he could see the poor Mexican hanging on a small oak.

"Take him down," Bill ordered and a young officer who seemed poised for the job climbed up a tree and began to saw him off the limb.

"Not like that," Crossen shouted, but it was too late. The limb creaked and Rodriguez's crumpled, broken body fell twenty feet to the ground. Bill watched numbly as it fell—as shapeless and lifeless and unheroic as all the other corpses he had seen.

No one made any attempt to cover him, but Bill stepped forward, removed his jacket and put it over the man's face and shoulders.

He walked to the sergeant and ordered him to return the body to his office. "Who is in charge of this?" he asked.

"Captain Wells."

"Tell him to see me."

"Captain Wells," the sergeant said sarcastically, "will see you if he finds that necessary."

"I see," Bill said. "You tell Captain Wells to get his ass over here or I'll call the governor."

"Yes, sir."

It took ten minutes for Wells, a heavy-set, bespectacled man to reach Bill's office. He entered and Bill handed him a list.

"What's this?"

"The roster of foremen on Nimbus Dam."

Wells studied the sheets. "There are sixty names on this list."

"That's right."

"What charges would you like to press?"

"Murder."

"All sixty?"

"Every stiff on this dam site," Crossen yelled. "I don't give a shit."

"Hold on, son," Wells said. "Hold on. I don't have anything against Mexicans. Do you understand?"

"No."

"Well, my wife is Mexican, do you understand *yet*?"

"I understand more," Bill said.

"I don't like murder any better than you do, but I also know the law."

"What is the law?"

"I cannot arrest a man without cause—"

"What do you suggest?" Bill interrupted. "You *know* they did it. You've read the papers?"

"I have. I think you had a lot of guts, but that doesn't give me a clue."

"What will?"

"I could make a suggestion," Wells said.

"What's that?"

"A reward. A *big* reward."

"Name it."

"Ten thousand dollars."

Bill reached in his desk drawer. He pulled out a check-book and wrote the check for the designated amount.

"You're really serious," Wells said.

"Yes."

"This," Wells said, holding up the check, "this might flush the bastards out. Ten grand, that's lots of drinking money. . . ."

Wells left and Dunby entered.

"You've got a nerve," Bill yelled. "You've got a fuck-ing nerve to show up here."

"I was gone when it happened," Dunby said. "I was screwing a broad. Is that a crime?"

"You're not getting paid to screw broads."

"I couldn't stop a mob no matter what. . . ."

Bill paced the room. "This was not spontaneous. This was planned. For weeks, maybe *months*. You never heard any of it?"

"No," Dunby said. "What's all the fuss? One god-damned Mexican . . ."

"Get out," Bill yelled. "Get the hell out of my sight."

But Dunby did not move. He looked at Crossen. "I told you when I took this job you weren't buying me off, and firing me won't get me off your back. You're still the same fucking traitor from San Tomas. Don't ever forget it."

"Go tell the world, you syphilitic bastard. Go tell them. I *know* you spend all your time in whore houses."

"And how do you know that?"

"I know *everything* on this dam site. *Everything.*"

Chapter XL

Bill Crossen's responsibilities had increased in the wake of O'Gara's departure. Presently there were four major construction projects: a shipyard in Oregon, two bridges in northern California, another aqueduct in the Central Valley, and all of these projects demanded his presence some of the time. His consulting firm was receiving greater acceptance than he had expected and that staff was growing.

It had been Henry Goldman's mission to meet with Bill on behalf of the Democratic Steering Committee to involve him in civic responsibility. They met downtown, in Goldman's now mostly ceremonious, large, private office (Persian rugs, oil paintings, marine antiques), and seated across from the elderly man, Bill felt anxious about being there.

"Many of us," Goldman said, "have watched you carefully—that is, most of us in the Democratic party, and we are all admirers of your talent, your energy, even a good many of your decisions."

"I'm very flattered," Bill said.

"I suppose you realize that you are rapidly becoming a very public figure."

"I *am* aware of it," Bill said. "But I don't seek the publicity."

"Be that as it may," Goldman continued, "we *do* have a tradition in San Francisco that men of means, men of skill, men of talent devote *some* of their time to public service."

"If you are referring to my peers," Bill said, "that's about all they are good for. . . ."

Goldman, reflecting on the waywardness of his two sons, said, "I may agree with your assessment, but not necessarily with your tactlessness."

"To the manor born," Bill said. "I *still* use the wrong fork at dinner parties."

"We are getting away from the subject of our meeting," Goldman said.

"So we are," Bill agreed. "However, I donate handsomely to the 'right' causes."

"I know that," Goldman said, "but it is not only money we need. We want your talent."

"What would you suggest?"

"There are a number of commissions: Police, Fire Department, Parks and Recreation . . ."

"All worthwhile," Crossen said, "but I could offer them little."

"Is there something that *does* interest you?"

Crossen looked at the trim, well-preserved man. "Yes. Farm labor. Industrial labor . . ."

"The Mexican question," Goldman said.

"Exactly."

Goldman shook his head. "A very unpopular issue."

"Unpopular with whom?" Bill asked.

"Californians."

"What about the Mexicans?"

"My boy," Goldman said paternally, "trust me. I've been in politics all my life. The whole thing's a blot on the state's honor. I wouldn't touch it with a ten-foot pole."

"Why not?"

"It would only hurt you."

"How?"

"Politically."

"Who is talking about politics? You asked me whether I would be willing to give some civic service. I said I would."

"Civic service is the stepping-stone to politics."

"I have neither the inclination nor the time for that," Crossen said.

"That is your choice; however, I would not put the art of politics behind me. It is an art in the right hands."

"You just don't have enough artists," Bill said.

"Quite true," Goldman agreed. "Why does the Mexican issue interest you so much?"

"It is being mishandled. We need the labor from Mexico for the harvests. We need some for construction. We close one eye and let them in, and when we're finished with them we throw them back over the border."

"From what I understand, you're not above using Mexican labor."

"That's right."

"And you house them in condemned quarters."

Bill reddened. "I'm not very proud of that."

"How do you intend to change that?"

Bill stood and paced the room. "I *am* guilty of all the offenses you cited, sir. Do you think it is possible for a man to change?"

"I've seen it happen," Goldman said.

"My foreman was hanged on the Nimbus Dam; you may have read about it."

"I have indeed."

"I killed him," Bill said almost unemotionally. "I and the system did."

"Perhaps that should teach you about the ingrained prejudices that exist."

"Everyone accepts it. No one does anything about it. I'd like to try."

Goldman looked at the earnest face of the young man before him.

"I shall speak to the governor."

"Thank you," Bill said.

Bill's presence at home was sporadic but his absences were scarcely noticed: Marjorie's hours were equally full. Under the tutelage of Madame Cheyne, a disciple of Solari, she worked for hours on fingering, balances, runs, octaves, chromatic exercises. She spoke to Solari several times a week and often placed the phone receiver on top of the piano to substantiate her progress.

Although Madame Cheyne, a woman close to sixty, was a technical perfectionist, she lacked not only the attraction of a Solari, but also his warmth and humor. With this woman, Marjorie felt the envy of an aging pianist who saw in her, now twenty-seven, about to begin her career, the very symbol of her own failure. Marjorie once mentioned this to Solari, who dismissed the complaint.

"Don't worry, love, I'll take you in hand a week before the debut. You are doing fine, just fine. The sixth variation is shapeless still. Work on it. . . ."

"Take you in hand," she thought, and felt herself stirring, knowing full well that his hands, his lovely, strong, sinewy fingers could easily span Rachmaninoff's huge chords and could gently hold her close to him, as if spanning another chord equally well known to his fingers.

Solari had suggested a two-bedroom suite at the Huntington Hotel on Nob Hill to be occupied by himself and

Marjorie and asked her to announce her isolation from Bill, her friends and family one week before the concert.

Solari, besides his teaching duties, had also assumed the role of manager, and after Marjorie's acceptance of this arrangement, began negotiations with Merola, the impresario, and made contact with Pierre Monteux, San Francisco's loved and venerable conductor.

It even amazed Marjorie how nonchalantly Bill accepted all these demands, never questioning her motives, never asking about Solari, never quarreling with her about unattended domestic responsibilities during this period of preparation.

"I've spoken to the accountants," Bill said one evening, "and they have strongly suggested that I spend some income or the government will take it in taxes."

"I've heard you're a millionaire, Bill," Marjorie said.

"Several times over, if I can trust the figures."

"That's quite a feat for twenty-nine. Aren't you proud of yourself?"

"Money is only a landmark now."

"But you did it all on your own. That's quite remarkable."

"I didn't, Marjorie. Don't forget O'Gara and Levey."

"You would have succeeded no matter where you went."

"That's academic now. It doesn't really matter."

"What does?" Marjorie asked quietly.

Bill faced her. She had lost weight, he could tell. She was wearing a simple white blouse, a pair of denim slacks. Her hair was drawn back severely, giving even greater intensity to her face.

"Selda keeps asking me that question," he said, "and it's true, I *did* have to think of something to indulge in. That's strange, isn't it?"

"Not really, Bill, that's you. . . ."

"All those years of poverty"—(it was an unusual admission for him)—"and now that it's over, I'm not really aware of it."

"I've never experienced that, Bill . . . and I am not saying that coldly."

"I know, Marjorie, there are a lot of things you could teach me."

She was almost taken by surprise by the intimacy of the conversation.

"Well, did you think of something you wanted?"

"I thought of a house," he said, "but somehow it doesn't make much sense at this stage of our life. I'm gone half the time and after your debut you'll be traveling . . . I've considered buying a yacht."

"Really?" Marjorie smiled. "That sounds like great fun."

"What do you think people will say?"

She touched his arm. "I always have to tell you, darling: To hell with what people will say."

"That's right. You always have to tell me. Maybe you could give me some confidence lessons."

"Me?" She laughed. "My God, the only place I feel confident is in a conservatory."

"I've watched you in those places. They are so forbidding, so cold, what is it like?"

Marjorie looked surprised. "You may not believe it, but 'those places' really make me feel at home."

"They need paint, the hardwood floors need polish, the windows are filthy."

"No, no," Marjorie protested, "they are monastic, perhaps, but there are rooms for pianists, singers, halls for ballet, studios for chamber music. There are skylights, filthy skylights, I admit, but they provide an ethereal illumination, white, blue, slightly yellow, when the sun shines.

"The acoustics are perfect, or as near perfect as you can get. The pianos may be old but they are tuned daily, often twice daily. People care little what they wear. They work and they sit on floors, there are very few chairs. They drink coffee, they chat. Pianists work their fingers, violinists exercise their bow arms, ballet students do stretching exercises. There is talk only of music, the dance. The world outside is very distant. There is ecstasy and despair but only as it relates to work. No one asks where you live, how you pay for the study, who you sleep with. A charwoman may pause as you finish an etude and say, 'I've seen Schnabel at that piano'; the doorman will reprimand you as you leave: 'Don't open that door, it's heavy. "Guard those hands, lovey," that's what Myra Hess always said.' "

"I can understand that," Bill said. "It was like that at MIT. I remember those laboratories, that intricate equipment. . . . I recall professors, men who had Nobel Prizes, men who held great academic chairs, and soon you were part of them. The quest was truth and the path was logic, and if you could measure up, you didn't care about sleep or food or anything else. . . ."

"Do you ever miss those days?"

"I do. I've started a development company," he said. "I've hired some young engineers . . . perhaps I'm trying to recreate that atmosphere."

"But it's an organization for profit, I take it?"

"Yes. It's a little too early to set up the William and Marjorie Crossen Foundation."

Marjorie laughed.

"At twenty-nine you're hiring 'young' engineers?"

But Bill did not laugh. "Einstein worked out the theory of relativity at twenty-two."

"And Mozart wrote his first concerto at six," Marjorie countered.

And after they had gone to bed, Marjorie lay awake and realized that perhaps Bill might slowly open up. She had never heard him talk about poverty, about insecurity, she had not even known that he would observe a music academy, or react to the observation.

She watched his even breathing, felt the presence of his very taut body, and knew that any closeness that would grow from their union would have to come as spontaneously as winter turning into spring. He was not a man who was comfortable with emotion: She had seen today the tip of the iceberg; it would serve no purpose now to dredge deeper. There was a dignity in privacy that Marjorie respected. She could be accused of having the same quality.

She was reminded of a story about Barbara Stanwyck when she was married to Robert Taylor. "I'd wake up an hour before he did," she had said, "and just *stare* at him."

The following morning Bill faced Dunby in his office at Nimbus Dam. Bill was holding a letter and a receipt for $200. He had phoned Dunby and told him to show up quickly or face the consequences.

"That was pretty tough talk, wasn't it, Crossen? 'Either you show up or you'll go to jail.' "

"It worked," Bill said. "You're here."

"Well, what the hell do you want?"

"I have here a signed statement by one of the foremen that states that they paid you off to be away from the dam site the night of the murder."

"Horseshit," Dunby said.

"I have a copy of the receipt that you signed. It's for two hundred dollars."

"Let me see that," Dunby said and Crossen gave him the receipt.

Dunby looked at it and tore it up. "So much for that," he said. "We can both play at the same game."

"Perhaps," Bill said. "I told you it was a copy. I have the original."

"So what do you want?"

"I could go to the sheriff with this and you would be arrested as an accessory to murder."

Dunby stared at him for a long time. "You're one smart Jew," he finally said. "What do you want me to do?"

"I want you to meet me at my attorneys'. You can bring your own."

"*Then* what?"

"I will have documents drawn which will end your allegations in exchange for this signed letter from the foreman."

Bill looked at Dunby. "It's blackmail, pure and simple. Yours, and mine."

Dunby shook his head. "Yeah, you're right. Have the documents drawn up. I'll sign them. I don't have money for an attorney."

Crossen looked at him. He had been a colonel, he thought, and the prison camp had broken him. He had received a considerable sum after his release, but he could handle neither affluence nor liberty. He looked at the man's shiny serge suit, his well-polished shoes and almost felt compassion for him.

"All right," Bill said. "We'll consider it a deal."

He stood, and Dunby followed suit.

"I'm not young, like you," Dunby said.

"I know," Bill said and thought, You didn't have a father like mine, either.

Part Four

Chapter XLI

Yachting has always been a gentile sport. The New York Yacht Club, the St. Francis Yacht Club, the Los Angeles Yacht Club, the Corinthian, the Royal London had simply banned Jews. It was not really a very severe hardship. Very few Jews had a penchant for the sea, and fewer still could afford a sizable yacht and the crew to maintain it.

Bill Crossen's motives for owning a yacht were singular. Ownership, per se, meant little to him; the vicissitudes of the San Francisco Bay were not much of a challenge. A sailboat to him was a thing of beauty because its very shape and substance resulted from the logic of all of its parts. How many times he had looked at vessels at the marina on his nightly walks: sloops, ketches, yawls, brigantines, and he had studied their shear and entry, observed their rigs and roller reefing . . . and he followed these yachts under sail, white, like floating gardenias in the blue-gray waters of the Bay.

But, unlike most aspiring boat owners, his admiration was not that of a sailor, but that of an engineer. He studied water lines and hull shapes and entry and displacement. He watched as a mathematician and a boat became not a thing of beauty, not an object of pleasure, but an equation; and after an extensive search for a vessel to suit his purposes he made a successful offer of $190,000 for Emil Sulter's ninety-six-foot yacht *Argonaut*.

It was only after the purchase that Sulter's broker discovered that Bill Crossen was a Jew, and though the mooring at the St. Francis Yacht Club was part of the purchase, membership in the august society, it was quickly pointed out to him, would be denied.

Crossen cared little about this and was amazed at the publicity caused by his purchase. Herb Caen tactfully wrote that, "membership was not sought."

It was another innocent action of Crossen's that kept the columns alive: Bill renamed the famous *Argonaut*. He christened her *Equation*.

It is considered bad taste, and some say bad luck, to rename a vessel; but it is a crime close to rape to rename a landmark yacht like the *Argonaut*, which had been in Sulter hands since its construction forty years earlier. But once again Bill Crossen (who did not read Herb Caen, or the San Francisco newspapers for that matter), did not give a good damn, and proceeded to use the yacht for his own purposes and that was that.

Henry Levey at dinner at the Concordia Club with his son once said about Crossen "that you must observe carefully not the things he listens to or the advice he takes, but more to the things he does *not* listen to or the advice he does *not* take."

"Imagine what people will say," Hortense started her usual litany, "Bill Crossen buying Sulter's yacht and then renaming it."

"Bill earned the money he paid for it and Sulter took

it. I heard he was glad to get it. Bill's bid was twenty thousand above the next one."

"Linda called, Joanne called, everyone is very upset."

"About *what*, for Christ's sake?"

"You heard that Bill was turned down at the Saint Francis Yacht Club."

"He was *not* turned down, he never applied. It happens that the boat is moored at the club, and they're stuck with that."

"He still put himself into a compromising position."

"Compromising, hell. He had no trouble getting into the Marine Corps as a Jew."

"He's been nothing but trouble since he came into our family."

"I am tired," Henry Levey said, dropping his suspenders, "of defending Bill Crossen. The world is changing, Hortense. San Francisco is changing. Two black couples have moved into the Huntington Apartments. The Olympic Club is open to the public for lunch. The Okies are taking over the Golden Gate Park for picnics on Sundays and a lot of young people genuinely believe that they fought for something in World War Two other than the right to preserve a phony heritage in San Francisco."

"They are not buying ninety-six-foot yachts," Hortense persisted.

"That's right, because very few of them have earned that much money."

"Nouveaux riches," Hortense said. "Bill Crossen will end up broke. Why don't he and Marjorie have children? Build a house? Start a trust for the children?"

"We don't discuss his sex or domestic life in the office. I'd suggest you desist yourself."

"Do you really think that Marjorie is happy?"

"Marjorie is making her debut at the San Francisco

Opera House in eight weeks. How do you feel about that?"

"I am harassed. We are having two hundred guests for a champagne supper that night at the Fairmont."

"Whose idea was that?"

"Mine."

"So don't complain. Forget the social aspect of it, will you, Hortense? Do you know what it means to be in Marjorie's shoes? She's *our* daughter. How many other families in San Francisco have a virtuoso for a child?"

"I am not saying that I'm not proud. There are a lot of other things that worry me."

"Like what? What you'll wear?"

"No. Did you know that Marjorie is moving into the Huntington a week before her concert? Alone?"

"So what?"

"You know how Marjorie is about clothes. I wanted to take her shopping. She said that fellow Solari is taking care of all that."

"People are not coming to the concert to see what she's wearing."

"And what if she's successful? Then what? She'll be traveling all over the world. You know that Bill can't go everywhere that she goes."

"I hope not. We're rather busy at the office."

"Do you like the idea of your daughter gallivanting all over the world alone?"

"Marjorie will be *performing*, Hortense. Not gallivanting. She spent six weeks in New York alone and came back whole."

"We have friends in New York."

"She never saw them once."

"That's right. She was very rude. I must speak to her about that."

"I'd suggest you keep out of it. Stay out of Marjorie's

debut, out of Bill's yacht. Jesus Christ, stick your head in a bridge game. Wrap bandages for the Red Cross."

"The war is over."

"Yes, this one."

But Hortense did not stop agonizing over Marjorie. There were manners and morals that were strictly observed on Pacific Heights. If one was invited to a dinner party, one arrived ten minutes after the announced time. Hortense and Henry's group would have one cocktail before dinner and one glass of wine with dinner. After dinner drinks were offered but rarely imbibed. There were no bars in these large mansions, the liquor was kept in a closet in the butler's pantry and drinks were ordered from the butler and served individually from a silver tray. It was the hostess's duty to carefully seat guests, usually no more than sixteen, around the table to make the mix "interesting," shuffling married partners to offset those who were normally introverted with someone more exciting. The skill in this selection marked a good hostess from the average. The standard fare was a standing rib roast, which the host carved from a sideboard. Lamb chops were popular, so was fresh trout; and at times daring hostesses would try French dishes, soufflés for dessert, even Italian food was served occasionally. For the most part, food was wholesomely cooked, but plain. Mashed potatoes were a favorite as were freshly shelled green peas. The chinaware was Spode or Limoges, the silver heavy and solid, the goblets crystal.

Tables were carefully set on linens often handed down from generation to generation. There were central floral pieces, reflective of the season, and silver candle holders with candles in colors to match the flowers.

One stayed until ten-thirty, perhaps eleven, and the following day chose a carefully engraved card, crossed out the family name and replaced it with, *Hortense and Henry,* and then wrote a short note expressing gratitude in one paragraph and extolling the hostess's originality or cleverness in the next. The word *memorable* was de rigueur.

One sent wedding gifts (usually filling in a pattern of prechosen china or silverware or glassware) and baby presents, and it was considered good form to make donations to a designated charity when someone died.

These customs were rigid and passed from generation to generation. Marjorie, who preferred to retreat to her piano, chafed at all these obligations, yet Emily Post was as much a part of her life as Beethoven. She, like Linda and Henry Jr. before her, had taken etiquette lessons from Miss Dineen, one of the social arbiters of San Francisco society. Miss Dineen who appeared in their house twice a week for an hour and a half covered every possible social contingency that might have to be faced.

Marjorie was taught that only sturdy cotton underpants would do, as well as unadorned cotton brassieres. Slips were always worn under dresses. She was taught how to cross her legs without showing any thigh, she was tutored in the art of getting into and out of an automobile without her skirt crawling up her leg. When wearing light summer clothes she was warned against backlighting from a window which might (God forbid) outline her legs under her dress.

Miss Dineen was thorough and considered "modern." She was aware of the custom of slumber parties and counseled her girls to wear flannel pajamas carefully buttoned to the top. Summer presented special problems. Although she detested the fashion she knew that young girls were now wearing two-piece bathing suits and Marjorie recalled blushingly trying one on for her and feeling that miserable woman's cold hands making certain that the waistband covered her navel, that the seat of her pants would not divulge any fanny, the crotch would not show any pubic hair. The halter was another problem, particularly in Marjorie's case since she was full-busted and had prominent nipples. It could not be worn loosely as Marjorie might expose herself, bending down; and yet if worn too tightly it outlined those nipples.

Miss Dineen carried her duties too far, sticking her hand into Marjorie's halter, trying somehow to manipulate her breasts into a shape of decency. Marjorie pushed the woman away from her quite forcefully, saying, "Keep your goddamn hands off of my breasts," but Miss Dineen was not easily intimidated. She slapped Marjorie sharply in the face and said, "Young ladies do not swear, young ladies do not defy their elders, and unless you modify your behavior, you will be a spinster all your life."

"Yes," Marjorie said, crying, "just like you," and ran to her room.

She was fifteen at the time, and though she was revolted by the physical intimacy, she was too young and too protected to suspect homosexuality in the woman and when she complained about the fracas to her mother, her side of the story held no water. Miss Dineen would prevail, *not* only to make a lady out of Marjorie, but *not* having Miss Dineen in the household was a social gaffe that Hortense would not tolerate. Marjorie was instructed to write a note on her own engraved bread-and-butter notepaper apologizing to the woman; and it took three hated tries for that note to be acceptable to her mother. Again, MISS MARJORIE LEVEY was carefully crossed out and replaced by *Marjorie*.

Dancing school, conducted by Miss Miller, was another trial. She was a woman in her early sixties, she failed to use deodorant, and though she knew the basic steps of the foxtrot, the waltz, the rhumba, the cha-cha, her primary concern, seemingly her *only* concern, was the fact that in the rhythmic exercise the clothed genitalia of the male must not touch the clothed genitalia of the female; and even Henry Jr., who attended her classes on alternate days to Marjorie's attendance, would never forget the placement of his right arm around the back of his female partner.

"Your hand must be placed firmly on the small of her back, below the fasteners of the brassiere. Your hand must never curve around the side of your partner, as you may touch the sides of her breasts," she instructed.

Perhaps the net result of all these rigid instructions, guidelines, admonitions was to create a group of young people whose primary topic of conversation at parties and gatherings was to mock Miss Dineen, to mock Miss Miller; and their revolt, though gentle, was still a revolt, and there were a number of swimming parties in the summer where a girl would lose her halter diving in the pool, there was many a dress strap that fell during a dance, and there was many a male erection that the girls not only experienced through the thickness of their partners' gray flannel pants, but accepted as a pleasant mystery through their solid cotton panties.

Marjorie recalled the fear of her first menstrual period, and the visit to the family gynecologist, who (rather than her mother) tried to explain clinically the fact that she was now entering the reproductive phase of her life. Even Dr. Silverberg, whom Marjorie had known socially, explained this cycle in the most distant of terms, using vague charts in old medical books, and he left it to Murphy, his aging nurse, to show the poor girl the use of proper absorbent fabrics that would get Marjorie through these "distressing days." She left the office white-faced, having received a book called *Growing Up,* which was a masterpiece of euphemistic writing describing sperm and eggs with such finesse, one thought they were rare flowers raised at the Bouchard Gardens in Victoria.

There were mothers on Pacific Heights who were

314

perhaps less rigid in their thinking, who realized that girls would be girls and boys would be boys; but still they adhered to the teaching of the Miss Dineens and the Miss Millers, and though the children did not observe each chapter and verse preached to them, they were, most of them, frightened stiff of going "all the way." They did realize the stigma of premarital pregnancy, and they learned to respect the potency of that hard, throbbing organ they felt on the dance floor.

O'Gara, drunk, once mentioned to an equally drunk Levey that he actually had liked "young Jewish broads."

"Why?" Levey had asked.

"They were always afraid of getting knocked up. They liked to have their cunts tickled, their breasts fondled, they even realized that it was hell on the guy, but they would not put out. . . ."

Levey smiled.

"Don't laugh. They sucked the hell out of you, I'll tell you that, Henry. I've had some great times with Jewish broads."

Chapter XLII

It had taken O'Gara only three months to run into all of the problems Crossen had projected on the Broadway Tunnel. He had not only encountered everything that Bill had predicted but had encountered the obstacles in such an accurate sequence it was as if his doom were projected on the big board of the stock exchange. Many a man would have walked away from the project, but not O'Gara, whose will to show "those bastards" quickly ground him into bankruptcy.

Although all of it was an intellectual victory for Crossen, he had the decency to keep it to himself, a feat that Levey appreciated as he sat in O'Gara's large, tasteless house in Seacliff.

"What now, Patrick?" Levey asked.

"I don't know."

"We could have gone broke together. If it hadn't been for Crossen, you know we'd be in it together."

"That's one smart kid."

"Yes," Levey said, pausing, "that he is, but I didn't come here to talk about him."

"What did you come here to talk about, Henry? It's not a wake."

"I want you back. We've got more work than ever."

"That's good of you, Henry. What does Crossen think of that idea?"

"I didn't ask Crossen. I don't need to ask Crossen."

"You still the managing partner?"

"Of course."

"I'm over the hill, Henry, let's face it. What would I do? Be a bookkeeper, a stock clerk?"

"You saved my ass in Panama once. You remember?"

"Sure, Henry, and you saved mine in Chile."

"And only you and I know why the S.S. *Douden* went down," Henry said.

"Or the S.S. *Corros,* which came to naught."

They both drank hard and tried to laugh.

"There were good years, Henry. Tough but good. We both got sucked into too much shit."

"I know."

"You should have booted Hortense. I should have kicked out Mavis. She was my third one, though.

"I always wanted to build a little hotel in Mexico, the South Pacific, remember, Henry?"

"Yes."

"Twenty rooms, a good restaurant, a bar, maybe run three or four whores . . ."

"I think about it sometimes."

"That would be all paid for now."

"Yes," Henry said. "We'd both be dead. Booze, broads, the tropics."

"What a way to go."

"That gives me an idea, Patrick. A real good idea."

"Go ahead."

317

"Take a trip. A long trip. I'll put you on the payroll. Scout projects, you know the routine. . . . Take six months. Take a year. The tropics, the world, south of France. Find a good spot and I'll visit you."

"You were one of the best, Henry. I'd put you up against any Irishman and you were still one of the best."

O'Gara stood. "I couldn't come back in the firm. Not now. I'll let you know about that trip. That sounds good. That sounds real good right now."

"Don't think about it," Henry said. "Do it."

"I'll call you in the morning."

The two men walked to O'Gara's front door and O'Gara watched Levey's limousine disappear. He walked calmly to his study and opened his desk drawer.

At nine the following morning Mavis reported the suicide to Henry Levey and asked him to the services. At nine-thirty Bill Crossen faced his father-in-law, and after Levey had told him of his meeting with O'Gara, he asked Bill Crossen only one question.

"You would not have let him back into the firm, would you?"

And Crossen said, "No, but for your sake, I'm glad you offered."

Levey turned his back on Crossen and looked at the busy street below him but his eyes were unseeing.

"All right," Levey said, "so we both fight. We both have a Polish background. Childhood poverty. Lots of energy. Good schooling. Work, work, more hard work, but *why*"—and now he faced Crossen—"why are you so *hard*? Already you've had success beyond the measure of most men your age. Is there no room for mercy? For mistakes? For weakness, error?"

"Henry," Crossen said, "I'll try to answer you. Our background is similar, I agree. Our reception in this town was similar, agreed. And yet you stood here telling me

318

that O'Gara said over and over, 'Henry, you're one of the best.' Did you not tell me that?"

"Yes."

"One of the best, despite the fact that you're a Jew."

"He didn't say that."

"No. But we both know that's what he meant. And you're flattered. You feel good because O'Gara, may God rest his soul, thinks you're a good Jew. San Francisco has gotten to you, *too*, do you realize that?"

"It's not that simple. O'Gara was also from immigrant stock. That was the greatest compliment he could pay me."

"Bullshit," Crossen said. "You've forgiven him all his life because he came into it with all these fucked-up prejudices. All his life he'd been waiting for you to prove yourself a rotten Jew. You never made it."

"You still haven't answered my question."

"What question?"

"Why are you so hard?"

"Mr. Levey—Henry," Crossen corrected himself, "we are not *that* much the same. I have demons besides my Polish background. I was in the march at Bataan where you measured existence in minutes. That march took a week. I was in San Tomas prison camp where you measured existence in days. That took four years. I may feel some pain in your society, some shuns, some slights, some cold shoulders, some resentment; but that's child's play compared with what I've been through. I hardly think about it anymore. You think I bought the *Argonaut* from Sulter and everyone thought I wanted to throw that boat in their teeth. Nonsense. I bought that boat because it is a challenge."

He paced the room now.

"You did not survive in that march unless you were hard. There was no room for mercy. There was no room for love, for compassion. You were always within

319

an inch of some yellow-bellied bastard's bayonet, one foot from his spiked boot. One day, one week away from his evil, rice-fed, goddamned brain . . . I'll trade you demons, Henry!" he shouted. "I'll trade you demons any time. . . ."

"Sit down," Levey said and Bill did as ordered.

"I'm sorry," Henry said, "but tell me something . . . I am her father . . . what about Marjorie?"

"What about her?"

"You *are* tough. Case-hardened may be the word. My little Marjorie . . . can she cope with you?"

"*Your* little Marjorie, Henry? You make her sound pathetic. *Your* little Marjorie is brilliant. *Brilliant!* She not only has talent, but she has *guts*. If you think I'm driven, then you don't know Marjorie. Hours mean nothing to her, fatigue means nothing to her, comfort means nothing to her—and I daresay San Francisco means nothing to her."

"Then why does she debut here?"

"You're right. San Francisco means *something* to her. Now. It won't for long."

"Why do you say that?"

"Because Marjorie will explode on the horizon like a Rubinstein, a Pablo Casals."

"And she may not," Henry said, and Crossen looked at him perplexed.

"She may have poor notices. Mixed notices. Then what?"

"She won't. She *won't*. Marjorie will reach the *top*."

"She may not."

"She may not," Crossen agreed.

"Then what?"

"She will prevail."

"But how about you?"

"What about me?"

"O'Gara failed. You were ready to dismiss him. What if Marjorie fails?"

"She won't."

"*What if she does?*"

"I won't leave her. You have my word."

"All right," Levey said, and Crossen now turned to face him.

"I have the requisitions for the Blue River projects. I need your signatures."

"They can wait," Henry said. "I've got to get ready for the funeral."

"They can't wait," Crossen said. He looked at his watch. "I've got to be in Salinas at one."

Levey signed the twenty documents.

"There is another matter," Bill said.

"What is that?"

"The Broadway Tunnel."

"What about it?"

"I've got the bids right here."

"What do you want to do? Break us, too?"

"O'Gara hit all the shit there was. From where he stopped I can go through like greased lightning. . . ."

"No!" Levey shouted and stood facing Crossen. "I don't need that blood money and neither do you. . . ."

"Sentiment has nothing to do with business," Bill said defensively.

"I said *no*, dammit!" Levey continued to shout. He reached for his overcoat. "I am going to the funeral of an old friend. Fuck the Broadway Tunnel. I don't give a damn if they ever get through it. Let it be a fitting memorial to an aging engineer."

"I'll do as you say," Bill acquiesced.

"You bet you'll do as I say. Now get your coat. You're going to that funeral with me."

"I'd rather not," Bill said.

"I am not giving you a choice," Levey said, sternly . . . and Bill walked to his office and got his coat.

When they lowered O'Gara's coffin in the ground, Levey recalled his first heart attack and wondered whether he would soon be buried himself, and Bill wondered whether he, his stubbornness and his irrefutable logic had indeed killed O'Gara. Oh, Jesus, he thought. Oh, Jesus Christ.

He was one of the last to leave the graveside.

Chapter XLIII

Selda had returned from Saudi Arabia twenty pounds lighter, her hair two inches shorter, and seemingly ten years younger. She had acquired one of those deep tans that only olive-skinned people can attain. She had asked Bill to visit her.

He kissed her warmly. "You look wonderful. Absolutely wonderful."

"Thank you. Thank you. I've never felt better in my life."

"I take it you had a successful rendezvous."

"Rendezvous, hell, Bill. I'm getting *married*."

"To Mr. Wednesday?"

"Indeed."

"But what about his wife?"

"First things first, Bubba. I'm getting married. Congratulations? You're going to congratulate me?"

Again Bill kissed her. "Congratulations," he said.

"Saudi Arabia is a female's dream. Not scenically,

mind you. It is all desert, barren machinery, heat, heat, heat—and men. Hundreds of men: engineers, architects, physicists, bankers, doctors . . . and very few women.

"It was a whirl. Hot days spent in a pool and hot nights on rooftop cafes. Conspiracies and sheiks and neon, hashish and opium and belly dancers, speedboat rides on the *Wadi al Batin* and jeep rides into the desert. I hardly ate, I drank a lot, I screwed my head off and turned down propositions four times a day, in elevators, in hallways, at the post office, the infirmary. I loved it. Saudi Arabia, the greatest aphrodisiac in the world."

"Mr. Wednesday," Bill insisted.

"All right. I lost my head but not my senses. We had been in Saudi Arabia for only six weeks when Joseph got a Dear John letter. Isn't that what you called them during the war?

"There had been trouble in that marriage. I was aware of that. Joseph did not write back. He wired. We had four months of guiltless bliss. I've been on a very long honeymoon."

"There are children, aren't there?"

"Two, yes. You think I can handle them?"

"You can handle anything, I think."

Selda grabbed her knees and tilted back on her couch.

"Imagine *me*, I thought I was finished. I had resigned myself to the library, Blum's candies and an empty bed for life."

"He's very lucky, this Joseph."

"Joseph Anderson. A goy."

"You expect me to react to that?"

"I never know *what* to expect from you."

"I am surprised you ever made an issue of it at all."

"My parents would never speak to me again. . . ."

"My parents," Bill said, "never spoke to me either, after I changed my name."

"That's right, I'd forgotten."

"I hadn't thought much about being a Jew until I came to this town."

"That couldn't come from Marjorie."

"Not Marjorie, no."

"How is she? I've missed her."

"Her debut is next month. We touch bases sometimes between the first and second movements."

"You must be very proud."

"I am, believe me. She's astounding."

"And how's *geschäft?*"

"I'm a partner. The firm is now Levey, Levey and Crossen."

"What happened to O'Gara?"

"Went broke on the Broadway Tunnel. Blew his brains out."

"My God!"

"I've opened a second firm of my own—Crossen Development."

Selda picked up his coat. "And you're still going through your sleeves."

"And I suppose you'll be quitting at the library?"

"Not a chance," Selda said. "I am not going to turn into a Jewish matron in this town."

"That's good. What if you have children?"

"I'll have children. Both my parents worked all their lives."

Selda rose and walked to the kitchen. She came back with a tray full of hors d'oeuvres and a couple of glasses of wine.

"I was just thinking," Selda said, "that you're slowly becoming a *mensch*. Four years ago you walked into this house, a scared, underweight kid . . . and here you are, actually *caring* about me."

Bill stood. "When is the big event?"

"Well, we've got legalities to worry about. I expect to

have Joseph move in in a few days. I hope I have enough drawer space."

Bill moved to the door. "When you're ready you can get married on my yacht."

"Your *what?*"

"My yacht. The *Equation.*"

"Where did you get a yacht?"

"I bought it from Emil Sulter."

"The *Argonaut?*"

"Yes."

"And you renamed it?"

"That seems to be some sort of crime. . . ."

"Well, well," Selda said, putting her arm around Bill's waist, "the Cohens have come a long way."

"Cohens, hell," Bill said. "You mean the Crossens and the Andersons."

"Dear God," Selda said, "my poor parents, they should only know. . . ." She looked in the direction of their photographs.

Bill slapped her on the fanny. "Stay off that candy. You look really marvelous."

Selda closed the door and sat on her couch. So much seemed to be happening so fast, but it was all exciting. How much did she owe to Bill Crossen or how much did he owe her? It was not a matter of settling accounts but these were indeed, as seafarers said, the synoptic hours.

Chapter XLIV

Solari had reserved a three-room suite at the Hunting-ton Hotel. There were two bedrooms, one for himself, one for Marjorie, a large living room containing the Steinway that Marjorie would use at the Opera House. They were all large rooms, high-ceilinged, wainscoted and furnished chastely but without distinction. Solari had ordered quarters facing an airshaft, not wanting to be distracted by the view of the Bay. He had arranged with the management to be called only at specific hours.

The rooms were filled with flowers: roses, carnations, a vase full of cornflowers. It was obvious that he had managed debuts before.

Marjorie arrived with two suitcases, wearing a tweed skirt, an olive-colored cashmere sweater. She looked even younger than she was standing in the cool light of the morning in the living room of the suite.

Solari came out of his bedroom and stood away from Marjorie.

"Let me see you," he said. He looked at her clinically.

"Turn, slightly," he said and Marjorie followed orders, and then he came forward and warmly embraced her.

"So pale, you look so pale," he said, and then he kissed her, gently, warmly.

"Come, sit down."

They sat on the couch, his arm not leaving her waist.

"Nervous?" he asked.

"Yes."

"The concert?"

"No."

"What, then?"

"You."

"Me?"

"I am not afraid of you, actually. I am afraid of myself."

"We have seven days," he said, taking his arm from her waist and pulling a typed schedule out of his coat pocket.

"We will study here, we will see the press, we will meet the maestro. We will have a dressmaker, makeup man, we will rehearse with the orchestra, have tea with the concertmaster. There will be hairdressers, masseurs, waiters, chambermaids. These quarters will be a circus."

"I told my mother I'd go shopping with her for a dress."

"Cancel that," Solari said. "What does your mother know about dressing an artist?"

"That will be an easy phone call," Marjorie said.

"And Bill? Where is your husband?"

"On the Blue River project in Modesto. I won't see him until the concert."

Solari said nothing.

"I *do* love you," he said, kissing her impetuously on the lips. "You look like a waif. . . . Come, get unpacked. I'll warm up that piano."

For months Marjorie had been furtively buying night-gowns, peignoirs and just as furtively hiding them in her suitcase. She carefully arranged them in a dresser drawer and listened to Solari playing Mozart beautifully. She could see those hands on the keyboard and she could feel them on the inside of her legs, and she felt flushed and busily arranged her toilet articles in her bathroom, hung up her other clothes and rejoined Solari.

He rose from the bench and walked toward her.

"Sit down," he said. He picked up her right hand and massaged it, then her left hand. He had placed some practice music over the keyboard and Marjorie played.

He watched and he listened, and at times he tilted her head back, straightened her shoulders. She remembered his hands on her breasts from New York, but Solari remained discreet.

They had begun at ten in the morning and they labored through exercises almost wordlessly.

"Looser," Solari would say sometimes, "build the attack, diminuendo, forte, *forte!*"

Over and over again he would sit next to her and replay the passage she had just finished to make a point, holding a finger on one key to isolate it from the others.

Lunch was served, left untouched and removed. The phone was taken off the hook. They worked and worked until night fell, and finally dinner arrived and was set on a small round table. An ice-filled bucket held Moet and Chandon, a candle was lit.

"I think it went very well," he said. "Very well. Are you tired?"

"No," Marjorie said, "but when—when are we playing the concerto?"

"Today is Monday. Perhaps Wednesday."

"Why so late?"

Solari smiled. "We shall play it here once. You'll play part of it for Monteux, you will play it at rehearsal and at the performance. It is too much as is. On Saturday night, at the performance it must sound as if you had simply *invented* it."

"So curious," Marjorie said. "So *new*. All of it so new . . ."

"Here, drink some wine. I want you to sleep well and have some rose in those cheeks tomorrow."

They returned to separate rooms and Marjorie had difficulty sleeping, wanting that man to share her bed.

She showered early the following morning and entered the living room wearing a robe. She was surprised to see the room filled with people and started to retreat.

"Don't go, Marjorie," Solari said.

"Just let me dress."

"No, no," he said taking her by the hand and introducing her to the assembled group.

"Monsieur Ponce, the designer; Madame Leon, Miss Damon, makeup; Mr. Walters, the hairdresser."

Marjorie shook hands and then Solari, still holding her by the hand, showed her an array of long black evening gowns on the couch: silk, satin, lace, chiffon, one more elegant than the last.

"Which do you like the best?" he asked Marjorie.

"They're all so pretty."

"By instinct, pick one," and Marjorie picked the simplest gown.

"All right, put it on."

She picked it up and started to go to her bedroom.

"No, no. Right here."

She whispered to Solari, "I've hardly anything on under this robe," and Solari laughed.

"It does not matter. Come, come," and Marjorie stripped off her robe and stood almost naked in the room, wearing flimsy, revealing undergarments intended for Solari, her cheeks now reddening visibly. It was a foreign sensation at first and strangely erotic, but everyone in the room was very clinical. She slipped the first dress over her head and Solari said, "Sit at the piano."

"Reach for two octaves," he said. "Reach, I said, don't lean," and Marjorie's hands spread on the keyboard.

Solari came over and put his fingers under her armpit.

"Too tight. Much too tight. Here, feel, monsieur," and Ponce's fingers replaced Solari's.

"Quite right. Scissor," he said.

Miss Leon handed them to him and he expertly slit the seam.

"How's that, Marjorie? Better?" Solari asked.

"Yes."

"All right," Solari said. "Now look at the breasts."

He walked behind Marjorie and cupped them.

"I want no folds, do you see this, monsieur? She has lovely breasts," and Ponce took pins and tightened the bodice in the back.

"Will madame be wearing a brassiere?" Ponce asked.

"No," Solari said. And now she felt Ponce manipulating her dress, her breasts.

Finally they gathered the clothes and scissors, the hair brushes, and pillows of pins and left. Marjorie reached for her robe.

"Don't," Solari said, and looked at her, standing alone, almost naked. He walked toward her and kissed her and steered her to his bed.

"Was that exciting?"

"Indecent," Marjorie said.

"Exciting?" he asked again, the fingers of his right hand slowly moving up the back of her leg.

"You're becoming an object," Solari said. "You're becoming public property. . . ." and Marjorie felt his fingers on her clitoris. She was moist, she knew, and she had been moist for hours.

"It is exciting for me, too," Solari said.

"Is it always exciting?" Marjorie asked.

"Middle-class Jewish question," Solari said, now undressed and kissing her lips, her cheeks, her closed eyes, the back of her ear; and Marjorie asked no more as his fingers, his tongue, his lips brought her carefully to climax after climax before he finally entered her and made her writhe and turn and gasp and shout and clutch him, feel him, caress him.

"You make an animal out of me," she said when they finally parted on the bed. "I say things, I make sounds, I can't believe I say and do these things. . . ."

Solari turned and faced Marjorie. He gently stroked her face.

"My little Marjorie. You look so pretty now, so frightened of your own emotions."

She kissed his fingers.

"But it's that quality, that purity, that innocence that gives you beauty. . . ." and Marjorie lay on her back and faced the ceiling.

"Why don't you want me to wear a bra?" she asked, her hands covering her naked breasts, still feeling Solari's tongue on her nipples.

"Because only you and I will know that secret and it will be erotic for both of us. I've told you how important that is."

"Yes," she agreed, because Solari had said so, and she knew how she felt and despite this middle-class morality of which he spoke she wondered how studied all of this was, how much he *really* cared, or loved her; and she felt her hand reaching over and running down his flat stomach and she felt him harden against her strong, supple fingers and he entered her again and she felt herself well up again and dismissed all the doubts and the fears and was grateful that Solari did not suggest, as he had in New York, that she play the concerto.

332

She fell asleep in his arms and awoke in them and then they showered and ate breakfast and began to work.

"What was the largest audience you've ever played for?" Solari asked.

"Twelve hundred at the Chopin competition."

"I see. All right. There will be three thousand, three hundred at the Opera House."

"Depending on attendance," Marjorie said.

"It's sold out," Solari said. "Standing room only."

"My God. That's wonderful." Marjorie clapped her hands.

"Some teachers," Solari said, "work on the principle that with the lights on the stage blinding the performer, with the darkened hall, with the security of the piano about you, playing a concerto in concert is no different than playing in your living room. I have seen great artists ruined by this tutelage. On Saturday night, Marjorie Crossen, I want you to stand in those wings and wait for your cue. I want you to walk gracefully, unhurriedly to the piano. I want you to nod to the orchestra and I want you to sit on the bench. I want you to take all the time you need to get ready, and when it feels right and your fingers feel good, I want you to nod to Monteux and begin.

"But more important, I want you to be aware of all those thousands of people out there, in the balcony, the mezzanine, the boxes, the orchestra. I want you to be aware of the orchestra and the ushers clutching their handful of programs, the electricians, directors, the stagehands."

"You're frightening me," Marjorie said.

"No, no. A thousand times no. You will have *no* fear, darling, because I want you to remember only one thing. No one, *no one* in that hall can play the piano like you."

There were tears in Marjorie's eyes as she finally sat at

the piano and played the concerto. All the months of practice since she had seen him in New York would, she hoped, now come to fruition.

Solari listened and said nothing throughout the performance, and when she finished he said, "The measure of a great artist is the ability to pour all he has learned into a performance. You have remembered everything I've taught you and everything Madame Cheyne has tutored. I've been in contact with her all along.

"The playing is very finished, Marjorie, very finished. I have some questions. Your notation in the second bar of the fourth variation is quarters, not eighths. Your run starting at bar forty-six is marked *brio*, and you have a double rest just before the coda."

"Yes."

"Why?"

"I know I'm deviating. I can change it."

"Don't. Just tell me why."

"I hear a rondo in the fourth variation," Marjorie said. "I see girls whirling on a meadow, their skirts flying out parallel to the ground. The dance stops. I need more time for the skirts to settle into place."

"Good. Good."

"But I can change it."

"No. For heaven's sake, no. You're not a student reading sheet music. You've got to interpret, you've got to make a statement."

"But will—" Marjorie started to ask.

"Don't explain, darling. You don't need to explain, but we must point it out to Monteux."

"My God," she said and stood up, "I must get dressed if we're going to see the maestro," and Solari smiled and walked to his bedroom and escorted the middle-aged conductor into the living room.

"Forgive the ambush," Monteux said sheepishly.

"My goodness, how could you do this, Solari?"

"The maestro and I are old friends. And what do you think, Pierre?"

Monteux was a small, muscular, heavy-set man. His hair was full and prematurely white, his face full, square and florid. There was a walrus mustache and his nose betrayed every good Bordeaux he'd ever tasted. His hands were small and delicate, his dress dandified, artistic.

"It will be the finest debut in years."

Solari poured wine and Monteux raised his glass in toast.

"In French we say, *C'est une uraie famille!* It means 'Welcome to the family,' and; may I add, it is a very small family."

There were three days left before the performance, two before the final rehearsal. Solari had earned his formidable fee. He knew every aspect of the business. He shielded her from second-rate reporters and radio personalities. He made her walk and chose her diet. He prescribed pianistic exercises like a doctor writing a prescription. He trained her like a race horse: a run here, a canter there, but mostly he created and preserved an air of calm. He controlled her fears, anxieties, uncertainties.

Before the final rehearsal he admonished her, "The orchestra is an instrument, played by one hundred and twenty gifted people, very gifted people, who will see in you—twenty-seven, pretty, self-assured—their own failure. Every ensemble player like Madame Cheyne is a frustrated soloist, and the envy will engulf you unless you use it."

"How?"

"With authority. Be pleasant, be warm, be firm. Just as with the audience tomorrow night, today at rehearsal let the musicians know from your first note that you are in command of your talent and in command of yourself and your God-given gift."

Half Svengali, half lover that Solari was, the admonishment worked, and the rehearsal went without a hitch. The players stood after the concerto and applauded with such genuine gusto that it was clear that any envy that might have been there at the beginning had quickly turned into admiration. The players were human, yes, but musicians also. The altar of talent was never desecrated.

Chapter XLV

Although Henry Levey's heart had always been in heavy construction—bridges, dams, tunnels, aqueducts—he could not deny Crossen's wisdom now in wanting to use the company's facilities and sizable assets to enter into more commercial work. The first two shopping centers that Crossen had built with his own money were extremely successful, and Levey could mount few objections to participating in the next five centers that were on Crossen's drawing board.

Monday morning at ten was the time for the partners' meetings, and with Henry Jr. attending purely as a formality, the sessions were usually sparring matches between Crossen and Levey Sr.

"The shopping center," as Crossen pointed out this day, "is unquestionably an economically viable project, but we should go back a step."

"I don't understand," Levey said.

"The shopping center is created by housing. New

housing. Tract housing. I have the figures. Five hundred new residences can support a shopping center. The process begins with a builder getting the acreage cheap, building the homes at a profit, and the ancillary land for the shopping center is gravy."

"You want us to go into the real estate business, too?" Levey asked.

"The money is in the package," Crossen said. "We can do the heavy engineering, a dummy corporation can build the housing. We step in and do the shopping center."

"Build crap like Jonas did in San Bruno, Ferndale? Never."

"If we don't build them, someone else will. I said we could have a dummy corporation."

"There is no such thing as a dummy corporation in San Francisco."

"Who in hell is financing Jonas? Goldman's bank. Who is financing Gate Village? The Hellers. Where is the money for Triangle Homes coming from? Gianinni."

"How about a compromise?" Levey said.

"Such as?"

"Let's build good houses. Architecturally sound."

"That costs more," Crossen said.

"You mean the profit margin is less."

"Correct," Crossen said. "The immortality syndrome does not come cheap."

"At my age that is a good investment."

Crossen nodded.

"Perhaps you're right. Often there *is* profit in quality. Besides, it will be a good challenge for Crossen Development. I've patented some new windows, prefabricated sidings, conduits. . . ."

Bill Crossen had a personal staff of twelve now: three engineers, one statistician, one demographer, two programmers, three secretaries, an attorney and an accountant. It was the latter who juggled his ever-increasing fortune between venture capital and solid investment. At age twenty-nine Crossen had found that the jump from an income of one million, annually, to two million annually took longer than the jump from two million to four. The last jump of four million to eight seemed almost effortless. His engineering patents and licensing of his products accounted for the major share of his income. His development company prospered selling computer expertise to other engineering companies, his shopping centers were gold mines and his share in Levey, Levey and Crossen was sizable.

His only folly at present was the rebuilding of the *Equation*.

He rarely discussed his wealth with Marjorie, who never questioned him about it. Her needs outside of her music were minimal and whatever she did need, she had sufficient income of her own to cover it. She tired of the stories of her friends, many of them malicious, about Crossen's Midas touch. Any given evening at any given party he was reported to be worth ten million, or twenty million; but all these figures were only that, figures, and she was grateful that Bill did not dwell on the subject himself.

"I would just like to be able to tell people to go to hell," Crossen recalled saying to Selda, and though certainly he found himself in that position now, he also learned that great wealth opened more doors, that business could be done with more gentility, that the money he was amassing gave him more and more an aura of infallibility. Bankers welcomed him and reserved the best part of a day for discussion in the most elegant boardrooms. There was never a question about approving loans, huge loans: betting on Crossen was betting on a winner and the terms and interest rates, conditions, all was simply carte blanche.

Suppliers haunted his office daily and young engineers offered their services for almost nothing to be "on the team," the Crossen team, the brain trust, the brain center, whatever was the popular nickname on Montgomery Street that week.

Herb Caen referred to him constantly as "young millionaire Crossen," "multimillionaire Crossen," "tycoon Crossen"; but Bill did not react to this, he laughed off references to his wealth and he was almost as close-mouthed with his family and friends as he had been with Selda in his first weeks in San Francisco.

But his wealth and his ever-mounting string of successes, plus his well-performed public service continued to fascinate the political power brokers of California.

"He is almost unassailable," Goldman said at one of their bimonthly meetings. "He's got looks, brains, a name, money, identity . . . a good war record."

"He's got problems," Almandi said, looking at Goldman.

"Name them."

"His youth for one. That may not sit well with older voters. The Mexican affair may not go down well with older voters either; there's still a lot of hatred. His wife . . . she's an artist, not a housewife. That's bad news."

"What else?" Goldman asked coldly.

"You know how I mean this," Almandi said, deferring to a Jewish Goldman, "but he is a Jew."

"I agree we'll lose voters," Goldman said, "but don't forget that the Jews *are* politically active, they *do* give money. Hitler has changed the Jewish question."

"You may be right."

"And *we can* teach the Mexicans to vote."

Crossen was ascending in political circles.

There was no question that his star was not only rising, it was catapulting. There were other young men in Pacific Heights that were prospering: young professionals, young entrepreneurs. However, no one could match Crossen's ascendancy or momentum or wealth.

None of this was lost on Henry Levey's friends, who never stopped talking about the qualities of his son-in-law, and none of it was lost on the wives of Bill's peers, who surrounded him now at parties and picnics, asking him questions on topics ranging from interior design to promiscuity, as if great wealth conferred omniscience, and no two people realized his popularity more than Marjorie and Elyse.

Marjorie, as was her style, "lived" with her husband's popularity, while Elyse not only teased him about it when they met (now more regularly) at Donen's penthouse, but found it quite aphrodisiacal.

"Well," she would say, referring to a party the night before, "Leslie did everything but give you the key to her house."

"I know," Bill said. "She phoned this morning."

"What did you tell her?"

"To forget it."

"Why? She's a very pretty girl."

Bill looked at Elyse, who was wearing a loose dressing gown.

"I think my life is complicated enough."

"Is that *all* I mean to you? Am I just a complication?"

"I didn't mean that."

"What *did* you mean? I have an investment in this affair, too."

Bill looked at her, but said nothing.

"Is it so difficult for you to say, 'I love you'?" Elyse asked him.

"You can tell that in bed, can't you?"

"I can feel you inside of me in bed," Elyse said.

"That's all?"

"That's all. Wham, bam, thank you, ma'am. That's how you make me feel."

"It was supposed to be 'fun,' " Bill half pleaded.

"It *has* been fun," Elyse said.

"So why are you complaining?"

"A girl would like to feel she's more than just good in bed. . . ."

Bill had returned to his office, and he did not recall how he had answered Elyse. He remembered the word *investment,* and his father's advice that you get nothing for nothing in this world.

Good in bed. She *was* that, he thought. She was beautiful, she was erotic, she not only could arouse him like no other girl had ever done—and she knew it—but she used that knowledge to make herself even more desirable.

And he was aware that it was not all free. It was not all fun. He knew that possessiveness would escalate, that the affair would reach a curve when the pain would overshadow the pleasure, and he knew that his guilt over Marjorie would also increase, and would rob him of more sleep, take away the few peaceful hours still allotted him.

Chapter XLVI

Stanley's Yacht Company in Stockton had been in business for seventy-five years, building the finest pleasure craft for the first families of San Francisco. Their foundrymen, shipwrights, their riggers and caulkers were often third-generation craftsmen in a company where skill and quality were key words and cost a subject never discussed. Traditionally plans drawn by one of the acceptable naval architects were sent to the firm, the keel was laid and usually a year later the owner's wife would be given a bottle of champagne, the vessel would be launched and that was that.

Bill Crossen did not stick to this formula. In the beginning Stanley's was unwilling to take an institution like the *Argonaut* and change it all. She had been originally built by Stanley's. Secondly, plans did not come from a reputable naval architect, but from Crossen's office itself, and lastly, Crossen was a Jew. These were a solid trinity of reasons to deny the space and talents of Stanley's

Marine Yard to Crossen, or so it had seemed in the world of yachting.

It is true the Goldmans had had a yacht built, and so had the Lehmans; and their Judaism had really been no problem, since their orders had simply been placed like an order for a box of Dunhill cigars, and the merchandise had been delivered just as effortlessly.

Crossen's plans were original and contained more innovative marine engineering (all carefully patented) than any set of plans previously submitted to the company.

At first the project was indeed called Crossen's Folly; bets were laid among old-timers about the vessel's instability, the foolhardiness of the sail configuration, the bizarre shape of the keel, the innovative use of beryllium masts, aluminum spars; there was little that the traditionalists could find right with the plans.

Bill almost enjoyed the horror in the eyes of seasoned shipwrights as he replaced a well-varnished spruce mast with one of lightweight aluminum, as he changed the hull shape from a full keel to a fin keel. There was hardly a corner of the cabin or the mounting of a turnbuckle that escaped the engineering eye of Bill Crossen, and only the largesse of his purse (he reportedly spent over $100,000 on the conversion) finally made the local naval architects keep their mouths shut, and repeated tank tests of models of the *Equation* so consistently proved Crossen's theories correct that apprehension turned into grudging respect.

Still, most of the old-liners persisted in stating that what may work in a model may fall apart in reality, despite the mounting evidence to the contrary.

However, the first sea trials of *Equation* left Stanley's men in awe. *Never* had a sloop performed like this yacht. Speeds of fourteen, fifteen knots were reached with ease in relatively light winds, and prediction after prediction of performance made by Crossen (not a sail-or) came true so precisely that all former prejudices and animosities were soon forgotten.

Crossen would come to the shipyard driving one of the company's pickup trucks, still wearing street clothes, and, shedding only his coat and tie, board the vessel. Accompanied by several of the younger men of Stan-ley's yard, he would take out the yacht and use chalk to specify changes in the hull; he would have sailmakers recut his canvas; he would have riggers change stan-chions and stays.

Nothing escaped his notice, be it the gearbox of the roller reefing, the workings of internal halyards, the brace on the steering column. One run in eight coats of var-nish would cause it to be stripped and refinished, one plug missing in the teak decks would be circled, and more often than not he would take a tool out of an experienced craftsman's hands and show him how to use it more efficiently, applying simple principles of phys-ics or hydraulics or aerodynamics.

He was never without a clipboard, a slide rule or reams of graph paper. He tacked two-inch strips of red gauze to every square foot of his very large genoa and studied the flow of the wind over its surface with a sailmaker.

"The luff is too short," he would point out, and once again the sail would be recut, reset and retested.

The *Equation* was ninety-six feet long. She had a beam of twenty-two feet (unheard of in racing circles), her decks were clear except for coffee-grinder winches and a commodious cockpit with a large destroyer wheel (never seen before, either).

Below was a spacious master stateroom aft with full sanitary facilities, a main salon, a galley and three guest cabins port and starboard, separated by a passageway inlaid in teak and ipol. The interior resembled an elegant sleeping car, and Bill insisted on efficiency rather than poshness. Everything fit, including the bedspreads chastely embroidered with the name EQUATION. Light fixtures were imported from Finland for their gracefulness. The galley was stainless steel, gleaming and sterile as a surgery. Only the chandelier, a lovely brass affair, was salvaged from the original fittings of *Argonaut* and hung above the dining room table.

When the final coat of paint had been applied, when the chaste gold leaf lettering graced the transom, and the yacht's pendant flew from the trailing edge of the mainsail, Crossen with the help of a handpicked crew of young engineers from his staff finally set sail for the home slip at the St. Francis Yacht Club.

Crossen had paid the considerable yard bill, he had shaken Stanley's hand; and as the graceful yacht headed down the delta of the Sacramento, old man Stanley turned to his yard foreman, his eyes on the slowly fading transom of the *Equation*.

"Well, that was one Jew that fooled me."

"What do you mean, Pop?"

"I fought him every inch of the way and he won every goddamned argument. I learned more from rebuilding that boat than I learned building yachts for fifty years. . . ."

He watched the vessel fade away.

"There ain't a conventional fitting on that vessel," his assistant said.

"That's right. And I've never seen such a keel or such a sail plan or such a shear," the foreman said.

"You'd think that beam would keep her dead in the water, and she moves like a panther . . . those boys are sure gonna be surprised at the Saint Francis Yacht Club when he sails in."

346

"Wait til he races them."

"He can't. He ain't a member."

"Don't seem right," the foreman said.

"It don't. I agree."

And there *was* excitement when Crossen and his crew pulled in. Some of the members actually left the bar to watch the trim yacht ghost into the marina, their eyes following her all the way to her berth. After lunch a goodly number of men walked about the boat, conversing quietly with each other, pointing, squinting.

One white-haired man finally approached Crossen, who was busy furling a sail.

"We'd sure like to see her. Could we come on board?"

Crossen gave him a hard look.

"If I can't piss in your club, you can't board my boat. Beat it."

Crossen's shipmates looked at each other and at the white-haired visitor. He left and before nightfall the remark was all over the club. It horrified Hortense and sent Levey into a spasm of laughter.

Linda and Hortense had lunch that day at El Prado. Hortense had her usual table near the door so she could not only monitor who was coming but see what they were wearing.

"What can we do, Mother?" Linda said seriously. "Everyone is talking about it."

"Your father thought it was hilarious."

"I'm almost ashamed to be downtown. How do you think *we* feel? Bob is so embarrassed he considered not going to work. Why did Marjorie have to marry that horrid man?"

"I don't know, Linda, I don't know. But she did."

"I used to be known as Henry Levey's daughter and I was proud of it. Now I am known as Bill Crossen's sister-in-law."

"Well, Saturday is Marjorie's concert. Perhaps they'll find something else to talk about."

"People are already talking about her living at the Huntington this week," Linda said. "I hear she's in a suite with that Solari."

"Who told you that?"

"I have friends. Wait until you read about *that* in the papers."

"Does her husband know about that?" Hortense asked.

"How should I know? We haven't seen them in months."

"People will talk, no matter what," Hortense said. "I'm not so sure I want Marjorie to succeed all that much on Saturday. What kind of life can that be for a young girl? Traveling all over . . . Are all your guests coming to the supper after the concert?"

"Yes."

"What will you be wearing?"

"A white dress from Magnin's."

"I'm wearing chiffon," Hortense said. "Ecru."

"That should be pretty, Mother."

"Yes. I wonder what Marjorie will be wearing? I was to take her shopping, but she canceled our luncheon. You know how she is about clothes."

"To tell you the truth, Mother, I don't give a damn what she'll be wearing."

"Now stop that, Linda. She *is* your sister."

"My little sister," Linda said, almost to herself, "always watching me get dressed for a party."

It was quiet in the suite at the Huntington. The piano movers had left with the Steinway to deliver it to the Opera House. The living room looked strangely naked.

Solari had ordered a light dinner for them.

"Have you spoken to your husband?" Solari asked.

"Yes. He was very supportive."

"Tell me about him," Solari said.

"He's complex," Marjorie said. "Brilliant, vulnerable."

"How?"

"He's not an old-line San Franciscan. They never forgive you for that. . . ."

"But you say he's successful."

"He is so successful they resent him even more."

"And you are close," Solari asked, "you and Bill?"

"I know why you're asking that, and I don't know whether I want to answer it. . . ."

"You don't have to, Marjorie." He held her hand.

"To many people it would seem like a strange marriage. I have my career, and Bill has his. We are in two separate spheres, and where we touch it is mostly with respect. . . . I'm not petty and neither is Bill."

"Have you told him about us?"

"No."

"How do you think he'd react?"

"I don't intend to find out."

"And what would you do if I said that I want you?"

"I don't know what you mean." Marjorie was flushed.

"If I told you I wanted you. More than twice a year. More than two nights, three nights."

"Are you asking me to leave Bill?"

"Perhaps," Solari said. "Perhaps in time."

Marjorie smiled. "Now who is acting middle-class?"

"You'd turn me down," he said lightly. "You wench."

She held his hand. "A sweet thought," she said. "I almost feel a touch of sincerity to it."

"Still think of yourself as a little waif, don't you?" Solari asked. "You're going to be a star. A very luminescent star . . ."

"Perhaps. And with no little help from you."

"You're a delightful pupil. . . ."

"Thank you," Marjorie said. "Thank you for everything. I have another mission in life besides my art."

"What's that?"

"My marriage. Sounds foolish for a girl who hops in bed with you, doesn't it?"

"Not really."

"I feel that Bill needs me. I truly do. He is tongue-tied emotionally, but I have patience."

"He must be very special to deserve all this. . . ."

"He is, Solari," she said, "he really is. I hope some day he'll know that."

"The beauty of working with genius," Solari said, "is that it does not end at the keyboard. . . ."

"A nice compliment," Marjorie said. "Will you be at the party?"

"No. I'll be in the wings. I shall see you through the concert."

"Then what?"

"I'll return to New York."

"But what about the reviews? What if I succeed?"

"You will succeed. I can see the reviews already. Take a rest. A month. I'll plan the first tour during that time. And now to bed," Solari said.

"I can't sleep."

"Yes, you can. I'll rub your back."

"That's all?" Marjorie smiled.

"That's all."

And Solari rubbed her back and Marjorie fell asleep, like a child; and Solari thought of Franklin Roosevelt who, it was said, though beset by more problems than twenty men could handle—personal problems, national problems, physical problems—could sip one glass of champagne, puff one Chesterfield cigarette and be asleep. The mark of genius, he thought as he looked at Marjorie, put a sheet over her shoulders and snapped off the bedside lamp.

*   *   *

Marjorie rose early, and though she thought of Solari's proposal and wondered whether she had hurt him, these concerns did not prevail. The thought of the sixth variation did. It needed sharpening.

Chapter XLVII

Henry Levey, trying to avoid Hortense's hectic preparations for the post debut party, decided to eat at the Concordia Club and had asked Bill Crossen to join him, which he did.

They crossed the broad, elegant dining room on the structure's second floor, and both Henry and Bill received many handshakes and felicitations from elegant Jewish families eating out this Friday night. They finally sat down at Henry's table, his waiter brought a martini for Henry, a basket of fresh bread, a plate full of butter balls.

"This is a great night for me," Henry said. "How do you feel, Bill?"

"I'm so out of my element. I simply cannot fathom the kind of talent Marjorie has."

"Well, you shouldn't be so modest, Bill. You're hardly untalented yourself. I've just spoken to Meyer and Kahn and I understand my federal income taxes have never been so high. No thanks to you, my boy, I suppose. . . ."

"That isn't talent," Bill said.

"What, then?"

"Logic . . . pieces fitting into pieces, gears meshing, wheels within wheels."

"Call it what you will," Levey said. "You haven't made those millions out of luck."

"Luck, no," Bill said. "Only a fool hopes for luck."

"And then you're not worried about Marjorie tomorrow?"

"No, not for a minute."

"Do you know what I did today?"

"What?"

"I had the chauffeur stop the car and steal her poster from a wall on Geary Street. 'What if they arrest me,' he asked. 'I'll go to jail.' "

Bill Crossen smiled.

"What a sensation to see your own daughter's picture all over."

"It is strange," Bill said, pulling an elegant box out of his pocket. "I want you to look at this."

Henry Levey opened the leather box stamped with the Shreve and Co. crest. Nestled in a fold of black satin was a lovely circular diamond on a very thin gold chain.

"It's magnificent. I love perfection."

"I'll have it in the dressing room before her performance."

Levey fondled the pendant and looked at Bill.

"I'm very touched by this," he said.

"Thank you, sir. I even bought some tails at Teldon's."

"A yacht, a diamond, a set of tails . . . perhaps I should start looking after your money."

"The yacht has paid for itself," Bill said. "I have fourteen patents pending on marine hardware I designed for her. I've already sold licenses on nine."

Henry Levey shook his head in amazement.

"I'd like to go out on that boat."

"She's fast," Crossen said, "I'll tell you that."

"But you can't race her, you're not a club member."

"They'll come to me. When that yacht boils out of the Golden Gate every yacht club will have their glasses on us, but I'll tell you a secret."

"What's that?"

"I still don't know who has the right of way, the starboard tack or the port tack."

"Oh, incidentally," Henry said. "I have a request from Hortense. . . . Would you please ride to the Opera House with us?"

Bill smiled. "She doesn't want me to show up in a company truck."

"Exactly."

"I'll do it, but it's a mistake. Look at the business we could get with all those photographers."

"I know," Henry Levey said, "I know," and seemed saddened that he could be so close to this boy, and not close to his own. It was too simple to lay it all on that young man's shoulders; a lot of the blame lay on his own and those of Hortense. The fear of poverty leaves so little time. But how long does that fear of poverty last? He had been secure for years, and Bill Crossen next to him was secure already. Would that fear ever leave either of them, or did that fear become the excuse for selfishness? He wondered, and wondered also whether Crossen ever shared those thoughts.

Chapter XLVIII

There were a great number of obligatory social events in San Francisco. At Christmas time the children of the rich had a luncheon in the Palm Court of the Palace Hotel, where Santa Claus would provide them with creamed chicken and small battery-operated toys; and after lunch everyone visited the City of Paris and admired the tree, laden with lovely ornaments and tinsel and lights, that filled the eight-story rotunda each year. At Easter time they rolled Easter eggs on the verdant lawn in front of the Conservatory at Golden Gate Park.

Rich gentile men had their annual enclave at the Bohemian Grove, where they were often joined by the president of the United States, senators and celebrated artists. There, living in tentlike encampments, they partook of libations served in five separate bars and ladies of easy virtue available in motels outside the enclave.

There were always balls and cotillions and coming-out parties; there were the annual regattas, the annual treks to Lake Tahoe, the teas at the deJung Museum and military festivities at the Presidio.

The San Francisco War Memorial Opera House, opened on October 15, 1932, was, however, the city's triumphant monument to civility and culture. Perhaps more than any other edifice west of the Mississippi, this structure divorced San Francisco finally from its roguish gold mining days of a hundred years before, and justified the label of Paris of the West, which San Franciscans so lovingly adopted.

It is a handsome structure, 180 by 282 feet at ground level. The stage block rises 150 feet into the air. Its architecture is reminiscent of Pallado's Basilica in Vicenza. The main facade gives entrance through five pairs of doors to the lobby, and then to the foyer, whose marble floors and vaulted, coffered, 38-foot-high ceilings provide an elegant background for yet another institution: the San Francisco woman. Understatement in dress was the rule of the well-bred. Black was the favorite color, and only the finest of fabrics and the most elegant tailoring would do. These women, whose legs were long and lean from much walking and climbing of hills, whose breasts were small but firm, whose faces were vivid from sea air, whose hair shone from grooming and brushing, these were the goddesses. At night the younger women wore mink stoles while the older generation donned sable and ermine coats. They wore little jewelry, with a preference for jade, as a tribute to their relation with the Orient; some wore small bands of diamonds; their evening purses were silk-embroidered and Parisian. And surrounded by straight, well-groomed, short-haired men in faultlessly tailored tuxedos or cutaways, looking like liveried help around the castle, the women basked in this hall illuminated by chandeliers and framed at each end by broad marble stairways leading to the upper levels of the house.

There is a golden horseshoe of boxes, twenty-five in all, belonging to the very first families in San Francisco. Each of these boxes has a separate inner room, many of them the scene of indiscretions by young or middle-aged scions more interested in sex than the works of Berlioz or Wagner. Below the boxes is the main floor; above them, a grand tier, a dress and balcony circle and the balcony. The house seats 3252 guests: or as any San Franciscan can tell you, one third more than the Paris Opera House. From the elliptical ceiling hangs the large chandelier, twenty-seven feet in diameter, not infrequently watched for motion in a city with an endemic fear of earthquakes.

Although the central foyer a half hour before a performance is a sea of elegance, of high compliments and gentility, the truly rich arrive by the carriage entrance, usually by limousine; and are slightly jostled by photographers, society columnists, reporters and ordinary citizens having a glimpse at local royalty.

It was here that Henry Levey's limousine arrived; and Hortense, looking handsome and trim, her hair a lovely gray, alighted, followed by her husband and Bill Crossen. They were indeed surrounded by the press tonight, but the questions were restrained and polite as were the answers. The opera light shone blue on top of the brilliant black car as it retreated quickly to its assigned space, only to be replaced by the next sparkling vehicle.

Linda and Bob, Henry Levey, Jr., and Joanne were already in the box, and all stood as Hortense and Henry and Bill Crossen entered. The Leveys sat in the first row on somewhat spindly, brocaded chairs, as did Bill. The rest of the family sat behind them.

They made small talk with the boxholders to their left, the Meehans, and to their right, the Haases; and they tried to look nonchalant as they opened the program, which contained not only the usual flattering biography but also a really stunning picture of Marjorie on its cover.

Marjorie had arrived at four with Solari and was overwhelmed by the banks of flowers from friends and all the leading families in the city; and there was one from the conductor, another from the concertmaster, one from Solari, even one, a modest bouquet, from Brogan. A messenger stood outside her dressing room door and delivered Bill's diamond pendant, and though Solari had voted against any jewelry during the concert, he could not, and did not, discourage Marjorie from wearing this present at the performance.

There was a dresser for Marjorie, to ensure that she would have time during the Berlioz to don her black gown, to have her hair brushed and her makeup applied.

Solari had suggested that the intercom from the stage be shut off, leaving Marjorie in silence until her performance.

Her mirror was bordered with telegrams, the messages warm, clever, often heartfelt.

At eight-fifteen she could hear the ensemble players walk to the stage, their conversations muted, and ten minutes later Pierre Monteux, splendid-looking and effusive, knocked on the door and entered. He shook Solari's hand and kissed Marjorie.

"Thank you for the lovely flowers," Marjorie said, "I hope you can join us at supper."

"I shall be delighted," he said. He looked about the room. "You have many admirers," he said. "Always remember this night."

"I shall."

Then Monteux turned and said, "I'll warm up the orchestra for you with a rousing Berlioz," and then he left.

The dresser, a heavy-set black woman, entered and Solari rose.

"Would you wait outside for a minute?"

The dresser left and Solari faced Marjorie. He picked up her right hand and rubbed it, then the left.

"All right?" he asked.

She nodded.

"Lead them," he said. "Don't follow," and then he kissed her and left. He turned before closing the door. "Now we begin," he said.

The black woman reentered the room and mercifully was quiet as Marjorie slipped into her gown and sat in front of the mirror to brush her hair. She slipped the pendant around her neck and felt its coolness on her breasts.

She was not afraid now as she thought about challenge after challenge in her young musical career, a career that even at her present age had spanned more than seventeen serious years. Her aptitude had been discovered when she was only 10 years old and an alert piano teacher at Grant School had made Hortense aware of her child's gift.

Hortense had received this news with curiously mixed emotions, wishing, perhaps, that the talent had been in Henry Jr. or Linda's hands. However, Henry Sr. was delighted and did everything possible to help his gifted child. There had been a succession of teachers, all of them excellent and all of them honest enough to know and say when the child had outgrown their mentorship.

In 1938, when Marjorie was fifteen, Hortense took her to Warsaw where she entered the Chopin International Piano Competition. Hortense would have preferred the event to occur in Paris or London, but dutifully chaperoned her daughter through the exercise, and they returned with a second prize for Marjorie and the memory of her white knee-length socks slowly descending her slim legs during the performance.

Sitting in the dressing room, Marjorie recalled her

parents' endless fights, her father encouraging her endeavors, her mother stating that it would ruin her social life; and still she practiced, and she performed to ever-increasing audiences and ever-increasing accolades.

In 1942, again accompanied by her mother, she won first prize in the Liszt-Bartok competition, usually held in Budapest but moved to New York because of the hostilities.

This victory not only established her among the forefront of young pianists but settled the domestic situation more firmly. There was no doubt now that her career could not be stifled, her father was pleased, her mother reluctantly resigned, and only Linda rebelled, feeling slighted by this inordinate attention to her younger sister; and that rebellion took shape in lording her physical attractiveness over Marjorie, of taunting her understandably jealous younger sister with her own active social life.

All this she recalled now, but still she was unafraid. Of course, there had been difficulties. Passages that took endless practice. Tempos that seemed insurmountably difficult, runs that were demonic, but she had always overcome these obstacles, always . . . and all of that now seemed long ago.

"Five minutes," she heard someone shout through the door, and she thanked the dresser and watched her leave.

Bathed in applause coming from the stage, Monteux opened the door and escorted her toward the wings. Marjorie paused for a second to adjust to the brilliance of the lights, and then Monteux touched her lightly at the elbow.

"*Après vous,*" he said, and she walked straight and regally toward the piano, center stage. As Solari had taught her she faced the audience and the orchestra and bowed slightly to acknowledge them. She looked at the balcony, the circle of loges and then turned and sat on the bench. She pushed it slightly closer to the keyboard and clasped her hands lightly together. The lights were lowered, the house became very still and Marjorie nodded to Pierre Monteux and he nodded in return. He raised his baton and the concerto began.

Marjorie sat straight and felt Solari's hands on her breasts. She was comfortable and knew each note, each passage, like a gardener knows his plants, some delicate, some hardy, some timid, some flowering.

And she realized now Solari's wisdom in choosing *this* concerto, a selfish creation by a pianist composer for a pianist performer, and though she knew that the interplay between orchestra and soloist was as intricate as a ballet, nonetheless it was the piano that struck the themes, the piano that set the tempo, the piano that reached each musical climax.

It was a measure of Marjorie's innate professionalism that she could so distinctly feel the response of the orchestra, and it was also a tribute to Solari that now she felt so at home. He had taught her to read that rapport during the final rehearsal. One hundred and twenty master musicians can easily work for or against a soloist, with the precision of their responses, the warmth of their tone, the brilliance of their tuttis, the crispness of their attacks; but tonight the San Francisco Symphony Orchestra was launching one of its own, and though Marjorie—with one eye on the conductor, another on the keyboard—could not see, she could feel the response of the musicians and could hear the virtuosity of their accompaniment.

She felt the benign authority of Monteux, known for his great melodic flair, and saw in his face a growing satisfaction in her performance. His eyes hardly left her. It was only when Marjorie closed her own in pianissimo

361

passages that she particularly felt his guidance, and as she reopened them, a slight smile played on his lips.

The Levey box was full of mixed emotions, but one thing was evident: Whatever those feelings had been before the performance—pride for Henry Sr. and Bill Crossen, a social triumph for Hortense, a modicum of jealousy for Linda and Bob, for Henry Jr. and Joanne— all these feelings became obscured as they watched Marjorie bathed in light in that darkened hall, playing with authority and grace and masterful professionalism. She became in those minutes a stranger. This was not the girl who cared little about clothes, the girl who would spill orange juice on the breakfast table, the girl who was chubby or moody or quiet; no, this was a performer, and what they were seeing was a poised young woman, an artist of great promise and stature bringing to fruition an endless number of hours of dedication and work.

None of them could have imagined the extent of Marjorie's triumph, none could have predicted her poise, the crispness of her runs, the warmth of her interpretation, the dominance of her tempo, her faultless demeanor, her absolute regality before those thousands of concert goers in her own city.

Bill Crossen's reaction was personal. He knew what performance meant. He knew what professionalism was. He knew what it took to be tested and not to be found wanting, and though he wanted to rise in that box and say, "That's my wife, *that girl is my wife,*" he knew also that Marjorie at this point was not his wife or Hortense's daughter or Henry's daughter or Linda's sister. . . . Marjorie, pulling her hand off that keyboard at the end of a run as if it were charged with electricity, was no one's wife, no one's daughter, no one's sister. She was in a world of her own, a world that only *she* knew and *she* dominated and *she* possessed. She was fitting the keystone into a proscenium that she had built with her own hands, her own sweat, her brilliance, and it fit.

And Bill Crossen *knew* that feeling, knew what it was like to know you were right, that your figures were accurate, your projections correct, your judgment indisputable. He looked at Marjorie and she was lit beautifully: Her hair shone and he could see his diamond caught by the Fresnel lamps, and he could see the perspiration on her brow and he felt both her frailty and her strength, and in a very strange way, he loved her, perhaps more than at any time during their marriage.

Selda, sitting next to Joseph Anderson in the orchestra, also loved Marjorie. But unlike Bill, she loved her as a girl, a warm, wonderfully warm girl who to her represented the quintessential beauty of Jewish culture, of rare talent and great vulnerability. She wondered how much of the fire she saw before her was kindled by Solari and how much of that fire would kindle Bill Crossen.

She looked at Joseph Anderson and realized that he loved her, and she felt warm about that love, and she knew, too, that much of it arose not from her beauty, about which she had never been secure, but from her warmth, a contrast to a barren, former loveless marriage; and watching and listening to each measure emanating from that piano she realized that inevitably the cold were drawn to the warm, the misunderstood to the sympathetic, and she grasped Joe's hand and he responded with his strong fingers, but she knew that it was she who had made the connection, and that it would be she who would continue to do so, but it was a role that came naturally.

Elyse and Lewis Wolf were in the Zellerbach box. She wore a black gown deeply slashed, and she felt Lewis's eyes on her cleavage; and though she *was* serene about her beauty—the almond brown of her eyes, the grace of her figure, the fullness of her breasts, the texture of her skin and the elegance of her hair—this beauty did not obscure an insecurity that night. Yes, eyes were upon her. Eyes were *always* upon her. She knew when she moved that men looked at her and when she spoke, men listened to her, but mostly what they wanted to see was carnal, what they wanted to hear was approval and what they hoped for was a sign of encouragement that might foretell her sexual acquiescence.

She could not compete with the innate talent that Marjorie possessed, and she could not compete with the coolness, the breeding that Marjorie displayed because that had not been available on McAllister Street. She looked at Crossen, four boxes to her left, and he was straight as an arrow, transfixed. She felt Lewis's hand on her thigh and she wanted to scream and despite all her poise and her beauty, she heard her father's voice—a voice she never stopped hearing: "You are a *hure!* You are a *hure!*"

Before the end of the concerto Solari slipped silently into the Levey box and asked Crossen to come with him. Crossen had never met the man but responded to his authority and joined him without question.

"Follow me, quickly," Solari said and they ran down empty foyers and stairwells until Crossen found himself in the wings of the stage, where he could now see Marjorie, closer, her back toward him.

"You belong here," Solari directed and left Bill standing there alone and somewhat puzzled.

Rachmaninoff had written his concerto well. It built and built, nuance upon nuance, theme upon theme until both pianist and orchestra rose to a chillingly beautiful climax, but that was not enough; there were four bars left and those belonged to the soloist and that final triumph belonged to the pianist and not to the tympani.

With the practiced flourish of a master, Marjorie's fingers left the keyboard. The concerto was finished, and the San Francisco War Memorial Opera House exploded, as the *Chronicle* reported the next day.

She stood and bowed to the audience and then to Monteux. The orchestra applauded, the string section tapping their bows on their instruments. Everyone was on his feet, the "Bravos" were deafening and Marjorie accepted the applause with dignity and grace and finally Monteux escorted her offstage.

Someone handed her a towel and she wiped the perspiration from her face. Still dazed by the brilliance of the lights from the stage she shook her head and stared into the blackness of the wings. A broad smile came over her face and she said to herself, "Son of a bitch."

She had not seen Bill approach, and feeling his hand, she collapsed into his arms. He held her, closely, very closely, and then she felt Monteux's hands and once more they left for the stage.

There were ten curtain calls. Only Horowitz had exceeded that, and finally she put her arm around Bill's waist and led him to her dressing room already beginning to fill with friends and admirers.

For the first time in many years both Henry and Hortense Levey held hands and cried. Surrounded by Marjorie's cheering admirers, they were finally overwhelmed by pride in and love of their daughter. Most of the boxes had emptied before they stood and had an usher escort them downstairs.

Marjorie embraced Monteux, and Solari, her parents, her sister and brother, Selda and, to her mother and father's surprise, Brogan. Champagne flowed and even electricians and stagehands came to pay their compliments. It was, as Solari had promised, an evening that could never be repeated; and later, standing in the receiving line at the Fairmont Hotel, Hortense could not believe that Marjorie, her worrisome little Marjorie, would hand her the social triumph of her life. The social pages of the *Chronicle* were almost as exultant as the music critics of the papers and as the critics of the radio stations.

The Gold Room of the Fairmont Hotel could accommodate 250 diners with great style. There were two bars, a small orchestra stage, a dance floor. There were ample waiters and captains to prevent the slightest misstep. The food matched that of the best kitchens on Pacific Heights, and San Francisco, as bitchy, as gossipy, as petty as it could be on the telephone during the day, could be equally elegant, gracious and correct in the evening.

It was often told that Hortense on seeing a homely newborn would never lie, but simply say, "Now, *that's* a baby," a definite noncomment; but here this evening, *no one* would have to lie, no one would have to feign compliments, for Marjorie, who they knew had talent, had *truly* emerged as an artist who would bestow honor on their group, and might well bring kudos to their city. Lines of well-wishers, eloquent and sincere, entered the room; and Marjorie and Bill and Hortense and Henry received a barrage of accolades that they knew were heartfelt, and they responded with grace and modesty and equal poise.

The evening was one of admiration and one of puzzlement. At first Bill Crossen's marriage to Marjorie had been a clearcut case of social climbing. Poor boy marries plain rich girl, all that fit into a slot. His early uncomfortableness in the crowd substantiated this, his quiet demeanor shored up their suspicions about his insecurity. But Bill Crossen had proven them wrong. He had not only succeeded, but succeeded with such speed and precocity that these assessments were suspect. Coupled now with Marjorie's success (that sweet, unaffected little girl, whose dance card was rarely filled), the situation produced a real problem.

Bill's phenomenal success, now merged with Marjorie's virtuosity, made them a couple who were unquestionably unique. They could not be slotted. One could no longer say it was a marriage of convenience, or a marriage based on greed or desperation. It was, as Mary Hillman said to Alice Fels in the powder room, "all an enigma," and Pacific Heights society was not able to deal with enigmas; for unless one could place people into convenient slots, unless one could label them as solid, old-line, pretty, nouveau riche, "on the way down," or "on the way up," then one dealt with a problem that could not be settled over one drink or two canapés or even on a week's cruise to Hawaii.

It was four o'clock when Bill and Marjorie finally arrived home.

"Welcome home," Bill said.

"Thank you," Marjorie said, "and did I thank you for my pendant?"

"Yes, you did."

"Did I really thank you? It's indecent, it's so beautiful."

"Don't think of it that way, Marjorie, it is as perfect as your performance."

"A lovely thing to say . . ."

"Are you exhausted?" Bill asked.

"Strangely, no."

"Aside from the beauty of the performance, perhaps what I found so admirable was your composure. All those people, didn't it frighten you?"

"Solari," Marjorie said, "you've met him?"

"Yes, briefly."

"Solari said to me, 'Remember, Marjorie, no one in that hall can play the piano like you.' I held on to that."

"Good advice."

"I felt very much at home with my piano, the orchestra."

"I noticed that."

"It is so strange, really," Marjorie said. "At first I had an element of revenge in this debut, here, in San Francisco, and yet . . ."

"What?"

"When it was all over, when I heard that applause and I watched the faces of the audience, the victory was really hollow."

"It's not that," Bill said. "You simply didn't find your adversaries at all worthy."

"Perhaps that's it," Marjorie said. "Perhaps that's very true."

"How would you like to sleep on the *Equation?*"

"The yacht?"

"Yes."

"I'd love that. I haven't seen it since you've finished her."

"Let's do it," Bill said, and they changed into comfortable clothes.

Before leaving their apartment Marjorie took his hand.

"I love you, Bill Crossen," she said. "I hear you have a half-million dollar yacht, and you look like you're going to run a streetcar."

He was wearing an old pair of tweed pants, rubber-soled shoes, a worn-out windbreaker.

"I'm going to have to get you some yachting clothes."

"I suppose," he said, looking at himself. "I've never noticed."

"I know the feeling. If you were to ask me what I was wearing when I was practicing I couldn't tell you."

It was almost dawn when they arrived at the boat, and the sun was well overhead after Bill had shown her every last winch, every last stanchion, after he had explained the curvature of the hull and the rake of the mast. They finally collapsed into the bed of the master cabin without making love, and though Marjorie did think of that, she was almost pleased at not having to compare Solari's sexual prowess to her husband's so soon after the former's departure. She rose some six hours later and managed to make some coffee in the shiny, efficient galley, and looking about the sleek yacht, she knew that both her performance of the night before and this very ingenious racing vessel perhaps represented very significant milestones in both of their lives, a kind of cold, clinical summit that might well excuse the lack of intimacy.

But no, Marjorie thought. There was more. This yacht, this *beautiful* yacht was the materialistic report card of a young engineer who was a genius, and her triumph of the night before was the report card of another form of genius.

Bill Crossen had chosen *her*. Despite her plainness, he had chosen her, and last night she was able to repay the compliment. Yes, there was more to marriage than respect, she had learned that from Solari, but there was also more to marriage than the bed. She could not deny the respect she had for Bill. She could not deny the pride he instilled in her. No, she concluded, despite their lack of warmth or playfulness, she felt very secure that she and Bill and their accomplishments were very solid pillars on which to build a marriage.

Part Five

Chapter XLVIX

The world was changing, even in San Francisco. Much youth had gone out of the new generation that fought the war, and many of the prewar frivolities were now viewed as just that. The birth of the United Nations in the city helped take some of the provinciality out of the town and the returning veterans often disagreed with their parents' assessment of Harry Truman as a simple haberdasher, but rather saw in him a decent man working very hard to return the world to normalcy.

But perhaps the biggest change occurred in the young Jewish community. There had been a goodly number, even from Pacific Heights, who had fought Hitler in cold trenches and in searing tail-gunner seats. There had been serious injuries and deaths among them, fighting a man who tried to eliminate Jews from the Earth. What they had been taught by their parents and by Rabbi Gold now all seemed very hollow.

They *had* met Jews not from German backgrounds

during the war. They had argued in barracks and fox-holes and learned of other facets of their religion. Yes, *Zionism,* for years a dirty word in their parents' homes, *did* have merit. Men like Herzl, like Ben Gurion *did* have a cause, a real cause, and the slaughter of six million Jews not only proved to be an outrage, but as they realized, a vindication of their principles and their "religion." Many of the boys from San Francisco had learned what it was to form a *mikvah,* to celebrate Seder, to gain some meaningful insight into Orthodoxy, and to question the wisdom of intermarriage and striving to emulate the gentiles.

And when these young men returned from the war, they left the bloodless temple of Beth El and sought out more meaningful rabbis, more serious congregations. They planned to raise their families in a more traditional religion than their parents had, not only as a testimonial to all their brothers who had died, not only in defiance of their parents, but also to try to embrace a very mature, sophisticated religion: Judaism.

For those young men who were married it was diffi-cult because their wives in their absence and in the religiously sterile atmosphere of San Francisco had re-mained relatively unchanged. But those wives who had done volunteer work, who had worked as nurses' aides or Gray Ladies at Letterman Hospital, those who had labored for the USO and the endless war charities had also begun to realize that their intellectual upbringing on Pacific Heights had been a sham, their ingrained preju-dices were hollow, and they welcomed their returning husbands' newfound maturity.

It was a hard period for women like Hortense who had always shied away from Zionism, from Herzl, Weitzman, the fervent Jews, but they also realized that an era was coming to an end. The endless process of the Nuremberg trials, the new glorification of Israel would make quiet, unobtrusive living among the gentiles an impossibility. It was, she said, a sad change in the life of the city.

Bill Crossen's reaction was different. He needed no introduction to Jewish Orthodoxy. He had been steeped in it in his childhood and had no love for it. But unlike Hortense or her group he did not try to join the gentiles. Deep down he had always felt they were his enemies. His looks allowed him to "pass," he had changed his name for expediency, and he was almost amused at the fervor with which a number of his peers now embraced Judaism as if it were a craze like chess or dominoes. He did not really understand. At the height of his despair in prison camp he could not fall back on his religion, as the Catholic boys did. He could not recall warm Seder evenings or the support of a family around him, because there had been none. Judaism to him was like living in an armed camp, and he had learned to become a guerrilla fighter. He had learned that the enemy was the world "outside," the enemy was weakness, the enemy was stupidity. This atmosphere did not create reverence or solace, but he had excelled in the fight. He had no empathy with Hortense and no admiration for the "new believers." He only knew where the battle lines were drawn, and he knew that the best defense was offense.

At this point no philosophical outlook prevailed. His mind was on the business at hand. He cared little about the changes in attitude of his contemporaries and less about the new stylish "Jewish" climate on Pacific Heights. Money, he felt, had no religion. The only altar money had was more money.

Following predictable laws of economics, Bill Crossen's ever-expanding empire demanded an equally expanding staff, and though Henry Levey chafed at the ever-higher cost of running his business, he could not deny that the profits increased geometrically. It was Bill Crossen who actually verbalized the dissatisfaction that both men felt as he paced Henry Levey's office.

"I agree," he said to Henry, "though you have not actually said as much, that we seem to have become more brokers than engineers."

"That's right," Levey said. "The best time I've had in years was running the Fish Hatchery project. Now I seem to spend more time with accountants than with engineers."

"But still," Crossen said coldly, "we can't bid on a project that would simply be enjoyable."

"Perhaps *you* can't," Levey said. "*I* can."

"That's true, but I have something in mind that might intrigue you."

"Go on."

"In the past two years we have gone from pure engineering to prime contracting to subcontracting."

Crossen paced Levey's office.

"My studies show that with the end of the war, the so-called baby boom will truly materialize. The need for housing will increase yearly, so *that* avenue is the correct one."

"Building those goddamned tracts," Levey said, "may be profitable, but it's neither a challenge nor engineering."

"Quite true," Crossen said. "When I analyze the figures I find that though we're making a handsome profit, so are our suppliers."

"What do you suggest?"

"Our biggest costs are steel, cement and lumber."

"Go on," Levey said.

"There isn't a steel mill west of Chicago, cement is an easy discipline and I have come to the conclusion that Brazil is a ripe country for a fast-growing hardwood."

"A steel mill. You want to build a steel mill?"

"Yes."

"Do you know what kind of investment you're talking about?"

"I do. I have all the figures. The bankers are falling over each other trying to lend me money."

"Sure, for five hundred tract homes, for a few shopping markets. They use the real estate for collateral. That's no big risk. . . ."

"I have the financing for the steel mill. I've even invented a furnace that will make Bessemer's look like the Model A."

"Jesus Christ, Bill, have you ever considered that we may be getting over our heads?"

"No, that hasn't entered my mind."

"You could go from shoestring to shoestring in *one* generation."

Crossen laughed. "I could. There is always a risk factor. There are unknowns . . . Russia, China, I have no control over that."

"I'm surprised," Levey said.

Crossen sat down and looked at his father-in-law. A handsome, balding man, beginning to show signs of aging. . . . "You're sixty years old. I'm going to be thirty. You want challenge. I'm offering it to you. Lumber in Manaus, steel in Montana, cement in Nevada, what are you afraid of? I'm handing you three challenges. Take your pick."

"There are things I like," Levey said. "My homes, my limousine, my trips to Europe, to Hawaii. I'm not worried about my bar bill at the Concordia or my charges at Jack's or D'Oro's or the Blue Fox. I'm too old to give all that up."

"No one is asking you to give any of it up. You want challenge? I'll give you all the challenge you want."

"And you," Levey asked, "you can only be in so many places at any given time. You have a young wife. You can't spend months in Manaus, in Montana."

"Marjorie is about to start her concert tours. She'll be gone more than I will."

"It's none of my business," Levey said, "but how can you sustain a marriage like that?"

"You said it," Crossen said and stood. "It's none of your business."

Bill Crossen had left that meeting and had neither returned to his office nor gone home. He found himself in cabin 12 of the Laurel Tree Motel in Tracy and he did not really know how he had gotten there.

He was certain of one thing, and that was that this room was not some sort of shrine to his affair with Elyse. He recalled asking for a cabin and the manager had said, "I remember you. I'll give you Twelve. You've been there before," and he had taken the key.

He sat on the bed, on a thin white cotton spread, and stared for hours at a poor reproduction of an even poorer painting of an unnamed ocean.

He could scarcely recall the drive to Tracy and recalled even less vividly his decision to make the trip.

He knew only that he had been ashamed of his behavior with Henry Levey, telling the older man coldly that his genuine concern about his daughter was none of his business.

He put his head between his hands and no longer saw the seascape. He knew he was crying but did not know why.

Why this endless cruelty toward Henry, who had been more father to him these past few years than his own father had ever been?

Why, why, this goddamned affair with Elyse Wolf, who was not good enough to kiss Marjorie's feet.

He rose, as if to shake these guilts, and managed to find a phone booth. He called Marjorie and told her he had business to attend to in Tracy, and as always she understood. He returned to his room and lay on the bed and thought of death at the prison camp. He saw the watchtowers and the men who manned them, he saw the dark blue barrels of shotguns eternally aimed at him, and he saw the wounds and death those guns inflicted on his comrades. He saw they body of Rodriguez dangling in the wind and the limpness of that body when it was cut down from the tree, and finally he fell mercifully asleep, dressed, unfed, unwashed.

Marjorie did understand Bill's absences. They had been frequent as her father's had been early in his career. But she was disappointed that Bill was not home now to share the letter she had received from Solari and once more picked it up and read it:

Dear Marjorie,

The accolades you received were not only deserved, but totally predictable. Unfortunately local criticism is never very objective. You are the hometown girl and are accorded a lot of attention. I don't mean to imply that your superb performance could not have withstood the test of any critic. (I am furious that Elder of the *New York Times* failed to attend, their normal boorishness.) However, we have now turned the first corner and are moving down a long road.

Fortunately your artistry precludes our having to work our way through the dreary Midwest to reach New York, though I feel we should play Cleveland and Philadelphia before reaching Carnegie Hall.

For your next concert I am suggesting Bach because his music is very demanding and I have found that eastern critics seem to downgrade performers playing Brahms, Beethoven or Rachmaninoff. They feel that these composers seduce audiences and do not give the artist a thorough test; these eastern bastards are so afraid of romanticism that they would prefer the sound of two freight cars heading into each other to a lovely rhapsody. At this time, we have no choice but to play their game, and you will win them over.

I should like to point out, however, that I do not want to play the part of musical Svengali. Your taste and artistry have now reached a level where it would be wrong of me to dictate your program, and you should never allow me to do this.

I was amused to see the *Chronicle* give as much space to the social aspect of your debut as to its musical importance. I mention this only because I have a very promising young student who is totally without funds, and any help would be welcome.

Ciao,
Solari

Marjorie agreed with the choice of Bach and recalled working her way through *The Well-Tempered Clavier*.

She wrote all this to Solari and she paid tribute to his wonderful tutelage and enclosed a check for $2000 for his student.

She thought about that first concert at the Opera House. Unknown to anyone in the audience, she had been aware of things other than her music during the performance. She had sensed the absolute, almost unreal quiet of the audience, the wonderful support of the conductor and the orchestra, the extreme kindness of everyone backstage. Of course, it had all been a victory, and like a strong opiate it was addicting. What was it, she wondered, that was so seductive? The applause? The warmth, the reverence for her music? Or was it all of these things, all of them in parts?

Or was it that she was in control, in total control, and this was the opiate? Perhaps the only one who could answer that was her husband. But these were questions she did not ask him, nor were they questions she would have liked to have been asked herself.

Chapter L

Linda Levey had married well. Her husband, Bob Seiff was the constant beneficiary of trusts bequeathed by close and distant relatives not because Bob was such a beloved nephew or cousin, but because Banner Foods, his grandfather's company, had always maintained a policy of keeping the money in the family.

Bob had studied law at a minor law school and had passed the bar, mostly thanks to familial influence. A few major accounts such as O'Gara and Levey, a trucking firm his family owned, an insurance company they also controlled allowed him to maintain an office and an aura of respectability. It was Linda, however, who knew that no one really needed his legal advice, that only his looks, his breeding and his money gave them the position they enjoyed in their group.

Linda and Bob were known as a handsome couple; their twin daughters were equally attractive. They had a lovely home on Broadway, they played golf, tennis, they entertained with panache; and until the emergence of Bill Crossen, Bob was really no different from a number of third- or fourth-generation scions in their group.

Linda deeply resented playing second fiddle to Marjorie now, and was further irritated by the fact that Bob Seiff was really a pawn in Crossen's hands.

"We own the majority of the stock in Daddy's firm," Linda said to Bob.

"Who is *we?*"

"Mother, myself, Henry Jr."

"So what?"

"We have the controlling interest."

"On paper," Bob said, "yes."

"Why not exercise that control?"

"Go over your father's head?"

"It seems to me that Crossen does that all the time."

"He *does* consult with your father."

"Is it possible," Linda asked, "for us to take control?" Her husband looked at her. "Legally, I suppose so."

"What do you mean, you suppose? You *are* an attorney. Is it or isn't it?"

"I don't like your tone of voice."

"To hell with my tone of voice. Is it possible?"

"Yes, it's possible. Why?"

"That's all I wanted to know."

"No one could run that firm outside of your father or Crossen. . . ."

"What about Henry Jr.?"

"Don't ask stupid questions. What does Henry Jr. know about engineering?"

"What do you know about the law?" Linda wanted to ask but restrained herself.

"We could sell the business," she said.

"Then what?"

"We could move to Hawaii. I've always wanted to move to Hawaii, you know that."

"Who do we know in Hawaii?"

"Who do we know here? I'm tired of being Bill Crossen's sister-in-law. I'm tired of your being the company legal counsel. Everything was fine until Marjorie married that son of a bitch. I'm tired of facing our friends, and the same endless parties. I'm even getting tired of San Francisco."

"You'll just be running away."

"Maybe I will," Linda said. "Maybe people will like us just for who we are."

"Who are we?" Bob asked in innocence, but the truth was not lost on his wife, and there was more to her suggestion of Hawaii than she was willing to admit. There was Buddy Feiger.

In that charmed circle of rich young men, no one was more popular, more sought after than Buddy Feiger. Blonde, blue-eyed, broad-shouldered and naturally gifted he had breezed through Lowell High and Stanford with little effort and much merriment.

He had followed in his father's footsteps and studied medicine, receiving his degree in the early years of the war. He was commissioned a first lieutenant in the Navy and his family's wealth and influence landed him a safe berth on Oahu, where he continued to study and received a degree in obstetrics and gynecology.

He returned after the hostilities with lieutenant-commander stripes and Lani, his wife, a lovely, long-limbed girl whose mother was English and whose father was Hawaiian.

They were accepted by their peers, but not by the older generation, and though they lived in a stately house, skied, and traveled and socialized as hedonistically as the rest of the group, Lani, a sensitive girl, felt the slights and the innuendos of Pacific Heights. After inadvertently hearing her father-in-law refer to her as "that pineapple," she wrote a terse note to her husband and returned to the islands.

Rejection was not an experience that Buddy Feiger was used to and he handled it poorly. He did not return immediately to Hawaii but pursued a series of young women in San Francisco.

Linda Levey Seiff was one of his conquests (actually an easy one) and they had spent a series of tepid sexual afternoons at the Alta Mira Hotel in Sausalito, in a small, poorly furnished room with a magnificent view of San Francisco across the Bay.

Linda was ripe, truly ripe. Dissatisfied with the professional lassitude of her husband, overshadowed by the ever-growing notoriety of her sister and brother-in-law, she was rebellious and eager for this alliance with Buddy.

It was only the incident with Elyse Wolf combined with the constant harping of his parents that finally forced Buddy to return to Oahu. But he found on his arrival that Lani had entered her own group and seemed reluctant to continue their marriage.

Linda had treasured a letter from Buddy Feiger. She had read one passage over and over again.

". . . and I shall never forget you, in your white half-slip after our lovemaking in that silly room at the Alta Mira. My life is so turbulent now, I cannot make any firm commitments. However, should you find a way to visit the Islands, or perhaps decide to move here, I can only say I love you very much. I am practicing here and have found a lovely home overlooking Kahala . . ."

The letter was carefully stowed in Linda's wallet. She knew the impracticality of moving her family to Hawaii, of risking divorce, of hoping for a positive decision from Buddy Feiger, and yet all the practicality of her life was also becoming increasingly unattractive. She felt no remorse in planting seeds.

Chapter LI

One Monday midmorning, Elyse Wolf returned home early from a canceled seminar in Berkeley. She parked her Packard convertible on the graveled driveway and walked briskly into the house. Perhaps it was the odor that made her immediately suspicious: cheap, heavy perfume, the scent of oleander or musk. An overturned bourbon bottle lay on the carpet, surrounded by the stain of its contents. She ran upstairs and found her son, almost two years old now, standing at the doorway of her bedroom staring at his father naked in bed, a heavy-set black woman astride him. She doubted whether Lewis had noticed her, she saw only the black, naked buttocks of the girl pumping up and down, another opened bourbon bottle in her hand. She scooped up her son and ran past her father-in-law's room where two black girls, also naked, surrounded the old man, one performing fellatio, the other's ample breasts caressing the older man's face.

There were tears in Elyse's eyes, but she didn't know whether they stemmed from pity or hatred. She walked into her son's room. His governess was nowhere about. She sat her son on his little bed, gathered what she could of his belongings, and, using the backstairs of the house, ran to her car, placed young Lewis beside her on the front seat and drove out of the estate.

She drove quickly, seeing none of the landscape, the Bay, the airport. She kept one hand on her youngster, deftly maneuvering her large car in and out of traffic. She left her car with the attendant on the portico of the Fairmont Hotel and, carrying her son, she walked toward the private elevator flanked by two small evergreens in stone urns. She found a key in her purse and when the elevator stopped, found herself in the elegant foyer of Arthur Donen's penthouse apartment.

She placed young Lewis, who was strangely quiet, on the large double bed in the master bedroom, removed her shoes, withdrew a pillow from under the bedspread and put her back against the ornately carved teak headboard. She looked at her watch. It was two in the afternoon. She felt beads of perspiration on her forehead, her pulse was racing; she watched her son tossing fitfully on the slippery satin spread and picked him up to rock him gently to sleep, a feat she finally accomplished.

She picked up the phone. She hired a nurse for the child and after her arrival placed the youngster in another bedroom with the elderly woman and returned to sit on the bed.

She had known that her father-in-law indulged in whores, but could not fathom that he would consort with black girls, particularly in his own home. She could not understand Lewis, her own husband, who, she knew, was guilty of every hedonistic sin except infidelity. The sight of his white, moist, erect penis appearing and disappearing between those black thighs—No! she cried silently. No, goddamnit, *no!* Again she looked at her watch. It was three o'clock now. For the first time since she had entered Stanford she wanted to call her mother, but she did not touch the phone.

She walked to her son's room and asked the nurse to order dinner for herself and her young charge. She kissed the boy and announced she would be leaving for a short while.

She returned to the bedroom alone and stared at the ceiling. Again she looked at her watch. It was four-thirty and she recalled Crossen's statement, "You have to make a decision."

She picked up the phone and called him.

"Bill," she said, "how about a favor?"

"Name it," he said cheerfully.

"Have supper with me. Tonight. Is Marjorie in town?"

"She's in Cleveland, making arrangements for her concert."

"Then no excuses," Elyse said.

"No excuses. Where? And when?"

"The usual place. As soon as you can get here. How about eight o'clock?"

"That will be fine," Bill said and hung up. He was learning that an affair, no matter how sophisticated, at some point would be demanding. He had noticed the stridency in her voice and almost feared their meeting tonight.

Elyse put down the phone and visited her son and the nurse.

"How was dinner?" she asked.

"Fine, ma'am," the nurse answered. "He ate everything."

"Good," Elyse said, "I'll be having guests. Are you quite comfortable here?"

The nurse understood and nodded.

"Good night." Elyse closed the door behind her and

returned to Donen's bedroom. She ordered dinner: soup, salad, steak, champagne on ice, a good red wine, and asked to have it all in her kitchen at seven-thirty. She toyed with lights and lit candles and ran a bath.

Bill Crossen downed a quick martini at home, an act totally foreign to him. He had had his fill of emotion these past weeks and questioned his wisdom in seeing Elyse. She had sounded distant, almost frantic. He felt like phoning Marjorie, but he didn't. He had nothing to fear except himself, he knew, dressing slowly, haphazardly.

Elyse, like an actress or a model, knew not only her best features, but also knew what would accentuate them. She had dressed quickly but decisively, and the front door was open when Bill arrived. Elyse was dressed in a long black silk skirt, a simple harlequin-patterned scarf tied over her bosom. She seemed smaller, frailer than usual. She was in stocking feet, her features lit only by candles and by outside spots illuminating the foliage around the penthouse.

"Good evening," he said, bending down to kiss her. "You smell wonderful."

"Thank you." She walked toward the coffee table. "A drink?" she asked.

"Just some wine."

She made a martini nevertheless and handed it to Bill. "Wine comes later. Cheers."

"Cheers," Bill said, clinking glasses. "I must say"—he turned Elyse in a circle holding her elbow—"that is the most ingenious use of a scarf I have ever seen."

She pulled one corner away from her breast and asked, "Am I showing?"

"You are now."

"I see." She released the material. "Hard day at the office?"

"They're all hard."

Bill heard the faint cry of a child, and Elyse looked up.

"My son," she said. "He must be having a nightmare."

"He's here?"

"Yes, he is with a nurse. Why don't you take off your coat?"

They chatted idly in short, stilted bursts of conversation. Bill had another martini, then hors d'oeuvres. He watched Elyse walk to the kitchen and return with two iced bowls of vichyssoise.

"Light those candles, will you?" Bill obeyed and they sat down for dinner. She had poured wine, and the lights of the Golden Gate Bridge, orange and brilliant, looked like a flaming necklace.

"What's this about?" Bill finally asked bluntly.

"I left Lewis today," she said. "How about a toast?"

She raised her glass, but Bill did not follow suit. "I don't understand."

"You will when I tell you."

"And when is that?"

"Eat your soup."

She rose and wheeled in the rest of the dinner.

Bill ate, but warily. He looked out at the bridge and watched the traffic crossing the Bay.

Elyse poured more wine. "You haven't eaten your dessert," she reprimanded him.

"I don't eat dessert."

"They're only fresh strawberries. Here, they probably cost three dollars apiece."

"The poor starving children in China," Bill said.

She rose, half threw herself on a large brocaded couch and patted the seat next to her with her hand.

Bill joined her and Elyse bent forward to pour two brandies in large, very thin snifters. She handed one to Bill. Her left breast had slipped out of the scarf and she slowly covered it with the flimsy silk.

She kissed him. Fully on the lips. Openly, warmly, gently, and she felt his arms go about her naked back.

He kissed her neck, more quickly, more firmly and she held his jaw with one hand.

"Slowly," she said, "slowly. I'm not going away."

He turned her and placed her on his lap. He could see the candles reflected in the opalescent darkness of her eyes, the light dancing about the edges of her hair.

"It is all done with one knot," Bill said, undoing the scarf.

"A clove hitch, engineer."

"No. A bowline."

His hands felt that back, and he looked at her firm breasts, perfect, with pliant nipples surrounded by slightly darkened areolas.

"Why this royal treatment?" Bill asked, sitting up on the couch.

"Why, have I treated you so shoddily before?"

"Indeed not."

Elyse covered her naked breasts with her arms. She looked at him and said, "I *need* you."

"Why?"

"I came home unexpectedly early today. There was the smell of cheap perfume and spilled bourbon in the house. And there was Lewis, *my* Lewis in *our* bed with a fat-assed nigger on his belly, his goddamned cock right up her big, black cunt."

"Stop it, Elyse."

"No. There was more. Our son, standing outside the door, his finger in his mouth, watching those obscene gyrations . . . dumbstruck. I picked him up and raced down the hall, and there was his grandfather with two more black whores. . . ."

Her tears were hot now and she burrowed her face in his lap.

"For years," she said, reaching for the glass of brandy, "for years, I've been playing games with you— cockteasing, bitchy, rotten goddamned games. I've stalked you and watched you turn from an insecure New York kid to a man who has licked *all* the hurdles. I've heard every goddamned bit of gossip about you and you've not only prevailed, you've surpassed them all."

"Enough, Elyse," Bill said. "Enough."

"Not enough. No, not enough. I know every one of those sons of bitches who gave you a hard time. I should. I slept with half of them before I got married.

"Only Lewis Wolf the Third, the warm, lovable, charming, drunk, *perverted*, goddamned Lewis Wolf the Third asked me to marry him."

She sat up, half-hysterical, half-drunk. "*He* asked me, and I said, yes. Yes. I wanted the view. I, too, wanted that fucking view of the Bay. . . ."

She found her black silk skirt and covered herself. "I kept my bargain. I played every game that Lewis wanted to play, *every* game his father wanted to play and all the time I loved you. I loved you, Bill Crossen. Do you know that?"

"No," he said honestly, "I didn't know that."

"I did, yes, but I didn't have the guts, or the integrity to tell you, to tell Lewis. There would always be time, and in the meantime there would always be another trip, another party, another toy, another bauble . . . and when I was ready . . . when I was good and ready . . ."

"Then what?"

"We're going to bed," Elyse said, standing.

"Elyse . . ."

"We're *going to bed* . . . now." She pulled him off the couch and pushed him toward the bedroom.

"I've had the greatest teacher in the world," she said as she poured brandy on his chest and lapped it up. "Use both hands," she said, "no, raise my back, there," and she reached a climax and another and so did Bill. She clung to him and said, "No, you're not going to wash up. You're not taking my fluids or your fluids from your body."

It was dawn when Bill Crossen fell asleep and it was three o'clock in the afternoon when he awoke and it was the first time in his life that he had missed a day of work.

There was coffee and a glass of tomato juice by his bedside. Elyse, dressed in a thin white robe bordered by navy blue piping, sat primly at the foot of the bed.

Crossen raised himself and sipped the coffee. He could see her nakedness right through the light woolen robe. He closed his eyes and saw her breasts, her thighs, her belly as he had the night before. He remembered the smells, the sounds, the feelings.

He looked at her. "You are one hell of a girl," he said.

"I've been told that before." She frowned.

He sat up in bed. "Now what?"

"You tell me," Elyse said.

"You can't leave Lewis."

"Why?"

"They'll eat you alive."

"Who is they?"

"His crowd. *Our* crowd. Pacific Heights. You can't threaten them. All the cards are in their deck. Stacked."

"Will you help me?"

"Of course."

"How much?"

"How much help do you want?"

"All I can get," she said and paused, thinking. "Why should it bother me that they were black?" Elyse wondered aloud. "How would I have felt if that house were filled with the prettiest girls in our group?" She looked past Crossen. "Lewis Wolf the Third has taught me that my services are no more valuable than any garden-variety whore's."

"Why must you torture yourself with that? Why?"

"Put yourself in my shoes," Elyse almost screamed.

"I am trying, but it still makes no sense."

"What doesn't?"

"Divorcing Lewis Wolf."

"What else can I do?" Elyse pleaded.

Bill rose, showered and shaved, and returned to the bedroom fully clothed.

"If you decide to go through with your plans," he said quietly, "you know I will support you all the way."

Elyse nodded and kissed him halfheartedly as he left.

He was not a man to push, she realized. He was not someone you could bully into marriage. She should tell him to go to hell, but she knew she wouldn't. Elyse and her son returned to Menlo Park.

Chapter LII

The Spring Regatta was a great traditional day on San Francisco Bay. It was this day that each yacht club entered their finest, fastest racers for the Farallon Islands Race. The course took them out of the Bay under the Golden Gate Bridge to the islands and back. It was a forty-mile sail and a lovely sight to behold from the hills surrounding the Bay.

Bill and Marjorie had invited Elyse and Lewis, the Lehmans, the Goldmans, the Blums and the Cohens, all young couples with sailing experience. Even though Bill Crossen did not belong to any yacht club, and could not officially enter the race, he could not be stopped from being on the starting line and he could not be prevented from racing his yacht. San Francisco Bay and the Pacific Ocean were in the public domain.

Everyone in racing knew about the *Equation,* and everyone was anxious to see what the old *Argonaut* could do after her bizarre conversion; and Bill Crossen did not disappoint them. Other famous yachts like the *Orient, Nepenthe, Summerwind* or *Swan* bobbed like nervous ballerinas waiting for the starting gun, but once the race began, *Equation* quickly showed her transom to everyone. She was faster downwind, crosswind and upwind, and the distance between her and *Summerwind,* the nearest contender, became so great as to prove embarrassing.

"*Equation,*" the *Chronicle* reported the next day, "an unofficial and unqualified contender, broke every record set for seventy-five years in San Francisco Bay and Bill Crossen, her owner-designer, should seriously consider the America's Cup next year."

Crossen had been intense during the race. He looked upon sailing as he did everything else, a battle, a mathematical or logical challenge, an engineering obstacle, and only after the yacht was safely moored again at its slip did he finally accept congratulations from Marjorie and his guests and indulge in the proffered French champagne.

It was a good party and all the participants shared in Crossen's pride in having won the race. Even members of the St. Francis Yacht Club came to the slip to offer congratulations.

"You can win," Elyse Wolf said, gracefully stretched out on the foredeck as crisp and beautiful as ever. "You can win, but you can't beat them."

"What do you mean?"

"Alice Lehman looked at the embroidered bedspreads and said, 'Gauche.' "

"Fuck Alice Lehman."

"Bill Goldman commented on the fact that the price tag was still on the sole of your deck shoes."

Bill Crossen raised his leg and looked at the sole of his shoe.

"He's right," Crossen said. "At least I bought them with my own money."

"That's true," Elyse said, "but that doesn't count."

"It all depends who's keeping score."

"Then what do you think of me?" Elyse was slowly getting drunk. "Is *my* price tag showing?"

"No, but your underpants are."

"Well," Elyse said, making no attempt to cover herself, "that's my only inventory."

"It's not," Bill said, "but you choose to think it is."

"What could I do? What could I *really* do?"

"You've got a brain, a good brain. Use it."

"And who am I going to prove it to? Lewis?"

"Prove it to yourself."

"Is that what you're doing?"

"Perhaps. It beats worrying about monograms on bedspreads."

"That may be true."

"It's difficult, I suppose," Bill said, "for a girl from McAllister Street to be a hedonist?"

"You're right," Elyse said. "Even that takes years of training. The Wolf boys have lots of experience."

"Then you have to make a decision, Elyse."

"You're right," she said. "I must admit, you're dead right."

Marjorie approached them with an open bottle of champagne and refilled their glasses.

"That was quite a race," Elyse said to Marjorie.

She smiled. "I expected no less. My husband is a winner."

"A winner," Elyse thought watching Bill, his arm about Marjorie, guiding her aft to the cockpit, "who is a winner? *You* are the winner, Marjorie," she thought. "You with your talent, your self-assurance, with your husband, *you* are the winner," and suddenly she felt once more the girl from McAllister Street as she looked at them all, standing in the cockpit on this obscenely large yacht as if it were their due, as if regattas and English hunts and homes on Broadway were all their due.

She pleaded a headache and asked Lewis to drive her home. It was she who picked up the gin, and she half filled a glass and drank quickly.

"What are you doing, darling?" Lewis asked.

"Drinking. Drinking gin. I want to get drunk and I want you to screw my brains out."

Lewis looked at her curiously, unbuttoning his shirt.

"The best offer I've had all day," he said, smiling, and walked upstairs.

It was shortly after the race that Bill appeared in Selda's library and asked to speak to her alone. At twelve o'clock she locked the door for lunch and they faced each other across a light oak table.

"I read about your race," Selda said. "Congratulations!"

"Thank you."

"Always the fighter, eh, Bill?"

"Always the fighter," Bill repeated almost to himself. "I wish that were true."

"Troubles," Selda asked. "You got troubles?"

Bill looked at her, at that incredibly kind, warm, loving face.

"Bill *has* got troubles. . . ." he admitted.

"Is it Marjorie? Elyse?"

"No, no. It's neither one."

"What troubles?"

He spoke as if he were in a trance. "A few nights ago I found myself in a motel room in Tracy. I finished Nimbus Dam months ago and have no more business in Tracy. . . ."

Selda said nothing.

"I had some words with Levey. I was actually unkind to him, and he doesn't deserve unkindness from me."

Bill stopped and wiped perspiration from his brow. "And then I was in that motel room. I couldn't tell you how I got there, or what I was thinking when I drove to Tracy, I was just *there* and I didn't know why or how I got there. . . ."

"Amnesia," Selda said.

"Perhaps . . ."

"It's not an uncommon symptom for men who've been to war."

"Maybe not," Bill said resignedly.

"You should get help."

"What kind of help?"

"A psychiatrist."

"No," Bill said almost too quickly.

"Don't dismiss it so quickly. Lots of my friends see psychiatrists. I did for months after my parents were killed."

"No," Bill repeated. "I'm not going to open that Pandora's box to anybody. . . ."

Selda looked at him and put her hand over his. "You asked me. I told you, I'm just a librarian."

Bill rose quickly and crossed the room away from Selda.

"I'm sorry," he said. "I'm sorry I brought it up. You won't say anything to anybody? Will you?"

"Sit down," Selda half commanded. "No," she said. "I won't say anything to anybody. You know that. But why won't you let anybody help you? You don't have to be *meshugge* to see a doctor. . . ."

"I know," Bill said. "I know all that. They made the same suggestion when I was discharged at Letterman General Hospital."

Bill's eyes roamed about the small library and Selda watched him.

"They mentioned you in *Fortune* again," she said. "Also the *Wall Street Journal* . . ."

"So I am told," Bill said abstractedly. "I *can't!*" he shouted. "I can't see a psychiatrist."

"Don't dwell on that," Selda said. "Dwell on Saturday."

"What's Saturday?"

"*My* wedding at *your* house."

"I haven't forgotten . . . I'm sorry to have bothered you."

"Stop it, Bill," Selda said. "Kiss me."

Bill did as asked.

"*Really* kiss me," and he tried.

"That's better. Order the lox and the champagne. No, order roast beef and champagne—I keep forgetting I'm marrying a goy."

"I'll order both," Bill said, standing and leaving hurriedly.

When the door had closed Selda buried her head in her arms. "I won't open that Pandora's box to anybody," Bill had said. Pandora's box, she thought. If you won't open it, Bubba, it will explode.

Chapter LIII

There was one love that Bill and Marjorie truly shared and that was a love for Selda, and Marjorie had overseen a quiet, elegant wedding for her and Joseph Anderson. They had asked for an unheralded union, but one that would include her groom's two children. Marjorie had borrowed her father's home in Menlo Park and the mansion with its sweeping gardens was a beautiful setting for the short ceremony performed by a municipal judge.

The ceremony was very informal and warm, and the following morning Marjorie got up early and found Selda in the loggia off the living room.

"This is so peaceful," Selda said. "It was a wonderful wedding. We are so grateful."

"We loved it ourselves," Marjorie said, "and why are you up so early? It's your wedding night."

Selda laughed. "We're hardly virgins. With Joseph's children around I don't want to play vamp."

Selda put her hand on Marjorie's. "And how are things with you?"

"Fine."

"Really fine?" Selda's look was penetrating.

"Yes," Marjorie said, staring into space, "really fine."

"You're getting famous, Bill's getting rich . . . are you really happy?"

"Bill and I don't go around asking each other whether we're really happy."

"You can't keep running, running, both of you. . . ."

"I don't feel I'm running, Selda. I don't think that Bill feels he's running."

"I am not trying to pry. I hope you know that. I love you both."

"I understand," Marjorie said.

"Your piano teacher . . ."

"Solari?"

"Yes. Do you still see him?"

"I have once," Marjorie said. "Before the debut."

"And you'll see him again?"

"I presume I will. You were the one who told me to enjoy it, Selda, and I have. You told me to take it for what it is and I have."

"That's good. And you have no regrets?"

"No. Sometimes I wish that Bill were warmer, more responsive . . ."

"Then tell him."

"I can't."

"Why not?"

"Bill is fighting something. I don't know what. It's no longer San Francisco, I'm sure of that."

"What, then?"

"I honestly don't know. There is a wall about him. Sometimes it opens slightly, but it can't be forced open, it can't be pried. . . . All I can give him now is patience."

"He's worth all that?"

"Oh, yes," Marjorie said with great conviction, "he is definitely worth all that."

Selda shook her head and smiled.

"If you get in trouble just come over. I still settle everything with chicken soup."

Joe Anderson's children appeared. A boy eight, a girl ten, both towheaded and shy, and Selda gathered them to her.

"Well, now you've been on a honeymoon," she said, and the children blushed.

"Have you got any breakfast for these Indians," Selda asked, and Marjorie rose and led them out by the hand.

Bill Crossen came into the room and sat next to Selda.

"That's quite a family."

"Yes," Selda said. "And quite a wife."

"You?"

"No, Bubba, not me. Marjorie."

"Yes, quite a wife."

"Do you ever think about children?"

Bill looked troubled. "No."

"You should."

"I know," Bill said, patting her knee, "we should."

"Here I am, the loudmouth cousin. The two of you have given us a wonderful wedding and I've got to put in my two cents' worth. Tell me to shut up."

"We love you, Selda. You know that."

"I know, I know. The great buttinsky. Jesus Christ, Bill Crossen, tell me to go to hell. If I don't understand, that doesn't mean it isn't right."

"Maybe it is. Maybe it isn't. Come, let's have some breakfast."

"What is in your craw, Bill?" Selda asked seriously, looking at her cousin.

"I don't know what you mean."

"You have everything a man could want, and still . . ."

"Go on."

"You're on guard. That's the right phrase. You're on guard. What frightens you, Bill? Something does. Marjorie senses it. What is it?"

"I didn't know I look frightened," Bill said, staring into space.

"Not to everyone, Bill, to be sure. Only to those who are close to you."

"What can I tell you, Selda? You don't get where I am without losing some bodies along the way."

"But that's the great American way."

"I know," Bill said. "There's a law in physics that states that every action has a reaction. They can't take my money away from me. They can't touch my power."

"What is it, then?"

He sat back on a comfortable rataan lounge.

"I have worked so hard," he said. "I have worked so hard so long. *Not* only to make money. That was part of it. Not only to have power. I *thought* that was part of it."

He paused and looked at her.

"I've worked so hard to drown out any emotion. I simply can't give in to that."

"Why not? You're not a machine."

"No, I'm not. I'm painfully finding that out."

"But why should that be painful?"

"It's something I'm not prepared to discuss."

"I see," Selda said, shaking her head. "You realize that by not discussing it, you're creating your own hell."

"I'm like a juggler," Bill said, "but instead of having three oranges in the air at one time, I have ten or twelve. I manage to be successful juggling those oranges, but the more oranges I get into the air the more I am questioned, questioned, questioned." He seemed almost angry. He looked at Selda. "I really love you, and I feel you love me. Marjorie loves me. I feel that also. No doubt you have some right to answers."

"I don't," Selda said. "But Marjorie does."

"Yes, Marjorie does, and yet it is she, my own wife, who questions me least, who leaves me alone, who . . ." He rose and paced the floor. "Jesus Christ, I am what I *am*. I don't have the energy or the time to probe my psyche. . . . Maybe I *am* happy with what I'm doing, maybe I enjoy running, running. Has that ever occurred to you?"

"You are running," Selda asked, "from what?"

"The inquiry is closed," Bill said. "I think Marjorie has a wedding breakfast set."

Selda rose and kissed him.

"As long as you know I love you . . ."

But the inquiry was really not closed. . . . Bill was fully aware of that. Lately, Dunby had been threatening once again to expose his past, there was the affair with Elyse which was becoming more burdensome than pleasurable and there were these periods of amnesia he had experienced which frightened him. Most of all there was the very real feeling that all the good things that were happening to him, even though all of them stemmed from his own abilities and determination, would have to be paid for in the end. He was not unaware of the possible challenges of running for governor, or that Marjorie would be away on tour a great deal of the time. And perhaps for the first time he admired men like Henry Jr., like Bob Seiff, even a Joseph Anderson, who accepted what life handed them and did indeed, unlike himself, stop running, running. He looked about Henry Levey's mansion and wished he had a similar retreat but knew that was not the answer.

Chapter LIV

Perhaps it was the fog which came in ever-greater frequency to San Francisco in the summer, but the mood of residents of Pacific Heights, Nob Hill and Russian Hill was usually set with the morning's first glimpse of the Bay, and if the towers of the Golden Gate Bridge were shrouded in white gauze, if the foghorns were wailing their endless litany, the cliff dwellers knew they were in for another dreary day: cool, moist, always forbidding, chilly on the canyonlike corners of city streets.

The well-to-do, although defending that same fog as giving "character" to the city, claiming it gave them vitality and freshness, nevertheless left for the warmer climates of Hillsborough, Menlo Park, San Rafael, Tiburon and Sonoma. The men still commuted to the city by train or car or by ferryboat, but the women enjoyed the swimming pools, the sunshine, the manicured proximity to nature. They would breach etiquette and serve steaks on paper plates and would substitute fresh fruit salad for elegant desserts; couples often slept on screened porches and the children were allowed to sleep in fancy treehouses built by the gardener.

There were summer dances out of doors, the wooden dance floors lit by paper lanterns. There were golf and tennis tournaments. Women wore shorts and men wore bermudas and both sexes would sport muted open-collared madras shirts; and though life was leisurely and informal it was no less structured than the days spent in the city.

The Wolf family had moved to their estate in Hillsborough, maids, butler, governess and all, and life continued in its merry way under the huge eucalyptus, amidst the vast expanse of neatly trimmed lawns.

One Friday afternoon Elyse Wolf returned from an assignation with Bill in San Francisco. She parked her Packard convertible on the graveled driveway and walked briskly into the house. She called, but no one answered. She ran toward the pool and found her husband passed out in his chair, a martini glass on the ground near his limp hand.

And she saw her son at the bottom of the pool, bluish, almost transparent; and dove in quickly, embraced the child and rose with him to the surface. He was wearing tiny navy trunks and his face and chest were blue and slightly bloated. She turned him over pounded his back and watched water flow from his lips. She put her ear to his wet chest but heard no heartbeat. She began breathing into his mouth, for what seemed hours, but there was no response. The child was dead.

It was all hazy to her from then on. She recalled running upstairs with the child. She heard herself calling frantically for the nurse, "Nanny, Nanny, goddamnit!" and then she wrapped the boy in one of his lovely small blankets and put him beside her on the seat of the car.

She waited in the emergency room of the hospital,

watching the frantic rush of doctors, nurses, and listening to the inhuman sounds of oxygen hissing from cylinders. She saw the ashen-faced young doctor and heard him say, "The child has been dead for two hours."

She had filled out forms, she recalled, and she had raced to the city and she was lying on Donen's bed once again, now aware of the dampness of her clothes, her hair.

She walked to his bathroom and dried herself and put on one of his bathrobes.

She recalled pouring herself a drink in the living room, and then a second and she returned to the bedroom and called Bill Crossen.

"Bill?"

"Yes?"

"I need you. Right away."

"It's two o'clock," he said. "I've got meetings."

"Right away! I'm at Donen's," she yelled and hung up.

She had gulped her drink and filled it once more when Bill rang the doorbell. She opened the door unaware that her robe had opened.

"Thank you," she said, "for coming."

"What the hell is going on? You've got a new costume."

Elyse looked down on her nudity. She was unaware of it and apologized.

"What's going on?"

"Sit down," Elyse said. "Want a drink?"

"No."

She looked at him and Bill noticed her tear-streaked face.

"My son is dead," she said, almost coldly.

"He's *what?*"

"Dead. Drowned."

"My God," Bill said, sitting next to her, putting his arm about her and letting her sob on his chest.

She finally sat up and faced him.

"Lewis was sitting next to the pool. Passed out. The governess was gone. She must have run away."

"Oh, Jesus," Bill said. "Oh, Jesus Christ, that no-good son of a bitch . . ."

"*I* killed him," Elyse said, staring into the vast living room.

"No," Bill said, turning to hold her.

"*I* killed him. Running around. Playing college. Trusting a dumb German governess . . . Sleeping with you."

"Don't do that, Elyse. Don't believe things like that."

"I *knew* Lewis was a drunk. I've known it from the first day . . . I—should never—never have let that child out of my sight. . . ."

Bill Crossen had seen many dead men in his life time. *Too* many. And now he could see that dead child, and he did not want to see him at all.

He rose and poured himself a drink and faced Elyse, who looked tired and frightened.

"It's not easy to face death," Bill said. "I won't tell you it's easy. I've done enough of it in my time. But I'll help. I'll help you all I can."

Elyse looked at him through her tear-filled eyes. "How can you help me? How can anyone help me? My father was right. Don't t"—Elyse held up her hand—"don't deny it. Everything I have, I've gotten through my looks, my body. And now I'm going to be punished for it." She looked at Bill.

"Lewis Wolf wasn't enough for me. First I had Donen, then I had you. . . . What did I expect? That the world would stand still while I went after everything I wanted? I killed that child, as if I'd drowned him with my bare hands."

"Don't," Bill said, "please, Elyse, don't do this to

yourself. . . . I know what it's like to have lives on your conscience. . . ."

"A child," Elyse said. "A beautiful, innocent little boy. . . ." She wiped the tears from her face with the sleeves of her robe and faced Bill quite soberly.

"I don't want to stay alive," she said. "I don't want to live with this the rest of my days. . . ."

"Do you remember Rodriguez, the man I made foreman?"

Elyse nodded.

"He was hanged," Bill said, "and I felt just like you are feeling now."

"Can you live with it now?" Elyse asked.

"Better than the day it happened."

"He wasn't your own flesh and blood."

"No," Bill admitted, "he wasn't."

"Go, Bill," Elyse said. "Go now, and thank you. This is my affair, not yours."

Bill looked at her and held her arms. "I love you," he said very gently. "You have given me more pleasure than any woman I've ever known."

"In bed," Elyse said.

"Not only in bed. You're very intelligent. You're very sensitive, you know all that. . . ."

Bill picked up the phone with one hand and dialed.

"Who are you calling?"

"A doctor."

"What for?"

"To give you a shot. To get a nurse. You need sleep, rest."

"You can't drug me forever," Elyse said.

"No, I can't. It's not the way out," Bill insisted. "When you're stronger, you'll fight."

"For what?"

"Yourself."

She did not answer him and submitted to the shot from the doctor who had arrived with a nurse.

Bill watched her go to sleep and covered her frail shoulder with a blanket. He bent down and kissed her forehead.

Sitting in the aft cabin of the *Equation,* his head between his hands, he wondered why, why it was his fate to be always surrounded by death.

The following morning he found Elyse somewhat subdued. She let Bill kiss her and he asked the nurse to step out.

"I've had two phone calls this morning," she said.

"Yes?"

"One from Papa. He was in tears. The other from Donen in Paris."

"Do you want to talk about it?" Bill asked.

"Yes," Elyse said. "I told Papa to bury the child. I told him I had already buried him in my arms. I can't face Lewis or his father or his brother."

Bill nodded. "I understand."

"Papa said he wanted to see me." She paused. "I told him I would see him in good time."

"What about Donen?" Bill asked.

Elyse slipped back on the pillow and faced the ceiling. "I don't want to see Donen, either. I've got to move before he returns from Paris."

"I'll move you across the street to the Nob Hill Towers."

"The Nob Hill Towers, my God. I can't afford that." She looked at her wedding ring. It was a ten-carat diamond, flawless, cold, beautiful and she slipped it off her finger and handed it to Bill.

"That's all I've got to my name right now. Sell it for me."

Bill handed back the ring.

"I *own* the Nob Hill Towers. I'll call the manager

when I get to the office. Get what you need and charge it to Crossen Development. I'll handle it."

"*You* own the Nob Hill Towers?"

"Yes."

"Please take the ring. It would make me feel better."

"Don't, Elyse. It's a loan, if you prefer."

"When will you get rid of this nurse?"

Bill looked at her. "When you tell me that it's safe. When you tell me honestly."

Elyse nodded her head. "I'm just about finished lying."

He rose from the bed, but Elyse held his hand.

"Please kiss me," she said, and Bill complied.

"Thank you," she said, and turned her head into the pillow.

Bill buried himself in work, but Elyse's beautiful, tear-filled eyes haunted him. He wanted to call Selda, but he did not. In an affair, he knew, you bear the pleasures and the pain alone.

Chapter LV

Henry Levey collapsed at his desk the following Monday morning.

He had ignored the warnings of his doctor after his first heart attack. He had not stopped smoking or drinking and he had not followed the dietary or exercise regimen that had been prescribed for him. "I'll live the way I like to live and if it's going to kill me, it will kill me," he said.

They called his son first and then Bill, and two physicians arrived shortly thereafter, Eldon Kahn, an internist, and Loren Baum, a cardiologist.

They opened his collar and placed him gently on the couch. Baum gave him an injection and an ambulance was called.

"It's not a stroke or heart attack," Baum said. "I've got a pulse. It's very weak."

Kahn started an IV, and Henry Levey looked very pale, his breathing shallow.

Bill stood with Henry Levey, Jr., and placed his arm about the young man's shoulder.

The stretcher bearers arrived and carried the patient to the ambulance. The two doctors rode with Levey to Mt. Sinai and Bill and Henry Jr. followed.

Hortense was called, as were Linda, Bob and Joanne. Bill phoned Marjorie in Cleveland. "Darling."

"Bill?"

"Yes. I am sorry to have to phone you."

"What is it?"

"Your father is ill."

"What's wrong?"

"The doctors don't know. He's very ill."

"I'll fly right home. I'll call you back as soon as I have reservations."

"I'm sorry, Marjorie. I love him, too."

"I know, Bill, I know. I'll be home in a few hours. Can you pick me up?"

"Of course. I love you."

At five o'clock in the evening the entire family had been assembled outside Henry's room, but there was still no word from the doctors.

At six o'clock Dr. Baum appeared. "We have an irregular pulse still. The blood pressure is very low."

"What can you do?" Linda asked.

"We're doing all we can."

"Would you like some dinner, Mother?" Henry Jr. asked, but she declined.

The wait continued. There was little small talk. Bill held Marjorie's hand. She was pale and shocked. At ten o'clock Hortense rose and faced Bill.

"It is all your fault. Working that man to death when there is no need for it at all."

"Shut up, Mother," Marjorie said.

"You all know it's true," Hortense continued.

"I said, shut up, Mother," Marjorie repeated.

"Don't talk to mother like this." Linda spoke up.

"You shut up, too," Marjorie said.

"Please," Henry Jr. pleaded, "why don't you all go home? I'll wait. I'll call you when there is a change."

No one moved. At midnight Baum appeared again.

"His pulse is getting weaker."

"Can I see him?" Hortense asked.

"No," Baum said. "He needs complete quiet."

Again Hortense approached Bill, pointing a finger. "If anything happens . . ." she began and Henry Jr. stood and hustled his mother aside. Marjorie rose and said to Bill, "Let's go home." She turned to Linda and said coldly, "Call if his condition worsens."

Bill followed Marjorie to the car. He opened the door for her and then slipped into the driver's side.

"I can take it, darling," he said. "Don't leave on my account."

"*I* can't," Marjorie said. "That bitch. The next thing she'll do is call Whit Boulton. That will kill him for sure."

Bill and Marjorie returned home, but made no effort to go to bed.

"You really do love your father," Bill said.

"Yes, I do. I hate the way mother has treated him. She practically flaunted her affair."

"Why did he take it?"

"I don't know. He was never a man who liked arguments. I hope he had a nice lady friend."

"I'm surprised," Bill said.

"About what?"

"You children actually knew about all that."

"Of course. You can't live in one house and not know what's going on. We used to stand outside their bedroom door when they were fighting."

"I like your father," Bill said. "I've always liked him. He's been very good to me."

"You were the son he didn't have."

At two in the morning Bill reached Henry Jr.

"Any news?"

"He's slightly better," Henry said.

"Thank you."

It was a difficult night for Bill and Marjorie. It was three in the morning when Bill was finally able to ask about her concert tour.

"It's going well," she said. "It's all going well. Bach is a challenge, but I'll meet it."

"But what—" Bill stumbled, and Marjorie finished the sentence.

"What if my father dies?"

"Yes."

"I just don't know," she said. "Take me to bed and hold me tight. Just hold me tight." It was the first request she had made in a long time.

They finally managed a few hours sleep, and the morning report from the hospital was somewhat more encouraging. Bill dressed and left for the office.

At ten o'clock Dr. Baum phoned Bill Crossen.

"I'm calling you," he said, "because I can't cope with Hortense's hysteria. Our findings are still extremely inconclusive and outside of intravenous feedings, the only treatment the man needs is complete quiet. It's his only chance."

"I understand. I appreciate your calling me. I'll try to help all I can."

"It's hard to treat the rich," Baum said. "They always want to control the treatment. Good-bye."

Crossen placed a call to Henry Jr. at the hospital and reported Baum's findings.

"Why did he call you? Why didn't he call my mother? She's paying him."

"Jesus Christ, Henry, don't you understand what I am trying to tell you?"

417

"No. All I understand is that it's *my* mother and my mother's husband." He hung up the phone.

Bill shortened his day at the office and found Marjorie at the piano when he entered the apartment. He sat next to her and embraced her.

"There's no change," Bill said, detecting tears in her eyes.

"I know, Baum phoned me, too. You know, Bill, when I first married you I couldn't understand your coldness toward your family, and now I feel *nothing,* except for Daddy."

"They're all under a strain," Bill said. "It's been a shock."

They ate dinner quietly and returned to the hospital. They sat in that pale green corridor, no one speaking, and finally Dr. Baum emerged from Henry's room. He looked at Marjorie and motioned her to join him.

The whole family watched as they walked down the long hallway.

"Your father knows you're here," Baum said. "He wants to see you and he wants you to go back to Cleveland."

"How is he?" Marjorie said. "I'd never forgive myself if he needed me and I wasn't here."

"Despite rumors," Baum said, "I am not God, just a doctor; but I *do* think he'd feel better if you'd pursue the concert."

"Can I see him?"

"For a minute."

They went to Henry's room, and Marjorie kissed her father, who was looking pale, immobilized by the intravenous tubing.

"Daddy," she said, and kissed him again, lightly.

"Kill them in Cleveland," he said.

She faced him, tears in her eyes. "I will, if you'll read the notices."

"I'll read them. Don't you worry. That Polish peasant stock is stubborn."

Marjorie felt Dr. Baum tugging on her arm and once more kissed her father.

It had been a difficult farewell at the airport for Bill and Marjorie. They were so filled with private thoughts, with things unsaid, unsettled, Henry's life hanging over their heads. They embraced at the gate.

"I won't call you unless I have to," Bill said. "I'll see you in Cleveland."

"It's all on your shoulders," Marjorie said. "All of it."

"I'll handle it. I'll handle it all."

She embraced him and she kissed him and held him and then she disappeared through the door leading to the airplane.

It had taken one month for Henry Levey's condition to stabilize, and though he was allowed visitors only once a day and then for only a few minutes, the crisis had passed.

In Henry Levey's home, Bob, as attorney for the firm, was seated with Hortense, Linda, Henry Jr. and Joanne. It was five o'clock and the butler had passed a tray of drinks.

"I think," Hortense said, "Bob has something for all of you to consider."

They watched as Bob opened a manila folder and looked at them all.

"This is not a pleasant task," he said, avoiding the gaze of Linda who had pushed him into this position, "but as you know we, seated here, represent the majority of stock in Levey, Levey and Crossen.

"Hortense, and I agree with her position, feels that Henry Sr.'s condition is due primarily to stress, and all of us know the cause of that stress.

"We can't fire Bill Crossen," he continued, "but *we can* dissolve the corporation, or better yet, we can sell it."

"But what about Dad?" Henry Jr. asked.

"We're only *doing* it for your father."

"You're not even asking him?"

"You know what he'd say."

"And what about Bill?"

"We'll have to tell Bill."

"Who?" Henry Jr. said.

"Bob will," Linda said.

"Yes, I'll tell Bill," Bob said, feeling somewhat sheepish, and Linda saw herself in Hawaii already.

All agreed that this move should be accomplished quickly while Henry Sr. could raise little objection, and the following Monday Bob appeared in Crossen's office.

"I must speak to you, Bill," Bob had said on the phone.

"I can't see you until Thursday."

"I think this matter takes precedence over anything."

"Really," Bill said. "All right, come in at seven."

"In the morning?"

"Yes."

Bob Seiff had probably never risen that early in his life but sat across Bill Crossen's desk promptly at seven.

"Do you always start at this ungodly hour?"

"Yes," Crossen said, "but I'm sure we're not here to discuss my personal habits."

"No, as a matter of fact, what I am about to say should not be taken personally at all."

Crossen looked at his tall, well-dressed brother-in-law.

"Say it."

"Hortense, Linda and Henry Jr., as majority stockholders in the firm, have decided to sell the company. Hortense feels that the business has become too big and is only a drain on Henry's health. You and Marjorie are, of course, invited to put your shares into the package."

"Have you asked Henry?" Crossen asked.

"No."

"How can you sell without Henry's consent? He started the business."

"We can't ask Henry. You know what he would say."

"He would tell you to go to hell."

"And kill himself continuing this business."

"You're all convinced that hard work is detrimental to the man's health."

"A man of Henry's age, yes."

"A man of Henry's age, my ass. When was the last time you worked hard?"

"I don't want any animosity, Bill."

"Animosity, hell. You're really going to do this behind Henry's back?"

"Yes."

"Well, I won't. I'll ask him."

"There's no use burdening him. Legally it is an open-and-shut case."

"I see," Crossen said. "Well, get up, open the door, go through it and shut it. You son of a bitch."

He watched his stunned brother-in-law leave the office, and he closed his eyes with his fingers and tipped back in his chair.

It was all coming too fast, he thought. The night with Elyse, Henry's illness, now this. There were endless conferences ahead of him, countless contracts, projections, blueprints, computer readouts. He placed a call to Marjorie.

"Bill?"

"Yes."

"How is Daddy?"

"On the mend."

421

"Thank God. I've been praying."

"Praying and practicing," Bill said.

"Yes. Exactly."

Bill recounted the details of Bob's visit. "I don't know what to do."

"You must ask Daddy," Marjorie said.

"That's what I told Bob."

"Then ask him."

"But what if they're right? What if I *am* killing him?"

"Bullshit," Marjorie said. "It's bullshit. Why all this sudden concern about his health?"

"I hadn't thought of it that way."

"Well, do."

There was silence on Bill's end.

"Bill?" Marjorie asked. "Are you there?"

"Yes, I am here, darling. I can't tell you how I admire you."

"Hang in there, Bill. You're the only friend he's got."

"Play your piano. I'll see him. I'll tell him what you said. Goddamn, I love you, Marjorie. . . ." he said and hung up.

Bill had seen Henry Levey twice weekly and had found him weak and lethargic on the last visit. Bill had assured him all was well, but the following day after receiving permission from Dr. Baum he visited Henry again. Bill was accompanied by an attorney and an accountant and fortunately found Henry somewhat sprightlier.

He quickly told Henry his family's plans and then he said, "As you know, Henry, I don't need the firm at all. I spoke to Marjorie. All we care about is you."

Levey nodded and motioned for Bill to come closer.

"When O'Gara quit," Levey said, "I told Hortense that he put his shares into a trust fund for his family, but that was not true. I bought his shares. They're in my name. I have control. I'll give you and Marjorie power of attorney for them until I get out of here."

"You don't want to sell the company?"

"Hell, no." He motioned to the attorney. "Look, I've been lying on my back a lot of hours and my mind is made up. Don't try to talk me out of it, do you hear? Draw up divorce papers for me to sign. And then serve them."

"But Mr. Levey."

"Do it, goddamnit! Did you hear, Bill?"

"I heard." He squeezed the frail, feeble hand, and later that day Bill summoned Bob Seiff and Henry Jr. to his office.

"I spoke to your father today in the company of two witnesses. He does not want to sell the company."

"I've already told you," Bob said imperiously, "what Henry Levey wants right now is purely academic. I *asked* you not to bother him."

"I *did* bother him." He pulled out a document of his own. "Your father," he said to Henry Jr., "bought out O'Gara when they split. Henry's shares and mine will outvote you, two to one."

"Those shares are community property with Hortense."

"Henry has also sued for divorce. It will be up to the judge to settle the estate. I think he will think twice before selling a man's business out from under him."

"I can't believe this," Henry Jr. said.

"There is nothing more to say now, Henry," Bob said, standing.

"There is for me," Bill said. "You're fired.

"*Who* is?"

"You and Henry Jr. I'll see you get your gold watches."

Chapter LVI

Selda had settled comfortably into her new marriage. She was a good surrogate mother, a warm, loving wife to Joseph Anderson.

She had phoned Bill Crossen that morning and they met in her small private office in the library.

"I've asked you over because I love you. Both of you. You know that."

Bill nodded. "What's on your mind?"

"There are rumors about you and Elyse Wolf. I hear she has left Lewis. People are saying she is living at the Nob Hill Towers and that you own it."

"I should have expected that," Bill said. "It's all gossip."

"I'm not preaching, Bill, and what you and Elyse do is your business. However, you should consider Marjorie. If there is something you want her to know, she should hear it from you first."

"I'm glad you told me. I have no intention of hurting Marjorie."

"I think," Selda said, "that she'll be very understanding."

"What makes you so sure?"

"I love you both," Selda said again. "I'm very close to Marjorie. Take my word. She is a strong girl. Nothing will threaten her."

"That's good. Let me tell you, Selda, Elyse turned to me for help. I gave it to her."

"That's none of my business," Selda said.

"I'm not ashamed of what I've done," Bill said.

"You forget, Bill, you're talking to a hussy who flew to Saudi Arabia with a married man. Remember?"

Bill smiled.

"I had my share of guilt, believe me, but no one owns anyone else in this world. I simply don't want you to be unkind to Marjorie."

"I have no such intentions," Bill said. "She's going to be performing in Cleveland in two weeks and I'll see her there. With her father's illness and the concert, now is not the time to burden her with this."

"You know best," Selda said and Bill rose and returned to his office. He looked troubled, Selda thought, but knew she had said enough.

He had dinner with Elyse that evening. She looked thinner, drawn. He kissed and held her at arm's length to look at her.

"Are you well?" he asked. "You look so pale."

"Physically, I'm a horse," Elyse said. "Mentally, I don't know. I'm glad you're here. I have to move. We're becoming a cause célèbre in this town and I can't let that happen to you."

"Fuck them," Bill said. "I only care about Marjorie's feelings."

"Have you said anything to her?"

"No."

"That's good. I heard about her father. I'm sorry."
She looked at him. "No matter what, I've got to leave the Towers."

"In time, yes," Bill said. "If you move now, it will only be grist for their filthy mills."

"What *will* you tell Marjorie?"

"That we're friends."

"That covers a wide territory."

"Yes it does. What about Lewis? Have you seen him?"

"No."

"Have you spoken to him?"

"No. I've spoken to his father. I told him I'd see him when I could. He was very sweet. He always is."

"What choice does he have?" Bill asked.

The steel mill in Montana was rising and the plans for the cement plant were almost finished. The seedlings in Brazil were taking root. Tract after tract rose in the backwaters of San Francisco, San Bruno, Daly City, Hunter's Point. Crossen Development was a company worthy of any man's efforts. Increasing funds brought increasing opportunities, and Crossen learned that money begat money in such profusion that further endeavor almost ceased to be a challenge.

His engineering patents were making him richer, and his fertile brain continued to generate more ideas for new products. He was known in financial circles as a wide-gauge man, and though he now wielded more power than he had ever dreamed of, he recalled Elyse's statement that if their indiscretion became public San Francisco would still be able to force them to their knees.

He had gotten an urgent call from Linda that morning asking to see him immediately, and he agreed reluctantly, wondering what further burden would descend on him.

She seemed nervous. "I don't relish telling you what I have to tell you."

"Go ahead."

"You know what the rumors are about you and Elyse Wolf."

"I didn't know there were any rumors."

"There are. Unfortunately. A lot of rumors. She has left her husband. And she is living at the Nob Hill Towers."

"I have heard that. She can live where she pleases," Bill said.

"I didn't even know that you *owned* the towers."

"I see," Bill said. "I didn't know it was any of your business."

"It wouldn't be, if it didn't involve the family."

Bill raised his eyebrows at the mention of that word.

"Bob hired a private detective, that's how we learned all these horrid things. . . ."

"Elyse Wolf is living at the Nob Hill Towers. I own it. What else? Do you have pictures?"

Linda reddened. "You don't understand, Bill. This sort of behavior is not tolerated in our group."

Bill turned his swivel chair so that he faced the airshaft outside the window of his office.

"What do you want?" Bill asked.

"Restore Bob's position as legal counsel for the company and none of this will go any further."

"Your father used to lecture me about family," Bill said almost to himself. "What about Marjorie? Have you considered *her*?"

"I hardly think you're in any position to lecture me about Marjorie."

Bill turned once more and faced his sister-in-law.

"People have tried to blackmail me before," he said. "It is not a wise course to choose."

Linda stood. "I'll give you three days to think this over."

"Shall we synchronize our watches," Bill said, standing.

Linda had never seen such coldness in anyone's eyes. She stood and left.

In Marjorie's absence, Bill Crossen was the only family member who now paid daily visits to Henry Levey, and it was a happy day when he was able to transfer his father-in-law to his estate in Menlo Park. Bill sat with him during the hour's ride and shortened the period by talking not only of Marjorie's forthcoming concert, but also of the affairs of the company.

"I've thought a great deal," Crossen said, "and feel that retirement on your end would be foolish. No one has entered your office since you left and no one belongs there but you."

"You've been very decent, Bill," Levey said. "I very much appreciate it. I *do* have some plans of my own."

"Are they private?"

"They are, but I can trust you, I feel."

"You can."

"I have a friend, a widow. Her husband worked for me. She is a lovely woman. I can give her some security and she may bring me some companionship."

"Now you're talking," Bill said, happy to see some hope in Levey's outlook. "Marjorie so much wants the best for you. I will be building a penthouse on top of the Nob Hill Towers for us. I'd like you to have a floor. That way we can keep track of you, you scoundrel."

Levey smiled. "And I would lecture you about family. Jesus. I understand they've refused you membership in the Concordia Club."

"Yes, they have."

"Why don't you buy it?"

"What for?"

"Buy it and burn it down."

They reached the country home and Bill helped Levey to a divan in the library. He asked Bill to open the French doors so he could see his lovely manicured acreage.

"You, too, Bill, will have to make decisions."

"Like what?"

"You own the biggest yacht in San Francisco. If you build a penthouse on Nob Hill Towers, you'll have the best view in town. . . . I can understand those acquisitions are symbolic—still . . ."

"Yes?"

"There are other ways to measure success than with a profit-and-loss statement. . . . I hear they are considering offering you a chance to run for governor."

"I've heard the rumor. It's nothing more than that."

"It *is*," Levey said. "I've talked to Goldman. They are *very* serious."

"*They* may be," Bill said. "I don't know whether *I* am."

"Why not? It's a great honor."

"I suppose . . ."

"What do you mean, you suppose? It's the greatest honor this state can confer on a citizen."

"I know," Bill said. "There are other options."

"Such as," Henry asked.

"The business."

"The business," Henry said. "I keep asking you over and over again: How much do you want? How much do you need? I hear you're worth several million—I don't really give a damn. Look at the Rockefellers. Even *they* got tired of earning money."

"Only *one* of the Rockefellers," Bill said. "The old man never had time for politics."

429

"Quite right. But a term as governor would not break you."

"That's true. I haven't thought about it from a financial viewpoint."

"What, then?"

"Don't ask," Bill said, "please don't ask."

"Well," said Levey, changing the subject, "tell the lawyers to get moving on my divorce. I don't want to get married in a wheelchair."

"You're quite a man, Mr. Levey. Were you frightened in the hospital?"

"You've seen a lot of death, Bill. I wasn't frightened. Do you know what bothered me most?"

"What?"

"Wondering whether Whitney East Boulton, M.D., was using my paisley robe. I had just bought it from Sulka."

Crossen laughed. "I'll have it sent for tomorrow."

"Good. I used to love that woman, can you believe that?"

With Marjorie in Cleveland, Bill Crossen spent that evening alone on the *Equation.* He loved the precision of its interior, the fusion of metals and wood, the teak, the oak, the brass, the chrome, the stainless steel fittings, the parabolic curves, the lightness and the grace of the vessel. He lit the kerosene lanterns and sat alone in the cockpit, shivering slightly in the fresh wind from the Bay. He could pick out the Levey house on Pacific Heights, and he could see the towers on Nob Hill, and he remembered coming through that Golden Gate years ago with his head filled with calculations, plans, projections, with his mind set on selfish achievement, on sinking roots: He had lived by his wits then and he still did. He thought of the seeming stability of the Levey family, the rigidity of the social patterns of San Francisco; and now, thinking of that scattered family, those fragile tentacles of solidity in those very solid homes he wondered whether *his* stability, his money, his holdings were just as teuous as the span of the gull drifting silently above him.

He thought of Linda in his office, frightened, threatening; and he thought of Elyse, pale and insecure; and he thought of Marjorie, two thousand miles away, perhaps the only solid element in his life, and he worried about her, too. He had indeed been able to program his performance these past years, but it was based on solid data, on firm questions and logically reached conclusions, and now, now that so much of that solidity he had respected was crumbling around him, he wavered. He flickered like the flame of his kerosene lantern, surrounded by jealousy and avarice and ecstasy and despair. For the first time since he had arrived in San Francisco, he, too, was frightened.

How many people had he used in his lifetime? His parents, his teachers, the men under his command? His wife, his in-laws . . . and he had kept running, running, always running, and the pursuit and his wits had made him rich, it had made him powerful, perhaps even untouchable, except that he had to live with himself. He snuffed out the kerosene lantern and crawled into his bunk. What does it take to get a good night's sleep, he wondered, as once again he saw the stump of a man's neck after the head had been cut off by a samurai sword. The stumps of legs, of arms, the distended bellies of men underfed, ravaged, diseased . . .

Chapter LVII

Cleveland proved to be more difficult for Marjorie than her debut in San Francisco. She was neither the "hometown girl," nor the untried artist. The reviews of her first concert had preceded her and though George Szell was a very knowledgeable conductor, and the orchestra a very finely tuned instrument, Marjorie found now an atmosphere of curiosity, rather than one of total support for a newcomer.

Solari had been aware of all this and in his excellent handling of his pupil was able even here to overcome most roadblocks. True, the press was now more demanding, the conductor at times more argumentative. Still, Marjorie's vast talent was the decisive factor, and her training was ample enough to scale a steep artistic mountain.

Solari had followed the same monastic regimen as the one in San Francisco, and Marjorie and Bill had agreed not to communicate until after the performance, and though he was able to protect her from most intrusions, Solari was unable to prevent a call from Linda reaching Marjorie early in the morning three days before the concert.

She spared Marjorie nothing: the fact that Elyse Wolf had left Lewis, the attendant publicity, Elyse's presence at Nob Hill Towers, the endless vicious gossip delighting the Pacific Heights crowd.

Marjorie listened without comment.

"Have you finished?" she asked coldly after Linda had graphically explained each detail of the Wolf affair.

"I think that's quite enough," Linda said.

Marjorie did not comment.

"What are you going to do?"

"Go back to sleep."

"I mean about Bill?"

"I shall see him after the performance."

"What makes you so sure? Would you like to speak to Bob?"

"What for?"

"I think you have ample grounds. . . ."

"For what?"

"Divorce . . . Marjorie, are you there?" Linda asked after a long silence.

"I am here. . . ."

"You haven't answered my question."

"You must be a very unhappy person. Good night, Linda."

Marjorie sat up in the bed, propping her pillow behind her back. She could hear the first sounds of the city stirring, auto horns, trucks, buses; and she could see dawn beginning to define her large, well-furnished room.

It had been a good union, she and Bill. He was an exceptional young man, far more exceptional than any outsider could fathom.

433

She had seen him emerge from a war-hardened, ghetto-scarred boy. She had watched his unending energy result in triumph after triumph. She had never cared for the financial success—they rarely discussed it—and she felt that all that money was only the report card that he produced for his labors.

She had watched their friends respond to Bill with rudeness and animosity, she had watched that change to quiet respect, and in the last year she had seen that respect turn to awe and then to a strange worship. The other young men had finally stopped trying to compete, although many of them were successful in their own right, and she had seen the women, her "friends," cluster around him at parties, touch him, tease him, try desperately to isolate him; and she had watched him handle this attention with a mixture of amusement and boredom.

She knew, perhaps sooner than anyone, that Bill Crossen was no longer fighting Pacific Heights because it quickly stopped being a match for him. His goals, like her own, were within himself, and the small appurtenances like memberships in clubs, chairmanships of charitable organizations, board appointments to the symphony or the opera were of no importance whatsoever.

As a wife, as a woman who slept with Bill Crossen, she was aware of Elyse Wolf, and she was aware that her great beauty, her grace, her wit, her background, similar to Bill's, might be a challenge.

After her own transgressions with Solari she had almost hoped that Bill might find some erotic pleasure with that girl, perhaps to assuage her own guilt or to affirm the solidity of their own union, a solidity she still felt very deeply.

Ultimately, she sensed it was only *her* achievements and her drive and her talent that would merit Bill's love. She had felt that from the very beginning. She had never complained about his cold, abrupt lovemaking, always suspecting that she could give more or receive more, a fact substantiated by Solari; and yet she felt that this part of their life might either fall into place or if not, should then be weighed against all the other qualities she so admired. Perhaps Elyse Wolf might awaken that sexuality, or perhaps she might, like Marjorie herself, find that the physical love that Bill Crossen gave her was *all* the physical love he was capable of giving to anyone.

She had seen his face as he watched her practice or after she had finished her debut, and she had seen his face as he watched her, exhausted or exuberant or crushed, and she had known that there was love in that face.

Marjorie Levey knew that she was plain, and yet she felt good about herself. She did not have the exotic features of an Elyse Wolf, the tiny waist of her sister Linda or even the high, solid cheekbones of her mother; and yet she knew that the plainness of her face and figure were offset by her intelligence, her talent, her inner peace and her patience.

Solari had proved that. She cared little how many women he had slept with or how many more he was destined to sleep with. She felt no jealousy. She had long ago stopped worrying whether that first night in New York she had simply been another conquest, another notch on his gun. No, now she felt his need for her. His love and his desires were real. She felt this as a woman, despite her inexperience, and though there was no way to moralize about her indiscretion, no way she could justify this selfishness, she did remember Selda's advice, wonderful Selda, who had said, "You're human, so what? Don't be ashamed of that."

She did not fear the concert or her schedule and she did not fear losing Bill Crossen. And this morning she did not leave her bed to crawl into Solari's arms, and she respected his discretion in not making an issue of it as they sat in the sunlit parlor of their suite eating a light breakfast and sipping a sinfully expensive champagne, which Solari explained would take the edge off the mathematics of playing Bach.

Chapter LVIII

It was a rare occasion when Bill Crossen's appointment secretary would consult with her boss. She was a bright, attractive young woman who had been instructed once (and only once) about scheduling Crossen's time, and it was a duty she fulfilled with much charm but great rigidity.

The request by a superior court judge of the State of California for a specified hour, however, meant a shuffling of the schedule and Crossen reluctantly agreed to the appointment. Alan B. Jessup was a stalwart of the Democratic party and a name often referred to in O'Gara's heyday. He was a heavy-set man dressed in a well-tailored suit; he was carefully manicured and barbered. He left his chauffeur in Crossen's outer office and seemed, as many had before him, surprised by the sparseness of Bill's small quarters.

"Judge Jessup," Bill said, standing, "please have a seat. A pleasure to see you. To what do I owe the honor of this visit?"

Jessup still looking around the plain, pictureless walls, finally faced his host and said, "You don't care much for personal amenities."

"Not really. Why?"

"My coat closet is bigger than this hole in the wall."

"*My* coat closet," Bill Crossen said lightly.

"Yes," Jessup said, crossing his legs and tossing his raincoat on a bookcase, "*your* coat closet. I am going to be brief and direct. I understand that's the way you like to deal."

"You're well informed."

"I am here representing a group from the Democratic party and I want to know your feelings about being the next governor of California."

There it was, finally, Crossen thought. All the rumors, the columns had been right after all.

"I'm flattered by the offer, but I can't accept it until I know what kind of man you're looking for. I have never been interested in politics."

"Politics, maybe not," Jessup said, "but there certainly has been enough publicity about you."

Crossen blushed. "That was not of my own seeking."

"That is the second reason I am here. We have had enough machine politicians, we have had enough patronage compromises. This state is moving and moving fast, and what we need is a young apolitical candidate who not only understands the progress in California, but is ahead of it. Can you suggest a better choice?"

"I am an American-born Jew of Polish ancestry," Crossen said. "I was born and raised on the Lower East Side of New York."

"There is an old saying in politics, Mr. Crossen, and I can state it, being Jewish myself. 'When you've had enough of the wops and the micks, turn to the hebes.' "

"I am not that type of hebe," Crossen said. "I don't

go to temple, I've changed my name. I have no close family ties."

"A modern Jew," Jessup said. "All in your favor. War hero. Prisoner of war, self-made multimillionaire, famous, attractive, aggressive." He lit a cigar. "What about your wife? Does she plan to continue performing?"

"Of course."

"That could hurt," Jessup said.

"Why?"

"The voters want their women at home, especially the governor's wife."

"Then you have the wrong man," Crossen said.

"You'd do nothing to stop her?"

"Certainly not."

"Well, it would mean votes. I don't know how many. How do you feel about the Mexicans?"

"The same I've always felt."

"Good. That's a plus for you. Tell me," Jessup said, somewhat sternly, "is there anything we should know?"

"Like what?" Bill asked.

"We call it in politics a burr up your ass. Anything the other side can bring up to embarrass us?"

Crossen was quiet for a minute.

"There is a man, a Colonel Dunby. He makes threats about my war record."

"You have an honorable discharge, don't you?"

"Yes."

"Forget it. They'll bring up a lot of other dirt."

"Like what?"

"That filly at the Nob Hill Towers."

"Nothing to it," Crossen said.

"Good," Jessup said, giving him a nudge. "That kind of stuff may even be good for you."

"I am neither a speechmaker nor a handshaker," Crossen said. "All I know about California is where its rivers run, who owns the land, where to get cheap labor and how to make use of the easterners and the mid-westerners, when they come to settle here."

"What you know about California, *we* know, Mr. Crossen. A financial statement from the Wells Fargo Bank is all that is necessary. Your feeling about California has been correct. It has made you rich. Very rich. Perhaps now is the time for you to pass your expertise on to the electorate. . . ."

It was flattering, all of it, no doubt about it.

"It would be a personal sacrifice," Crossen said. "My business would stop."

"Not stop, exactly," Jessup said, "just be put in a blind trust."

"I equate the two," Crossen said.

"I can believe that. But at your age, with your ability, the governorship is only a stepping-stone."

"To what?"

"To anything you desire. My God, boy," Jessup said, "do you realize what I am offering you at your age?"

"Perhaps not. Perhaps not all of it. *Who*, precisely, is offering me all this?"

"The people who can put you in," Jessup said emphatically.

"And who are they?"

"You will meet them, if you agree to that."

"I don't see how I can turn that down. Where and when?"

"The boardroom of the Prudential Bank at noon tomorrow."

"I'll be there."

Bill Crossen had visited the Prudential Bank boardroom before, as he had most of the other boardrooms of major banks with which he had done business. He even knew all of the men around the highly polished, large, oval table: Goldman, Lehman, Crocker, Hellman, Roth,

Wilder, Call, O'Leary, Jessup, Saranoli. They were the power-brokers of the Democratic party, and most of them were twice his age. After a few pleasantries it was Lehman who began. "I think," he said, "that Judge Jessup has already told you why we have asked you to come here. Your accomplishments in the state speak for themselves. You have provided much housing, *good,* low-cost housing; you have brought water to the south of the state; you have begun heavy industry, built freeways, shopping centers, schools, athletic facilities—but you know your accomplishments better than we do."

"You are very kind, Mr. Lehman, although I don't deserve all the credit you have bestowed on me. The credit for the quality of the housing we have built belongs to Henry Levey. He taught me that quality can be profitable. The canal systems I have built were planned before World War Two. I simply modernized construction and expedited their completion. Hunter's Point, Castro Valley, Santa Rosa, Fresno were all areas that any demographer could have chosen as well as I did."

"Modesty is a good quality in a man," Goldman commented, "however, you *will* admit that you had a hand in all these projects, and all of them succeeded."

"I cannot deny that."

"For a man your age, the accomplishments are sizable."

Crossen said nothing.

"You said to Jessup," O'Leary said, "that you're not a political animal."

"That's right, sir."

"I would dispute that. Most of us at this table feel that you've been able to wind the legislature around your finger."

"Only for the common good," Crossen said.

"Yes," O'Leary said, "only for the common good. And it is for that common good we'd like to think of you as a candidate."

"Gentlemen," Crossen said, "I am naturally honored by all your flattering words and the offer of high office, but what kind of governor do you really seek?"

Ross, the oldest of the men, looked at him.

"A good question, Mr. Crossen. I think I can say without exaggeration that no man in this room really needs *any* governor for survival." There was slight laughter in the room. "Most of us are no longer in the acquisitive stage of our lives. However, we would like to protect what we already have."

"How?" Crossen asked bluntly.

"We know there has been growth, tremendous growth, and we expect that growth to continue."

"I would agree."

"On the whole, we feel the growth has been orderly, and most of all we want that orderliness to continue."

"As you see fit," Crossen said.

Hellman picked up the innuendo.

"Hold on, Crossen. Hold on, boy. This is not a dictatorial board. There has been much change in California already."

"I know," Crossen said. "Lots of blacks, lots of Okies, some Mexicans, the city is filled with people who weren't born here."

"All right," Lehman said, "it's on the table. Why screw around? We've never asked a Jew to run, either."

Bill faced him squarely. "This is a free country. We won the war. All of us, the whites, the blacks, the Okies, the Mexicans. The war is over. They can live where they want."

"Are you saying," Lehman asked carefully, "that you don't object to the changes that are taking place in San Francisco, in California?"

"I didn't say that, Mr. Lehman. I am not a native San Franciscan, as you are, and I haven't felt the social

442

changes as much as you. However, they *are* taking place, and they will continue to take place."

"And what do you suggest?"

"I don't suggest anything. I'll keep on doing just what I have been doing. If there is manpower, I'll employ it. If there are employed, I'll house them. They must eat, we must create employment for them. Throwing up your hands in a fit of nostalgia will do nothing for this state. The days of the landowner and the slaveholder are over."

"He's right," Crocker said. "He's dead right. You can't close the borders. You can't wall this city. But a man working eight hours a day is a lot less dangerous than a man loitering around Fillmore Street."

"And a lot less hungry," Crossen added. "Look at New York with their Puerto Ricans."

"Then you would follow the same formula that you have been using," Crocker asked. "Am I correct in that assumption?"

"If you offered me the chance," Crossen said measuredly, "and I accepted—" he paused carefully, "that would be my philosophy."

The men nodded.

"I may add," Crossen said, "that I am not a bleeding-heart liberal. I have, even in my short lifetime, used a lot of labor. I am not afraid of labor, but I also believe in rewarding it fairly."

"Well," Goldman said, "if the state profits as well as you have personally, there will be few objections."

There was laughter around the table, and Bill Crossen rose and left.

Crossen had made a good impression, unquestionably. He was a fine-looking young man; his face would look good on a poster. He was apolitical, and he had never lost an election. He was Jewish, but did not pursue his religion. He had the support of an old-line family in the city, his wife was talented and might become famous, he was childless, but that problem might be overcome.

"But what about us?" Saranoli asked coldly. "Let's face it, we don't give a shit who sits in Sacramento. How will he take care of us?"

Saranoli was reputedly the biggest kingmaker in California politics. Son of a streetcar conductor, he had, with the aid of the closely knit Italian community, been mayor of San Francisco twice.

"The answer to that," Goldman said, "is how badly he wants the job. For a young man he has everything now. Money, power, respect, looks. It is true, he can continue in private life and become twice as rich, twice as powerful, but in a lifetime there are such things as diminishing returns. The governorship of California, perhaps later federal appointments, offer gratifications, satisfactions, rewards of incredible dimensions which no amount of private capital can provide. . . ."

It was a shrewd assessment, and the decision was made to support Bill Crossen. Jessup phoned him the next day and gave him the news. It had only been one day since the meeting and Crossen, alone, carefully deboned his rex sole at Jack's. None of the men at the Prudential Bank, none of the astute men at surrounding tables could fathom the reaction the offer had caused in Bill.

"We're all running," he had said to Elyse. "We have to keep running." And though he made that philosophical observation partly as therapy for that stricken young woman, he knew also that he was speaking for himself. Though at times he became bored with the endless financial success of his ventures, bored with their predictable outcome, he knew this offer, this tempting offer was yet another chance to run. To run and keep running. He also knew that a decision to continue that pace not only might ruin his health, but the cause of that flight, the *true* cause of that flight, might well be his undoing.

He also remembered his statement about power. It was one of the first ones he had made to Selda, and he knew that all the money he had amassed had given him power and that the governorship would give him even greater power. But he had also learned that raw money spoke for itself. More and more doors opened for him, the atmosphere became increasingly more genteel. What was his *need* for power? he wondered. Who was left to tell to go to hell?

Despite Rodriguez's death, he had enjoyed his work on the state housing board; he had enjoyed the accolades he had received from the Mexican American sectors. He *did* take pride in the success of his projects in the poverty-ridden valleys of San Joaquin and Imperial. There would be more opportunities now. He could, perhaps, he thought, become a *good* governor and almost smiled thinking that he had come to this state, this town for no other reason than to take care of William Crossen. And though he had succeeded, and succeeded far beyond his own dreams, that success, the money, the prestige, the power had really given him less gratification than he was willing to admit.

Crossen slept on board the *Equation* that night and realized how few really good friends he had made in the years that he had been living in San Francisco. Although in the early years there had been few opportunities to get close to Marjorie's group, his success had certainly opened enough avenues to closer relationships. It had been (he knew) his own choice. He was busy, he traveled a great deal, and it was his nature to be close-mouthed, introverted; and only tonight, as few other nights that he could remember, would he like to have

445

been able to discuss his options, mostly with Marjorie. But even there he knew he would not open up sufficiently to get answers to questions he needed answered. He could not deny that the invitation to enter politics at such a high level intrigued him. The offer itself certainly was a tribute to his performance, and the opportunity to see whether the challenges of government would be conquered as well as those of engineering and business also intrigued him.

He needed no further income. His business and investments would easily take care of Marjorie and himself for the rest of their lives, and he had to admit that many of his activities were repetitious, and less challenging. More dams, more canals, more housing, more shopping centers; the saying that success breeds success, he learned, was more true than he had imagined, and much was accomplished by the well-oiled machinery he had set up lately with very little effort on his part.

The governorship would be a new challenge, and he had to admit that the more he thought about it, the more he coveted it. The work details at San Tomas were another matter, and he had trusted Colonel Dunby's assessment of the situation. Already most of the Levey family had turned against him. The affair with Elyse, though a matter easily dismissed by a private citizen, could be blown out of proportion if he entered public life. The San Tomas experiences, the horrors of that camp, the sights, the sounds, the smells, the deaths, the mutilations, the tortures, the screams . . . all that would be revived.

He had used men, his *own* men in prison camp for his own purposes. There was no denying that. It was not only a matter of survival, it was a purely selfish act. Of course he had rationalized it. If he had not taught the Japanese captors engineering, he might not be alive today. But it was treasonous, that he had used his own men, for his own purposes. . . .

"You must work it out," the psychiatrist had told him when he was discharged at Letterman General Hospital. "See your priest, see your rabbi. . . . I would even suggest some professional help."

But he knew no priest, he knew no rabbi, and there was no time for "professional help," and the nightmares remained.

Perhaps, he wondered, this race for the governorship might not be the All-American dream at all, but nothing more than a public purging of all the hells and deaths he—*he*, Bill Crossen—had left in his wake. He did not sleep that night at all. And he did not sleep the following night, either.

The second night, he finally resolved that he would *refuse* the offer. He would say no. To hell with them. At this point, he was his own man. Once committed he would not be. He *knew* why they had sought him out. He was young, yes, successful, yes. He was ingenious, yes, but in their eyes he was not wild-eyed. He was, he knew himself, conservative. He knew, like them, he wanted the order of the day to continue. He knew what they meant about the "business climate," and he was in accord. He was safe in their eyes because he would protect their investments, respect their real estate; *safe* because he would respect their aristocracy. How safe, he wondered, would he really be? Could he, as governor, find himself in a stark motel room in Tracy, not knowing how he'd gotten there? Sweat appeared on his forehead. The only solution would be to turn the offer down, to keep running, to keep drowning himself in work, to remain as anonymous as possible. Perhaps that was the only answer, after all.

Chapter LVIX

Selda had arrived early at the concert hall in Cleveland, and she had picked up the ticket held for Bill Crossen. She had that afternoon spoken to the management and had been given a backstage pass to use after the performance.

She had a fine seat in the orchestra section and buried herself in the program notes, reading about Marjorie's past performances, and other random erudite notes about the city's cultural endeavors.

The lights dimmed, the orchestra quieted down and George Szell, tall and elegant, appeared and opened the performance with a wonderfully frivolous "Gaieté Parisienne."

Marjorie followed Offenbach. She looked quite regal and composed in a lovely white gown, and Selda watched as she nodded to Szell and the piece began. But it was all lost on Selda whose mind was on other things, and it was not until the following morning that she understood what had transpired. The reviews once again were superb. Even Fisher of *The New York Times* and Waldring of the *Herald* praised not only her mastery of the piano, but her knowledge of Bach as well. Her technique was deemed faultless, her ear superb, her taste flawless.

Throughout the performance, though, Selda saw not a finished artist but a young woman to whom she would bring much consternation at the end of that performance.

Selda stood in the wings bearing a bouquet of roses, and when she appeared after her first bow, Marjorie could only say, "Where's Bill?" as an assistant handed her a towel.

"He'll be all right, sweetheart," Selda said.

"But what's wrong?"

"Take your bows and don't worry."

The audience was as enthusiastic as the one in San Francisco. They stood, cheering, and the conductor motioned the orchestra to stand. Marjorie shared the applause with Szell and the players, but she could not wait to return to Selda.

"Has he been hurt?" she asked when they finally pushed through well-wishers to her dressing room.

"No, Marjorie, no," Selda said. "He'll be all right. He's just worn out."

It took almost two hours of festive formalities before they reached Marjorie's hotel suite and finally settled themselves on an overstuffed couch. It was one in the morning and Cleveland was asleep outside the window.

And it had only been three nights earlier that Bill had rung Selda's doorbell. It was dinner time and he was dressed in a pair of work pants, a shirt open at the neck. He was unshaven, his hair uncombed.

"Selda," he said.

"Bill, come in. Would you like some dinner? We're eating."

"No. No thanks. What time is it?"

449

"It's seven o'clock."

"My God. What day is it?"

"It's Wednesday."

She pulled him in the door and closed it. He seemed to be shaken.

"Come. I'll put some food into your belly. You look awful."

"No, thanks. I—" he paused. "I—need . . . to talk . . . to you."

"Of course, but . . ."

"*Now.*"

"All right, all right." She pushed him toward the living room.

"*Now, alone,*" he said.

She quickly steered him to her bedroom and went to tell her husband and children of her plight.

"I'll eat later," she said. "Go ahead without me."

She returned to Bill and shut the door behind her.

"When is the concert?" he asked.

"Saturday."

"Last Saturday?"

"No, this Saturday."

"That's good," he said.

"What is wrong with you?"

"I don't know," he said, and paced the small room and then sat down on the bed and wept.

Selda placed her arms about him but he continued to weep. Then he stopped.

"I have so many conferences, luncheons, staff meetings. . . . What day is it?"

"Wednesday."

"My God."

She looked at Bill. He seemed almost as frail as the first day he had entered her home, and she decided quickly that he needed medical help.

"Stay where you are," she said, and half ran to her

husband. She explained the circumstances and asked him to call a doctor, then she returned to Bill.

"Sit down," she said. "You'll be all right. You're *vermischt*. I've called a doctor."

"No," he half shouted. "No. No. I can't see a doctor."

"You have to, Bill. You have to."

He started to run out of the room, and she called her husband who gently restrained him.

"Who's this?" Bill asked.

"Joseph, my husband. You know Joseph."

"Yes. Hi, Joseph," Crossen said. "I'm way behind. I've got to go. I'm supposed to be in Cleveland, I have two board meetings. . . ."

Dr. Aranoff arrived in less than an hour, and after a short examination suggested that he take Bill to Mt. Sinai Hospital.

"My cousin," she said to Aranoff, "is ill, no doubt, but I would appreciate his anonymity. It has been rumored that he may run for governor of California."

"I understand," Aranoff said. "I know Bill Crossen; he doesn't remember me now. I'll handle it all."

Selda accompanied the doctor and Bill to Mt. Sinai Hospital, where he was quietly admitted under a false name to a private room; and Aranoff sedated him sufficiently to put him to sleep. He observed his patient until that had been accomplished, then joined Selda in the hallway.

"He was in the war, wasn't he?"

"Yes," Selda said. "A prisoner of war for four years."

Aranoff nodded. "I see."

"What is it?"

"Disorientation. Partly shock, partially amnesia. Low blood sugar, I suspect . . . it's common."

"And what's the prognosis?"

"Good. If handled right. I'll call a psychiatrist, Dr. Goodstone. He's the best."

"His wife is performing in Cleveland on Saturday. He's got to be there. . . ."

"Out of the question," Aranoff said.

"You don't know Bill Crossen."

"No. Not well," Aranoff said, "but I know these symptoms."

"Should I phone his wife?"

"Not now. Wait until Goodstone has seen him."

"How long will he be asleep now?"

"Eight hours, at least. Go home. Get some rest. I'll have Goodstone here in the morning."

It was dawn when Bill awoke, and Goodstone was already seated at the foot of his bed, his kindly Jewish features radiating reassurance. He was a man in his sixties. His suit looked as if he had slept in it, not only the night before, but several other nights. The jacket seemed threadbare, his bow tie was askew.

"You're in a hospital, Mr. Crossen. I am Dr. Goodstone. A psychoanalyst."

Bill stirred slowly, trying to get through the haze of the drug. He noticed a bottle above his bed, a needle in his arm.

"What's this all about?"

"Just glucose. Seems you haven't eaten in a few days. Your blood sugar was very low last night."

"What day is it?"

"Thursday."

"I've got to be in Cleveland on Saturday."

"I know," Goodstone said, "I spoke to your cousin, Selda."

"I've got meetings, board meetings."

"I know that, too."

"Does anybody know I'm here?"

"I do," Goodstone said. "Your cousin Selda does.

She brought you here last night. You're registered under an assumed name."

Bill nodded and said nothing and neither did Goodstone. Goodstone watched Bill finally raise himself in bed.

"Do you know, Mr. Crossen, why I'm a psychiatrist?"

"No."

"I flunked out of engineering school, I couldn't hack the math. I still can't."

"How are you on brains?"

Goodstone laughed. "A sense of humor," he said. "That's good."

"I mean it."

"Do you want a list of my degrees?"

"No. I want to get out of here."

"I know," Goodstone said. "Everybody who's in a hospital does."

"I can't stand confinement," Bill said.

"I understand. A man who was a prisoner of war needs an open door."

Bill looked at him somewhat more sympathetically. "You seem to know a lot about me."

Goodstone rose, walked to the foot of the bed and sat on it facing him.

"That's my business. You have a reputation for very high intelligence. Now listen to me carefully."

"Go on."

"The physicians here have run blood tests. I've seen the results. You're low on sugar, low on hemoglobin, and you've got a touch of jaundice. You are lacking elements but we can put all those back into you. The more you cooperate the quicker we can accomplish this."

"By Saturday?"

"No. Not by Saturday. A week, perhaps."

"But Marjorie's concert . . ."

"I know about that."

"I *must* be there."

"You cannot be there. Selda has offered to go. The sooner I can build you up, the sooner we can talk. Man to man. Do you understand? I need to deal with someone who has the strength to fight back. Not someone flat on his ass."

"Is that a medical term?"

"Yes," Goodstone laughed.

"And what if I were to walk out of here? Pull this damned needle out of my arm and walk out of here?"

"You have that right. You're not committed."

"You wouldn't stop me?"

"Why would I do that? I didn't come here to punish you. I am here to help."

"What are my chances of getting to Cleveland?"

"Always the engineer. You want a probability curve?"

"Yes."

"In your state of mind, you would not be able to reach your home. You would not be able to pack your clothes. You would not be able to reach the airport, and you'd scare the hell out of your wife if you *did* manage all that."

"What the hell is wrong with me?"

"You are asking for the solution to an equation without giving me any of the input."

"You did learn something in engineering school."

"Yes," Goodstone said, "I did. Even medicine, believe it or not, has some logic in it. . . ."

"They have asked me to run for governor of California," Bill said.

"So I have heard. Would you like that?"

"I don't know. They'd never let me run if they thought I was a looney."

"You wouldn't want them to, would you?"

"I suppose not. But they know I'm here."

"Who are *they*?"

"Lehman, Goldman, the goddamned newspapers, I bet."

"No one knows you are here. Only Selda, and Dr. Aranoff and myself. I told you we've registered you under an assumed name."

Goodstone rose. "You are not in a locked ward. You are in a regular hospital. You can walk out of here anytime you wish. I'm prescribing several more shots and infusions for you to regain your health and to let you sleep. You can refuse those. I'll be back tomorrow morning. If you want to see me before then, please don't hesitate to call. I can be here in half an hour."

"Thank you," Bill Crossen said. "Why am I so damned sleepy?"

"We've put enough Demerol in you to kill a racehorse."

"Never send a boy to do a man's work."

Goodstone walked by the side of the bed and looked at the level of the IV bottle.

"As soon as this is empty, push the bell," he said. "Efficiency is not a strong point in this hospital."

He left and joined Selda in the corridor. They walked down the hall and sat in the reception room of the hospital on the first floor.

"How does he seem?"

"Better than I thought. He feels compelled to go to Cleveland."

"You can't let him go to Cleveland."

"I can't stop him," Goodstone said.

"He is here by doctor's orders."

"Granted, but he is not insane. I can't commit him, and if I committed him I could not do it under an assumed name."

"Are you putting nurses with him?"

"No. I told him he could walk out. If he doesn't trust me, then I'll never be able to help him. I told him he would get another shot, so he should go back to sleep soon."

"I understand what you are saying, Doctor," Selda said, "but we must *help* him."

"I intend to."

"But you don't understand."

"What?"

"I told you before, they have asked him to run for governor of California. He can't be *here* under an assumed name very long."

"I am aware of that, too."

"Then what can you do?"

Goodstone looked at her with his very kind eyes. "We are dealing with a man who has lived under the pressure of a good many crises for a good many years. I can't put someone like that together overnight. . . ."

"I understand. He should have seen you right after the war."

"Why do you say that?"

"That's when I first met him. When he was discharged from the service."

"Perhaps that's true," Goodstone said, "but he didn't." He looked at the sadness in Selda's face.

"There are things we can do to speed up his recovery."

"Name them."

"I am dealing with a very intelligent young man. That is a help. Secondly, I need all the input I can get from people who know him well. You, for one."

"I'm available."

"How about his wife?"

"She'll help, but she has a concert on Saturday."

"Yes. I want you to go there."

"Me?"

"Yes. Bill Crossen is in no shape. Who else could help?"

"Mr. Levey, his father-in-law."

"Who else?"

"I don't know," Selda said. "Bill has very few friends."

"All right. There is you, Marjorie, Mr. Levey. We'll get started in the morning. You'd better go home and get some sleep."

Selda did not go home but instead took up a vigil outside Bill's door all night. Her husband brought her dinner, a nurse brought her a blanket, and she passed the hours without trouble, reading and thinking, and sometimes dozing.

It was Goodstone, wearing the same rumpled suit, the same benign smile, who woke her at seven in the morning. He sat next to her and proffered a cup of coffee.

"Thank you," she said.

"He didn't leave," Goodstone asked.

"No. He didn't."

"His blood sugar is almost normal. The hemoglobin is coming up. I saw the lab reports a minute ago."

"Do you think he can go to Cleveland?"

"Out of the question."

"Then *I* should go."

"Yes."

"How long do you expect he will be here?"

"As short a time as possible. This atmosphere is very damaging to his personality. You say money is no problem?"

"None."

"I know a private clinic in Sonoma. Perhaps Sunday or Monday I can move him. After I see him, I want to talk to you."

"Good," Selda said. "I guess you know what you're doing."

"Don't be so sure," Goodstone said.

"I'm sure," Selda said. "You remind me of my father."

Goodstone laughed. "I seem to remind *everyone* of their father." He rose and entered Bill's room.

"Good morning," he said. "Jesus, why don't they let you shave?"

"I don't have a razor."

"Buy one."

"You'd let me use a razor?"

"Why not? I haven't even thought of suicide. Have you?"

"No."

"Good. I'm glad they got that needle out of your arm. Your blood is responding fine."

"I had some eggs for breakfast."

"Order a steak for lunch. You want some books? A radio?"

"No, thanks."

"Your cousin Selda is flying to Cleveland."

"What will she tell Marjorie?"

"That you're ill. Is that a crime?"

"Perhaps I should call Marjorie. . . ."

"Perhaps you should, but I wouldn't. She has a big concert ahead of her."

"I know," Bill said. "I could still make it."

"No, you couldn't. You might get to the airport. You'd never make it to Cleveland."

"Jesus Christ! Why not?"

"I *did* study stresses and strains in engineering school before I flunked out. There are too many of them in your psyche right now to support the kind of man you really are. Does that make sense?"

"I suppose."

"It will take six hours for Marjorie to return from Cleveland to see you. The world won't end in six hours."

"I need to see my secretary," Crossen said.

"That can be arranged. When do you want to see her?"

Bill looked at his arm, but instead of his watch he noticed a plastic band with a name on it.

"Clever, isn't it? For three dollars," Goodstone said, "they put your name on your wrist. Anytime you forget it, you can reassure yourself at a glance."

"It's not even my name."

"That's right," Goodstone said. "We'll get a refund."

"I've never been without a watch since I was six years old."

"I can believe that," Goodstone said. "That's probably one of the reasons you're here. . . ."

There was silence in the room and then Bill looked at Goodstone.

"I woke up in the middle of the night. I tried the door. The corridor was empty except for Selda. She was asleep in a chair. . . ."

"You're on the fifth floor," Goodstone said. "The window isn't bolted, either. I want you to understand something, my boy. I am not your father, and I am not your mother. I am your doctor, and you're my patient. You trust me and I'll trust you, and that's where it ends. I don't love you and I don't expect you to love me."

"You know, Goodstone, they made a mistake when they flunked you out of engineering school."

"That is the mosaic of life, Crossen. The trick is simply to make more right decisions than wrong ones."

"My secretary," Crossen said, "and a razor."

"Yes, sir," Goodstone said. "And I'll send up some straws so you can weave a basket."

"You have a sense of humor, too," Crossen said.

"Yes. I have been known for that and for the fact that I look like everyone's father."

"You don't look like mine."

Goodstone left and the last statement stuck in his craw.

Chapter LX

Miss Godden, Bill's private secretary, a woman ten years his senior, well groomed, intelligent, sophisticated, sat at Bill's bedside.

"I'm sorry to have you see me like this, Miss Godden," he said.

"I'm sorry to see you here."

"You are an executive secretary. And a good one," Bill said. "If I've never told you, I should have."

"You have, Mr. Crossen. You have. Thank you."

"I'll be incommunicado for several days, weeks. . . ." He seemed suddenly vague, and Miss Godden waited apprehensively for him to continue.

"I have also," he continued, "been asked to run for governor of California."

"Congratulations."

"Thank you. My absence from the office, my unavailability will raise questions, *many* questions."

"I understand," she said sympathetically.

"In my frame of mind," he confessed, "I don't have the answers to these questions, and I will rely on you to supply them."

She rose and patted his hand. "You didn't hire me only because I can type and take dictation. . . ."

"Exactly."

"You can count on me. I've always felt you were much too accessible, anyhow."

Bill looked at her. "If things work out that way," he said almost haltingly, "do you think you could live in Sacramento?"

"You bet. I could even live in Washington, D.C."

She stood.

"Oh, one more thing," Bill said.

"Yes?"

"How much do you want for your watch?"

She looked at the small watch on her wrist.

"It's just a cheap watch."

"May I have it?"

"Of course," she said. She unfastened it and handed it to him.

"I'll return it or replace it."

"Don't worry about it," she said, "and get well soon."

"Thank you."

She rose and left.

Goodstone, as was becoming his habit, appeared again at seven in the morning to find Crossen dressed, sitting in a chair reading the national coverage of his young wife's triumph.

"Class," Crossen said, "*that's* class. Look at these reviews."

"I read my *Chronicle* this morning, Mr. Crossen. I saw her debut in San Francisco. You should be very proud."

"Proud," Crossen said, "and humble," but Goodstone did not pick up on the remark.

461

"Hold your hands out in front of you and close your eyes," he said. Crossen obeyed and finally Goodstone told him to drop his arms and open his eyes.

"What was that all about?" Crossen asked.

"I used to be an M.D. before I became a psychiatrist."

"I see."

"I have reserved a cottage for you at San Ysidro. It has a fireplace. A king-sized bed. A thousand acres. Horses, a pool. A restaurant. It is in Sonoma. I'll drive you there."

"Marjorie. When am I going to see Marjorie?"

"I suggested to Selda that they return by train. She will be in San Francisco on Monday night. I presume you can see her Tuesday. . . ."

"I am not a cowboy. What the hell am I going to do at San Ysidro?"

"Regain your health. Talk to me."

"You don't look like a cowboy, either."

"Really? Most of my women patients think I sell Fuller brushes at night. I understand you crave anonymity. I can get it for you there."

"I appreciate that. Will Marjorie be able to stay with me at San Ysidro?"

"In good time."

"What the hell does that mean!" Crossen shouted.

"I see you've got a watch again. Perhaps I can teach you that your whole life is not made up of beating a clock. You're wasting a lot of time sitting here. . . ."

"You're taunting me," Crossen said.

"Nothing of the kind. I am telling you the truth. Remember what I said?"

"What was that?"

"I don't expect you to love me. . . ."

"You said that," Crossen agreed. "I wonder if anybody loves me."

*   *   *

Marjorie phoned Bill the next morning and found him not only rational but extremely sweet.

"I've read every notice, darling, every one, over and over again."

"Chalk one up for the Crossens," Marjorie said.

"Yes. I tried so hard to get there, I—" he hesitated. "The doctors—" he hesitated again, "no one thought I could make it."

"I love you, Bill," Marjorie said. "There will be other concerts, other nights. . . ."

"I love you, too, Marjorie. I have," he spoke very slowly. "I have never felt like this."

"Selda and I are getting on the train today. I will see you in a couple of days."

"I can't wait to see you," Bill said, almost on the edge of tears.

"I know," Marjorie said. "I know. I feel the same way."

Marjorie and Selda shared a comfortable drawing room on the Super Chief traveling west, but they spent precious little time watching America pass their window. Neither the wheat-laden Midwest, nor the mountainous Rockies elicited much comment from the women.

"Perhaps the greatest worry I have," Marjorie said that first morning, "is how devastating Elyse Wolf really was."

"Forget it," Selda said. "A good piece of nookie."

"I'm not blaming Bill, Selda, except I'll never be an Elyse Wolf. I'll never look like Elyse Wolf."

"All right. Be realistic. Solari? Was that the guy's name?"

"Yes."

"Good in bed. Suave, exciting, overwhelming, yes?"

"Yes. Incredible. He asked me to live with him."

463

"What did you say?"

"No."

"Are you sorry?"

"No."

"If Bill Crossen wanted Elyse Wolf, I'm sure she was his for the asking. Obviously he didn't."

"I guess you're right. But why the breakdown?"

"It *had* to come, Marjorie. I expected it years ago when that boy first showed up at my house."

"The prison camp?"

"The prison camp, to some extent, sure, but more. His background. I remember my parents talking about his father. A miserable, domineering, unbending Jew. . . . I've talked to Dr. Goodstone. He feels the problems go way back."

"But what about me? Have I done nothing to make his life better?"

"I think," Selda said measuredly, "that Bill Crossen loves you more than any woman alive. . . ."

"But should I tell him about Solari?"

"My instincts say yes, but Bill has an analyst. Dr. Goodstone. Talk to him."

"But saying nothing might hurt him even more?"

Selda threw up her hands. "I am not judge or jury. I've got instincts. That's all. I love my husband. I've asked *him* about Bill, and he said he cannot understand how anybody, any engineer, could accomplish what Bill has accomplished in so few years."

"But at a price?" Marjorie asked.

"Yes. At a price. Everything has a price."

Chapter LXI

Bill Crossen's cottage, a three-room affair of grooved wood painted white, commanded a view of manicured lawns, cutting beds of flowers, vineyards and gentle, oak-covered hills. It was pleasantly but not opulently furnished, with chairs of flower-patterned prints and window boxes. There was a fireplace in both the living room and the bedroom of the cottage, and there was a large porch on which he sat with Goodstone, Crossen wearing denims and a sport shirt, Goodstone acknowledging the rural setting by unloosening his necktie.

"All right, Bill," Goodstone said. "I am going to be totally honest with you. I understand about the offer of the candidacy, and I realize that you do not have the luxury of a lengthy analysis."

"That is quite right."

"So we will have to make do with the little time available and the fathomless experience I have had in this field."

465

"Modesty is not your virtue."

"Modesty," Goodstone said, "is *never* a virtue. I want you to know that I've spent a good deal of time with Selda already, and some hours with your father-in-law."

"Why Henry?" Bill seemed agitated.

"I wish there were ten *more* people I could talk to to help me, but you seem to be a very solitary soul."

"What does Henry Levey think of all this?"

"He loves you, Bill. He will do anything to help me help you."

Crossen put his head between his hands.

"Goddamnit, I don't want to bother Henry. He's been ill himself."

"Yes, he has. But he is doing fine. He's being very cooperative."

"I don't *want* his help."

"Why not?"

"He's my father-in-law."

"I know that. What's wrong with that?"

"He's not my father. My father's not here."

"What if he were?"

"He wouldn't help."

"Why not? You're his son."

"We're very different."

Goodstone looked at Bill a long time before asking the next question. "What *was* your father like?"

Bill hesitated, then said, "Cruel. Very cruel."

"Was he physical?"

"What do you mean?"

"Did he beat you?"

"He slapped me across the face."

"What else?"

"He kicked me."

"What else?"

"He choked me."

"What else?"

466

"He spit at me."

"What else?"

"He shadowed me."

"Shadowed you?"

"I had two paper routes when I was a kid. I would collect once a month. He was behind me all the way. House after house."

"You hated him," Goodstone said.

"He was my father."

"Forget that. You *hated* him."

"He fed me. He housed me."

"And you brought in money since you were six years old?"

"Yes."

"You hated him, goddamnit, Crossen. Why not? I already hate the son of a bitch and I don't even know him."

"What good does all that do now?"

"For me, nothing," Goodstone said. "For you, everything. You want to be my governor, I want you on solid ground."

"Governor," Bill laughed sarcastically. "Well, this episode should put an end to that adventure. . . ."

Goodstone was quiet for several minutes. Then he said, "An end to the adventure. I understand you taught yourself Japanese in three months."

"Yes."

"And so you sailed on from high school to NYU to MIT. All on scholarship?"

" 'Sailed' may not be the right word."

"I did not mean financially," Goodstone said. "I meant academically."

"That's true. I had no problem. Phi Beta Kappa, summa cum laude, all they had to offer."

"Fun?" Goodstone asked. "What did you do for fun?"

Crossen was slow to answer. "There wasn't much time for fun."

"I see. Girls?" Goodstone asked. "No girls?"

"I had no money. No time."

"You weren't celibate?"

"No. But practically."

"And then the war."

Crossen put his fingers over his eyes and Goodstone watched the motion.

"Yes. And then the war."

"All right," Goodstone said, standing and pacing the room. "If I were in your shoes, listening to my questions, I'd say, what's with this guy? Playing hopscotch with my life. Father, mother, school, the army. All in one hour . . ."

"*You* said that," Crossen answered. "*I* didn't."

"I know. You must realize that I am under pressure, too."

He sat down again across from Bill.

"Listen to me, and try to believe me. In the first place we are all traumatized. You, me, Selda, Marjorie, that guy raking the leaves down there. Life is wheels within wheels.

"Some people, like you, have run the wheels too fast. At this point you are *overtraumatized*, but other than that you are an extremely functional man. I don't intend to break you into an unassembled jigsaw puzzle and fit you together again."

"Your approach amazes me," Crossen said.

"Why, did you think you were the only decisive son of a bitch in town?"

"I did until this happened."

Goodstone shook his head. "I believe that."

"When is Marjorie coming?" Bill asked.

"In three days."

"Is she walking?"

"No, she is taking a train. That was my doing."

"Where are my baskets?"

"I would have sent the material," Goodstone said, "but I thought in twenty-four hours you would put the Indians out of business. Tell me about San Tomas. . . ."

Chapter LXII

The following day Goodstone waited for Crossen to rise, but was surprised to see him enter the front door of the cottage, dressed, shaved, a better tone and color to his skin.

"This is a very pretty place," Crossen said.

"How long since you've looked at a tree?"

"Strange you should ask that. Trees are always in my way. Roads, dams, bridges, culverts . . ."

"All right," Goodstone said, "enough trivia. This Ito fellow at San Tomas . . . tell me about him."

"We spent two years together at MIT."

"Were you friends?"

"I had no friends."

"You *thought* you had no friends. . . ."

"Whatever."

"What happened to him?"

"He left suddenly and returned to Japan. I couldn't understand it until Pearl Harbor."

"Where did you first see him again?"

"On the March on Bataan."

"Did you speak?"

"No."

"But he recognized you?"

"Yes."

"And you survived the march, obviously."

"Yes."

"Because of him?"

"I'll never know."

"And then you met again at San Tomas?"

"Yes. He summoned me. We spoke."

"About what?"

"MIT, mostly."

"What, specifically?"

"About the courses I had taken after he left."

"He spoke English?"

"That's right."

"He made me sanitary officer, but there was a price."

"What was that?"

"He wanted lessons."

"What kind of lessons?"

"He wanted to learn what he had missed at MIT."

"And you agreed?"

"Yes, but . . . he used me and I used him."

"How?"

"I worked on my future at San Tomas."

"How?"

"I built the Delta-Mendota Canal in miniature. I built scale models of heavy machinery I intended to patent. . . ."

"What's wrong with that?"

"Nothing, so far. Except—" he hesitated.

"Except?"

And Crossen shouted, "I used my own men, American prisoners, to build that canal, to lay out the state of California! Weak, disease-ridden men in that Philippine heat, that humidity ... That's how I assembled my daily work details."

"Did you kill anybody?"

"What do you mean?"

"Did anyone die on those work details?"

"Men died every week. Malaria, malnutrition ..."

"There were five thousand men at San Tomas. Did only men in your work detail die?"

"No."

"But you'd like to believe that?"

"Of course not. The men were very weakened already."

"I understand you got drugs to your men. Quinine, Sulfa. Is that right?"

"When Selda shipped them."

"Why did you do that?"

"I knew they hated me. I had to do what I could to ..."

"To what?" Goodstone now shouted. "To survive?"

"Yes, to survive."

"And men were beaten at San Tomas?"

"Yes."

"And kicked?"

"Yes."

"And choked?"

"Yes."

"And spat on?"

"Yes."

"And they cleaned up vomit and piss and shit?"

"Yes ... it was a prison camp," Bill said.

"I know," Goodstone said, "and you don't like to be beaten, choked, spat on. ..."

"I could have taught Ito and his Japanese cohorts all I learned at MIT without working on my own project."

"Of course. You could have built hypothetical projects."

"Yes."

"But you were crafty, is that what you are saying?"

"Crafty . . . well, I did it all for myself. . . ."

"Why?"

"Because I didn't want to waste time during imprisonment."

"Why not?"

"I was getting older."

"You were twenty-four when you got out?" Goodstone asked.

"Twenty-four, yes."

"And you wanted to get to work, to build, to invent. To make more money and more money."

"I suppose."

"Suppose? Why?"

Crossen flinched. "That's me, I guess. . . ."

"What does that mean?"

"Driving, mean, selfish, tough, brutal, son of a bitch," he said.

"That what you think of yourself?"

"Yes."

"Really, yes?"

Goodstone walked to the window and faced the pastoral landscape.

"Selda told me that your only motive when you came to San Francisco was to get power. Do you remember saying that?"

"Yes."

"Do you know what you were saying?"

"I thought I did. . . ."

"You were saying you wanted power so no one could ever hit you again, choke you again, spit on you again . . . that's that you were saying."

"The army didn't think my conduct was so exemplary."

"Fuck the army! Did it ever occur to you while you were in prison camp, that Eisenhower had his dinner flown from Twenty-One in New York to London three times a week? Do you think he worried that that flight crew might hit a storm? Get shot at? Have engine failure?"

"Why am I so tired?" Crossen asked.

"You are not tired. You can't face hating your father."

"I send money," Bill said. "They send it back."

"Fine," Goodstone said coldly. "Don't send money."

Now Bill faced him. "So you *are* harking back to Freud."

"You bet your sweet ass, my boy. His principles are as solid as Archimedes'. His theories as watertight as Newton's. . . ."

"And with enough money, you can even have your sins washed—"

"Bullshit," Goodstone interrupted. "If you want to wallow in grief, do it. If you want to sanctify those nightmares, be my guest. . . ." He rose.

"Wait," Bill said. "Please wait. You swear pretty good."

"Learned it in engineering school," Goodstone said, smiling and sitting down again.

"It's strange, you know, but after you've reached a certain pinnacle of success, no one ever swears at you anymore."

"I'm multifaceted," Goodstone said.

"Yes," Bill answered, "with a superb sense of humor."

"Refined, eloquent, urbane," Goodstone rattled off. . . . He patted his battered coat jacket. "Win the award each year for one of the ten best-dressed analysts in San Francisco. . . ."

Goodstone rose and faced Crossen. "Let's get back to the nightmares," he said. "What are they like?"

Crossen said nothing.

"Can't you remember them?"

"God, yes."

"What do you dream about?"

Bill faced him squarely. "Death, death, death."

"What kind of death?"

"The men in the march. The men in prison camp."

"Go on. . . ."

"I see Rodriguez. Rodriguez cut down from that tree, limp and lifeless. . . ." He hesitated. "Elyse's child . . . blue and drowned in that pool." He shielded his face with his hands.

"Go ahead and cry," Goodstone put his arm about the young man. "It's not a sin. You feel you caused all those deaths?"

Bill nodded.

Goodstone sat facing Crossen and waited for him to compose himself. Finally Bill looked up.

"I'm all right now," he said.

"You are a bright man," Goodstone said. "I want you to give me some honest answers."

"I'll try."

"You—you, Bill Crossen—personally bombed Pearl Harbor?"

"No."

"You, Bill Crossen, personally hanged Rodriguez?"

"No, I might have just as well. . . ."

"*You*, Bill Crossen, founded the Wolf family, and their useless genes produced an alcoholic son?"

"No, but . . ."

"*But what?*"

"Your theory doesn't hold up," Crossen said.

"Why?"

"What would you say to Elyse Wolf if you were treating her?"

"I am not treating her, I am treating *you*. . . ."

"I said it before, with enough money you can even buy off guilt."

"Wrong," Goodstone said. "I also treat patients for

nothing. You *want* to believe you caused all those deaths. There is a name for that neurosis. It's called the crucifix complex."

"You have a name for everything."

"No," Goodstone said, "we don't, but your problem is common."

"So it has a name, so what?"

"I'm going to try to explain the nature of that beast," Goodstone said.

Bill looked at him.

"It stems from a need to play God."

"God?"

"Yes, God. You like to feel omnipotent. You *like* to think you have that power to cause death. . . ."

"Why would I want that?"

"Because ever since you were a little boy you wished your father was dead."

"No," Crossen said.

"*Yes.* Don't you remember the nightmares you had then? The fantasies? Come on, *think.* . . ."

Again Bill covered his face, but this time Goodstone pried his hands away and faced the sobbing man.

"Look at me," Goodstone commanded, as he stared at Crossen's tear-streaked face.

"Look at me and tell me I'm right."

"*You're right,* damnit," Crossen said. "You're right. Night after night I lay in bed wishing that son of a bitch were dead. I had endless fantasies. Knives, guns, trucks, the third rail of the subway . . ."

"And you, an abused child, take responsibility for that?"

"I don't know."

"Look," Goodstone said quietly. "Life is a tragedy. We each owe it one death. The men in the prison camp, your work details, Rodriguez, Elyse's child . . . they have paid their debt. If you believe in God, then their destiny was preordained."

"And if you don't?" Bill asked.

"Then it was preordained by nature."

"What about murder?" Crossen asked. "What about a man who shoots another and kills him?"

"That is a different pathology," Goodstone said. "We are talking here about a classical case of crucifixion complex. Nothing more. The urge to feel responsible for deaths not caused directly. There is a difference.

"California," Goodstone continued, "has the death sentence for criminals. There is a cell in San Quentin called the *death* cell. There are men waiting to enter that chamber. It is called *death* row. Only the governor has the right to pardon. Have you considered that responsibility?"

"I have," Bill said.

"Seriously?"

"Yes."

"Has it become a decisive factor in your decision to run?"

"It has."

Goodstone smiled and said, "Do you think you've given an inordinate amount of your time to that question? Be honest."

"Yes."

"More than another man in your shoes?"

"Probably . . ."

"Then the equation comes out? Would you say?"

Crossen looked at him and managed a smile. "You son of a bitch," he said to Goodstone.

"Aah, good," Goodstone said. "The steel is returning to your backbone. I've got to leave. I have other patients. I'll see you tonight."

And Crossen stood at the door and watched the

rumpled little man disappear down the path in front of his cottage, his bald pate reflecting the sunset. He heard Goodstone start the engine of his car and heard the wheels spin on the gravel driveway, and he felt as helpless as he had as a small boy climbing a tall commode, begging his father to help him down, and he recalled the words: "You're such an idiot to climb up there, you get yourself down. . . ."

Chapter LXIII

Marjorie met Goodstone in his office the morning she returned to San Francisco. It was a large room in the Post Building, its furnishings as unkempt as Goodstone's suits, yet its chairs and couches were covered with well-worn leather, the lighting pleasant and warm.

Goodstone rose and embraced Marjorie and congratulated her on her triumph in Cleveland.

"I saw your debut here," he said. "You were magnificent."

"Thank you."

"I told your husband I flunked out of engineering school, and I must admit I hated the piano lessons my mother foisted on me, but," he held up his hand, "I *do* have some skills. I barbecue steaks like Roy Rogers and I play a mean harmonica."

Marjorie responded to the warmth of the man immediately.

"Before you ask, I will tell you that your husband is

479

not insane. He is not going insane. There *are* technical terms for his breakdown whose only use is to classify his problems for actuarial purposes, they mean very little.

"When I first saw him he was overworked, undernourished, both contributing factors to his illness; but he was under a great deal of emotional pressure, perhaps the one fact of his life he is least able to deal with."

"Is he all right?" Marjorie asked.

"Physically, yes. A little weak, but I keep sedating him. He is young. Very vital. An incredible young man, really."

"Yes," Marjorie said, "I agree, but what about these pressures? Was it Elyse Wolf?"

"Partly," Goodstone said. "Minimally."

"What else?"

"A great deal," Goodstone said. "A very traumatic childhood, a monster of a father, an endless need to survive in a tough neighborhood, demanding universities, prison camp . . ."

"I know."

"But more," Goodstone said. "There is friction in *your* family, he has guilts about his behavior in prison camp. He has been asked to run for governor of California, he runs a large corporation. . . . I mean, I can usually remember to go to the Chinese laundry or the shoe repair shop, but I can rarely remember both the same day. . . ."

"And I can only see to the end of the piano keys," Marjorie said. "What can I do? When can I see him?"

He grasped Marjorie's hands in his and looked at her.

"Imagine all those pressures, Marjorie. All the ones I have listed. A man without his strength would have cracked long ago."

"But he puts them on himself," Marjorie said.

"Quite true. He has a need to feel guilt. To some

extent that is a Jewish trait, but in his case the need is pathological."

Marjorie looked at him. "And you can treat that?"

"Of course."

Marjorie stared at an earthenware lamp, whose shade was still covered in cellophane.

"You want him well, is that right?"

"Yes."

"Why?"

"I love him."

"Not good enough."

"I respect him."

"Still not good enough."

Marjorie leaned back in her chair and stared at the smoke-stained acoustical ceiling. "All my life my older sister has been a threat. . . ."

"Go on."

"She was prettier than I was. She was more popular."

"And you took that out on the piano."

"Yes. Until Bill came along."

"Go on."

"He was good-looking, he was frightened. . . . I wanted to throw that good-looking Bill Crossen into Linda's teeth."

"Good. Good. Now we're getting somewhere. And how did you fare?" Goodstone asked.

"Better than I expected."

"How?"

"I didn't know how extraordinary Bill was. No one did. He didn't just work for Daddy. In less than a year everybody was listening to Bill Crossen."

"You respect that."

"Yes."

"Why?"

"He was *my* man. I *do* have pride."

"And the piano?"

481

"My work flourished."

"Yes. Why? You were rid of Linda, why the compulsion to stay at the piano?"

"Because it pleased Bill. I could see the pride he had in me. He would spend hours watching me practice. It was only then I could see love in his eyes."

"Love or respect?" Goodstone asked.

"I don't know."

"When did you first know about Elyse Wolf?"

"My sister phoned me in Cleveland."

"What did you feel?"

"At first . . . I thought about Linda. . . . I had watched Elyse," Marjorie said. "I had watched all the other bitches flocking around him when he became so successful."

"And how did you feel?"

"I was surrounded by Lindas."

"Good." Goodstone rubbed his hands. "Boy, no wonder Crossen loves you."

The remark startled Marjorie. "Do you think he does?"

"I'm certain of it. . . . Why do you question it?" Goodstone asked.

"I *knew* he respected me. I didn't know he loved me."

"And so you turned to Solari."

"You know about that." Marjorie blushed.

"Of course I know about that. What the hell difference does it make?"

"Selda, she told you?"

"Of course Selda told me. I'm not a stargazer."

"I'm not very proud of that situation."

"I don't hand out report cards," Goodstone said. "Why did you turn to Solari?"

"I didn't," Marjorie said. "He seduced me."

"I believe that, but you became a consenting party."

Again Marjorie turned red. "Yes."

"Why?"

"I felt a need."

"For what?"

"Love," Marjorie said.

"Not good enough."

"Physical love . . ."

"Still not good enough."

"A climax, damnit!" Marjorie said.

"Good enough," Goodstone said, handing her a Kleenex. "These have gone up in price."

"What?"

"Kleenex. The whole economy is going to hell."

"In music," Marjorie said, "we call these rondos."

"What?"

"The little fugues stuck between major movements."

"Very good. I call it tap dancing," he returned to Marjorie.

"You're saying that Bill was no good in bed."

"That's cruel," Marjorie said.

"*Be* cruel."

"He was not as good as Solari. I've only slept with two men in my life."

"Fair enough," Goodstone said. "He was selfish, is that right?"

"I suppose."

"He masturbated, essentially?"

"You are very blunt."

"Perhaps," Goodstone said and turned to face the window. He put his fingers together in front of him.

"I want you to listen to me carefully," he said. "I have a nice house in Sea Cliff, two sons at Harvard, I own one hundred and sixty acres near Bakersfield, and do you know why?" He turned and faced Marjorie.

She shook her head.

"Because most of my patients from Pacific Heights have affairs. Did you know that?"

"It doesn't surprise me.

"Good. Now let's analyze an affair. Let's think about it. Your kind of upbringing, *my* kind of upbringing, does not really prepare us for the complexities of sex. It is a dirty word. It is not mentioned. You learn about it from your peers, who know as little about it as you do. Parents, *nice* parents, don't discuss the subject. A gynecologist hands you a book, *Growing Up*—am I right?"

"Yes."

"And the author of that tome should be crucified, beheaded, whatever.... 'The sperm enters the egg,' bullshit. You are barely being taught the mechanics of the game; he doesn't *dare* mention the word penis, or the word vagina; he doesn't touch on premature ejaculation, he never touches the subject of masturbation, and yet *that* is what you're handed. *That* and the little sordid tales that come over the fence."

"Linda," Marjorie said.

"All right. In your case, Linda. Kinsey," Goodstone said, "has shown us that Bill's sexual behavior is average for young American males. I am not offering this as an excuse for him, I am only saying that Bill's behavior in bed is 'normal' statistically, and I am *not* saying that you don't have the right to expect more."

"Thank you."

"Solari comes along," Goodstone continued. "He's older. He's experienced. He knows how to handle a woman. He knows it's amateur hour for you. It is very gratifying for him."

"And me."

"Yes."

"But what about Elyse Wolf? She's not older?"

"No, she's not. Not in years. But I suspect in experience."

"How do you think Bill behaved with her?"

"At first, I am certain he behaved the same as he did

with you. But a girl like Elyse would change all that. Did you and Bill ever practice cunnilingus? Do you know what the word means?"

"I do," Marjorie said, "and we didn't."

"Did you with Solari?"

Goodstone did not look at her and waited for the answer.

"Yes," she said meekly.

"Why?"

"He taught me."

"Good," Goodstone said. "God bless those dirty-minded musicians."

"Why did you say 'dirty'?"

"Wonderful," Goodstone said, facing her. "Wonderful reaction. It is *not* dirty. *Anything* consenting adults want to do in bed is *healthy*. Healthy. Sustenance, support. Wonderful."

"Why don't you write a book?" Marjorie said, "*Growing Up Right*."

"What, and knock myself out of the box? Forget it." He smiled. "But there is more to an affair. I don't mean to champion infidelity. It is unreal."

"Why?"

"The atmosphere is unreal. You are in a room with Solari, an apartment, a motel. And so is Bill with Elyse. You are in a cocoon sealed from the world. No laundry, no dishes, no problems, no phones, everything is pointing *one* way: the bed. That's romantic, that's libidinous, but it is unreal."

"Then you are against it. . . ." Marjorie asked.

"No. I am not saying that. We are all born with sexual drives," Goodstone said. "They are not all equal, but they *do* exist. An affair is only an outlet, the answer to a cry in the dark, but it not *the* answer. . . ."

"What is?"

"To learn from it. That is the answer. I have spoken

485

to you and I have spoken to Bill, and I have the feeling that you have the basis for a very good marriage."

"I'm happy to hear that," Marjorie said.

"Are you?"

"Yes."

"Do you realize that, despite Elyse, Bill might never be a Solari?"

"Solari," Marjorie said, "has asked me to live with him."

"And what did you say?"

"No."

"Why?"

"Because I want with Bill what I had with Solari."

"Why?"

"I want our marriage to succeed."

"Good."

"I have to tell Bill about Solari."

"Why?"

"I can't let him walk around with that guilt about Elyse."

"It's not a major guilt."

"*Anything* I can do to help I want to do," Marjorie said.

"I appreciate that. But it won't help him now, this schoolgirl confession. Do you trust me?"

"Yes."

"Then don't tell him. He is walking a very narrow tightrope right now. I need no further sway."

"Can I *ever* tell him?"

"Yes."

"When?"

"When I tell you."

"I have to live with myself, too."

"I know," Goodstone said. "He's ill, you're not."

"There is a lot of steel behind that benign look of yours, isn't there?"

"You bet," Goodstone said. "Jesus Christ, you're both sexual amateurs. I have patients that have three affairs concurrently."

"And how do you feel about that?"

"If they function that way, then it's all right. They just get screwed up on the names at the wrong moment. That's where I come in."

"You are saying *anything* goes, is that it?" Marjorie asked.

"No," Goodstone answered, "I am not saying that at all. Freud, psychoanalysis, even we respect morality. We do not understand that word fully. We question it more than the average man. We *know* that a man reading over you for ten minutes, evoking his legal duties to make it societally all right to have intercourse is not the answer to all human needs. We *do* know that. I *do*, strangely enough, believe in monogamy, and I do feel that the Bible, though flawed, is about as good a document as the Constitution; but I also know that hard and fast rules are juxtaposed to not-so-hard and fast human egos and human needs, and it takes the skills of men of my profession to not only allow you to live by those rules, but be happy with them."

"I bet you are a hell of a harmonica player."

"You bet," Goodstone said, slapping his knee.

"Will you help us?"

"I am trying to."

"I mean will you help us both?"

"If you want me to, I will."

"Thank you."

Goodstone stood and paced the room. "We're going to Sonoma now. I had not intended to tell you this, but you, too, have such extraordinary intelligence, I will."

He looked at Marjorie, who looked frightened.

"Elyse Wolf's child drowned while Bill and she were in bed. Give or take an hour. Elyse discovered the child and she brought him to the hospital. Afterward she phoned Bill and asked to meet him." He looked at Marjorie, who was now crying.

"Why?"

"Bill said she always called herself a whore. And he agreed."

"And what would you say to Elyse Wolf if you were treating her?"

"Bill asked me the same question."

"And what did you say?"

"I said I was treating him, not her."

"You know that's not an answer," Marjorie said.

"That's right," Goodstone answered. "Let me just say that Elyse Wolf is not a whore."

"What else?" Marjorie asked.

"Whatever else I could say would cost fifty dollars an hour. . . ."

"And a box of Kleenex."

"Yes," Goodstone said, "and a box of Kleenex." He rose, put his arm around Marjorie. "Let's go see your husband."

They arrived at San Ysidro and Marjorie left the car and ran up the grassy slopes to Bill's cottage. He was standing at the screen door waiting, and when Marjorie entered, they embraced warmly and tenderly, even tearfully.

"I have them all here," Bill said finally, pointing to a coffee table filled with reviews, scores of them. "Congratulations!"

"Thank you. Thank you," she said, looking not only at him but around the spacious, sunny room.

"Dr. Goodstone is outside," she said, "but he said he'd see you later."

"How was your trip?"

"Hectic, Bill. Selda, thank God for Selda."

"She phoned me. She said your performance was magnificent."

They sat on a small divan holding hands, Bill wearing denims, a blue shirt open at the collar, Marjorie in a simple, straight white dress.

"I am sorry," Bill said finally. "I am so sorry I wasn't in Cleveland."

"Bill, please," Marjorie said.

Bill avoided her eyes.

"There was so much. So much all of a sudden. Everything came rushing at me. There were days, nights, two days, three days, I don't know, I couldn't tell you where I was or what I did. I don't recall eating or sleeping, or where I was. . . ."

"You don't have to explain."

Bill looked at her. "I do," Bill said, almost wearily, "there's so much I have to explain. . . ."

"Not now, darling," she said, embracing him. "Not now."

"You've been talking to Goodstone."

"Yes. This morning."

"Quite a guy," Bill said.

"Yes. Quite a guy," Marjorie agreed. "I feel we should follow his advice."

"Which is?" Bill asked.

"Not to probe. Not to explore. To enjoy each other . . ."

"Does he feel I'm that sick?"

"Not at all. I'll tell you honestly, Bill, he said you were walking a very narrow tightrope. He wants nothing more to sway it."

"I appreciate what you're saying"—he looked at her— "it is difficult for me to listen to anyone, you know that . . . and yet I respect his talents. He is proving things to me like an engineer. He uses logic, not emotion . . . once I got out of prison camp I thought I'd never need anyone again. . . ."

"I've only spent the morning with him," Marjorie said, "but underneath that warm delicatessen look is a very steady man."

"You bet," Bill said. "Perhaps we should follow his advice."

"So they have formally asked you to run for governor?"

"Yes, they have."

"Congratulations. Congratulations, Bill."

"I thank you."

"What are your leanings?" Marjorie asked.

"Up in the air. What are yours?"

"I want you to run. I feel very strongly about this."

"Why?"

"You'd make a fine governor. You have so much to give . . . but that's not all. . . ."

"What else?"

"I'd like to be married to a governor."

"They have told me that your career would cost me votes."

"I can give up the piano."

"You will like hell," Bill said. "I told them that. Nothing will tamper with your talent. Not even the presidency. . . ."

"That is a lovely thing to say."

"That is the truth."

Goodstone entered the room. "Hi, Bill," he said cheerily. "Where's my basket?"

"You haven't brought me the straw."

"You're terrible," Marjorie said to Goodstone, then changed the subject. "I brought a picnic basket," Marjorie said. "I'll fetch it from the car."

"Quite a girl," Goodstone said after Marjorie left. "I think she's even brighter than you. . . ."

"I happen to agree with that assessment," Bill said, "but why do you say that?"

490

"You don't have to analyze *everything* I say. I have pipelines other than Freud. . . ."

Marjorie returned and placed a checkered tablecloth on the table on the porch. She had brought good French bread, ripe cheeses, a bottle of chianti, and they ate like horses.

When they had finished eating, Goodstone reached into his pocket and brought out a man's watch.

"There," he said, handing it to Bill. "You look silly with that lady's watch on your wrist."

Bill thanked him and Goodstone stood. "Well, now that I have eaten your food, sipped your wine, justified my unconscionably high fee, we shall go. It's time for you to get some rest."

"You mean Marjorie isn't staying?"

"Not today."

"Why?"

"I flunked out of engineering school. Not medical school. . . . We'll both be back tomorrow."

Bill sat and shook his head. "I don't understand. . . ."

"I didn't ask you to love me, do you remember that?"

"I'll be here tomorrow, Bill," Marjorie said. "You have to trust the doctor."

They embraced and Bill watched them walk toward Goodstone's car.

"Don't forget the baskets," he yelled as Goodstone and Marjorie drove away.

Chapter LXIV

"Why," Marjorie asked when she returned that evening to Goodstone's office, "won't you let me stay with Bill?"

"I'm decompressing him like a diver. He's had enough emotion for one day. It takes a tremendous amount of strain for a man in his condition to project rationality."

"You mean he's not."

"He is, but it takes effort. Normally it doesn't."

"Then you're saying he is sicker than you indicated before?"

"No, I am not saying that. There are two sides to all of us: the physical and the cerebral. When the physical is functioning well it supports the cerebral. He is not all that strong yet. . . ."

Goodstone held up his hand. "Look, Marjorie, I told you earlier today that I feel strongly about his confinement at San Ysidro, and I *want* you there. As soon as possible. Tomorrow, perhaps."

"Good," she said.

"Good, yes, but there are things you must know first. . . ."

"Go on."

Goodstone stood by the dark window and faced her. "Circumstances," he said, "particularly his chance to run for governor, interfere with the orthodoxy of his treatment. Normally I should not be seeing you both, and I must tell you right off that much that Bill has told me I cannot divulge because of the patient-doctor relationship."

"I understand," Marjorie said. "I don't mean to pry."

"When I deliver you to Bill, the natural course of events will lead to bed."

"If Bill wants that."

"He will, but don't expect Solari."

Marjorie looked at him.

"In the first place, he is weak physically, and in the second place you can survive without a climax."

Marjorie blushed.

"For a while," Goodstone added.

"What else?" Marjorie asked.

"Not much," Goodstone said. "Your intelligence and tact will carry the day."

"What a nice thing to say."

"It's true," Goodstone said. "However, don't expect too many revelations from him. It is difficult for me to open him up and I'm a professional."

"There are things I'll have to say," Marjorie said.

"Say them," Goodstone said loudly. "He's not a fragile tea cup. He's tough. Plenty tough." He looked at Marjorie and added, "Like you."

"Is that good or bad?" Marjorie asked.

"It is neither. There are survivors and nonsurvivors. You are a survivor."

* * *

John Haase

Bill had picked fresh flowers for the cottage. There was a fir in the hearth and he was genuinely happy as he helped carry Marjorie's luggage in.

"I'm going to let you domesticate this place," Goodstone said to Marjorie. "Bill and I are going to take a walk."

She waved at them as they left the cottage and reached the lawn and stretched out.

"How did you sleep?" Goodstone asked.

"Fine."

"Any dreams?"

"I suppose."

"What were they?"

"I don't remember."

Goodstone looked at him. "I understand. The mind is not a computer. Any decisions about the candidacy?"

"No," Bill said.

"I've told you that *not* making a decision is also making a decision. . . ."

"You've told me that. I still don't understand it. I've never shied away from decisions."

"You've been ill. You're under medication."

"I haven't taken your pills for days."

"I know."

"How do you know?"

"Jesus, Bill, give me *some* credit. Those pills are placebos. You *are* getting your medication."

"You son of a bitch."

"Good. That's a good decisive statement."

"I'm sorry," Bill said. "I didn't mean that."

"Don't be."

"I've never let anyone run my life before. . . ."

"That's what you thought."

"What do you mean?"

"Your father has run your life all along."

494

"I have admitted to the hatred. What else do you want?"

"Hatred is a wasteful emotion. That's all I'm trying to tell you. This decision about running for governor . . ."

"Yes?"

"It must not stem from hatred, or revenge, or the desire for power."

"What, then?"

"It must be what you want. *You.* What *you* want. Be selfish. That's fine. Ask yourself, 'Is that what I want for me? Or do I want another ten million dollars or do I want to sit on a tropical beach for the rest of my life and drink rum?' All valid choices."

Bill shook his head. "I—still—don't know."

"I told you—you're under sedation."

"*Why?*"

"I'm letting you run in neutral for a while."

"How long?"

"Not long, and don't fight it. I'll let you shift to first gear very soon."

"You are all disciples," Bill said. "All slaves to Freud, you analysts."

"To some extent—like Marjorie, we all play variations on a theme. Some of Freud is pure bullshit."

"In *your* opinion."

"Yes. But don't underestimate it."

"I wouldn't. Any guy who sneaks drugs into my food . . ."

It was Bill, really, that first afternoon who made it comfortable for Marjorie, questioning her about her career.

"After New York, what?" he asked.

"My first tour," Marjorie answered. "Sixteen cities. Three months . . ."

"Your career is very demanding, isn't it, Marjorie?"

"Yes."

"And maybe I should ask you the same question Selda always levels at me. Are you running or is it a joy?"

Marjorie sat back on the flowered chintz couch. "A little of both," she said, "but after a while, after the prizes and the debut, the talent becomes self-evident. It is God-given and one should not waste it."

"But the hours and hours of practice—I've watched you. I've watched the sweat pour from you."

"I'm not aware of that."

"And could you stop?"

"If there was a good reason to. If you asked me."

"You know I'd never do that."

"If we had a child."

Bill nodded.

"It is strange," Marjorie said. "I'm doing well at this point. I know that, and yet I'm on the bottom of the ladder. I am a beginning virtuoso. I'm not a Rubinstein, a Horowitz, I'm not a Crossen, do you know what I mean?"

"I do."

"It takes years of concertizing, years of study, years of practice and decisions, decisions, musical decisions, until people will hear me play and say, that is Crossen, not just Marjorie Crossen, that talented young woman. You have to have your *own* sound, your *own* rhythm, your *own* intellectualism. *That* makes you a Myra Hess, a Wanda Landowska.

"Yes," Marjorie said decisively. "The night of my debut, that was the night which sealed my fate. . . ."

"You make it sound so ominous," Bill said.

"No, no. Nothing like that. It all came together that night. It was ecstacy."

"I can understand that," Bill said. "It is like saying no to five hundred men who are saying yes, and you *know* that you're right."

"Exactly." Marjorie's eyes sparkled.

Bill kissed her and said, "I'm getting hungry."

"I brought some steaks and potatoes. I'll give it my best. . . ."

They spent a lovely evening together and they made love lightly and playfully. Before they went to sleep, Marjorie said, "I have to ask you a favor."

"Name it."

"Daddy is coming to see you tomorrow."

"Why? He's been ill himself; he shouldn't come all the way here."

"He's coming because he loves you."

"What is the favor?"

"I want you to take my brother back in the business. He is my father's son. I think he'd like that."

"I've already done that," Bill said. "Also Bob. I acted very hastily."

"I am not so sure of that. I might have done the same."

"Your father once lectured to me about family. I should never have forgotten it."

"Well, consider yourself part of it, Bill. He loves you very much."

Chapter LXV

Henry Levey, well dressed and well groomed, but using a cane for support, arrived the following morning at eleven. He embraced Marjorie, then Bill and seated himself in an armchair, facing them.

"I want you to know," he said, looking at Bill, "that you have used up all your sick leave and I am tired of everyone at the office wondering where you are and acting as if I were incapable of making a decision."

"You've returned to the firm?" Bill asked.

"Yes. I felt a hundred percent better after my first day back at work."

"That's good," Bill said. "That's very good."

Levey looked about the cottage. "This looks very cozy," he said.

"The most expensive loony bin in the country, I am told," Bill said.

Henry and Marjorie exchanged glances and Henry

said to Marjorie, "I have a favor to ask of you. Would you leave me alone with Bill for a while?"

"Certainly." Marjorie rose, picked up a book and left the cottage.

"Bill," Levey said. "I heard about your collapse and it saddened me. I have scarcely been able to think of anything else because I love you like a son."

"Thank you," Bill said respectfully.

"I have been trying to think of a way to help you. . . . I can't give you money, you have more than I do. . . . I can't minister to you, I'm not a doctor. . . ." He looked out the window. "Perhaps I can tell you something which might help a little." Again he paused. "I have never told anyone this in my whole life. . . .

"Linda Levey," he said, "is not my child. She is Whitney East Boulton's child by *my* wife."

"My God," Bill said.

"I didn't know until she was eight years old. . . . That's when I got that news . . . and I collapsed. Just like you. I had fought the same fight you have. I was smart, hours meant nothing to me, competition was rough, and I was rougher. I had everything I wanted. Almost everything. When Hortense told me, I felt cheated and vulnerable, distraught; for the first time in my life, I had lost control."

"I'm sorry," Bill said.

Levey shook his head. "We didn't have psychoanalysts in those days. I got drunk, and I stayed drunk for days, weeks. I screwed everything that was loose," and then he turned to Bill.

"But I survived."

"What about Hortense?"

"She wanted a divorce. Some uncle had left her a great deal of money all of a sudden. She thought she could do without me now. But I wouldn't give it to her."

"Why?"

"There were lots of reasons. I told you divorce was frowned upon. I had two other children of my own. . . . I wasn't going to make life *one* bit easier for Hortense or Whitney."

"But you've sued for divorce now."

"Yes," Levey said. "*Now* I have. When I heard that Hortense tried to sell my business, when I realized that my health was undermined, I decided that *now* was the time. It was *my* decision. Do you see? Let her have that goddamned Whitney. I'll piss on his grave before I die, I swear. . . ."

Bill looked at Levey and saw the steel in his eyes.

"I'm not telling you all this because I want sympathy. I am telling you this because I want to prove to you we're all fallible.

"I've always been a fighter and you've always been a fighter. But even fighters lose a bout here and there. The sooner you realize that, the sooner you'll get better."

"You've been so good to me, Henry," Bill said, "so very good to me."

"Look, son, if I hadn't listened to you, the firm might have gone belly up."

"You would have found a way."

"I have much to be grateful for myself," Levey said. "You have done wonders."

The door opened and Goodstone entered holding Marjorie by the hand. "Well, Levey," he said in mock sternness, "playing amateur analyst, are you?"

"Shut up," Bill said.

"Like hell I will. One engineer is bad enough. Two engineers are always a disaster."

"Professional jealousy," Levey said.

"Right," Bill agreed.

"Did someone say something about lunch?" Goodstone asked.

"No," Bill said.

"Well, they should," Goodstone said, helping Levey out of the armchair.

They went to a pleasant little Italian restaurant in Sonoma with mock grapes on mock lattices and posters of Siena and Florence on the walls. They lunched on ravioli and finished several bottles of chianti.

Bill tapped the side of his glass and everyone quieted down.

He spoke slowly, self-consciously. "I am not very good at gratitude," he said, "I know that. However, I have had more quiet hours than I've had for years, and I would like to tell all of you how grateful I am for your support.

"I would like to say one other thing: I have the *Equation* standing by with a crew of six. This was meant as a surprise for Marjorie before Dr. Goodstone tried to drug me to death.

"However," Bill continued, "as soon as he feels I am able, I mean to sail that boat to Hawaii. It should take us ten days. . . ."

Marjorie kissed him.

"That's two thousand miles of open water," Levey said.

"I know. Child's play for the *Equation*."

Goodstone said, "Columbus, to the best of my knowledge, never changed his name. A Jewish captain? Whoever heard of such a thing?"

Chapter LXVI

At the urging of Dr. Goodstone, Bill remained another week at San Ysidro, and though the psychiatrist was well aware that he could not cure lifelong fears and hatreds, he tried as best as he knew to fully use the time available.

"You must forget this business of your using people—forget it," he said.

"What about Marjorie. Does she know about Elyse Wolf?" Bill asked.

"Yes."

"And how did she react to that?"

"She didn't jump for joy when she heard the news. What do you expect?"

"Elyse was a bitch," Bill said. "A beautiful bitch."

"And you fell like a ton of bricks . . ."

"Yes." Bill avoided Goodstone's eyes. "I didn't realize all of it until the child drowned," he said. "But I *must* tell Marjorie about it."

"You will. In good time."

"And when is that?"

"You'll know."

Bill nodded, unconvinced. "How would you like to sign up as second mate on the *Equation?*"

"Good God, I get seasick in the bathtub."

"That bad, eh?"

"Not really. You're going to have to stand on your own two feet. How *do* you feel about the governorship?"

"Torn."

"Why?"

"I'm not worried about the office," Bill said. "I *am* worried about the campaign."

"Dunby?" Goodstone asked.

"Partly."

"What else?"

"My sudden conversion to the Mexican cause."

"What else?"

"I could lose."

"You could. What would *that* do to you?"

Bill looked straight at Goodstone. "I have never lost before."

"Perhaps that would be therapeutic."

"I don't intend to spend the rest of my life putting Bill Crossen together," Bill said.

"I don't, either," Goodstone responded, "and I see no need for that." He stood. "If you run, you'll win. If you win, you'll make a good governor. But have the right motives. The boy-wonder shit has got to come to an end. You have vast wealth. You can use it for good. You've left the Lower East Side. You've mastered Pacific Heights. You've weathered your first affair."

"Where shall I find this vast fount of altruism?" Bill asked.

"Within yourself."

"Do you think it's there?"

"It's in all of us."

"Even *you?*" Bill joked.

"I thought seriously of going into the rabbinate, did you know that?"

"And you became a drug pusher instead."

Goodstone laughed. "That's right. That will end when you leave here."

"And when will that be?"

"I've been studying the tide tables," Goodstone said.

The ship was dressed. The brass glistened, the brightwork shone. A crew of six young men in their early twenties wore white pants and navy shirts with EQUATION printed on their backs.

It was a lovely sunny morning in July; a slight breeze drifted over the blue waters of San Francisco Bay. Henry Levey, Goodstone, Henry Jr. and Joanne, Selda and Joe and Linda and Bob sat in the padded cockpit sipping champagne. There were shipfitters from Stanley's Marine putting final touches on rigging and turnbuckles. The sailmaker once more checked the ample sail inventory. The American flag flew smartly from the well-varnished flagpole and a stack of green bananas was hoisted halfway up the mainmast. Even the *Chronicle* had sent a photographer and the following day published a lovely photo of the gleaming yacht finally powering out to sea, the cheering farewell committee standing at the dock.

Charles Stockwell, the oldest member of the young crew, was at the wheel. He was a veteran of four TransPac races and handled the large destroyer wheel with great finesse. Smaller yachts, like pilot fish, accompanied the sleek vessel on its path to the Golden Gate, their horns tooting, their crews waving and wishing good passage.

Marjorie felt young and giddy and alive as she watched

all the merriment and saw Bill in the aft cockpit, his feet against the sternpost.

Bill heard the mainsail being raised and felt the boat heel slightly in the morning wind. He did not look forward, but knew the genoa was being raised, and he felt secure in the competence of the almost silent crew.

They had been active years since he first set sight on the hills of San Francisco, coming in on a troop ship, and though physically the city had not changed that much, he now knew it was now part of him. He watched as *Equation* passed Coit Tower, graceful as ever, and he watched the homes that climbed Telegraph Hill. He could see the early morning traffic on Lombard Street, where his motel had been. He saw the crumbling arches of the Palace of Fine Arts, and could make out Vallejo Street, where Selda lived. The course out of the Bay spanned all of Pacific Heights. He saw the stately Levey mansion, Linda and Bob's house and Nob Hill Towers. He saw Henry Jr.'s home and the Haas mansion and the Zellerbach estate.

They passed the eucalyptus forest of the Presidio and finally were under the Golden Gate Bridge, that graceful red-colored span dwarfing the 120-foot mast above him. He felt the Pacific swell increase as they passed the lighthouse and he watched the skipper set his course for south-southwest.

Ten miles out he could see the shoreline heading south to Mexico and north to Oregon and he was not unaware that he could soon be the man, the *one* man who might govern this state, this rich, restless, sun-drenched, desert-filled, mountain-topped, ocean-coasted state. And he was not unaware of all the wealth he had accumulated, of all the respect he had earned, nor was he unaware of Marjorie, only twenty feet behind him, who had the sensitivity to leave him alone at this hour on the stern of his boat.

He heard the soft chime of the ship's bell. It was high noon. He turned and watched the airfoil of his sails, and satisfied, he took Marjorie by the hand and led her to the bow.

The *Equation* cut cleanly through the swell, and he watched the white spume boiling port and starboard. He put his arms about her and Marjorie nestled on his shoulder.

"How long do you figure for the crossing?" she asked.

Bill said, "I knew there was something I forgot."

He loosened the strap of his watch and threw it overboard.

"First night out," he said, "we don't have to dress for dinner."

Once past the harbor of San Francisco, he watched the coastline. Rugged toward the north, softer toward the south, and he was aware that this state, this state of California, larger and more populous than many, many countries, might soon be under his rule.

It had been only six years ago that he had entered this state under the same bridge, a khaki figure, like thousands of other khaki figures, carrying discharge papers, medical records, a wallet full of back pay. And he had emerged out of that khaki morass. He had emerged with his brains, and his energy and his drive and imagination; and if money was the report card, then he had passed; and if the accomplishments were the report card, they could be looked at; and if California wanted him, he thought, they would be getting their money's worth. Not unlike Marjorie, he had supreme confidence in his abilities, but after his breakdown he questioned his stability.

Goddamn that engineering mathematics. Everything for him had to come out. Everything always had to balance.

Chapter LXVII

Bill Kraft, although only twenty-six years of age, was a respected navigator, and though Bill Crossen's skills were not unformidable, he was, as agreed, the owner, but not the master.

Again by agreement, though they carried radio and other mechanical and electrical navigational equipment, Kraft used a sextant, weather permitting, and celestial navigation when the nights were clear. It was almost paradoxical that Bill, who so coveted the latest in technology, became almost fetishistically pure on board his yacht. At night he relied on kerosene for the lamps; during the day he had canvas bags ready to catch rainwater; he liked holy stone for his teak deck and tallow for his cooking.

They were a lively crew on board the *Equation*, but Marjorie soon found that Bill, though not much older than the rest of them, unobtrusively earned a certain respect, a deference, which taught her more about his obvious demeanor as supervising engineer on all of his projects.

However, the formality of owner vis a vis crew diminished gradually as the air became warmer, as more clothes were shucked, and more men preferred sleeping on deck between watches.

A boat in itself is a sensual object. Its confluence of curves, its womblike interior, its beauty stemming from the composite of each of its parts can easily explain its classification in the female gender.

A boat, however, can also be sexual, particularly if seven men are confined in a relatively small space with one woman, and that woman belongs to only one man.

None of this was lost on Marjorie, whose various outfits drew much comment and whose lighthearted teasing drew laughter. It was not lost on Bill either, who found these minor flirtations aphrodisiacal and found himself thinking less and less about Elyse Wolf.

The elements could not be faulted. The July weather was perfect. The seas were calm and blue during the day; an almost full moon illuminated the water at night. The trades were steady but undemanding. The *Equation* averaged a respectable eight knots an hour, and without discussion neither the skipper nor the crew made any effort to gain further speed from the yacht, though it would have been easily achieved.

They were under spinnaker, that lovely, multicolored parachute whose rainbow-colored fabric was traversed by the design of a pair of dividers. The air was warm, the sun was hot, the night sky was star-filled and the kerosene-lit cabin was a delightful haven.

It had become a habit for Bill and Marjorie to have cocktails on the foredeck, which was ample and comfortable on the ninety-six-foot yacht; and the crew, except for minor sail changes, would leave them alone until sunset.

It was during that ritualistic hour, the eighth night out, that Bill broached the subject of Elyse Wolf to Marjorie.

"I know you know, Marjorie," he said. "I know from Goodstone that you know, and I appreciate your not having said anything."

Marjorie was wearing white shorts, a Venetian gondolier's striped shirt. She wore no shoes, no socks. A bandana covered her hair.

"I *do* want to discuss it, Bill, I *truly* do. However . . ."

"What?"

"Is *this* the time? It's so beautiful. All of it"—she waved her hand—"is so beautiful. I'm so happy."

Bill turned away from the sunset and put his head on his hands.

"I'm happy, too," he said. "*Very* happy. You're the last person in the world who deserves this. . . ."

Marjorie looked at him. She said. "I will never be as beautiful as Elyse Wolf. I will never look like my sister Linda. . . ."

"I told Elyse, Marjorie, that there were times, when you left that piano after hours and hours of practice that you looked prettier than she ever did."

"That is a lovely compliment. Thank you."

"But not an excuse," Bill said. "Unfortunately." He hesitated, then continued. "I spent a long time with Goodstone on the subject. He did not approve but he understood."

"What did he understand?" Marjorie asked.

"The temptress and the tempted . . . the animal in all of us."

"Did *that* make sense to you?"

"Sense, perhaps," Bill said, "but it evoked no pride."

"Are you afraid of the animal within you?"

"What do you mean?"

"Are you afraid I'm a china doll, easily broken? Are you afraid I'm half etiquette and half woman?"

"I don't know," Bill said. "Until I knew you, they were all Elyse Wolfs. Not as rich, not as stylish, but . . ." he stopped.

"Go on."

"Whores. Elyse called herself a 'hure.' "

"And to you, what am I?" Marjorie asked. "The *nice* girl, the girl reared in Pacific Heights, the girl in cotton underpants with no sexual organs, climaxes, *wants*, needs . . . ?"

"I suppose."

"You're wrong, Bill," Marjorie said, now kissing his face, tears in her eyes. "You're wrong because I betrayed you before you did me."

"How?"

"Solari. The great Solari. All talent. All sensitivity. Damnit, Bill, he seduced me the way Elyse did you . . . and why didn't Goodstone tell you about that?"

It had grown dark, but neither of them had noticed it. Michael, the youngest crew member, came forward to announce that dinner was served, but Bill asked him to serve it to them on the foredeck and he disappeared.

"I *wanted* to tell you, Bill. I knew you were harboring this guilt about Elyse, and I knew you shouldn't. I am just as big a 'hure' as Elyse Wolf."

"Don't say that," Bill said.

"Why? Where am I different?"

"I *do* know," Bill said, "that I am cold in bed. I spoke to Goodstone about that, too. I know I didn't make you happy. I doubt whether I've ever made *anyone* happy. . . . You deserved better than what you got from me."

"Not deserved, Bill. Not deserved. We are not born in this world with a sexual due bill. . . . I suppose you got the same whitewashing from Goodstone that I did."

Bill stared at the luminescent wake of porpoises on

510

the starboard side and waited until Michael had served their dinner and left them alone once more.

"He *did* whitewash it, Bill, but he did linger on the animal in all of us."

"I know," Bill said. "I got the same lecture."

"Did you feel it was just a lecture, or would you admit that there was some truth to what he said?"

"*I* was wrong," Bill said, "and *you* were wrong, damnit. It's hard for me to understand that you can *pay* someone to say it was right."

"Goodstone never said it was right. Not to me. He only said the urges were human. . . ."

Bill turned and placed his back along the lifelines. He looked at Marjorie, dimly lit from the skylight below her.

"I don't know how to apologize to you, Marjorie, I really don't know. . . ."

"There is no need to apologize, Bill, but I must tell you something. . . ."

Bill watched her.

"Elyse Wolf is only a symbol for me. In sailing I've learned you call them storm-warning flags. . . . When I first heard about Elyse, all I could think about was Linda. Linda *is* prettier than I am. . . . I know that. I can't change my face, although my mother tried like hell. I can't change anything. . . ."

"I don't want you to."

"But there are other Elyse Wolfs in this world."

"Yes, I suppose there are," Bill said.

Marjorie sat next to him and kissed him fully on the lips.

"Do you know what Goodstone said? He called us sexual amateurs. . . ."

"Perhaps he's right," Bill said. "Shall we go below and do a little homework?"

Marjorie laughed. "I feel so much better. I feel so very much better."

He and Marjorie walked aft and entered the master cabin. It was lit with three kerosene lanterns, and Marjorie turned down the double bed. She slipped off her jersey, stepped out of her shorts and jumped into bed naked. A beam of moonlight played with her breasts. Bill sat next to her and kissed them.

The sun was hot and bright when they woke, and Bill looked about the stateroom at the teak and the brass and he heard lines being worked topside. He felt the grinding of a winch, the snap of a shackle, and he knew it was his, all his, even the girl lying next to him with her head buried in a pillow, and for the first time, for the first time in years he felt a measure of peace.

Chapter LXVIII

The homing instinct in man is as strong as in swallows, as strong as in whales, and though Bill and Marjorie and their good crew had had as idyllic a crossing of the Pacific as anyone could hope for, the vastness of that ocean does have an effect: Though one knows that in midpassage the horizon will never include the sight of land, the eyes strain nevertheless, searching, searching.

They knew now that they were nearing the island, not only by charts and calculations, but by the proliferation of birds—gulls, petrels, terns—which circled their yacht in greater frequency, by the appearance of other boats, by the presence of aircraft passing above them.

Although Bill did not stand formal watches, he did frequently take the wheel to let the helmsman eat his breakfast. The smell of bacon reached his nostrils and Marjorie came up the companionway to give him a plate.

"Do you know, my love, I have done everything on this voyage except make a decision," Bill said.

"What decision?"

"Whether to run for governor or not." He looked at her, her face and arms, her legs, deeply tanned. "Goodstone told me, not making a decision is also making a decision."

"Good advice," Marjorie said.

"Perhaps," Bill said. "I lay awake last night and thought, there is no need to stop. We could sail on and on and on."

"Would you like that?" Marjorie asked seriously.

"I think that luxury is premature."

"Why?"

"I have your career to consider, for one thing."

"And what if I said I'll chuck it?"

Bill grabbed her hand. "I know you would. But you can't."

"My career will only stand in your way even if you decide to run."

"Your career will never stand in my way," Bill said quite definitely. He paused. "I suppose," he said, staring at the horizon, "that most men contemplating politics are pure of heart . . . and yet . . ."

"What?"

"We have so few good men . . . the process must be corrupting. Perhaps the office is. . . ."

"It doesn't have to be," Marjorie said. "Who needs to corrupt you? You can have anything you want, materially."

"I *am* aware of that. I'm not afraid of that."

"What does frighten you?"

"Compromise. Management, labor, Jews, non-Jews, small business, big business, blacks, Mexicans, federal rights, states' rights." He looked at Marjorie. "You haven't really seen me on a construction site. I can be one hell of a bastard."

514

"As long as you're on the side of the angels," Marjorie said.

"And whose side are *they* on?" Bill answered.

"God, state and Emily Post," Marjorie joked, but Bill did not laugh.

"The question," he said intensely, "the *real* question is what will happen if I decide *not* to run. . . . This opportunity comes only once. The momentum is building now. It can't be revived. I *know,*" he said, "I have that office in my pocket. I know that. My boys from MIT have made projections. We have calculated county after county, cities, towns, hamlets. We have programmed issues, and we have studied voting patterns and we have planned where to spend money and where not to. I could run against FDR with Jesus Christ as his running mate and win by a comfortable margin. . . ."

"I think, Mr. Crossen," Marjorie said, "you have made a decision."

He looked at her. "I think I have."

Marjorie walked toward the cabin. She yelled at Michael. "Everybody topside," she said. "Bring champagne and some glasses."

Michael complied and they faced each other around the binnacle.

"Has anyone sighted land?" Michael asked.

"No," Marjorie said, raising her filled glass. "Here's to the next governor of California."

The Pacific did not lay serene for the entire passage. The Molokai Channel, that wind funnel created by three thousand miles of open ocean on either side, gave both *Equation* and its crew a thorough baptism. Bill estimated the winds at force ten and foul-weather gear and safety harnesses became the order of the day.

The *Equation* buried her lee rail as they hurtled through the channel at better than eleven knots.

515

There were two men at the helm and two men on the foredeck, and Marjorie secured everything below. The wind was high, the swells deep and menacing, but the yacht was solid and though their faces were repeatedly stung and drenched by spray from the top of the waves, they plowed on like a solid locomotive for ten long hours until they sighted Diamond Head and felt the winds abate, the seas calm and their arrival at Ah Wai harbor was festive and welcome.

The navigator rolled up his maps. Sails were furled and covered, canvas slipped over the wheel, the binnacle, the winches. Lines were hung up to dry, flags were raised.

"Well done," Bill said to the crew. "Well done, indeed. I'll buy the mahi-mahi and the rum."

"I'll buy a woman," the skipper said, "if you don't mind."

"With your tan," Marjorie added, "you should sell, not buy."

Marjorie and Bill arrived at their suite of the Royal Hawaiian Hotel. The desk clerk had handed Bill a batch of telegrams and letters. Reality was closing in on them, but Marjorie walked out to the balcony and looked past the bougainvillea, the palms, the hibiscus, to the ocean beyond.

"There's still time," she said to Bill, reentering the room.

"Time for what?"

"Tahiti . . ."

"Yes. I'll hang a picture of it in my office in Sacramento, and no doubt wonder whether I made the right decision."

Part Six

Chapter LXIX

Three young men, Charles Willard, Tom Frisbie and Walter Allen, had been with Bill Crossen from the beginning. Their training at MIT and the University of Pennsylvania and their expertise in computer science, in modern scientific analysis in the new field of communication, had made them invaluable to Crossen in his early days on the canal, later on Nimbus Dam and subsequently in Crossen Development.

It had been a symbiotic relationship, they with their specific disciplines and Crossen with his visionary and imaginative administration all helped make the enterprise function. The stock Crossen had given each of them had made them all early young millionaires, and though they joked sometimes about Crossen's humorless approach toward life, there were no jokes about what he had done for them, and their loyalty was legendary.

Once Crossen had the candidacy offered to him it was

quite natural that he would enlist his friends to conduct the campaign.

"I don't see the difference," he said, pacing his small office, "any difference between a political campaign and a construction project. There is the same goal: to come in at a profit, to come in on time, and to safeguard the equipment and personnel. *Me,* in this case."

They laughed.

Bill did not laugh. "There are fifty-eight counties in this state, from Alameda to Yuba," he said somberly. "I now want definite voting patterns of those counties, including the *number* of votes, and I want projections of how much time to spend in each county, or perhaps whether to ignore some altogether.

"We have from June until November, and though I am used to working sixteen hours a day, I *am* new to politics and don't know whether I can smile that long or wave that long or kiss babies—Jesus," he said, "what am I getting into?"

Now Bill smiled, and Frisbie said, "*You* want to be governor. Not *me.*"

"All right," Bill said, dismissing the levity. "I've spoken to the political pros and they have assured me of several comforting facts: California has always had more registered Democrats than Republicans, but until 1953 because of factionalism among the scattered Democratic clubs, the Republicans usually managed to come out on top. The California Democratic Council is now the leading volunteer political organization in the country and they will be behind us one hundred percent.

"The other important development is the organization of the Mexican American Political Association."

"In the bag," Willard said.

"Not quite," Crossen answered. "I've been told that although the Mexican Americans are sympathetic to me,

I cannot assume that *every* Mexican American will vote Democratic."

"I agree," Frisbie said.

"Of course. With their numbers they should hold a club over the heads of *both* parties. The one that will give more to the Mexicans will get the vote."

"What are you willing to give?" Willard asked.

"I'm going to name a Mexican American as secretary of agriculture."

"Hold on, hold on," Allen said. "There *are* a lot of farmers in this state. It's still the biggest business."

"I am aware of that," Bill said. "I am quite aware of that." He paced the floor as they watched him.

"I'm a Jew," he said, "that's a minus. I have no children, that's a minus. I'm rich and young and that can work both for me and against me. . . . I *have* gotten notoriety out of the Mexican affair on the dam, and I know that will work against me. . . ."

He looked at his friends. "It was the Mexican business which started me in politics. . . . Let's say it gave me religion. I intend running as a Jew, committed to the welfare of the Mexican workers, that's it. Win or lose." He paused. "But," he said, "I don't intend to lose."

Walter Allen had been silent during the recitation. He looked at Crossen now.

"It's all very admirable, Bill. Really it is. I am happy you're running and I think you could make one hell of a governor."

"Something is troubling you?"

"Yes," Allen said. "Politics is *not* like a construction project. You are not dealing with engineering problems, with site vagaries, with supplies. You are dealing with people. And you are dealing with an opponent who will throw everything in your path that he can to defeat you. There are so many variables that even a computer won't help."

"Variables, yes," Bill admitted. "But you are forgetting *one* thing."

"What's that?"

"We'll be throwing an equal amount of shit at the opponent. . . ."

"You *are* becoming a politician, aren't you?"

"Perhaps," Bill said. "But don't forget *he* doesn't have a computer."

"We could offer him the services of Crossen Development," Frisbie said.

"Yes, we could," Bill answered, "but that's conflict of interest."

"Whose?"

"Ours."

But there were more than computer experts who now surrounded Bill Crossen. Old politicians, young politicians, state senators and representatives . . . There were the kingmakers and the lobbyists, and Bill listened, learned, agreed and disagreed, and on an unusually warm day in February in Fresno he addressed the thousand delegates of all the Democratic clubs of California, the Democratic office holders, state and county functionaries, the Young Democrats. He was the last speaker and the delegates were restless.

"Ladies and Gentlemen," he said.

He looked so young, Marjorie thought, in his blue suit, his chastely patterned tie, but he looked handsome and straight and serious and his voice was strong and calm.

"I am deeply grateful for the opportunity to address you, and knowing the hour is late will sincerely strive to be brief." (Applause).

"I came to this state thirteen years ago after spending four years at San Tomas prison camp during World War Two.

"I was by profession an engineer and had the good fortune to join the firm of O'Gara and Levey as a civil engineer. Those were heady days, both for an engineer and for California. Victory was ours, our state's population was growing, and expansion and improvement were the dominant factors.

"Starting as supervising engineer of the Delta-Mendota Canal, not far from this hall, continuing to Nimbus Dam, to Glen Falls, to Waterford, I not only learned my way about this state, I know every tree that was in our way, every mountain we had to traverse and every valley we have crossed.

"Unlike my colleagues," Bill held up his hands, "I can tell you that California soil has gotten under my fingernails and I assume will stay there for the rest of my life." (Laughter)

"You will hear, or have heard that I have become rich, and I will not deny that. California has been good to me, but despite that, I still get around in a truck, I still prefer well-worn boots to shoes and it was an act of God which made me buy this suit." (Laughter)

"But let me tell you that my job has not only made me rich, personally, but rich in knowledge about where this state has gone and where it should go from here.

"The war has changed California, as you know. We have grown by leaps and bounds. We have more blacks, more Mexicans, more midwesterners, more easterners and we are richer for that." (Applause)

"But we are only richer if we know how to use all the talent, all the sweat, all the diversity to make our state even stronger, even healthier, because the sum is greater than its parts if we know how to harness all these assets.

"I shall have critics. Of this I am aware. They will say I am young, and I cannot deny the calendar. However, may I say in my defense that my four-year imprisonment has seasoned me beyond my years. I do not recommend the experience to anyone.

"They will say I belong to the Jewish faith. It is a heritage I'm proud of, and may I add that belonging to a minority confers only a sensitivity to other minorities, and basically this is what makes up the fiber of our American society." (Applause)

"There will be those who will think me liberal because of my convictions, and those who will think of me as conservative because I have succeeded in the world of business. To them I can say only that both accusations are true and the convictions are firm."

He paused and looked intensely at his audience.

"I have my fingers on the pulse of this state. Believe me. I know where it's going. The heartbeat is strong. The patient is healthy and will continue to grow. If chosen, I shall give you all my energy, all my wisdom, and all my compassion. I have never in my life considered failure as a viable option. Good night."

It was eleven o'clock at night, the hall smoke-filled. The delegates stood and cheered.

The following day the *Chronicle* reported that Bill Crossen's forthright speech, his posture, his hard-hitting honesty made him the youngest candidate yet picked in California by the CDC, the most powerful body in partisan politics.

And it was with equal strength that he won the California primary that first Tuesday in June and faced Robert Jones, his Republican opponent.

They had done well, the Republicans, in picking Jones as his opponent. At forty, he was older than Bill, but still young. He was a conservative attorney, a state senator from San Diego who had been a minor football star at USC. He had a good war record, a wife and five blue-eyed, towheaded children, and their family portrait, appeared on billboards across the state in great numbers quickly. Fortunately, for Bill, Marjorie was pregnant.

"I can deliver a son to you," Marjorie said to Bill, "or a daughter. Perhaps twins. The likelihood of quintuplets is small."

Bill laughed. "I demand not *only* quintuplets, but they must be blond and blue-eyed."

"The governor has spoken," Marjorie said.

"The governor has."

"Have you considered losing?" Marjorie asked.

"Not for a minute. We had hoped for Jones to win the Republican nomination. They are so predictable, it is laughable."

"Daddy said the Republicans are pros and very rich."

"I agree with him. However, professionalism has its predictability, too, and that will help us. As far as money is concerned, we have no worries."

"And what about us? What will it do to you and me?"

Bill held her hands and looked at her. "I've been studying Eisenhower. I know the criticism he is getting. His golf, his weekends at Camp David, his afternoons at Burning Tree, his large estate. He scoffs at all of it. We've never had such trouble-free times in our country. He stopped the war in Korea in a week. His policies are strict but not ruthless. He is dealing from strength because of his past success. I intend to follow that example. . . ."

"And us?" Marjorie asked again.

"I know what you've asked. If I am elected we'll live in a home in Sacramento. We'll have dinner together. I won't be scattered over ten construction projects, and you, after the baby is born, will be home with me, for a period of time."

"For a period of time, indeed," Marjorie laughed. "You will be governor and I'll trade Debussy for diapers."

"Does that trouble you?"

"No," Marjorie said. "I, too, had a say in the conception." She kissed him. "I wonder what the Joneses are doing this morning?" Marjorie asked.

Bill looked at his watch. It was ten o'clock and Sunday. "They are emerging from church. All seven of them, all dressed up. And they are smiling and reverent."

"Was that your last printout?" Marjorie asked.

"Yes. And tomorrow I'll be in Napa Valley and assure them that not all the water will go south."

"And what will you tell them down south?"

"I'll tell them to drink Napa wine and to trust me. . . ."

"You are a son of a bitch," Marjorie said. "But it just so happens that I love you."

"Politics makes strange bedfellows," Bill said.

"Well, how about some breakfast, bedfellow?"

"How about some lox and eggs," Bill said.

"You know we never ate that in Pacific Heights."

"How well I know. Bob Jones should have a tutor from your neighborhood. They could *really* teach him how to be a gentile."

Levey had been right. The Republicans and Bob Jones were giving Bill a run for his money, and neither the expertise of his three friends nor the judgments of his newfound political allies could foretell the tough fight ahead.

They had done their homework well. Despite Bill's neutralizing of Dunby, they had found others from San Tomas who questioned Bill's war record and that put him on the defensive.

They did not attack his Judaism specifically but made him disclose his assets. The figure of ten million dollars raised eyebrows in many a California household, and again Bill was on the defensive.

His lack of political experience was attacked, his eastern background was attacked, his yacht was attacked, even Marjorie's talent was made an issue.

But Jones was not immune either. He had received a football scholarship under questionable circumstances. His frosty-faced blonde wife from South Carolina could trace her ancestry to the Ku Klux Klan, and Bob Jones's voting record in Sacramento was like the Sermon on the Mount for Bill Crossen as he spoke in Monterey, in Tulare, in Calaveras and Imperial.

"Mr. Jones voted against schooling; Mr. Jones voted against housing; Mr. Jones voted against canals and dams. Mr. Jones voted against farm labor and higher education. Mr. Jones, ladies and gentlemen, is *against*. And I am a candidate *for*. I am *for* you, and I am *for* California, and I am *for* progress and I am *for* the sensitivities of our people. You have the choice. . . ."

It became a bitter race, a tight race, a race watched nationally with the approach of fall, and Bill's eventual victory was small, very small; but finally, relaxing with his friends Willard, Allen and Frisbie, the day after the election, he was both appreciative and unusually light-hearted.

"We made it," he said. "I told you so. The equation came out."

"*You* didn't win it," Allen said.

"Who did?"

"Marjorie."

"What do you mean?"

"*We* watched the computers," Allen continued. "What put you over was the birth of William Crossen, Jr., six weeks ago. . . ."

"You mean I was behind?"

"Yup," Frisbie said. "Two points."

"You didn't tell me. . . ."

"Nope."

"Why?"

"We were confident, too. We had programmed the effect of the birth on the election and our advantage was two point eight percent. That's how it went. We won by point eight percent."

Bill sat quietly in their midst. "I am grateful to all of you. I hope you know that. Whatever you want from me you can have. . . . Just name it."

Frisbie removed his little tin badge from his lapel and handed it to Bill. It was red, white and blue and showed Bill's face and read FOR CALIFORNIA.

"I know what I want," Frisbie said.

"Name it."

"I don't want to see red, white and blue. Not in ribbons, not in banners, not in garlands or in flags. I want no coffee, no chicken, no handshakes or bearhugs."

Bill laughed.

"You won't join me in Sacramento?"

"No. I'll work on my net assets. When they reach the size of yours, I'll call."

They all laughed.

Willard said, "I have computed that my wife, my pretty, hopefully still young wife may be amenable to spending forty-eight hours in bed with me . . . and if they demand a recount, use an abacus, don't call me."

There was sweetness to victory. Unquestionable sweetness. The *San Diego Union* reported that Bob Jones failed to appear at church that Sunday. So did his wife and the five towheaded children.

Chapter LXX

On January 5, 1955, the *San Francisco Chronicle* reported that William Crossen was sworn in as the thirty-second governor of the state of California and the second Democrat to be so honored in the twentieth century. He was also the youngest man to hold that office.

It was a brief ceremony as Bill had requested, held before the joint session of the state legislature in the assembly chambers of the ornate Capitol Building. The chief justice, Phil Bibson, administered the oath of office at 2:47 in the afternoon, and following this Goodwin Knight handed over the keys to the governor's mansion, a hundred-year-old Victorian building suspected of being a fire trap.

Bill made a short acceptance speech, which was constantly interrupted by the applause of a strong, newly elected Democratic majority in both assembly and senate, and reaffirmed all the beliefs he had stated during his election campaign.

Although one thousand people had assembled before the ornate capitol, the persistent rain made the outdoor activities brief, and after Bill introduced Marjorie, family and close political allies all retired to the governor's mansion for a sit-down dinner for two hundred.

Everyone was there who counted in politics as was everyone who had been invited from San Francisco: the Sterns, the Zentners, the Haases, the Habers, the Hellers and Kahns. All of those who had so grudgingly allowed Bill Crossen into their midst now each claimed a stake in his success and outdid themselves proclaiming their intimacy with the new governor.

There was a fine dinner of vichyssoise and squab, of California wines and French champagnes, and as the hour grew later the party narrowed to only close friends.

They had all watched him this day, during his inauguration, during his speech, during all the ceremonial functions incumbent on such a day.

Henry Levey, acccompanied by his fine-looking, gray-haired fiancée, was proud, genuinely proud, for this boy who had not only followed in his footsteps but gone beyond them. Selda was proud, not only because Bill was her cousin, but also because he was the first Jewish governor in California history. Although not raised in Orthodoxy, her parents' death had given her a great deal of insight into that sophisticated religion.

There was Elyse and she was not alone. She had returned to Lewis after he had spent six months in a sanatorium.

She managed to congratulate Bill and did so gracefully.

"It is from the heart," she said and kissed him.

Hortense had come alone but also shook his hand.

"You have more to be proud of than I do," she said. It was almost a pathetic statement for this strong woman, and it struck both Bill and Marjorie.

"There will be much volunteer work," Bill said. "I hope I can count on you."

Hortense nodded and turned away. There were tears in her eyes, and Marjorie put her arm about her shoulders.

Henry Levey, Jr., and his wife shook Bill's hand, and young Henry said, "Now I know why you don't eat lunch. . . ."

They all laughed.

The party was thinning out. Brogan had hung on a good Irish dinger, Henry Levey consumed his sixth Scotch and soda, the orchestra played on and the room was pungent with the aroma of flowers.

At eleven o'clock Bill surprised Marjorie by taking her hand and steering her upstairs. He entered the freshly painted nursery and they stared at their infant son askew in his handknit blanket.

"Kiss him good night," Bill said.

"Why?"

"We're leaving."

"We are?" Marjorie was startled. "Where?"

"For the *Equation*."

"Tonight?"

"Yes."

"I can't go like this." Marjorie scanned her lovely silk gown.

"Everything is on board. Don't worry."

"You're crazy."

"Yes," Bill said, bending down and kissing the baby. Marjorie did likewise. She placed her lovely fingers on his navel and the tip of his nose.

"He almost spans a tenth," she said.

They descended the circular staircase and spotted Henry Levey.

"We're leaving for the *Equation*," Bill said. "It's moored on the Sacramento."

"The *first* night? Think about noblesse oblige."

531

"To hell with noblesse oblige. I'll be at my desk at seven as usual."

"And all twelve pencils sharpened," Levey added as he watched them leave. He shook his head.

Marjorie was already in bed in the aft cabin, still only lit by kerosene lanterns, as Bill made one final tour of his decks. He bent down to retie a mooring line and saw a highway patrolman standing in front of his car. It was his guard, and Bill waved and the patrolman waved back. He thought briefly of the guard towers at San Tomas, but no one ever waved from there.

He returned to the aft cabin and shut its door. Marjorie looked lovely by the yellow light of the kerosene lamps. Her hair shone, her eyes sparkled, even her chaste white linen nightdress looked elegant.

"And what, may I ask," she said primly, "is on the governor's mind?"

Bill sat on their bed and slipped off his highly polished black shoes. "Something your father said."

"What was that?"

"Noblesse oblige." He blew out the lanterns. "That phrase didn't surface much when I was delivering papers on Delancey Street."